CW00741734

'Every secret and spirit, uneasily buried to stay dead, rises up to be reckoned wi evocative debut. A young couple returns to the ruins of a family homestead in the outback of the far north and need to grapple with the ghosts of the past, and their separate legacies of childhood and orphanhood. Manton understands instinctively what haunts us, and why, and her rich prose, threaded with powerful metaphors and images, brings the remote and beautiful landscape and the spirit of the unquiet past to life.'

Cate Kennedy, author of *The World Beneath*

'*The Curlew's Eye* is a story of loss, hope, family and the secrets we carry wherever we go. In the ancient landscape of far northern Australia, two young parents try to make a home away from their traumatic pasts. The narrative builds like the oppressive tropical wet season. I could feel the heat, smell the dirt and rain and storms, sense the aura of the remote property: the restless dread and unease. I could also see and hear the birds, especially the haunting cry of the curlew. A promising debut that weaves together memory, grief, fear and truth with magical realism.'

Karen Viggers, author of *The Lightkeeper's Wife*

'With prose both lyrical and minimalist, Manton conjures Australia's remote Top End in all its magnificent starkness. A page-turning debut as unsettling as it is compelling—be prepared to burn the midnight oil.'

Fiona Higgins, author of *The Mother's Group*

Karen Manton lives in Darwin and Batchelor in the Northern Territory. Her short stories have won five NT Literary Awards and are published in various anthologies, including *Best Australian Stories*, *Award Winning Australian Writing*, *Review Australian Fiction* and *Landmarks*. She has been awarded the Eleanor Dark Flagship Fellowship at Varuna Writers' House, the NT Writers Centre Hachette Mentorship and the Arts NT Varuna Residential Fellowship. *The Curlew's Eye* is her first novel.

THE CURLEW'S EYE

KAREN MANTON

ALLEN&UNWIN

SYDNEY•MELBOURNE•AUCKLAND•LONDON

This is a work of fiction. Names, characters, places and incidents are products of the author's imagination or are used fictitiously. Any resemblance to actual events, locales, or persons, living or dead, is entirely coincidental.

First published in 2021

Allen & Unwin
83 Alexander Street
Crows Nest NSW 2065
Australia
Phone: (61 2) 8425 0100
Email: info@allenandunwin.com
Web: www.allenandunwin.com

 A catalogue record for this
book is available from the
National Library of Australia

ISBN 978 1 76087 951 8

Map by Isak Pollock/Mika Tabata
Set in 12/17 pt Minion Pro by Midland Typesetters, Australia
Printed and bound in Australia by Griffin Press, part of Ovato

10 9 8 7 6 5 4 3 2 1

The paper in this book is FSC® certified. FSC® promotes environmentally responsible, socially beneficial and economically viable management of the world's forests.

For my family

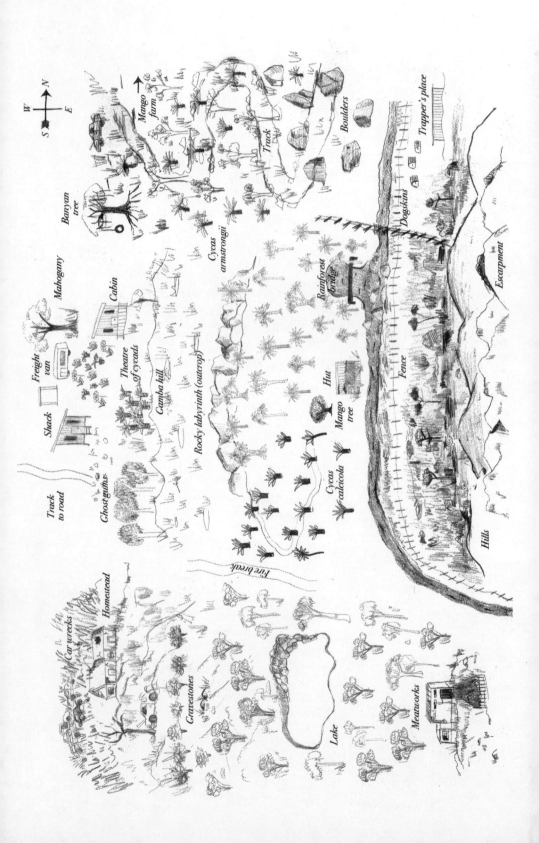

There's nothing in the lake, Magdalen.

There is, Joel—I can feel it.

You can see all the way to the bottom. There's nothing there.

I'm not seeing anything, says the girl.

The water is a breathing silence, its darkness a body. And all around the quiet earth, the listening stones. Above, the dome of night is stuck with pinpoint stars.

She is very still, his sister. Her stillness frightens him. But he says nothing. He waits, while the present and the past and the future mingle in the breathing silence, the breathing water.

I can feel it, she says again.

And her body shifts in the dark.

1

The fire burned in a wavering orange line by the road, flaring now and then as it devoured the head of a pandanus or licked its way along a dead branch. Above, kites circled through rusty clouds, waiting for a scurrying marsupial, a snake, to flee the flames.

Greta slowed and eased the four-wheel drive off the highway.

'Is that a controlled burn?' she asked as she pulled over.

There were no fire units in sight.

'It's pretty late in the season for that.' Joel opened the door and got out.

The three boys crowded at Toby's window to see.

Greta went to stand with Joel. As she rounded the bonnet an animal leaped out of the fire and stood on the edge of the road, disoriented. 'Is that a dog?' she asked.

She called out to it but Joel said, 'Leave it.'

It was a dingo sniffing the air, snout raised to the gliding birds and strips of airborne ash.

A row of gamba grass ignited with a rush close to the road. The dingo was gone suddenly, streaking back into the very heart of the fire, through vivid flame to the darkness behind where the ground was already known and charred.

'What are you doing?' Greta breathed, trying to follow the animal's shadow behind the shimmering light.

The sun dipped below the horizon. A restless call came from the car. Joel was buckling up, telling the boys to do the same. She returned to them, slipping behind the wheel.

'How long till we get there?' Raffy's foot pressed into the back of her seat.

'About eighty kilometres,' replied Toby.

He had his own map across his lap with a texta line marking the few thousand kilometres they'd travelled from the south-eastern coast up through the red centre to the point where the desert gave way to the tropics.

Greta turned the key. The vehicle rumbled awake.

'What's up ahead?' Joel asked Griffin, who was seated between his brothers with a pair of binoculars aimed at the windscreen.

'I'll keep you posted,' the boy said.

Greta pulled back out onto the highway and they left the fire behind. Dusk moved in around them; the sky quickly deepened to night. A full moon rose directly ahead, as if the road were leading into it. The higher it rose the more silver it became, casting an eerie light over the land.

The children were asleep by the time Greta's headlights lit up the sign: *Old Mine Rd, Lightstone 35 km*. This was the turn-off that would take them to the property; it had been part of the highway in the past.

Greta felt a shiver of excitement and fear. She had imagined it for so long, this return to the place where Joel grew up with five brothers, a sister, his parents and two uncles. The father running a small meatworks, his mother managing seven children and the garden that fed them. Greta gathered it hadn't been an easy ride. Every family has its troubles.

The land was hilly, rising up above moonlit bushland and then dipping down to lower ground. She drove slowly to avoid potholes. A cattle truck loomed up ahead and she eased onto the dirt siding to let it pass. Eyes glinted at her through gaps in the trailer's slats. As the dust settled she moved on again.

They drove past farmland for quite a distance before reaching a T-intersection where Joel gestured left. 'Not far now,' he said as they crossed a floodway between tall markers and rainforest.

The road curved and narrowed to a single-lane bridge. The creek beneath flowed into a dark pond where slender paperbarks rose in the moonlight. As the car climbed to another crest Joel cautioned Greta to slow down.

'Here.' He pointed to a gravel track leading off to the right.

She pulled up to a rusted gate, chained shut. Joel got out to shove the gate open over stones. She drove through and waited for him, engine idling. In the rear-vision mirror he was red-tinged from the tail-lights, hooking the chain into place. He climbed back up into his seat and rested his elbow on the lowered window. His fingers tapped the roof.

Greta moved the vehicle on, glancing at Joel, thinking he might speak. But he was silent. Among the silhouettes of cycads and sand palms and eucalypts, the shadows of boulders loomed. They leaned in one to the other, a communion of stone. They knew who she was and watched her pass. But she did not know them. They were the stone strangers. Her foreign breath wavered. Loose rocks rattled under the wheels, the grasses swish-swished at the car door.

A piercing wail cut through the night. A woman, a child, a bird.

'Bush stone-curlew,' murmured Joel.

Again the awful cry, once, twice, to end in a crescendo shriek. The night was scoured open. The stars quivered. A terrible loss, a terrible grief. Greta peered out for a glimpse of this feathered agony, but the shadow plants kept their secrets. She kept the car moving forward and the further she went, the more she felt the pull of a dreadful, echoing abandonment. The cry had gone right into her. And with it a question, *What is it? What is it?*

In the silence afterwards the memory of the wail went with her. The night was altered. A weight, a stone had dislodged.

The track went over a small rise. Ahead was the sudden glimmer of a corrugated-iron roof. The moon was a spotlight on it. This was the shack where they would live. Slowly the little house drew near, the ground was bringing it to them.

Greta pulled up by a water tank on stilts.

'We're here,' said Joel quietly.

The car shuddered to silence.

Together they listened to the hiss and tick of the cooling engine, the chirp and rustle of creatures in the darkness. One of the children rattled in a breath. The driver's door creaked as Greta opened it. She walked to the front of the shack her husband's uncle Pavel had built years ago. For the most part the walls were not solid. They were flywire, tacked around the outside of the house frame. There was a row of louvres either side of the front door. The rear of the building was set close to the ground. The front stretched out over a slight incline, ending with a verandah that was roofless and missing most its boards.

Joel led the way up rickety wooden steps to a couple of planks laid like a bridge over gaps to a screen door. Greta looked out across the moonlit landscape. About twenty metres in front of the shack the ground dropped away. In the distance water gleamed silver. On her right, the land sloped up to the dark shape of another house. The old homestead where Joel grew up, she guessed.

The door behind her scraped open. Joel stepped inside. 'Here it is.'

She followed him in. His torch shone around a single room, with a stone wall halfway across that had a pantry alcove behind it. A raggedy wicker couch was the only furniture. The kitchen bench was a wooden slab. Behind it was a sink but no stove, no oven. No cupboards either, just open shelves under the bench and in the pantry. Louvres above the sink looked onto a pokey back verandah and a concrete laundry trough.

Joel brought in a camping lantern from their trailer. The flame hissed alive. It was a lighthouse in the middle of the floor. Together Greta and Joel lugged in the swags and unrolled them. Then he carried in each sleeping child. They smelled of sweat and the hot chips they had eaten. She carefully removed Griffin's binoculars and dragged off his shirt, and wiped Raffy's face with a damp cloth. Toby she let be.

When Greta was done she lit another lantern and took it out the back to the shower, which had a corrugated-iron enclosure with no roof. There was only one tap. The pipes grunted and gave nothing at first. Joel came in and hung his clothes over the wall. She opened the tap further. A burst of warm water splattered her skin, the dirt at her feet. Joel pulled her in close. His heart was a muted beat against her ear. Softly her fingers pressed against his scars. The raised and tormented skin. Along his left arm, across his chest and reaching to his back. They were a comfort to her, the scars. His body was the only known thing.

He left first, shaking the water from him. She listened to his feet shudder the steps on the back verandah. The flywire door slapped behind him. She ventured out naked to let the unfamiliar air dry her and the moon light her skin.

Inside, Joel was already stretched out on the swag. It smelled of other places they'd been. She lay down beside him. He hooked his arm around her head and pinched her ear.

'Here we are again then,' she said. 'At the beginning.'

He drifted from her quickly into sleep. She could feel his body sinking into the swag, the floor, the ground beneath.

Greta scanned the dark room, the shadows of the children, the unknown land outside the see-through walls. Beyond the silence of the verandah, the world was brushed with silver-grey light. Every plant or tree was fixed in a night pose, cast in a paralysis of stiffened arms, spiked fingers, a fountain of hair. A termite mound gleamed its tower strength, pointing to the stars. The ground was a strange sea of ashen light and dark shapes. She felt herself hovering over it all. She might be in a dream, or she might be here for real. The boundaries were suddenly thin. Some part of her had travelled out and was wandering.

How far they had come. How distant from that morning, two months ago, when Joel's older brother Mick had phoned.

She remembered Joel's low voice in the dark, and branches scratching the window; the boys' soft breathing in the adjacent room, the shapes of them under the indigo blanket with its pattern of sprawling blue flowers and the tired satin edging; the sound of surf down on the shore.

After the call, Joel had explained that Mick and his new business partner up north wanted to fix up the old family property, buy out Joel and his brothers and build tourist cabins for backpackers and grey nomads, with a cattle agistment on the side. Mick would pay Joel up to the end of the year to finish the first cabin, put in fences and clean up the place. He wanted a garden too, for tourist appeal.

'What a nut,' Joel had laughed softly.

'It's an idea,' Greta replied.

She saw a rambling vegetable garden, tropical fruits, bees and honey. A different experience for the children, a known income for a while.

'The build-up is the worst time of year.' Joel's fist bumped a gentle rhythm against the wall behind him. 'And it'll be feral. Weeds, gamba, fallen-down buildings. No one's been there for years except squatters, wild pigs and stray cattle. Mick won't pay much either. I could go on my own maybe.'

'I'm not letting you go without us.' She kissed him fast.

A wave broke with a loud smack down on the rocks.

'Lightstone', she'd whispered over and over to herself. She liked the ring of the name.

Four to five months was longer than they usually stayed in one place but they would do the work and move on, as they always had these past twelve years. As Greta had for years before she met Joel. Before Toby took a hold in her womb and posed the question of a joint future.

'We can give it a try,' he'd replied to her misgivings. And his fingers had touched her belly where that little heartbeat sang on the other side.

'Just as long as you don't build me a white picket fence.'

'Never. I'm strictly barbed wire.'

Fencing, bricklaying, bar work, cleaning. Farmhand, kitchenhand, shop assistant. They found work wherever they landed. The children were homeschooled or did short stints at a local primary. It kept them out of the rat race. No long-term career, no mortgage or brick-veneer home.

It would be the same up north, she'd thought. But now, lying here, she was not so sure. It was different somehow, the stopping. Already she felt pegged to one place. There was a magnet under this little house. Beneath the swag, the floorboards. Even the soft rhythm of Joel's breath seemed drawn to it. He was recalibrating in his sleep.

The warm air pressed in; it was an atmosphere. And the moon had shifted, casting light on different shapes and lending a view uphill to where the shadow of Joel's childhood waited.

The child with the softly whistling nose tossed and turned. Greta rolled on her side to watch her three sleeping boys. She was overwhelmed with love for them. It struck her that in all these years, every highway and meandering track they'd taken together had been heading for this destination. A shack perched halfway up a hill in an other-world of bizarre shadow plants and dark sentinel trees, where the earth rose in sharp-pointed mounds and the rocks could see at night. It was true for Joel and herself and each child born along the way.

Every road had been leading here, to this place.

The girl's breath is quick, panicked. She's fleeing through a narrow passageway. On either side of her the walls are rock. They have a sound, a deep hum. Her fingertips brush against the stone, as light as passing feathers. Every turn becomes another corridor. Outside the cicadas chant their fever-pitched rhythm. She can see nothing of that world except for a sliver of sky above her, a wound of light. There's a shout behind her, footsteps thudding near. The rocks tilt, press close, suck her in.

2

Greta woke before dawn into that bluish, liminal space that seems to have no time. Beside her, Joel snored softly. The boys were flung across their swags, night dancers fallen from the sky when the stars faded.

She pulled on jeans and a singlet top, and found her boots. The screen door opened with a little squeak. She crept over the planks and down the wooden steps which wobbled under her feet, soft with hidden rot. Joel's friend Gabe had lit a clearing fire around the shack the month before. You'd need a compass to find the shack otherwise, Joel said, the gamba was that thick.

She walked to the edge of the hill. On her right four ghost gums stood quiet. Below her was a rocky amphitheatre where cycads waited like actors cast under a spell. Their trunks were black, their hair a spill of green fronds. She stepped down among them. From there the land fell steeply to an outcrop of boulders. They were gentle shadows obscuring the world below. She could hear the creek running through that hidden valley. Above it wisps of mist trailed where cool and warm air mingled. On the other side of the valley hills rose in shadow curves lined with trees. There was a dim light between their trunks. They stood slightly apart, like people. Everything ended with the giant arm of an escarpment. Pale blue light spread up in an arc above it, pushing back the night.

The place she'd come from felt so far off it mightn't exist, with its pale dune grasses, the green-purple melt of waves, the wind's icy sting.

'We're going north,' she'd told the children. 'For an adventure.'

They'd paused in their game to stare at her, eyes bright under their beanies.

Greta heard a faint rustle, a throaty grunt. Her eyes darted to the noise. A wild pig was just a few metres from her, beside a boulder. She froze. Those curved tusks could cleave her in two. The pig snorted, and then a skid in the dirt, a clatter of stones and it charged downhill through the gamba. Greta stayed rooted to the ground, unable to move.

Two black cockatoos glided past. Their wing beat was slow, and slow too their raucous screech, *Why, why have you come here?*

They took the mist with them. A fierce line of orange seared the top of the ridge.

The hot eye of the sun appeared. The shack and the water tank flared with light. Griffin flung open the front screen door, binoculars around his neck, and balanced his way across the plank to the steps. Raffy came after him. They paused at a dome-shaped pizza oven to the side of the shack. Greta watched them go to the open shed behind, where a red ute and a quad bike were parked, and a rusted bedframe leaned against a stack of tyres. Nearby they found an old rail freight van, red with small rectangular windows up high. The four palm trees behind it gave a tropical postcard look. Griffin tried the door but it wouldn't open. A stately banyan tree caught their attention next. It was further away from the shack, and closer to the slope downhill, with a sprawling network of branches and aerial roots. A shout went up about the platform above them and a ladder nailed to the trunk.

A couple of thumps on the water tank made her turn to see Joel. He smiled and came over, settling his hat with one hand.

'Toby and I'll start up the bore and go for a drive, check out which fences are left.'

'I don't know how you'll find the fences,' Greta murmured, 'with all this grass.'

'Gabe could only do so much.'

A firebreak had been burned around the shack, up to the homestead on one side and as far as the banyan tree on the other, and from there down to the creek. Patches either side of the track out to the road had also been burned, she remembered from last night. But the slope down to the outcrop and the lake was a sea of grass, as was the paddock behind the homestead, and the land beyond. They were hemmed in. One live match was all it would take.

'Gabe's lent us a generator for now.' His fingers lifted a damp strand of hair from her cheek. 'I'll start it up later, for the fan in the afternoon.'

She'd noticed a pedestal fan in the pantry alcove and wondered if it worked.

Two sharp points jabbed her back. Toby laughed when she turned, and held out a forked stick.

'Your mother was just looking for that,' said Joel. 'For her water-divining. In case we have to sink a new bore.'

'You need two pieces of wire for that.' Toby had all the facts.

'Yes, but your mother's magic. She finds water with a two-pronged stick.'

Toby solemnly passed the stick to her. He wore the same style leather boots and long-sleeved work shirt as Joel, and a new broad-brimmed hat.

Joel gave Greta's black plait a tug and called Toby to help unhook the trailer from the four-wheel drive. They then drove away with a toot of the horn.

'Muuuuum!' shouted Raffy from the banyan tree.

She turned to see his hopping figure on the platform.

'Griffin's gone off down that hill!' He pointed.

Griffin. The child who must be followed.

They went down from the banyan tree into a valley of cycads, punctuated with rocks. The males had cone-shaped heads pointing fierce to the sun, the females wore necklaces of shining green and bronze baubles. They fascinated Greta, these ancient plants. She'd been reading about them. Raffy called her over to one of the rough, woody trunks with its crosshatch pattern.

'It's like fossilised reptile skin.' He put her hand against it.

Rings scarred the bark at intervals, leaf scars where a new head of fronds had sprouted after fire. Her finger traced one of the memory lines.

Raffy crouched to pick up burned cycad nuts, then hurried off again, faster now, boots skidding on little stones. Greta tried to keep up. The harsh sunlight made her squint. She wished she'd grabbed her hat and a sensible shirt. The woolly butt trees gave no shade. Their leaf shadows dappled the ground, shoals of fish flickering. Everywhere was a repetition of the same plants and rocks. There were no landmarks, no reference points. No escape from the sun.

She picked up her pace after that vagrant Griffin. He was a notorious wanderer, disappearing to chase a lizard or spy on a bird.

The sound of the creek grew louder, she glimpsed it between trees below.

'He's gone,' panted Raffy.

'Not to worry.' Greta held out her forked stick. 'I have my diviner. It's multipurpose, for water and for children.' She closed her eyes and pointed it downhill.

A shout answered.

'It works!' Raffy exclaimed.

Griffin was below them, up to his knees in bright green grass. He had no feet, only legs. Behind him loomed seven black, curvacious boulders. Raffy ran to his brother and they both disappeared.

Greta hurried after them. The rocks were wise, ancient souls, weathering the eons. Among them pandanus palms stood guard, with their heads of spiky, double-edged sword fronds and bright orange fruits. Their trunks were whipped with black scorch marks.

'There's a spring under me,' Griffin announced, feet prodding the damp earth.

A whistling kite passed over them and trilled.

Raffy was wide-eyed, taking in the boulders, the bird above, the pandanus. He'd woken up in a strange chamber, in a fairytale he'd never read. He tiptoed away to avoid disturbing a sleeping giant. Griffin followed him, leaving Greta alone.

She too felt unsure of this place; these bodies of stone that might not want visitors. She could almost hear them breathing. They knew something.

There was a shuffling behind one of the boulders, footsteps. She edged around to see what was there. Nothing. Just a fallen branch with grey twigs as slender as birds' necks and knots in the wood for eyes.

The kite whistled again.

Greta left the silence of the boulders and walked towards her children's voices. They were following the creek where the water tumbled between copper-coloured rocks and over skinny tree roots. On either side great swathes of grass had been flattened by wet season waters and dried all facing one direction.

'What's this?' Griffin shouted from up ahead.

He was standing on a rock mid-stream, tugging at dreadlocks of dead fronds and grass twisted around the forked branch of a young paperbark tree.

'Careful,' warned Greta, uncertain of what he might pull loose.

Raffy tried to join his brother, but Griffin elbowed him away. 'I've nearly got it!'

He dragged it free at last, a triangle of twigs with five wire strings dangling down, each one knotted with slivers of bone and fine twists of metal.

'Chimes!' He held out his find, triumphant.

'Someone's made them,' Raffy said.

'Someone has,' Greta agreed.

The bones were tiny, as from a little bird. Likewise, the metallic objects were petite, crafted from thin nails, screws, the miniature spring of a discarded toy. They made no recognisable shape, sign or animal, though Raffy searched for one.

'It's a secret code.' Griffin passed the chimes to his mother and moved on.

'The mother carries everything,' Raffy comforted her, and hurried after his brother.

They couldn't go far, stopped by a fence that continued across the creek. A metal flap hung from the lowest wire, above the water, to stop debris dragging on the fence in the wet season, and animals crawling underneath in the dry. On the bank opposite, wild dog skins stretched along the neighbour's barbed-wire fence with a sign: *Keep Out! Trespassers will be Shot!*

Rusted forty-four-gallon drums were lined up beside the sign, each painted with white letters. Griffin sounded out the message. *This—is—my—land—fucker!*

'Look at those strange cows,' pointed Raffy as skinny Brahmin cattle walked in a weary line behind the fence.

'Not as strange as these stone igloos.'

Griffin passed Greta the binoculars and pointed up the slope behind the cows. A stone, domed structure sharpened into view. Two more were nearby. The stones were painted white. The next one she found had chicken wire across the front.

'I think they're cages,' she said.

'There's a bridge here!' Raffy called them back to the fence on their bank.

He'd found an inviting gap in the barbed wire. Beyond it was a wooden footbridge across a pool of dark water fed by the creek. Both the bridge and the water disappeared into a rainforest of paperbarks, fig trees, pandanus and vines.

'Can we cross it?' asked Raffy.

'Not today,' said Greta, noting rotten, sagging planks.

A ta-ta lizard waved, as if beckoning them across.

'Whose land is it, anyway?' Griffin asked.

'It's part of this property,' she told him, and then wondered. It was a question, after the sign over the creek.

'No-man's-land,' piped up Raffy.

'There's no such thing as no-man's-land,' said Griffin. 'Aboriginal people lived here, didn't they, Mum?'

'Yes,' she said.

Her fingers held the wire between the barbs.

'White people took it,' Griffin announced.

'We're white,' said Raffy.

No escaping it, thought Greta.

Griffin kicked a stone under the last rung of wire, forcing it from the stubborn earth. 'Well, I wish we weren't.'

'Me too,' added Raffy, with a quick glance to his mother.

She had no words for them. Her fingers tapped the wire. 'Come on, let's go back to the house.' She cast a look across to the fence with the dog skins and the warning.

As the boys charged ahead, Greta hung back at the gap in the fence. If she were alone, she'd duck through and cross that little bridge into the dark thicket of vine and paperbarks to snatch a glimpse at whatever lay beyond. The footbridge glowed in the sunlight. Everything was very still. Only the creek moved, flowing on, on, into the next world.

———

As they came over the brow of the hill towards the shack, Greta saw Joel standing where she'd been at sunrise. She wasn't sure if he was looking out over the unkempt property with apprehension or resignation. Something had shifted since their arrival in the dark. He was not at ease.

In the distance, the escarpment was the burnished answer to his gaze. She drew near to him, but he pulled away.

'I want to show you something.'

He called the children to the four-wheel drive. Greta hung the chimes from a tap at the side of the verandah. Toby leaned out the car window and yelled for her to hurry.

The boys' voices and bodies were all song and scruffy pushing and pulling as Joel drove out to the road. The mystery they had entered the night before under that swollen moon was gone. Dust from the track rose up and dulled the landscape in a brown-grey light.

Out on the sealed road Joel picked up speed. Trees rushed past backwards. The children yelled to feel the wind through their hair. The car rattled over the bridge. In daylight Greta could see the dwindling creek, the shrunken waterhole shaded by paperbarks.

'We saw the neighbour's fence down at the creek, seems he won't want us visiting.'

'Trapper,' said Joel. 'Been there forever. His father and mine hated each other.'

They went over the floodwater crossing. Not far on, Joel braked and turned onto an unmarked track. A rock flicked up under the chassis and made a bang loud enough to silence the children.

'We're at the bottom of the hill in front of the homestead now,' Joel said, driving carefully through the bush until he came to a clearing and a dam.

The water shimmered. The sides were steep, stony red earth for the most part, except for one spot where a cluster of boulders led up from the water to the bank. They'd be the only way out if you fell in, thought Greta.

Joel turned to face the three in the back seat.

'See this water?'

The children nodded.

'This is the lake. It's poison.'

They stared back at him, quiet.

'Don't ever swim in it or drink it.'

The children dared to look at the lake again.

'I'm showing it to you so you know.'

He turned from them to gaze out across the still expanse of water.

'Pretty small for a lake,' Toby observed.

'It was a small quarry once,' said Joel. 'And then a dump for mining equipment. Machinery, rubbish. Those forty-four-gallon drums are leaking chemicals. That's where the poison comes from.'

'Why'd you call it the lake?'

Joel shrugged. 'We just did. Used to punt around it on our raft.'

The children looked across the water and then back at Joel with new respect—their father, who'd grown up near a poison lake.

'You're never to come here alone,' Joel continued. 'Not through our land, not any other way. Always with an adult. Never only kids. Got it?'

They nodded.

'You can see all the way to the bottom of this water because of those toxins,' he said. 'And what you'll see is a whole lot of bones. In the wet season the water level rises enough for an animal to drink from it. Most seem to know it's poison and leave it alone, but every now and then one makes a mistake.'

Joel shifted to point in the opposite direction, to a long unused track. The grasses almost hid it. 'The old meatworks is down that way. And you don't go there either, you understand?'

The children nodded again. They were thinking of the bones, Greta knew.

A gentle breeze ruffled the water's surface. The silver arms of a drowned tree begged the sky for mercy.

'There it is then,' said Joel. 'That's the lake.'

3

It followed Greta, the poison water. Now she'd seen it, she couldn't shake the image. It lingered with her through the night and was there in the morning, waiting. It mixed with the humid air and pressed in on her. Like the clouds rising behind the escarpment and travelling towards the shack, giant messengers with pending news.

To distract herself she focused on arranging the shack. Home is where the heart is, she always told her boys. Home is anywhere you make it.

She whispered it now as she rolled up the swags and stood them by the couch, fat and upright; and while she set up the cast-iron stove, with the coffee pot sitting on top, sporting its slightly melted handle. The shelves under the bench and in the pantry were covered in dust and termite wings and gecko dirt. She wiped them all down. Raffy followed her to line up enamel cups and plates. Joel and the other two boys brought in boxes of gear and clothing from the trailer, and then they all looked for besser blocks and planks by the open shed to make shelves.

'One shelf each,' Greta told them.

Raffy claimed the top one with his T-rex. Toby put his juggling balls, magic tricks and diabolo underneath. Next was Griffin's world, with his bird book, binoculars and a copy of *Journey to the Centre of the Earth*, which Joel was reading to them. She and Joel would share the last shelf. She took up half with her jewellery-making and bead boxes. A couple of shops on the east coast sold her necklaces, earrings and bracelets on consignment, and she sometimes took a stall at a local market. Keep the boat afloat, that's what the beads were about.

On either side of the shelves she stacked milk crates, one for each person's clothing.

'This room has shrunk,' Raffy noted.

She laughed. 'It'll be smaller again when we pick up the fridge and some furniture.' They would be driving up to Darwin the next day to pick up the second-hand deals she'd found online, and shop for food and building supplies. 'We'll have to hurry up and finish that verandah.'

Raffy sang to himself as he arranged new treasures on the louvres by the front door. A bright green feather, stones glinting mica, a kapok pod oozing white fluff.

'I know what you might like,' she said, and slit open the masking tape across a box.

'What did it say?' asked Raffy, pointing to the black texta letters she'd sliced through.

'*Fishermans Creek*.'

'A box from where *you* grew up.' He kneeled beside her, ready to be fascinated.

She took out a rolled kilim and three embroidered stockings in unopened cellophane packets. Her aunt had sent them one

Christmas when she was a child. They'd been put in a cupboard and forgotten.

'Here.' She handed him a jar of shells. 'You could put these on the louvres too.'

He stood up, excited, turning the jar in his hands to see pipi, limpet, fan and cone shells, as well as a crab's exoskeleton, complete with legs, claws and eye-like marks on its back.

'Look!' His finger followed a line of black and red glass beads weaving between the other shapes.

'My mother's necklace,' she answered. 'I broke it.'

He paused. 'I hope she forgave you.'

All Greta remembered was her own mortified child-face in the mirror and the necklace clutched in her fingers, with no catch, and the sound of beads scattering across the floor.

The lid was too tight for Raffy to open. She unscrewed it for him.

He held the jar up to her nose. 'It smells of olives and sea.'

In a rush she recalled her mother Vivian's rare laugh, sunlit fish scales, the sound of the surf, sand-clogged fingernails. Quick as slides on high speed in the old family projector. There and gone.

'Toby says this is a real-life bullet hole.' His foot smoothed back and forth over a hole in the floor. 'Uncle Vadik did it one Christmas.'

Joel had told them about this escapade during a monotonous stretch of the highway.

'Do you think he tried to shoot Pavel?'

'I'm not sure,' Greta said. 'He was very drunk.'

'Why would he shoot his own brother?'

'Families have wild weather sometimes.'

She was craving coffee and went to the camping box for the grinder and beans. She leaned against the sink to turn the handle. The gritty sound and aroma were a comfort. Raffy's back was a silhouette at the louvres. He was intent on the shells, arranging them one by one.

She'd just set the coffee pot on the stove when Griffin bumped through the back door carrying a toolbox upright. He eased it onto the bench.

'He's heavy,' the boy said, puffing.

Greta thanked him and opened the box to take out a tin. Her father's ashes were inside, sealed in plastic. Frank would have scoffed at an urn, the expense and show of it, so they'd decided on his favourite tin where he kept items he didn't want to lose—his and Greta's birth certificates, his watch if it wasn't on his wrist, a torch, a twenty-dollar note. And right at the bottom were precious secrets—a photo booth shot of him and Vivian the night they met, the head scarf she'd worn on her last day, the wedding ring she'd left behind.

'When will you let him go?' asked Griffin.

'When I'm ready.' She smiled at him. 'In a wild, beautiful place he'd like.'

What would it cost you, she heard Janna say, *to bring him back as he asked? You don't have to live here.*

Janna, still there in Fishermans Creek, ever angling for Greta to return, if only for a visit. Janna had been less trouble as a twelve-year-old, reading tea-leaves and fortune lines. Still, she was a saint to have cleared out that old cottage wobbling on its salt-bitten stumps four years ago, storing the boxes of unsorted gear, furniture and Vivian's photographs in her ex-boyfriend's shipping container on her property. She'd sent the ashes in their tin and the box of a few belongings to the orange farm where

Greta and Joel were working at the time. There'd been no funeral, at her father's request.

Griffin barged out the back door again as Raffy turned to her with a question.

'Do you think Pavel would mind us living here?'

He'd finished with the shells and was balancing the jar by his mother's bead boxes. Then he moved through the room with his arms out, as if testing the space and his great-uncle's approval.

'I'm sure he'd be glad,' said Greta. She crunched a lone coffee bean she'd found on the bench. 'It sounds like he was a gentle soul, Pavel.'

'And Dad helped him build this shack anyway.'

His toe explored the bullet hole again.

'You know there're stone steps here under the verandah.' He opened the front door. 'You can see them down there through the gaps.'

'They must be the original ones.'

'Pavel made them up to his little house.'

She stopped herself from saying, 'Don't fall,' as he walked out over the makeshift bridge, peering down. When he'd made it safely to the ground and crawled under the verandah, she went back to the open box. Her father's oil lantern was wrapped in a hand-knitted olive jumper. She lifted it out and pressed the woollen to her face. The smell shot her back to his kitchen. There he was at the stove, boots planted on the crusty lino, eyes staring into the aluminium saucepan and its lump of burned tuna mornay.

'Don't send me there, Gret,' he'd said.

But what else could she do? After the fall out on the reef, the wound on his leg that wouldn't heal. He couldn't travel. And he couldn't live alone.

'You can't come with us, Dad. You know you can't.'

She might never forgive herself for those words. She knew he wouldn't last at the respite place in Adelaide, far from the waves, the quiet river. She knew it when she saw his hand on the child-lock gate.

His watch slipped from a sleeve of the jumper. The face had yellowed and the wristband was broken. She set the time and watched the second hand do a revolution.

The last things in the box were her mother's sewing scissors, and a spider conch shell in bubble wrap. Greta put the wrapped shell on a louvre above Raffy's treasures.

The coffee pot bubbled on the stove. She turned off the gas and poured herself a cup. Griffin's hand-drawn calendar stared at her from the end of the bench. Days one and two were crossed off. The remainder stretched in wavering lines from the beginning of September to the new year, followed by a line of question marks.

Outside, Joel sounded the earth with a crowbar, breaking up soil, edging in under rocks to lever them out. He and Toby were levelling ground for the cabin. Two bedrooms, a bathroom and a balcony at the escarpment end, with a skillion roof, was the plan. Greta could hear Joel explaining the importance of foundations, if they weren't right the cabin would be skewiff forever. He'd chosen a site by a beautiful scarlet gum, not far from the shack. Close enough for bedrooms, distant enough to be a separate dwelling.

Mick would pay Gabe to help, Joel said. Gabe, who'd lived on and off with Joel's family. No one knew where Gabe was just now, only that he was off working somewhere. He came and went. Hopefully he would appear well before he and Joel were due to go fencing and mustering for five weeks in late October. Gabe had rung about this plan during their drive up north.

'It'll see us through,' Joel assured her, since Mick was paying them only a little more than supplies.

You'll have to master the run of this place before then, Greta told herself.

Again the lake came to her mind's eye, whispering of underground aquifers. Where might the poison leak? She imagined hidden channels of toxic water trickling around buried rocks, seeping through the soil into the bore, gushing from the kitchen tap.

There was not always reliable phone reception here either, she'd realised, on the theme of threats and emergencies. It was as if the faintest breeze could deliver or erase it on a whim. Best to walk up nearer the homestead, Joel had advised.

She pushed the lake aside in her mind, unrolling the kilim to stand on it and feel the rich colours underfoot.

Raffy came flying across the plank bridge and through the door. He was breathless. 'No one can find Griffin.'

'He was just here,' she said.

'Well, he isn't now. He's completely gone.'

She checked her father's watch. Maybe half an hour had passed since Griffin was inside. The binoculars were missing from the shelves, she noticed. 'Ah, Griffin,' she sighed, and went out into the glaring sunlight, as if she might see the boy with her mother perspective.

She scanned downhill across the gamba and outcrop of rocks to the lake, and up the slope to the homestead. The place expanded while she looked at it, an endless stretch of bushland to the escarpment. This land could swallow him, make a dead leaf of a child. She shivered.

Raffy ran to check the shower and the outdoor toilet. Toby joined the search, climbing up the banyan tree to use the platform as a lookout. Greta looked in the red ute that Gabe had left. There was no boy in the four-wheel drive or the trailer.

From the mahogany tree near the rail freight van a flock of white cockatoos watched the humans, their yellow crests fanning and contracting.

Raffy went to Joel who kept on with the crowbar for a few moments, then stopped. 'Griffin!' His voice rang out sharp across the valley.

The cockatoos took flight with loud squawks. *Griffin, griffin, griffin* echoed back the escarpment. Raffy hurried over to Greta to watch for any sudden reappearances. But the place was silent and nobody came.

'Cut it out, Griffin!' Joel shouted.

The rocks, the burning sun and the wandering child. They'd snapped his patience. He threw down the bar with a clang.

The branches of the mahogany squeaked bravely. The door to the cargo van opened. A shape appeared in the doorway.

'Griffin!'

He kept his head low to hide a sheepish grin. The binoculars were around his neck. He tried to move away, but Joel's hand was too quick.

'There's no hiding here!'

Griffin kept his eyes averted. He waited for Greta to move closer and wriggled free.

Joel was a coiled spring. 'If you get lost out here, that's it! You're gone! We might never, ever find you.'

A blue-winged kookaburra flew in to claim the mahogany branch above him. Griffin sidled away.

Joel moved off with a glance to Greta. 'Those kids need to go to school.'

Toby followed him back to the crowbar. Raffy turned in little circles, watching his shadow on the ground.

The kookaburra started up a raucous laugh, then with a flash of blue wing took off.

Greta walked across to the freight car, noticing how the ground was uneven, and that stones lined patches of dirt. She was walking the sunken map of Pavel's garden.

The van was from another era, perhaps the old North Australia Railway. It had been fitted out with a table and bench seats, cupboards and a bench. A rusted fan hung from the wall at the far end, above where a bed might have been. Raffy snuck in under his mother's arm.

Griffin reappeared and pushed past them both. He stood on the bench seat behind the table to look out one of the windows. 'There was a golden tree snake winding up this tree.'

He searched through the binoculars for the vanished snake. Greta could see a palm trunk frilled with green vine leaves. Higher up, a cluster of red berries hung among the fronds. A white pigeon with black-edged wings feasted there. Griffin focused on it, and then pulled his bird book from his back pocket. 'What I'm really looking for is a hooded parrot.'

The pigeon flew away, and he sat down to slap a rhythm on the table. 'We could make this a cubby.' He smiled at Raffy, pleased with the find.

Greta ran her hand along the faded blue laminex benchtop, and noticed the lino floor had buckled and cracked.

You could patch this up, she thought, make a room of one's own. All it needed was a lick of paint and an air conditioner.

The idea of fixing up the freight van took hold while she threaded beads onto a necklace wire after dinner. She worked at the camping table out on the back verandah. Her father's lantern glowed beside her. Joel had told them that his parents lived in the van when they first came to Lightstone, when his brother Mick was a baby. Greta imagined her mother-in-law, Maria, with a new baby and then toddlers in the cramped space. Was it like the train she'd fled in across Europe, in the same freight car where Fedor and his brothers were also hiding? Greta saw them cowering in the dark, hearts thudding to the clacking rhythm underneath, being carried into an unknown future.

Raffy came outside to see what she'd made. He picked up a pair of earrings and dangled them at his earlobes. 'How do I look?'

'Real flash.'

'Raffy!' Toby called. 'Dad's going to read to us now.'

Raffy dropped the earrings in the tray and hurried inside.

There was a snap of wicker as Joel sat down. 'What chapter are we up to then?'

Greta put the necklace aside and wandered out to the edge of the hill to have a moment on her own. The cooler night air was a comfort after the glare of the day. Joel's voice drifted after her. She stepped down to the bowl of rocky ground where the cycads were and found a boulder to sit on. With the night the land had changed. The world of silhouettes had returned. There was no moon yet, just a spill of stars above. Far off, a dingo howled its long, high notes. Others joined in, calling their age-old song. She looked back to the shack. The lantern flame flickered.

The unseen valley drew her in again. Her eyes followed the line of rocks and trees from the outcrop down to the glimmer of that poison water, so pure under the moonlight, so alluring. Even it might alter under the spell of this night, turn innocent.

In the humid darkness a woman's feet search the ground. She's moving downhill. Her steps are erratic, lurch and pause. Loose stones clatter ahead of her. Her breath is uneven because of her fear, and the weight she holds. Clasped against her is a squalling child, under one year, face twisted in a purple contortion, a small and shivering fist at the swollen, pulsing ear. Every cry escalates. The mother holds the baby's head in her hand, the hot skull of pain. The weight of the body, the weight of despair.

The father's angry yell barks from the house back up the hill. The dogs rattle their chains and yelp his disquiet. She turns her head to look back towards the muted light of the house beneath the glinting iron of the roof. She hears the thud of a fist slamming into gyprock, the renewed commotion of the dogs.

She draws the child closer into her breast, to muffle the cries. The baby writhes, arches back, howls curling from its wet mouth.

As if the night could be her last hope, the mother holds her child out, an offering to the darkness. She pleads with the night, whispering her terrible supplication.

The child shrieks, a sick and twisted wail.

The air is shocked silent. The trees darken. The rocks close their ears against the sound.

And the still lake breathes its quiet, the dark mirror for a moon caught in the tendrils of a horrified tree.

4

The school was an old community hall, weatherboard with louvres down both sides. Near the front door were three flagpoles, flying the Australian Aboriginal flag, the Torres Strait Islander flag, and the national one that Griffin never liked to see flying alone. He'd been admonished at his last school for omitting it in his school project and refusing to sing the national anthem.

Greta thought her angel ruffians might have clung to her on their first day, but Griffin and Raffy bolted for the climbing frame under a blue shade cloth, and Toby went to the oval, which was unnaturally green. A three-legged dog romped across the grass after a shoal of children chasing a soccer ball.

Greta went inside to find the teachers. There were two, she'd heard, and only thirty students. The classroom was one large room. Pegs for bags lined the back wall and a fridge hummed in one corner. The smell of lunchboxes and pencil shavings was in the air. A divider curtain down the middle had been pushed to one side. The louvre windows gave a split view of the playground, the oval and a bush block.

Wooden desks scoured with graffiti faced a blackboard that took up most of the end wall. Beside it was a slightly open door with *Teachers Only* stencilled on it.

'Hello?' Greta called.

'Hello!' A woman came through the door, laughing.

She wore a bright orange headscarf. Her smile was infectious. She was called Miss Rhianna and she was the sun.

She shook Greta's hand and gave her the enrolment forms. 'Don't read it all at once, you'll get a headache!' Her voice was husky, she might be a singer.

'When did you arrive?'

'Last week.'

'Still finding your feet!' She chuckled and moved out to the porch. 'Let's find your boys—Toby's twelve, Griffin's nine and the little one's six, right?' She looked across the playground. 'Ah, I see them! Straight into it!'

Greta waved to Raffy. He came over and considered Miss Rhianna, taking in the diamante stud in her nose and the eagle claw tattoo above her ankle.

Miss Rhianna passed him the school bell. 'Here, can you ring that for me?'

Another boy ran up. 'I'll help you,' he offered.

It was heavy. They worked out their fingers on the handle to ring it together. Children started heading for the schoolhouse, lining up at the bottom of the steps. Rhianna took Raffy's hand and eased him in among them.

Greta sat at a lunch table to fill out the enrolment forms. The children were inside by the time she finished. As she was leaving the school grounds a mobility scooter zoomed up the path. She stepped sideways just in time. An older woman was driving it, with a toddler on her knee and a boy standing at the back. He jumped off at the school door.

Greta wound down the car window and continued along the road to a T-intersection. A *Welcome to Lightstone!* sign greeted her on the corner. An arrow pointed towards the general store and post office. The main street was lined with white frangipanis. The air smelled of them. Immediately on her left was a swimming pool. She slowed the car to read the opening times on the gate. A faded yellow shade cloth hung above the inviting water. On the other side of the road an abandoned church stood in the middle of an unkempt block. A dirt road separated it from an oval over-looked by a shady rain tree. Behind it was a frighteningly high, old-fashioned metal slide and a set of swings. The buildings on her left were boarded up—a bakery, hardware store and a couple of unmarked shopfronts. Last in the row was one with a sign: *Op Shop, Saturdays.*

She headed for the general store further up on her left. The park opposite ended with a thicket of trees and bushes. Glancing across, she caught sight of a model castle among the dark trees. Greta was so surprised she stopped in the road, engine still running. It was a salmon orange colour, a couple of metres high and wide, with a stone wall. Greta stared at it, almost unbelieving. She'd have expected a giant crocodile, or a bull rider. Instead, a change-ling monument dropped by a raven from another hemisphere, or tipped out of a fairytale book to take root where it landed.

A ute behind her beeped. She turned left into the general store car park. Over the road she noticed the pub, and next to it a high-fenced yard with faded signs: *Timber Yard, Scrap Metal, Sand and Rocks.*

The store was raised off the ground, with a low-roofed verandah that wrapped around one side of the building, leading to the adjacent post office. Two old petrol pumps were outside, both out of use. An elderly woman wearing sunglasses sat at a corner table on the verandah, watching people come and go. She nodded as Greta went into the store.

There was no air conditioning. The shelves were lined with tins and packets of food, and a few hardware items in one section. Vegetables, dairy products and bread were crammed into a loudly humming fridge. She bought a few groceries and a chocolate muffin. Outside she read the local noticeboard. There was a reward for a dog lost on Fireworks Night and a poster for last year's Rosella Festival. The pub had a family meal deal and karaoke on Friday nights. A ride-on mower, a tractor and a tinnie were for sale.

She paused at an ad for an old 35-mm SLR camera, with lenses, filters and camera bag, as well as black-and-white film, developing gear and an enlarger. Who'd buy it now, she wondered, with everything digital?

The camera was an Olympus OM-2—light, easy to carry, Greta remembered. She'd used her mother's one back in year twelve. Just as well Vivian hadn't lived to see the end of film photography. *Digital, never!* she would mutter, and suck on her cigarette so hard it popped.

Greta whisked the ad from the board.

'You must be Joel's missus.'

Greta turned, conscious of the ad in her hand, and saw it was the old woman at the table who'd spoken.

'Heard he was back.' She smiled at a young man coming up the steps, and stood to leave with him. 'Tell Joel we'll see him round.' She was a little breathless.

Greta smiled, 'I will,' and then followed the verandah around to the post office.

There was a queue inside. She filled out a form for a PO box.

'Come at the worst time of year,' said the woman behind the counter. 'That build-up is here already.' Her nametag said: *I'm Dee and I rule!*

Greta passed over the form and money. Dee slid a key towards her and Greta smiled her thanks. The bell above the door clanged as she left. Dee would be putting two and two together. *This is the wife of Joel, who's back in town. We'll see what we think of her.*

Across the road the strange castle beckoned. The three-legged dog from the school found her there. She pushed aside low-hanging branches and the woody tendrils of a vine.

The air smelled of flying foxes. Above her dark greenery trembled. She walked around the castle's stone wall. It had a little gate that said: *Make a Wish.* The moat was empty, its waterwheel still. There were three cylindrical towers, the largest in the middle. None of them was ramrod straight; they had a curvaceous sway. Each had three windows one above the other, and a spiral staircase leading up to a moss-coloured roof. Every window had a green, curved overhang, like an eyelid. Even the tower roofs had these eye windows. The entire structure gave her the feeling of an Escher drawing. She couldn't tell if she was watching or being watched. Or if the castle was innocent or sinister. A sign—*Pavel's Castle*—was fastened to a rock at the back. Joel's uncle, surely! Why hadn't he mentioned it?

The foliage above her was suddenly alive with disgruntled squawks. She'd disturbed the flying foxes. Black wings stretched along slender branches, jostling for space.

She ducked under a low branch and escaped to the shade of the rain tree by the oval. Delicate white flowers were strewn across the ground. Ibis stabbed their curved beaks at the lush grass lining the cricket pitch. The rest of the oval was yellow dry, like the park behind her. She ate half of the muffin and put the rest back in the bag for Joel, feeling a niggle of guilt that she'd stopped so long.

Greta came back to find the shack empty and a note from Joel on the bench, held in place by the spider conch shell she'd left on the louvre. It was unwrapped. She wondered if Joel or one of the children had discovered it. She picked the shell up and clutched it tight, sliding her fingers between its bony ones.

Joel's note was wordless, just little sketches of barbed wire, fence cutters, a stick figure holding a crowbar and a pile of rocks sprouting a flower. The boys loved these quick cartoons he left in a cutlery drawer or pegged to a tent rope. He didn't say much, Joel, but he had a wry humour and his own way of expressing himself. A quirky little sketch. A pretty feather on the dashboard for her. A pearly shell to shift her mood. She wondered sometimes if it was the travelling that had held them together, the being on the road and not settling in one place. It kept them occupied, distracted. He wasn't one to delve. She'd liked that about him.

'Tell us the story of how you met, tell us again,' Raffy would plead, nose pressed to the window, watching the reflectors with their red eyes pass, listening for the tyre to edge onto the ridged white line and give him a fright with its noise.

'Well, he was a surprise, that's for sure,' Greta would begin.

First she'd seen the surfboard swirl in along a narrow, foamy channel. With no surfer in sight, she'd panicked. But then two hands grabbed the rocks below her feet and he hauled himself up like a sleek, dark merman with the sun a pink ball behind him. He smiled at her for an introduction and leaned down to rescue his board. There was a cut on his ankle, and watery blood trailed across his foot. He peeled the wetsuit to his waist and inspected the board. Old scars glistened across his torso, welts glowing white against his olive skin.

'Where are you headed?' he'd asked.

'And the rest,' Toby liked to chime in, 'is history.'

'Or the future,' Griffin would add, 'depending on how you look at it.'

Greta drew a second flower on Joel's sketch and listened for the red ute as it ambled along in search of bedraggled fences to repair, replace, reinstate. She was worried for him working in this heat, the sun bearing down on him hour after hour. She saw his boots on the cracked earth, his body shrouded by the terrible grasses, the endless infestation of them.

She'd often worked on fences with him, singing the wire into place. But here he wanted to work alone or with Toby, urging her to start on a garden.

'Plants aren't my thing,' he said. 'I kill them.'

So he was down the hill, marking his lines. She would mark hers here, by the shack, reinventing Pavel's garden beds and creating her own. Garden tools and the plants that she'd bought on their trip to Darwin were waiting for her. A native gardenia, quinine bush and a sandpaper fig. A bush apple and native hibiscus. A couple of water pots.

Nothing had prepared Greta for this earth. The ground was rock-ridden. With every jarring slam of the spade another landscaping dream evaporated. She chipped pointlessly at land-locked stones, shifting crumbs of soil around them. Her shirt clung wet to her skin. Blisters stung her palms. She gave up on the spade and smacked the hoe into stubborn dirt. Stones, gravel, clay smarted back with their tougher resolve. The ground didn't want her. After an hour all she'd made was a haphazard patch of dents. After two hours she was too light-headed to keep on. This was a task for dawn.

Defeated, she headed for the shack. Inside was no comfort. It was a box of stifling air. The sun was overhead, beating down on the roof. She couldn't drink enough water to quench her thirst.

She moved onto the verandah, across the floor's scaffolding to a hammock she'd strung up between two posts and collapsed into it.

The ruin on the hill shimmered behind a heat mirage. Even from this distance Greta could hear the odd noises it made, the shifting roof, the slip of a beam. A whirl of dust strutted across the front of the burnt-out house. There must be a breeze there. She willed it to herself. Nothing came.

The closest shade was at the banyan tree. It had become a hub for her children. Not only for the ladder and platform, but for the track they'd worn from it down to the creek. The shadows under the tree tempted her. She slipped on her thongs and made her way there.

Aerial roots enmeshed the tree like woody snakes around its trunk, propping up the branches. Joel and Toby had strung up a tyre swing on one branch. Repairs on the platform and its three-walled cubby would be the next project. Joel had built the cubby for his sister, he'd told them. It was her escape from raised voices, frayed tempers, her father's belt.

Magdalen was the only girl and the last child in the family. Dead by her early teens after a terrible car accident on the highway, a fire that gave Joel his scars. He rarely talked about it, or his sister. Greta knew only that she'd followed Joel around and had trouble at school, and was often unwell with ear infections. She'd left school after year three. Joel took Magdalen with him wherever he could. On fishing and hunting trips she was the car DJ, choosing tapes to play. When she lost it and spiralled into a meltdown, only Joel could calm her. Greta knew even less about the five brothers. They'd drifted apart when they left this place, after losing their mother to cancer, their sister to the car accident and the house to flames.

She wanted to believe it was different once. Here, under the banyan's vast shade, she saw another kind of vine—invisible, encircling each child, binding them to this place and to one another. And the vine that held Joel to Magdalen was the strongest. Greta was jealous—not of the love, but to have a sibling.

She reached out a hand and gave the tyre a push. The branch creaked, the rope moved in a slow twist. She turned the swing faster, around and around. In the whirling O of the tyre she glimpsed a little boy. Gavin from Fishermans Creek. He hadn't come to her like this in years. Odd for it to start again here. He'd had a tyre swing too, at the caravan park where he lived. They'd spin each other around and around. The ground would tip afterwards, they'd walk crooked.

Greta grabbed the tyre and held it still. The boy was gone.

A soft tinkling came to her from the other side of the tree. Griffin's chimes were dangling off a low-slung hook at the end of a chain hanging from a branch. She wondered if the hook was for a car engine or a carcass. Her fingers tapped the chimes to make them ring. She ventured out of the tree's shade.

The sun was fierce. The gamba was as tall as her and all around. The dry, yellow stems whispered. A narrow track wove between them, it might take her somewhere. A few steps in she glimpsed a black shadow and froze, thinking wild pig.

A loud screech ripped the quiet. Three black cockatoos squawked upwards, their wings and the blood sign of their tails stark against the cloudless blue sky.

In their place was an abandoned car, marooned on a mound of red earth. Its rusted bonnet pointed skyward. The boot was sinking into the ground. The back wheel was off. Next to it was a mangled nest of metal cables. An axle jutted up through the centre like a bony arm. Leaves and crushed glass covered the car's floor. The seats were metal cavities. The steering column was a headless neck.

A warm breeze shivered through the grasses. Someone coughed. Greta spun around.

A girl of about thirteen or fourteen was staring at her, hands poised against brittle stalks she'd pushed aside.

'God!' Greta stumbled backwards. 'I didn't see you there.' She smiled awkwardly.

'Careful of snakes,' said the girl. Her words were slow, a little slurred. She didn't smile.

A shiny black ribbon eased from a lughole in the car's front wheel. Greta watched the slender tail disappear into the grass. The cicadas screeched louder. The air was a suffocating vibration.

The stranger didn't move. She wore no hat, but her skin was terribly pale. A blue vein pulsed at her temple. Her arms and legs were spotted with small red bites. One at her knee was infected, raised into a pustule. She smelled of stale sweat, campfire smoke and gamey meat. Her dress had been white once and was dotted with blue daisies. A dirty lemon cardigan clung stiffly to her arms. Greta wondered at her wearing it in this heat. She was strong-boned—tall for her age, perhaps. She seemed young. Innocent. Greta tried to take her in without staring. The girl was listening to the odd notes of the chimes under the cicadas' racket. Her eyes were on the shack.

'You live here,' she said.

'My husband lived here,' said Greta, 'when he was a boy.'

The girl didn't look at her.

Greta tried a smile. 'We've come to clean the place up.' She paused. 'Joel's brother asked us to fix it.'

She waited for the girl to speak. Nothing.

'He's got five brothers. That's a lot, isn't it?'

The girl twisted a grass stalk tight around her fingers. 'Joel,' she murmured.

'You know him?'

The girl was rattled then. She breathed in with a shudder and looked from Greta to the escarpment. Her fingertips were strangled white.

'I meant does your family know him—he would've lived here before you were born.'

'I'm on my own,' the girl said.

She waited for a last ripple of notes from the chimes and then moved away, her hands parting the long dry stalks. Greta tried to keep sight of her, but the grasses took the girl quickly, and all Greta saw were yellow rods shimmering in the heat.

———

Greta was surprised to see Joel outside the open shed when she got back. The fences must have frustrated him. He was chopping wood for the outdoor oven. Toby was keen to make pizza after school. He'd already swept the hearth free of leaves and twigs and the skull of a small mammal. Greta was looking forward to trying it out for bread or a stew in the cast-iron pot. It was a friendly oven with its brown stones and bright mosaic door. The children had been proud to learn Joel had built it with his uncle. She wondered if the chips of coloured tile Pavel used for the door were broken for the mosaic or by someone else's temper.

Greta watched her husband chopping with a steady beat, not pausing. She could sense an agitation in him. As if he'd met an adversary down there at the fences and was gathering his resolve. Splits of wood jumped out, warning her back.

She told him about the girl, her voice sounding between blunt thuds.

'Can't think who that might be,' he replied.

'I was wondering if Trapper had a daughter.'

He stopped and caught his breath. 'He doesn't have kids.'

She let him begin with the axe again, and then said, 'I wonder if she's been squatting here with someone. We might have put her out.'

The wood split. He wiped the sweat from his face with his arm. 'Kids roam places for fun if nobody's there. Word'll get round we've moved in.'

He was in a world of his own again, wielding the axe.

'Well, I hope she's not in trouble or something, on her own.'

Another piece of wood broke open.

He smiled at her then, one hand holding the axe. 'You're too kind worrying about people, you are. Just like my mother.'

5

'Here,' said Greta, handing Toby the camera ad with its mud map. 'Don't let me get lost.'

She crunched the red ute's gearstick into place. For all its quirks she was growing fond of this vehicle. There was a distinctive rattle inside it, and a squeak from the fan belt, but it felt trusty, like it would go forever. It reminded her of the truck her father drove when she was a kid, with the tray full of fishing nets and crab pots.

Toby studied the arrows and lines leading to a hand-drawn star and a name. 'Who's Brynn?'

'I don't know, but she's selling her camera.'

They buzzed along the road, past bushland and across a creek that was a gaping dirt channel. The car dipped to a floodway by a billabong that had retracted to leave a wide stretch of baked mud. A white egret paused in its fishing to watch them pass.

Toby called out for Greta to slow down as they climbed a hill and saw a tractor tyre painted white against a fence. The gate was open. The car skidded lightly up the steep dirt driveway to a small dwelling with grey fan palms planted along the wall. A flock of indignant guineafowl immediately surrounded the car. Greta stepped out into a cacophony of squawking. The three boys followed.

'Anyone home?' she called, moving tentatively towards the house. The birds hustled her on, red chin skins flapping, blue faces bobbing alarm.

'Here,' a voice answered.

To the right of the building was an outside laundry. A woman was at the clothesline with a knife in her hand, working on a dead wallaby strung up by the hind legs. A bucket was underneath.

'I'll finish this now I've started,' she said. 'I thought you'd come earlier.'

Greta felt slightly chided. On the phone the woman hadn't specified a time.

'I'm Brynn,' she added, for the benefit of the children, perhaps.

Greta introduced them. They gave little waves, not wanting to shake hands. The woman was skinny and wore faded denim overalls with a black singlet underneath. Her silver hair was cropped short and her eyes were dark and held a savage sorrow. Her feet were bare and tanned with dirt.

Toby edged closer to watch her cut away skin from the wallaby's ankle and peel it downwards. The flesh gleamed white and pink. The smell of it smacked Greta's nostrils. Toby picked up a severed arm and tapped the stiff black claws.

'Have them,' said the woman. 'They make good back scratchers. Give one to your brother.'

Toby held out the other arm for Griffin, who folded his arms against the gift.

'The camera's on the back verandah.' Brynn pointed the way with her knife.

Raffy and Greta walked around the side of the house, while Toby and Griffin stayed to see the wallaby's belly slit open, the guts spill into the bucket. Brynn yelled at the dogs. Toby's voice lilted on the breeze, explaining why dogs couldn't eat offal and how to check hearts and livers for worms. His father's meatworking days here, and his grandfather's fastidious, fiery reputation, were serving him well these first few days in the playground. He put them to use with this Brynn.

Greta and Raffy found the camera equipment in a box on a coffee table. They sat on the sagging couch to go through it.

'Take a picture and let me see it.' Raffy struck a pose.

'This one doesn't work like that.'

Greta opened the camera to show him where the film canister fitted. 'You have to wind on the film for each picture, wait till you've finished the film, take it out, and then develop your negatives and prints. Until then, you don't really know what's there.'

Raffy was intrigued.

'Are you a photographer?' she asked as Brynn arrived with Toby and Griffin.

'Not me,' said Brynn. 'Henry.' She sat beside Greta to roll a cigarette. 'No point keeping it locked away. He'd want it used.'

'Why doesn't Henry want it now?' asked Raffy.

'Henry's dead,' said Brynn. 'Cancer got him.'

'I'm sorry,' said Greta.

Brynn lit her cigarette. She took a long drag and exhaled slowly.

'Can you blow smoke rings?' Raffy wanted to know.

Brynn laughed. 'Ha! You're funny!'

Greta looked through the box to find a slide viewer, a light meter, developing tank for negatives, a tin of developer powder and an orange safe light. Raffy asked to hold the safe light. Why was it orange? He had a thousand questions.

'You'll need a darkroom,' said Toby, looking at all the paraphernalia.

'There're dark rooms in that old house,' called Griffin, swinging in the hammock. He stretched its red net around himself to make a cocoon. 'Dad says any walls left are burned black.'

'I've got my eye on the old freight van,' said Greta. 'I think your cubby's my darkroom.'

'No way!' Griffin sat up too quickly and had to struggle against capsizing.

In a second box on the floor Raffy found another contraption. 'What's this?'

Greta carefully took out the enlarger. It had a domed hood and the lens on a bellows. 'This is a vintage one.'

Brynn nodded, pleased Greta understood.

Toby and Raffy moved closer to see. Greta described how a hidden globe inside could shine on a negative and project the image onto photographic paper. It reminded Raffy of how they'd looked through a cardboard pinhole to see a solar eclipse.

'I'm not a photographer myself,' said Brynn, leaning back. 'It's all too arty for me. Too technical and bloody time-consuming.' Her hand tapped the developer powder tin. 'There's more of these in the coolroom, and film in the freezer, black and white only. Don't let me forget them.' She looked at Toby to make him the reminder.

Greta thanked her and unwrapped the three extra lenses. There was a 28-mm wide-angle lens, a 135-mm short telephoto, and a 300-mm long lens for close up.

'It's a good kit, Brynn.'

'Our grandmother Vivian was a professional,' said Raffy, picking up a sachet of silica to squeeze. 'She taught Mum.' He paused. 'And then she walked into the sea and died.'

'True?' asked Brynn. Her dark eyes were on Raffy.

He nodded. 'We weren't born yet. Mum was just a kid.'

'I'm sorry to hear that,' said Brynn.

Raffy's voice fluttered to a whisper. He kept his gaze on Brynn. 'Not a soul knows where she went except her.'

'Oh, Raffy,' sighed Griffin, and tipped himself from the hammock.

Greta looked through the camera's viewfinder to check he'd landed safely. Click.

'Gotcha,' she said.

'There isn't even any film in that,' he replied and shimmied off the verandah into the garden.

A couple of hens stepped in line behind him. Toby hurried after them. Raffy hung back for a turn in the hammock.

'Cuppa?' Brynn asked.

Greta followed her into a small sitting room with a piano and an armchair. Raffy soon joined her to see Henry's photos stuck on the walls and curling at the edges. A cocoon hanging from a leaf. A green tree ant's nest of eucalyptus leaves welded with white silk thread. The lightning shots impressed him most, jutting through night skies, lighting up rocks and termite mounds.

'Henry was a storm chaser,' Brynn called from the adjoining kitchen. 'Up at all hours and out in terrible weather. I was always waiting for him to be struck.'

She came to lift the piano stool's lid. A stack of photos was inside.

'Pick one you like and you can have it.'

Raffy took out a bundle and sat with his back against the piano, near the pedals. Above him numerous ivory keys were missing. The whole instrument was bowed and out of alignment. The top was gone, so its innards could be seen. It used to live outside, Brynn explained.

Greta admired the garden sprawling down the slope. She explained her own plans for the shack.

'The soil's the challenge here,' said Brynn. 'I'll take you up to the export yards next time I go. Get yourself a tray of cattle manure. Mix it with dirt and sand from Ronnie.'

'I haven't met Ronnie yet.'

'You will.'

When the tea was ready they went back to the verandah. Brynn smoked another cigarette, quiet now, as if she'd had enough of talking. Greta wondered if Henry and the lightning photos had silenced her. She drank her tea and began repacking the camera equipment.

'Raffy, choose your photo and find your brothers,' she called into the room behind her.

But Brynn suddenly snapped out of her reverie and stood to fling the dregs from her cup.

'Can't let you leave without some plants. This way, my girl.'

She walked swiftly along the narrow track. Her back was ramrod straight. The dogs scampered up, excited. A small black pig followed.

'Don't pat,' Brynn warned Raffy, pointing to the pig. 'She bites.'

She selected a pawpaw for him to carry, saying, 'You can grow anything up here,' and that was how it seemed as they passed the mottled backs of watermelons and the spiky heads of pineapples.

Raffy kept close to Greta, keeping an eye on the pig that trotted beside the wallaby-skinning woman. He stopped short at a dead thing on the ground and squatted to poke it with a stick. Its soft brown, spiny shell had split open. Greta could see he was thinking baby echidna.

Brynn laughed. 'Jackfruit.'

She pointed up the tree trunk beside them where hefty green, stubble-skinned fruits were hanging out from the side of the trunk. 'Good for curry when they're green, dessert when they're yellow.'

A little further on they stopped to see an impressively large pumpkin fenced in with a riot of greenery. 'See my winner?' said Brynn, opening the gate. 'I grew her for the Darwin Show but couldn't part with her.'

It was sagging underneath, an overgrown orange moon dropped by the night. She passed her hand over the pumpkin's barnacled skin. 'Must be a hundred kilo. I'd have won if I put her in the show.'

'It has its own private cage,' Griffin smiled as Brynn shut the gate against the pig and its relatives. The idea reminded him of those unusual cages they'd seen over the neighbour's fence. He asked Brynn about them.

'Trapper's critter world.' She rolled her eyes at Greta. 'An albino monitor, he says. A flying possum. A talking cockatoo and a three-horned goat. Freaks of nature, he'll tell you. He lures tourists occasionally, panning gold in the creek, selfies with his menagerie.'

She stopped to uproot turmeric and galangal for Greta. 'Stick those in the ground, give them plenty of water. They'll grow.'

For a nursery she had a couple of trestle tables holding seedlings in pots, with a shade cloth overhead. She packed a crate with young plants. Griffin read out the labels. Snake bean, custard apple, kaffir lime, tamarind. The boys carried off pawpaw and banana plants in pots to the ute while Brynn found rolls of wire and shade cloth.

At the last moment she sent Toby to the coolroom for the developer and film, where he could also see the wallaby again. Then she gave Raffy a bag of hose adaptors, and an old sweet potato sprouting roots like tentacles for him to plant. He held it warily like it might move. She led the way to the car with pots of eggplant and cherry tomatoes.

The pig trotted on one side of her, Raffy on the other.

'You'll keep your pig then,' the boy suggested.

'I will,' said Brynn. 'I like her. We have the same mood swings.'

A whiff of bushfire smoke was on the air. She paused to register the wind's direction. 'That's a fire at the wrong time of year. Some twit with a match or a welder.' She shut the ute tray with a slam.

Greta went to collect the camera equipment and enlarger. When she was done she handed Brynn a wad of money and slid in behind the wheel. A soft clucking came from the back seat. She turned and saw a black hen nestled on Toby's lap. Griffin held a brown one. Raffy's was the smallest, and white. The boys grinned at her.

'Don't say no,' Brynn told her. 'They're layers.'

'Thanks.' Greta gave her a wry smile. 'For everything.'

'I'll sell you some guineafowl if you're interested. Always let you know when a snake's around. Chase off a dingo if they have to.'

She stooped to pick up a brown feather with white spots and placed it on the dashboard, then slapped the car roof. 'I'll come by in a few days.'

The ute moved forward. The guineafowl dispersed. Greta imagined them at her place, rounding up the children, the man, herself and the new hens.

She tooted the horn and waved out the window. In the side mirror the steely woman watched them go.

'I was thinking,' said Raffy as Greta turned onto the road. 'You know how Henry was a lightning chaser?'

'Sure.' Greta gave him a quick smile in the rear-vision mirror.

'I think it's why he liked Brynn. I think she was his lightning bolt.'

6

Two whistling kites glided in circles above Greta. She was standing in the middle of a rough garden bed edged with rocks. Shallow dents marked the ground where she was trying to dig holes. She struck the earth with the hoe. It bounced and dinged back. Across the valley the escarpment glowered heat. She hit the ground again. Next to her, various seedlings waited in their pots. Clouds assembled overhead like curious onlookers. Her thoughts drifted out of her and mingled in the heavy air.

She was glad of the excuse to pause when a ute rumbled up to the shack. It was Brynn, with two rockmelon vines, a wild passionfruit and trellis.

'I'm here for a stickybeak. And a coffee.'

Greta took her up to the verandah. She and Joel had laid decking the day before.

'Homey!' Brynn admired the retro lime-green table with matching vinyl chairs, and the pair of well-loved wicker armchairs facing the escarpment. 'I like the table!' Her hand patted it.

'Joel says he needs sunglasses to look at it. I thought it was tropical.'

Greta set up the coffee pot. Brynn leaned against a verandah post to light a cigarette. Together they put the trellis at the end of the verandah for the passionfruit vine. It partly obscured the view of the ruin.

'But no one will cry over that,' Brynn said.

'No,' Greta agreed.

After coffee they planted the melons in the rough garden bed Greta had made from the water tank to the verandah. Brynn chatted as she worked, and Greta slipped in a few questions about the town and how long Brynn had lived here.

'Must be eight years now,' Brynn answered. 'It was Henry's idea. He loved the place, not that he had long here in the end.'

When they'd finished she stretched her back and said, 'Well, that's it for me. I'll see you next time.'

She promised to return in a few days, and offered to share driving up to Darwin for shopping. Her last advice was about bananas. 'Plant three together. They like friends.'

Afterwards, showered and wrapped in a sarong, Greta sat in a wicker chair and put her feet up on a milk crate topped with a square of plywood. Toby had made it to double as a coffee table and footrest.

There was a breeze lurking up on the hill. She heard the homestead's iron roof lift and clang. Good place to fly a kite, she'd suggested. But Joel seemed to be avoiding the old house. There was a risk of falling beams, he warned her, and walls that might collapse. 'Don't take the kids.'

He hadn't taken her either.

She was tempted to venture there now, while he was checking

fences and the children were at school. She could try out Henry's camera.

The incline up to the homestead was steeper than she'd expected. It was a bald hill, scattered with bronze-coloured rocks, a few sand palms and skinny saplings with wide leaves like green, yellow and red flags. The sun bit through her shirt, and the tripod's makeshift rope strap dug into her shoulder alongside the camera bag.

Every few steps the boulders multiplied. She imagined they had eyes. At night they might speak. For now they let her pass, and held quiet their secrets.

She paused out the front of the ruin, taking in the place. The station owner, Donegan, had bought two half-destroyed houses for a song after the '74 cyclone and trucked them to the property. Fedor and his brothers rebuilt them into a home. Maria planted around it for shade. It was a luxurious move after the freight van, silver bullet workers' van and open shed where they'd been living. They called the new place 'the homestead' among themselves.

After the fire and twenty-three years of abandonment, the stumps had sunk, skewing the face of the house. The verandah was lashed with charcoal fingers. Its floor had collapsed. The windows of every room were long, melancholy eyes. Decaying shutters were pinned back to the walls.

She passed a Hills hoist in the grass on her way to the back of the house, where rusted cars were lined up with crooked towers of used tyres and car parts. The paddock behind was overrun with gamba. Among the trees and termite mounds were the shadows of other wrecked vehicles. The grass hummed with insects and heat.

How must it have been for Joel's father to arrive here with his brothers, fleeing a terrible incarceration? And his mother, escaping her own secret traumas? After Europe's colder climates how did they adjust to life on this bald hill, with its relentless sun, the unforgiving soil? She imagined Maria hoeing the tough earth, pregnant, breastfeeding, running after toddlers in the heat and pining for mountains, music, tulips.

At the side of the house a section of wall was missing. Greta stepped inside. Dead leaves crunched under her boots. The noise was too loud, announcing her. A spell might break, incite an avalanche of ant-eaten wood. Something was here still. The imprint, the after-breath of souls.

She was in the old kitchen. The walls were blackened but the room was intact. A single window shutter was still propped open—the old, tropical kind that pushed out and up. An upturned enamel bath was at one end, and a cast-iron oven at the other. The oven door hung loose from its hinge and the flue reached for the sky through a missing section of roof. Here Maria would have stirred her chicken soup and sliced the salami Uncle Vadik made.

Down the hallway the frame of the house was bare in places. The fire must have rushed through, licking one room and destroying the next. She felt a surge of sadness to look on the devastation of a family. It made her think she shouldn't take photos.

The living room's ceiling was gone. Flaps of iron roofing clung together at odd angles so shafts of light beamed down. One lit up a long mound of charred debris. The family table perhaps. She conjured it back to life in her mind, with children around it and Maria lighting a candle in her crystal candlestick, the one possession she'd brought in her suitcase, miraculously unbroken.

'Stolen!' Fedor would growl—which was a lie, because the children knew the candlestick was a secret gift from a rich count to their mother's mother's grandmother.

Greta had spliced together a strange mix of Joel's anecdotes and her own images over the years from glimpses he gave—an incident, a trait, a song or story to amuse the boys. She interwove them. But standing in the actual place where they'd lived, her knowledge felt scanty. The images were fading in real light, pieces were missing, fractured. All she had were tenuous threads. And her imagination.

She focused the camera on a thick wreath of black strands under one of the shafts of light. It took her a moment to realise it was a burned car tyre. The noise of the shutter lifted something in her. She breathed easier. Joel wouldn't care about photos, she told herself. He'd say the past is the past.

A light wind breathed around the building. Flaps of metal squeaked above her. A window shutter pulled and rattled, eager to speak.

She stepped onto the sunken verandah. Greta imagined Fedor with his gammy leg limping to and fro, muttering his discontent, shouting for Maria.

She retreated back into the house and made her way to the next room, which was less touched by the fire. A cast-iron bedframe was still there. Something gripped her heart to see it. Had Maria died in this bed? Was this where Joel had read to her by lamplight? And lifted her for the last time, her body shrunken and yellowed?

Greta set up the tripod and camera. Perspiration stung her eyes. The empty bed blurred and sharpened in the lens.

The roof was gone from the next room. The sky was vivid blue against the charred beams. Two bunk frames remained. She knew from Joel that all six brothers had slept in one room. Mick, Lars, Seb, Radek, Danny and Joel, their real names morphed into easier-to-pronounce ones for the new country where they were born. Half of them blond-haired and blue-eyed like their father. Half of them black-haired and brown-eyed like their mother.

Across the hallway, Magdalen's room was not much bigger than a walk-in wardrobe. A stained and mouldy mattress lay on the floor, with yellow stuffing bulging from its side. There was a hole punched in one wall. Next door was the bathroom. Its floor had fallen through, and the green ceramic basin lay on the ground below.

The last room in the house was gone, sheared off. A row of concrete stumps made a line through the grass.

The most fascinating space is one that's disintegrating.

She could hear her mother's voice, see her walking through sunlit dust motes in a derelict warehouse and her own little red boots following.

Watch your step, or you'll disappear.

Retracing her way she stopped again at Magdalen's room. A glimmer caught her eye through the hole in the wall. A set of chimes was curled up on the exposed noggin. She drew them out. They were like the ones Griffin had found, except the triangle at the top was made of three metal pipes. The strings were knotted with miniature bones, rusted nails, a snail shell, diagonal mirrors.

The sound of Joel's quad bike pulling up interrupted. She laid the chimes on the mattress and hurried out through his mother's room.

He pushed the hat off his head. His shirt was soaked and his hair was wet, except for a few strands that stood upright in the breeze.

Greta handed him her water bottle. He gulped and wiped his lips with the back of his hand.

'Careful in there.' He nodded to the homestead.

'I know.' Something like guilt wrapped around her.

'Curiosity killed the cat.' He noticed the camera hanging from her neck.

She looked back to the house. 'Must've been some fire.'

'It was.'

He squinted at the sunlit roof, arms folded. Then he smiled wearily at her and she sauntered with him to the edge of the old garden where the ground began its descent to the lake. A stony incline led down to a belt of turkey bush dusted with pink flowers. After that it was mostly rocks and trees down to the water. Woolly butt, stringybark, ironbark. The trunks were like poles. The lake shimmered in between.

Joel kicked one of the empty forty-four-gallon drums next to him. It tipped and somersaulted, shuddering down over stones until it banged against a gutted station wagon. The car had nose-dived into a red bead tree. A tussock of gamba fountained through the roof.

'Magdalen was born in that car,' he said.

'Your sister?'

He nodded.

His sister's birth was a panic, he'd told her once, not long after they met. She remembered snippets. A father sleeping off his vodka, two older brothers out pig hunting. Another one playing darts. The younger children unsure what to do. Except for six-year-old Joel, kneeling on the kitchen bench to reach the car keys kept in a jar at the back of the cupboard, with the salt his uncle had spilled across the bench biting into a cut on his knee. And his mother's dress was wet, clinging to her, which had puzzled him—was it from the shower, or from the rain hammering the roof? Afterwards, he used to dream the roof had disappeared and rain was pelting on him and his mother inside.

Greta had assumed they'd found a doctor, a hospital.

Wrong, wrong! a white cockatoo shrieked overhead.

She saw that little boy again, kneeling in salt and holding the keys out to his mother.

'I have to go,' Joel said, though he lingered. 'I'll see you late afternoon.'

'The kids want to eat at the pub tonight. For a treat.'

'Uh-huh.' He took another swig of water then held out the bottle.

'Take it,' she said.

His fingers brushed her wrist.

She watched the quad bike buzz down the hill. The shack was a small nut, closed in on itself.

Now a flock of white cockatoos screeched out of the blue sky. Their wings flapped white light as they landed in the branches above the stopped car. The lake gleamed. The ground creaked in the heat.

Greta turned back to the homestead. The sun had recast the light and shadows around the building. A portrait of a ruin was taking shape in her mind.

The shutters moved on their hooks. Tappety-tap-tap.

To take them or leave them—Magdalen's chimes.

Who would care? She went in. They were on the mattress where she'd left them. She snatched them up. A tremor shivered through her as she stepped out across the sunken verandah. She was a thief.

She wove her way quickly between the rocks and sand palms, heading for the shack. There was a strange ringing in her ears. The saplings' leaves rattled at her. The stones were singing. They had seen.

7

They pulled up outside the pub on sunset to a cloud of flying foxes rising from the castle's forest. Their wings beat softly through the air, shadows against the gold and pink clouds. A mother flew low over Greta's head; she could see the baby clinging to its chest. Toby was impressed by the gothic show. He wanted to know where they were going.

'To feed,' said Joel. 'They'll be back at three a.m., making a racket to wake the dead.'

He took the children across the road for a quick visit to Uncle Pavel's castle. Griffin was amazed at his great-uncle's talent, the size of the model, the unlikely salmon colour. He dawdled behind the others and Greta had to call him away.

The pub had a verandah with bar stools and a bench that over-looked the street. It seemed the store and the pub were designed for everyone to watch everyone else.

As soon as they entered, three men at the bar turned to stare. One nodded at Joel. For a moment no one said anything. Then the woman behind the bar straightened up from leaning on the counter. She had dyed blonde hair with a jet-black streak on one side.

'Well, look who's back, after a couple of sweet decades.' Her mouth was a sarcastic twist.

'Not that long, is it?' Joel's smile was quick.

She kept her hands on her hips as if she might not serve him. Then she snatched his ten-dollar note, filled a schooner and set it down hard. 'Thought you must be dead.'

Foam slid to the counter. The change clinked against the glass.

Toby begged for money for the arcade machine he'd spotted. Joel let him take some coins and the boys disappeared.

The woman tilted her chin at Greta to ask what she'd like.

'G and T, thanks.' She'd treat herself for the end of the week.

Joel introduced Erin who'd already turned to the spirits shelf. An elaborate J snared in Celtic knots was inked across her shoulder blades. The low-scooped back of her t-shirt seemed designed to show it off. She took her time to find the bottle.

'Where's your brother Danny?' Tonic hissed from the bar gun into the glass.

Joel shrugged. 'Who knows? Says he'll turn up to give me a hand.'

Greta passed him a menu to order fish and chips, and reminded him to bring some glasses.

She took her drink and a jug of water. An older man at the bar nodded to her as she headed to the table. One or two others watched her go.

Joel ordered the meals then crossed the room to join her. On his way a burly man stepped in front of him. Joel's glass tilted, spilling beer.

'Back then, are ya? Thought you lot were gone for good.'

After a long stare the man pushed past. Joel sat down opposite Greta. He was silent. She wished they'd ordered takeaway. She hadn't considered that the reason they'd not yet visited town together might be that Joel was avoiding it.

'Must be strange to be back,' she said.

'Yeah.' He sipped the beer.

The music was too loud for conversation. Joel focused on the giant TV screen. Nearby, Toby was behind the wheel of a racing car arcade game, with his brothers either side.

Suddenly a boisterous laugh cut through the music. A woman's arm snaked around Joel, trapping him in a headlock. 'Who says you're allowed in?'

'Cyclone Tori!' Joel's frown disappeared.

'This yer missus?' She shook Greta's hand and sat between them at the head of the table. 'Dee said you were in town. Aunty Hazel too, outside the store there—let's me know the latest.' She nodded at the arcade machine. 'That your lot over there? Mine'll be the ones pushin' in.' She grinned at Greta. 'Axel's a real life junior sedan racer. The younger two are Barnie and Skye. Trouble with a capital T. God love Miss Rhianna, I say.' She thought for a moment and said, 'Your kids go to school on the bus, do they? Ride their bikes to the road gate?'

Greta nodded.

'I can pick 'em up and drop 'em off with mine on Wednesdays— it's my Darwin supplies day. Our troopy'll fit 'em all in. Chance to have a cuppa.'

Greta thanked her and offered to help with children and car pooling too.

'Us women have to stick together,' Tori answered.

After a while the buzzer on the table vibrated and blinked red lights. Greta called Griffin over to help collect the meals. When she returned Tori was still talking.

'What's up with Schmick Mick? Livin' the flash life in Sydney, I heard.'

Joel offered chips to her children, against her protests.

'Done nothin' to that place all these years. No burn-off, no cattle, nothin'. I thought he said he was managin' it.' She sucked air through the gap in her front teeth. 'That's what happens when people go down south. Don't give a shit. Weeds, gamba. It's a fuckin' fire risk, Jed reckons.'

'Ronnie'll slash it,' said Joel.

'He'll have his work cut out for him.'

'I'll burn it with the first rain.'

'You'll be waitin' a while, if it's like last year. Latest, shortest wet ever. People are sayin' it's the climate change.'

'You're still with Jed then?'

'Bad habits die hard!'

Joel offered her a piece of fish.

'Nah, I'm all good, mate. I'm just here to drink and sing karaoke.' She smiled at the singer on stage, whose voice was full of passion and slightly off-key. 'You could get me a beer, though. And one for your missus.'

'Not for me,' smiled Greta. 'I'll drive.'

The air vibrated with music, Greta could feel it passing through her feet.

'I grew up with Joel,' Tori said, 'swimmin' in that lake, till we knew it was poison. We all loved it. So clear, you know? The new doc couldn't believe it when she found out what was in it. I'm waitin' for a cancer.' She half laughed. Her fingers tapped the table in time to the music. 'Joel's sister Magdalen hated it, creeped 'er out y'know.' She glanced at Greta. 'Maria too—his mum. She was real superstitious. "If you stand too close, it'll take you," she'd say.' Tori stopped suddenly, as if another thought had taken hold. When she spoke again it was with a kind of reverence. 'I've wondered since if she was one of those people who can see things, y'know? Like second sight. I reckon she had it.'

Joel came back with a drink for Tori. 'Complimentary for you, they said.'

'Cheers.' She thanked him, and explained to Greta, 'I used to work here so they look after me. I'd like to still work here,' she continued, 'but the farm I run with my brother keeps me too busy. What are you doin' here?' she said to Joel then. 'Go and catch up with the fellas at the bar.' She gave Greta a knowing look. 'It'll do him good.' She took a gulp of beer. 'So the old place is still there, the one that got burned?'

'Only just.'

'A huff an' a puff an' you'd blow it down, eh?' Tori swivelled to face the stage and whistle at the singer, then turned back. 'We lived there half the time, us kids. Maria'd feed us till we dropped. She loved people, you know, always huggin' you breathless, singin', tellin' stories. It was all good if Fedor and Vadik weren't around, thumpin' fists and ravin' on.' Her hand swept over the table as if to clear it of unseen crumbs. 'She could really sing, Maria. Deep voice. Real deep. Like some kinda weird angel.'

Greta saw Maria creeping into the night to sing softly across the valley, and little Joel sneaking through one of the casement windows to follow her.

'She came here for karaoke once.' Tori's fingers turned her glass. 'Sal persuaded her—Sal from down the meatworkers' hut. Loved 'er karaoke, our Sal. But Maria, God! She killed it. They turned the machine right off. Just listened to her voice. Sent chills down yer spine.'

The children finished eating and moved on to the pool table, counting the coins left between them. There was a call for more talent up on stage.

Tori yelled out, 'You ain't heard nothin' yet!'

A few onlookers chuckled and someone called out, 'Go, Tori!'

She laughed and turned back to Greta to continue her story. 'Yeah, that was a legend night, Maria singin' at the pub. Never happened again, but. Old mate Fedor hit the roof.' She sucked in her breath. 'You could see the blood clots along her hairline.' She traced her finger along her own forehead.

The music cranked up louder. Tori stood and drained the last of her beer. 'He could be a brute, Joel's dad.' She made her way to the stage.

Raffy came to sit on Greta's knee. 'It's too loud!' he said.

She would have liked to stay and hear Tori sing, but Raffy complained that his ears were hurting, so she signalled to Joel, who was at the pool table with Toby. He took the cue for a last turn. The ball hit another with a sharp crack and both shot into the pocket.

Outside the flying foxes were gone, though the smell of them hung in the air. The moon had eased above the rain trees. The rest of the sky was dark with only a few stars peeping through. A semi-trailer carrying a digger was parked in the street. The driver was checking the tyres.

'Ronnie!' Joel called and went to shake his hand.

'Look,' whispered Toby, 'there's a giant from Uncle Pavel's castle.'

Raffy punched his brother's arm.

Ronnie stood under the streetlight, feet wide apart. He was much taller than Joel, and wore a yellow high-vis shirt and blue overalls. His grey hair stuck up in tufts.

The boys peered inside the open door of the truck. A pit bull sat on the passenger seat, pink tongue lolling.

Joel called his sons over to shake hands and Greta followed.

'We'll visit Big Ronnie's place tomorrow after school. He might let you ride the grader.'

The boys stayed close to hear about a slip-on water tank and pump Ronnie would lend Joel to bolt onto the red ute if there was a fire. The conversation then turned to the cabin.

'He's a schemer that Mick,' Ronnie chuckled softly. 'You'll be buildin' a resort before you know it.'

Raffy was captivated by a movement inside Ronnie's shirt pocket. A little face poked out, pink nose quivering for air.

'That's me little possum,' said Ronnie. 'Poor bugger lost its mum.' His forefinger pushed the little head down. 'Don't tell 'em inside or they won't let me have m' Guinness.' He winked at Raffy.

The possum wriggled up again.

Ronnie gently took it out for Raffy to see.

'Don't worry, she doesn't bite. Just sniffin' for food.'

He waited for Raffy to bravely touch the possum's head, and then let it hide in his pocket again.

'Some rocks've come up with the gradin' today,' he said, reaching into the truck's cabin. 'You boys might like 'em.'

He dropped one into Raffy's palm. It was chunky, purple with a partial tan coating.

'Amethysts.' Ronnie also gave a stone each to Toby, Griffin and Greta.

The boys huddled under the streetlight to see them better. Ronnie stepped up onto the truck's tray to open an esky, pulled out a large frozen fish, wrapped newspaper around it and passed it to Joel.

'Barramundi,' he said to Greta and stepped down.

Joel whistled his thanks. Ronnie smiled and rubbed the back of his neck.

Griffin measured his own height against the fish. He'd never seen such a big one.

Inside the pub Tori was belting out 'Bow River'. Ronnie looked over that way. Joel shook his hand again.

'Do you think anyone will see it?' Raffy asked his mother in a low voice.

'What?'

'The possum.'

The road away from town felt narrower on the way back, in the darkness. Greta wound down the window to keep alert. The noise of the karaoke and Tori's voice were still with her. She shuddered to think of Joel and Tori and other children swimming in the lake, while up at the homestead Maria with the beautiful voice tried to warn them about the poison water. The woman with second sight. The singer who'd been gagged.

Things unravelled, Joel had told her.

She saw the turning wheel of Fedor's moods, Vadik's drunkenness and Maria trying to protect her children. And Pavel building his castle.

The air blowing by the window was a relief, and the shadows of the trees and hills too.

In the back seat a tussle brewed. Griffin wanted to hold the barramundi. Toby wouldn't give it up. She waited for Joel to intervene but he was distracted with his own thoughts and not interested in their battle. She glared at the rear-vision mirror. 'Stop it!' She said.

Her eyes clicked back to the road. A bovine shape loomed. She swerved. The car skidded towards a ditch. She swerved again, and the car fishtailed between reflector posts, clipping each one. Her hands argued with the wheel. The vehicle was possessed. Suddenly she was hurtling into the bush, with Raffy calling out behind her in a frightened voice, and light bouncing ahead onto saplings, termite mounds and leaves.

'Greta!' Joel cried.

She heard them in a strange way, as if she were travelling underwater. All she could see was the broad white trunk of a eucalyptus heading straight for her. She slammed her foot on the brake. The car lurched to a stop just before impact. The engine idled, light streamed up the tree. The whiteness of the bark dazzled her senses.

'I thought we were goners!' Joel's eyes shone post-fright.

'There was a cow on the road—we were about to hit it.'

'Could've been a buffalo!' Toby suggested.

'Scrub bull more like,' said Joel.

Greta stepped out and peered through the children's window. 'Are you all right?'

Griffin blinked at her, silent.

'Sorry for fighting,' mumbled Raffy.

She walked to the front of the car. The bull bar was jammed with gamba. She yanked the stalks free. Joel crouched to drag grass from the chassis. Above them the branches of the tree glowed white.

'Can we go home now?' asked Raffy in a small voice.

'I'll drive if you like,' Joel suggested.

'No, I will.'

She reversed the vehicle onto the road. There was no sign of the mystery beast. Toby leaned out the window to look behind him.

'I can't see anything.' He sank back, disappointed.

'It'll be long gone,' said Joel.

And something in the way he looked at Greta made her say, 'It was there. I saw it.'

Don't touch, Maria says to the hand with the ice in the red-chequered tea towel.

It is her son's hand.

Magdalen's cries whimper along the hallway.

Go to her, says Maria. Go and comfort her.

Shh, Joel says in a low voice. She'll sleep. She'll forget.

Turn off the lamp. There's too much light in here.

He switches off the lamp. Now in the dimmer room she dares to look at him. He is almost a man.

Her gaze shifts to the open door. The curtains billow with a strange breeze, transparent white veils across the windows. The embroidered flowers on the material whisper what they have seen. The breeze strengthens and moves into the room. Through the door, the windows, there is a stirring.

It is coming from the lake, she says, and she shifts herself in the chair, her eyes on the gap of the doorway to greet the phantom breath. One day it will take us.

Joel says nothing. She will talk of the lake now and tire him. She will conjure it up as a worse menace than his father's fist. He quietly straightens himself. Her eyes are closed. He moves out onto the verandah.

Nothing will kill him more slowly than this family, than the air in this house. The withering heart.

8

Greta gazed in disbelief at the entrance to the new firebreak. Along either side of the graded track tall grasses shimmered. She'd heard Ronnie's tractor slashing over the past couple of days while working on the garden and converting the freight car into a darkroom, but she hadn't imagined this. She was looking on a direct road to the poison water, to the meatworks, to the forbidden world below.

The four-wheel drive pulled up behind her. Joel came to speak with her.

'You've made a highway to the lake,' she said.

A flicker passed over his face. 'It had to be done.'

'True. But now the kids . . .'

'I'll build a yard fence. Keep the wild things out. And in.'

He looked up to a cloud that bloomed white overhead. One of the children beeped the car horn. He pulled a list for Darwin from his shirt pocket. *Industrial fan, chest freezer, air con* and *exhaust fan for dark room* were highlighted. She'd found everything second hand. Now the electricity was connected she would swoop on bargains.

'If I don't find these today?'

'Nothing for you,' she said. 'Nothing.'

He kissed her firmly on the mouth. 'Careful not to go too far and lose your way.'

'I'm not Griffin.' She smiled, and then added, 'He reminds me more and more of you.'

'You reckon?'

'I'm not sure why exactly. His mysteries maybe. Mr Elusive.'

He laughed gently. 'It's not just my birthmark he copied then.'

They both had a crescent stain on their necks. She'd been surprised and moved when Griffin was born with the identical little imprint in the same spot.

Toby tooted the car horn. Joel held up the list like a promise.

'Bye,' called Raffy as they pulled away. 'I'll bring you back an ice cream!'

She waved. She could eat that little boy.

Her father's watch said ten o'clock. Take the photos and be back by midday was her plan. Noon here was like midnight in Raffy's fairytales. Be home by twelve or mutate. The humidity was up ten percent since yesterday. Every day it increased. She took a drink from her water bottle and returned the watch to her back pocket. Then she walked up to the homestead to check her mobile for emails—a message from a craft shop about her jewellery, a hello from Janna wanting Greta's PO box, and a school notice about a regional schools swimming carnival at Lightstone pool in November. They felt like messages from an outside world.

She walked down to the crashed station wagon where Magdalen was born. Greta had never had much talent when it came to photographing nature or humans, but the car wrecks on this property fascinated her. So many of them, so many poses. Each one its own drama.

She set up the camera and tripod. A muscle twitched in her forearm and there was a tremor in her fingers as she adjusted the focus and shutter speed. *The camera is like an eye. The film is waiting for light to touch it.* Vivian's voice came to her, explaining aperture, depth of field. *How much light to let in, how much to keep out, that's the secret.*

She moved around the car, framing her shots, seeking different perspectives. The mangled nose of the bonnet. The mottled patterns of corrosion. She crouched to find a new angle, where the red bead tree's strength held back not just the car but the stony hill, the burnt-out house and its companion wrecks. The clouds above were witnesses.

A curlew cried nearby. She'd never heard it in the daytime. She stopped to listen. A quarrel of squawks came from further along in the turkey bush, and the curlew's shrieks cut in urgent and quick. *This is my place, it's mine.*

Greta crept in among the bushes to follow the sound. The leaves were fine green needles and the flowers were pink stars. The bird kept silent. It would be watching her boots pass. She searched through gaps between branches. No sign of the bird. But two white rocks came into view. They looked like strangers carried from elsewhere and planted here.

She pushed past the turkey bush to discover a line of tangled barbed wire part buried around the stones. Each one was roughly etched with a name. *Maria Elena. Magdalena.* Greta stared at them, shocked. She was sure these were graves, though there were no dates on the stones. She knew the year they'd died, 1994. She wondered if Joel had chiselled the names.

She pulled at a vine wrapped around Magdalen's stone. It cut her palm with a sting. She'd have to come back with secateurs.

The cicadas started up their rasping chant. The air pulsed with their noise.

She stepped back to take a photo of the stones. A sudden hiss from behind startled her. A long-legged bird rushed forward, wings held out in a warning banner. Its legs were slender, pale grey with a bulging knot at the knee. A dramatic black stripe stretched across each underwing. And it had a striking long eyebrow, creamy with a rufous tinge. The bush stone-curlew had found her out. It stopped about a metre away and hissed again. She didn't move. After a while the bird called a truce and folded its wings. The feathers were a haphazard mix—brown, grey, cream and black. There was something of the dishevelled messenger about it.

'Cryptic plumage,' she recalled Griffin reading aloud from his bird book. 'Reptilian eye.'

The bird quick-walked away into the bush. She spotted it again soon after, standing perfectly still among a cluster of grey twigs and branches. A second bird was next to it, huddled low on the gravel.

'No nest,' Griffin had told her. 'Just a scrape in the ground. Two eggs.'

She took a photo, swapped to the long lens and quietly positioned the tripod. Neither bird moved. Did they do this when dingoes or feral cats were after them? She focused on the eye of the one standing guard. It was watching her. A translucent eyelid slid across the yellow iris. Click. The nictitating eyelid. That elusive membrane. It reminded her of the camera shutter's magic, the black iota of a second when only the camera has vision.

You're shooting blind. It's all about trust.

Greta moved away to find a gap in the turkey bush. The incline down to the lake was rocky, with scatterings of sand palms and cycads. She hummed to feel light-hearted, but the strangeness of the lake affected her even this far off. She felt increasingly nervous moving among the trees. Vacant cicada shells clung to their furrowed bark. The empty eyes watched her. She picked off a couple for Raffy. Now she noticed the trees were oozing sap, caramel-like flows or trails of honey gathering in a bulging, amber gem with ants scurrying to and fro. Among the grasses she came across half-buried forty-four-gallon drums corroded and split open, packed with dirt, and numerous rusted car wheels and brake drums.

Closer to the water the ground was carpeted in leaves. She kept alert, ready for a death adder curled in its nest. Griffin had warned her. From where she stood, Greta could see how the dam was an uneven circle. On her side the bank was high and fell in a sheer drop to the water. As Joel had said, she could see all the way down to an underwater tip of rusty drums, discarded pieces of machinery, the bleached bones of a cow.

Her boot set off an avalanche of small stones. She watched them splash and drift to the sandy floor. It wasn't too deep, she guessed, four metres perhaps, more in the middle.

There were no fish or turtles. No long-legged egret tiptoeing along the waterline. Even the surrounding bush was strangely quiet. She listened for animal rustlings, bird calls. Nothing. The water was deathly still. And awake. So transparent, so clear it shocked her. It was unnatural. The place was a crystal-clear trap.

She took a couple of photos and then walked around to the opposite side where Joel had first showed them the lake. Not far from the bank a gutted car had sunk, bonnet scalped to one side, boot lid up like an open mouth. The back doors were torn off, the windows smashed. It was a cousin of the wrecks up at the homestead. Behind it the branches of the drowned tree reached up in a flailing paralysis.

A breeze stirred, the surface of the water ruffled. She watched the disturbance spread, the way it marred that pure transparency, as if the lake might erase a given insight. She waited for the distortion to settle, the ripples to disperse. The water resumed its glassy stillness. Once again she saw the buried secrets.

Nothing on the floor of the lake had moved, but she felt an alteration. The stillness was more intense. A loneliness closed in on her. The heat in the air was singing and the cicadas rasped their fast beat. The water was a frightening silence, an absence of the living. Imagined or real, she understood that inexplicable thing Maria and her daughter had feared. If you stand close enough it will take you.

Above the water the clouds were in conversation with each other and their reflections below. She set up the tripod and changed lenses again to capture these ever-changing shapes. They inspired her. *Contrast, shadow, light.* She could hear her mother again.

At last she crossed to the other side of the firebreak. On her left the hill rose in a wave of gamba. The shack wasn't visible, only a sky that glared cruel sunlight. Ahead of her a path of flat, grey rock separated the grassy hill from a rock-scattered incline on her right.

Greta checked her watch again. Eleven fifteen. She should go back now. But ahead of her a willie wagtail urged her on. Every time she came near, it flew on a little way and waited for her. She followed the bird to a hollow tree stump bound with termite mud. It danced there, tail jerking, head cocked at her. Just as she was about to take a photo, it hopped behind the stump. She edged around, eye to the viewfinder.

'God!'

She'd already taken the shot. But not of the bird. A dead wallaby's grin filled the lens. The willie wagtail tittered from its grassy

78

hide. She lowered the camera. How oddly similar to a car wreck this mummified corpse looked, with its furless body torn open to expose a clutch of ribs and sinews dried out like crisscrossing threads of rusty wire.

Further on, the path led her to three stone pillars. One stood alone, the other two leaned in to balance a spherical rock between them. When she passed them she felt as if she'd gone through a gate.

Ahead was the outcrop she could see from the shack, a network of rambling boulders and overhangs, corridors and chambers. The rocks were a range of hues, from grey to brown and black. Others had warm orange tones.

How must it sound in the wet here? she thought. With tumbling water at every turn.

The cicadas ratcheted up their song. Greta wandered among the formations in awe of their colours and textures. Tiny shells were embedded into the rock. Jagged lines of white or orange ran in lightning bolts through the stone. She was in a labyrinth, a parallel world. Heat radiated from the walls either side of her. Specks of quartz and mica glinted in the sunlight. Her children would love this place.

'Wouldn't go in there if I was you,' came a sudden voice.

A stout man stood behind her, blocking the entrance to the passageway she'd entered.

'Might run into the devil!' he snickered. A metal detector was in his right hand. His dark hair fell in greasy locks from under a misshapen leather hat. He reeked of sweat. 'You Joel's woman?' he asked.

She didn't like his eyes. They mocked. And his body was like one of those forty-four-gallon drums packed tight with dirt.

'I'm Greta.' She tried a smile and asked if he was the neighbour.

He snorted contempt.

'Find much?' She gestured to the detector.

'None of yer business, missy!' He drew in a breath. His shirt moved like a skin. 'I've got fossickin' rights!' he barked. His chest swelled with authority.

She wasn't sure what he meant, which annoyed him further.

'Me fossickin' request! Mick never said nothin'. Two months and consent is deemed!' He was clearly pleased with himself and pulled out a piece of paper to wave at her. 'I go where I like on this block, Joel or no Joel.' He frowned at her camera then took a few steps back to consider the hill.

Greta took her chance to escape into the open.

'Joel should've burned it all orf by now.'

'He's waiting for the first rain.'

'Is 'e?' He spat on the ground. 'Place'll be toast before then. I seen this place burn like hell!' His boot gave a triumphant little stamp. 'Not that I'd give a shit. Place's cursed.'

She adjusted the camera around her neck, which cut the grin on him. He glared at her.

'An' you can tell Joel one of my cows's gone through 'is shit fence!'

'He's fixing the fences.'

'Like fuck 'e is!' The greasy hair shook at her. 'Movin' star pickets's what 'e'll be doin'. Like 'is land-creepin' father 'n' uncle. Boundary fuckin' stealers. Whole fuckin' fam'ly. Migrators! Fuck 'em!'

She watched him go on down the track and steeled herself against the tremor she felt. Where was he off to, she wondered. When he'd gone she slipped back inside the passageway, curious to see where it went. Around the corner the corridor narrowed and the rock walls rose higher, leaning in at the top. The sky was a sliver of blue. She edged her way along, hands pressing against stone.

Sediment and shell, grit and fibre, iron. Each step became a tighter fit for her boots. The closeness of the walls started to unnerve her. Any minute her breath might disturb an underlying presence and wake the rocks to shift, press together. Suddenly she didn't want her children to know about this place at all. She saw the thin arm of a child snatched through a crevice. Heard a squeak behind a jagged crack. It was a relief to turn another corner and find an arch leading out to a rock platform.

Below were the valley and the creek. The descent was steep and rocky, and the cycads were a different species, with silvery-green fronds. At creek level the land flattened out in a grassy expanse. It seemed dry now, but Greta imagined it would flood in the wet season. There were a few eucalypts with creamy white flowers. The numerous pandanus had long beards of dead fronds. They mustn't have burned in years.

She drank water and splashed it on her face then set off downhill. Her boots slipped on loose stones. At the bottom she came to a mango tree with a sprawling head of leaves. She wondered why it was growing here. She wouldn't have expected it. The fruit were green, hanging ornaments. A flock of magpie geese feasted underneath. One honked a warning. A crowd of wings rose up.

As the air cleared a wooden hut came into view—a ramshackle outfit with the walls patched in places and the roof strung together with odd sections of corrugated iron that might lift off in a gale. The narrow verandah at the front had tree branches for posts.

There was something strange about it, as if it had only just landed when the geese pulled aside an invisible curtain.

Wouldn't go in there if I was you. Might run into the devil! What had he meant by that?

She hid in the shadow of the mango tree to see if anyone appeared. Insects flew from the leaves around her. There was no movement at the hut, but the sound of little bells came to her, alluring, beckoning. She took out the camera and focused on the verandah. A set of chimes dangled from the corner eave. Just like the ones from the creek and the homestead. Click.

Greta returned home later than she'd intended to find a bus parking alongside the shed. The door sighed open and Ronnie stepped out. He seemed almost startled to see her.

'Joel bought it off me,' he said, glancing back at it. 'Says it's a kids' bedroom till the cabin's done.'

'Really?' It was the first she'd heard of it. 'He's a man of sudden inspirations!' She'd learned to ride with them in exchange for a few of her own.

'You happy with it there? I can move it.'

'I'll sort it with Joel.' She smiled to reassure him.

He half turned to consider the mahogany tree. 'That's got some height in it.'

'I hope it doesn't come down while we're here.'

'They're known for it.'

He squinted out to the escarpment rather than meet her eyes. He'd run out of words.

'Do you need a lift back into town?' she asked.

'Nico's gonna pick me up in about half an hour—young bloke doin' some work for me.' He smiled awkwardly. 'Joel said you weren't here. I was just gonna drop it and go.'

'I'll make us a cuppa.'

He followed her to the verandah and sat at one end of the table with his left leg underneath, the other out to the side. She went inside to make the tea and returned with two cups.

He smiled politely. 'Kids happy at school?'

'They're loving it. New friends.'

The tea was hot, she gently blew into her cup. Ronnie kept his gaze on the ridge. His fingers were too large for the cup handle. She saw now that his middle finger was cut short, a thick stub.

'Rhianna is it?'

'Yes! They adore her.'

'My daughter went to school with 'er.' He paused to let the news sink in. 'She's over on the east coast now. Beautician. Lookin' after all those Gold Coast ladies.' He smiled at the thought of them and sipped his tea.

Greta curled her dirt-caked fingernails into her hand. 'Did you grow up here in Lightstone?'

'Nah. I come along after Joel's family left—must've been '97. They'd gone a couple of years before. Seb was here still; had a wreckers' yard up there at the old place. I only knew Joel by hearsay.' He smiled briefly at Greta, but the escarpment was his comfort. He kept going back to it.

'Wasn't till he come back with his brother Danny, 'bout fifteen years ago, that I got to know Joel. Danny was a bit wild, but Joel did some grading for me on that road past Brynn's place. It's bitumen now. Used to be dirt.'

'I didn't know he'd come back then.' As soon as she said it, she wondered if she had been told, and forgotten.

Ronnie shifted in the chair. 'Didn't stay long. Few months maybe.'

Greta was quiet, thinking.

Ronnie took refuge in the tea, drinking the rest of it without a pause. As soon as he heard a truck rumbling in he stood and eased his chair into place at the table.

'I'll be going then, Greta.' He smiled. 'Hope that bus isn't in your way.'

'It'll be fine,' she said. 'Last stop.'

'I reckon there's life in her yet.' He seemed lighter now he was going down the steps. 'Not sure if she'd make it to Adelaide. Halfway maybe.'

'I'll remind Joel of that when he says we're taking off in it.'

He waved to her from the truck, which did a U-turn and hauled away, churning up dust.

Why hadn't Joel ever told her he'd returned after his family left, she asked herself. And a voice in her answered, Why would he?

———

Joel and the children returned just before sunset. The bus caused a stir of excitement. Greta was on the verandah, drilling a hole for a hook into one of the posts, so she could hang up the chimes from the homestead.

'The bus is great, don't you reckon?' Joel came to give her a cold beer. 'Kids've got their own place.'

'Sure,' she said, screwing the hook into place.

'Where'd you find those?' he asked.

'Up at the old place.' Her fingers untangled the strings. 'Careful of my plants.'

He stepped back from the heliconias and ginger plants she'd planted to keep the galangal and turmeric company. The chimes tinkled softly.

'You don't want them here?' she asked.

He shrugged. 'Have them if you like.' He sipped his beer.

'Did your sister make them?'

'She might have,' he said vaguely.

'Come and sit with me,' she said, stepping down from the ladder.

A flock of lorikeets chattered past in a flash of red belly and green wing. Across the valley the escarpment had deepened from gold to russet. The merciless glare of the day was gone.

Joel sighed into the chair next to her. There was a silence between them. The sun had lowered, casting a softer light everywhere, except for the four ghost gums that were a luminous white.

'You never told me your mother was buried here.' Greta's fingers pulled at the beer label. 'Or your sister.'

He leaned forward, his gaze on the bottle in his hands. 'It's a long time ago.'

She looked at him. 'I don't have to know things if you don't want to tell. The kids might find them, that's all.'

'It doesn't worry me.' He leaned back in the chair. 'I've never been one for visiting cemeteries. The person's gone. No one's there.'

The daylight across the hill dimmed. Only the gum trees' branches kept their glow.

'I'm not a grave person,' he added, mock serious. 'I'm a funny man.'

She reached over to ruffle his hair. 'Is that so?'

'Not really.' He gulped a mouthful of beer. 'Danny's the comedian. Every family's got one.' He bent forward, wincing at a pain in his back, and moved the crate table closer. He hooked up Greta's foot to rest there next to his.

'Is he ever going to come and help you, this brother of yours?'

He shrugged. 'Don't bet on it.'

She drew in her breath. 'Anyway, I thought I'd tidy up around those gravestones. Plant a couple of trees. One for your mother, one for your sister.'

Greta felt oddly emotional. She could feel the jarring spade at her core.

'Sure.' His foot gently tapped hers. 'Are you all right?'

'Just tired. Staying up too late printing photos. And up early digging in the garden.'

'We need a fence around your vegies or pigs'll get in.'

'You and your fences.' She smiled.

'There's cows on the roam too', Joel said. 'I saw a few up behind the old place.'

She sat up straight, remembering. 'I think I met Trapper today, down the hill with a metal detector. He says one of his cows has gone through your shit fence.'

Joel laughed. 'That'll be him. Cranky bastard. Our fathers had a running argument over fence lines, stray cattle.'

'He's got a permit to fossick here, apparently, since Mick didn't reply to a formal request. Says he goes where he likes.'

'Like a mining company.' Joel gulped his beer. 'Let him. Might fall down a shaft. Step on an unexploded bomb. Do the world a favour.' He flashed a quick smile. 'Just joking.'

'I don't like it, with the kids. Him snooping around.'

'He won't touch them.' His voice was firm about it.

Greta wasn't much comforted by his talk of mine shafts and undetonated bombs.

'We can do this verandah roof tomorrow,' said her husband, oblivious to the threats all around. He left his chair to check the beams above him. He smiled back at her. 'Dawn start, before the sun's too high.'

'I'll have to ask my plants about that,' she told him. 'They thought I was working with them.'

She looked up through the gaps between the beams. The last tinge of pink sky was fading into twilight. Already she could see bright Venus. She didn't want a roof over this verandah. She wanted the stars. The welcome night.

9

Greta splayed out her damp hair on the pillow. The fan purred gently over her and Joel. There was a new kind of silence at night with the absence of the generator.

A gecko clicked, *cuk, cuk*, across the ceiling. Her arms ached from digging foundation holes with Joel, and helping with the verandah roof. The shack felt more closed in now, with another layer between the humans and the sky, the land.

This night was especially dark, with a new moon tomorrow. Sun, moon, earth would align.

In the distance a curlew cried out, wailing that deep lament. It was more than a call. There was something else in it. The sorrow of souls, layers of grief across the ground. The dark rocks would recast the notes, press them down into sediment lines.

When the curlew cried again the sound was so human Greta sat up to listen. She went to the back door with her torch. Griffin was outside the bus in his pyjamas, his eyes wide in fright. Behind him the moon was a skinny silver hull carrying a dark ball.

'Did you hear the bird?' she asked.

He was confused, still tethered to a nightmare. 'I saw someone. A face at the window.'

She remembered the terror visions of her own childhood, twig fingers scraping on a windowpane, the peering faces of shadows. Those other-worldly shades that entered a nightmare and were still in the room when she woke with a pounding heart.

'I don't think anyone's there. They'd need a ladder to see inside the bus.'

'Do you think?'

She guided him into the shack. He curled up on the couch.

'It's like when we first came,' he said softly.

He fell asleep quickly, as if he'd come up for just one breath in the real world then returned underwater.

Greta lay down again. She listened to the chirruping crickets, the gentle woof-woof of a barking owl. And then a different noise, like footsteps. The verandah boards creaked with a weight. She sat up, her back against the stones of the inside wall. Step, step, pause. Step, pause. She was not imagining it. And it wasn't an animal. It was a person looking for something. She heard a bump against the table.

There was a long silence after that. Only her own breath and the nose-whistling snuffles of Griffin. She fumbled for her torch but couldn't find it and so waited, ears on high alert.

The footsteps and a small, hovering flame roused her. She saw a hand holding her father's lantern and a face peering through the flywire above Joel. Greta's heart raced. She tried to think what she could use to defend herself—Joel's wrench maybe. It was under the kitchen sink. For now she couldn't take her eyes off the intruder.

The face seemed familiar somehow. Suddenly she recognised who it was—the girl from the wreck near the banyan tree.

Her eyes were fixed on Joel, watching him sleep. She never moved, just stared. It was unnerving, obsessive, this watching him while he slept. Her fingers touched the flywire, curious and tender, as if they might defy physics and reach in to brush his forehead. How did she know him?

Griffin coughed. The girl's eyes switched to him. The couch was pushed up against the flywire. There was almost nothing between her and the sleeping boy. She manoeuvred the lantern to see him better. His neck was exposed. The light fell on his birthmark. Despite the flywire and the shadows, Greta saw a change come over the girl's face—as if she hadn't expected to see the little boy and was discomfited by him, or his existence was against some surety of her own. There was something sinister, menacing in her gaze.

'Joel!' Greta called in a loud whisper. She stood up.

Her foot kicked the torch. She grabbed it and shone it on the flywire.

The girl stared back, aghast. Before Joel had fully stirred the girl was gone, a faint 'No!' singing into the night as she flitted across the verandah and leaped to the ground.

Greta flew from the room to chase her.

'What is it?' Joel's voice mumbled against the bump of the door.

The girl was a fleeting shadow, the lantern a disembodied light beside her. I'll never be quick enough, Greta thought. But the girl tripped and fell hard to the ground. Before she'd struggled to her feet Greta caught up and seized her arm.

'What do you want?' She clutched the girl's arm so tight she could feel the bone.

The girl raised her chin in defiance and yanked herself free.

She'll run, Greta thought.

And yet the girl stayed. Greta's finger marks were on her skin.

They were both quiet, each listening to their own and the other's breath.

When Greta had steadied herself, she asked again, 'What do you want?'

The girl flicked open her hand. An amethyst sat on her palm. 'I took this,' she said.

'Have it.' Greta wondered at herself, chasing off a child like this. 'Where do you live?' she asked.

'Down that way.' The girl's hand swept towards the valley.

'In the hut?'

In the torchlight the girl's face was a picture of innocence. She ignored the question, or didn't hear it. Her eyes were focused on Greta's face. She moved closer and stretched out her hand to touch Greta's cheek. She said, 'You are very real.' Her eyes locked on to Greta's. 'You have lost someone. Someone very young.' Her gaze didn't waver. 'It's a sad thing to lose a friend.'

A tightness wrapped around Greta's lungs. The curlew cried into the night. The girl shivered. Her right hand moved to her left wrist for comfort. It was then Greta noticed she was wearing a wire bracelet with rusted metal charms.

There was a sudden scuffle at the water tank, a chicken's panicked squawk, a metallic ding. Greta turned to shine the torch behind her. A rufous owl was perched on the tank with Raffy's white hen limp in its clutches.

When Greta looked back the girl was gone. She'd only turned her head for a few seconds. She shone the torch past the ghost gums and up to the ruined homestead, then switched it off. Only then did she spot the lantern's bobbing light disappearing through gamba alongside the firebreak.

'Wait!' called Greta, alarmed.

The girl didn't look back.

'If you drop that lamp in those grasses, we're all gone,' Greta whispered.

10

Greta sliced through the blue water of the local pool. The black lines of the lane wavered beneath her.

You have lost someone. Someone very young. It was unnerving, the way those blue eyes had looked into her. *You are very real.*

Where had she come from that first time Greta saw her by the car? And last night? *Down that way.* Near the outcrop, the hidden valley. The hut.

I wouldn't go in there if I were you. Did Trapper know the girl was there? The thought sickened her.

It's a sad thing to lose a friend. Gavin's face floated up to her from the pool floor. She sucked in water and came up spluttering at the wall. She'd reached the shallow end without knowing it.

Erin was there, skinny and tanned and wearing a black bikini. A section of plastic wrap covered a fresh tattoo above her left breast.

'Tryin' to get fit?' she asked.

Greta smiled, breathing hard. 'A few laps after school drop-off keeps me sane.'

'I can't swim yet.' Erin pointed to the tattoo. 'Don't let me stop you.'

Greta readjusted her goggles and swam on. She kept seeing the girl's distorted face against the flywire and the amethyst in her hand. It might have been a dream if Griffin's amethyst hadn't been missing this morning, along with the lantern.

At the deep end she stopped and eased herself up onto the ladder. The blue water rocked. Erin had gone.

Afterwards Greta went to the post office and checked the letterbox. There was one letter. She recognised Janna's handwriting.

Hazel smiled at her from her usual table. 'You've been swimming,' she noted. 'It's the weather for it.'

'Sure is.' Greta sat down with her, shy. 'The kids are in the creek every day. Joel says there's no crocs.'

'There's traps set up. But you gotta watch out. When the rain's coming, you know.' She nodded to a woman entering the store.

Greta wanted to ask Hazel about the girl, if she'd heard about or knew the mystery visitor. But Hazel spoke first.

'As long as you're not swimming in that lake.'

'Joel's warned us off it.'

The air was humid, close around them.

Hazel looked out to the empty car park. Her breath rattled a little. 'There was poison water where my mother grew up.' She cleared her throat. 'Not like that one where you are. I'm talking different water.' Her hand waved through the air to change the place. 'To get rid of us, you know?'

She stopped to breathe. A cough took hold of her. When it passed she spoke again. 'Makes people sick. More and more of that poison, little bit every day, kills you.' She closed her eyes and passed her hand over her face.

Greta felt her stomach drop and a horror run through her, for this story and all the untold ones, the ones she didn't know. They were quiet, the two women, their fingers almost touching on the table. The store door opened and closed with people coming and going.

A four-wheel drive pulled up close to the verandah.

'I have to go now,' Hazel said, slowly standing.

Greta walked with her to the car, with Hazel holding her arm and sucking air in quickly now and then, because of a sharp pain in her legs, she said.

Greta opened the car door and gave her a hand up.

'My son, Trenthan,' Hazel smiled.

Trenthan nodded to Greta.

'Thanks, dear,' Hazel said.

'No worries.'

'Slam it,' Trenthan told her, for the door.

Hazel's words stayed with Greta on the way home. *There was poison water where my mother grew up.* Flowing through everything, Greta thought, and she shivered as she turned into the property.

On the verandah she opened the letter from Janna. A faint smell of ylang-ylang wafted out. It was an invitation to 'our wonderful locals' to take part in the Fishermans Creek community arts and crafts show in January, when the town swelled with holidaymakers. *Sell your work, show off your talent!* A handwritten note urged Greta to send jewellery and frame a few photos. *They'll sell for sure honey, and I know you need the cash. You could deliver it yourself, have a beach holiday.* Greta turned the note over. *And can you give me a call? It's about your dad's place.*

Greta returned the letter to its envelope. Fishermans Creek was still chasing her, even this far away. But her father's house would slide into the river one of these days if it hadn't already. She knew that. And Janna wouldn't want his furniture and Vivian's photos in her ex-boyfriend's shipping container forever.

She watched Joel slam the crowbar into the earth over at the cabin site. He was digging foundation holes.

The wise man builds his house upon the rock. Even her atheist mother had quoted that to her husband, who'd built their house on a sandy hill. *A river changes course*, Vivian had warned. It was passing too close. And the tides were coming in. *Any minute we'll be a boat.* Wasn't that what Frank wanted—to sail into the horizon? Vivian beat him to it by walking there.

Greta took out her mobile phone to check the reception. It wasn't strong enough. She'd have to walk up to the homestead. Later maybe. She wasn't sure she could withstand the force of Janna. *Deliver it yourself, have a beach holiday.* Not yet, not yet, something in Greta said.

She could hear Joel muttering in frustration. She took him a glass of cold water filled with softly hissing ice.

'Thanks, you're a legend.' He drank thirstily. His shirt was sweat-soaked, his skin streaked with dirt.

A pile of rocks they'd both dug up over the past week were behind him. Greta was edging her garden beds with them. Griffin was making towers with the smaller stones. Odd little cairns would mysteriously appear by the front steps or the water tank, under the darkroom or along her garden paths.

'They'll do me in, these endless rocks.' Joel took up the spade.

For every one lifted out, another surfaced. Greta imagined them shifting underground and discussing where to emerge next.

She started filling the wheelbarrow from the pile. 'That girl was here last night.'

'What girl?' He kept digging and didn't look at her.

'The one I told you about—the one I met near the banyan tree when we first came. She was on the verandah, looking in. Round midnight.'

'Better lock up then, or hide things.'

He swapped the spade for the crowbar to edge around a stone and lever it up.

'I don't think she wants to steal.'

'What is it she wants then?'

'I think she wants to look at us,' she said. 'You in particular. And Griffin.'

He crouched to lift out the stone. 'What's that supposed to mean?'

'I thought you might know.'

He grimaced with the twinge in his back or what she'd said, perhaps, and let the rock drop onto a pile.

She left him to his digging and pushed the wheelbarrow across to her garden. The rock-lifting was giving her new muscles. Every day Griffin challenged her to an arm wrestle. *Arm strongii*, he called her, after the cycads. She must ask him about the species down in that hidden valley, near the hut where the girl might hide.

She couldn't understand why Joel would avoid talking about the girl. Over the years she'd learned to decipher his silences, his cryptic answers. He was hiding something. She wanted to hook it out.

She glanced over at him. He was digging with a passion, like he might excise an enemy. We are both wrestling with the ground, she thought, asking for some kind of leeway. And above us the white clouds plume, islands in the sky.

A koel bird called its pensive hopes of rain. Greta hoped these stones didn't mind being removed from their private underworld and relocated, unasked.

A shout came from Joel. The crowbar somersaulted up into the blue, then dived to bounce across rocks. He was staring into the hole he'd dug. She went to him and saw the rock embedded in both sides. It could be a hidden reef.

'We're going to have to haul that out with the four-wheel drive,' said Joel.

They took turns levering and digging to break more dirt around it and pass a rope underneath. When the rock was chained up to the car, Joel signalled for Greta to move forward. The vehicle strained, the tyres kicked up dirt and the rock jolted out. There it was, an uprooted giant's tooth.

Greta lay down next to it to watch the clouds. They were connected within the rock somehow. She could feel the hum of the hidden world underneath her. She wondered if Hazel would teach her something about this country. She mightn't want your questions, a voice in her said. Taking up her time. Pressing on wounds.

She went to find Joel in the shower. The water wasn't cold but still it was a relief. She could feel her thoughts becoming calmer, a sense of logic returning. Everything is relative, she told herself. The temperature of water, the nature of ground. Rocks versus sand.

The air inside the shack was warm, oppressive.

Joel turned on the fan and filled a tea towel with ice for the rash on her neck. She felt the heat sucked away. She picked up her father's watch from the bench.

'Forget them,' he said, reading her mind about time and children coming home on the bus.

He kissed her, and she felt a wave of warmth for him under

the tangle of her questions. He's always been a good kisser, she thought. He carried her off with him, and tripped on the swag.

'Don't break your kneecaps,' she said as they fell.

A tear of sweat dropped from his chin to her chest. She glanced over his shoulder to the beanbag dented with the shape of a child, Griffin's open bird book on the floor. Brynn's spiky-skinned, yellow-green jackfruit on the kitchen bench.

'You're distracted,' he said.

The sheets were a damp twist. The swag was a thin excuse for a mattress. She rolled him under her and sat up. The fan whirred air onto her back.

She pressed his hips close, to feel his bones against hers.

What had she been thinking earlier, to cast him as a stranger? The heat must have turned her head. He was the same as he'd always been, this man she'd plucked from the ocean all those years ago. He was returned, familiar.

11

It's all about light and darkness. About making the invisible visible.

Her mother's words kept finding her out, here in the van. This is the problem with the dead, Greta thought—thirty years later and a few thousand kilometres away they sneak in to see how you've set up your darkroom.

The windows were covered with foil and she'd built a cover over the exhaust fan to keep out the light. She hadn't painted the walls black, leaving them off-white to see better under the safe light.

Keeping the chemicals cool was her challenge. Her developer, stop and fixer solutions were in bottles, jugs and trays on ice. Twenty-three degrees by the thermometer—not bad for the tropics.

She'd just finished checking her timing charts when Toby knocked. Greta hesitated. The air conditioner rattled on the wall.

'Can I come in?'

She opened the door, remembering her mother's darkroom, the fierce instructions not to interrupt. She turned up the exhaust fan to suck away chemical vapours. Toby sat down to watch.

The image must be protected.

She gave her mother's answers to his questions about the light-proof bag, where she hid her hands to cut open the film canister, and wind the film onto a spool to put inside the developing tank. Even the camera is a miniature dark room, she explained.

There is so much light in our world. So much exposure.

Vivian didn't use a lightproof bag. Total darkness in the room was her way. Greta disturbed it only once, opening the door to let harsh light flood in. It came back to her—the quick shout, silent fury, ruined negatives quivering in the bin.

Greta went through the steps with Toby, pouring chemicals in and out of the tank, tipping it slowly back and forth—one, two, one, two, like a metronome. She kept her eye on the mobile's stop watch.

Time and temperature. If it's not right the image will distort. This is science, not art, she used to think, impatient with the many exacting steps.

'You will never be Vivian.' The art lecturer had winced at her slapdash ways, skipping exposure texts, guessing times.

When they'd finished and rinsed the negatives Greta pegged them on a line strung from one end of the van to the other. Toby peered at them closely, deciphering images. Here was a cycad's head of fronds, the thick fingers of pandanus roots. They didn't look real, more like X-rays of an alien forming in its pod, morphing into an unknown creature. The curlew was a white ghost, the scraggly turkey bush a filigree of fine white bones. And the day sky behind the bird was as dark as night.

'It's weird, all reversed,' he said. 'The dark is the light, and the light is the dark.'

Greta felt old next to this child of a digital era. She opened the door to air the van while the negatives dried. Toby came outside with her to search the sky for the Southern Cross, the pointers, planets. She remembered her mother's shadow on a dune, the red glow at the end of her cigarette.

When they were ready to print, Toby switched on Henry's orange safe light. Greta chose a negative of Magdalen's birth car to position in the enlarger.

'Wow,' he whispered, when he saw the light shine through the negative and the image appear underneath on the photographic paper.

When the exposure was done and she switched off the enlarger's light, he was shocked to see the picture disappear.

'Trust me, it's there,' said Greta.

The latent image, secretly in the paper. She remembered her own wonder when she used to watch her mother working. It had gone into her at an early age, the magic of light and mirror and lens, the luring of an image from white nothing.

She slipped the paper into the developer solution and gently moved the tray. There was a second of waiting, of wondering if it was a hoax, a mistake, and nothing would appear. But suddenly shadows emerged. Lines, shapes took form. From nothing came the shadows of rocks, the car, clouds above.

'I can see it!' Toby smiled.

He kept time for her, calling out when to lift the paper with tongs and move it on to the stop, then fixer, then rinse trays.

She pegged up the finished image. Toby stared at it, transfixed. Protection. Concealment. The invisible made visible.

'I never knew,' he said. 'I never knew what it truly was.'

It appealed to the illusionist in him. Toby the magician, with his box of secret drawers, his sleight of hand and clever card moves, had found something akin to a new trick.

He chose the lake for the next print.

The poison water looked other-worldly in its ethereal projection and the dim orange light. And again when it reappeared in the developer tray with the spiky pandanus and dark trees around it.

'It's like a memory,' Toby said. 'Or a daydream. You can choose when to start and stop it.'

'You're so right,' she agreed.

Latent memory. Switch it on and off. Project the picture you want, fix it.

Toby pegged up the finished print. Its steady dripping had a beat. He wanted to stay longer, to watch her develop a sheet of thumbnails.

'Next time,' she said gently, and he left then.

Now the darkroom was hers. She took out the next sheet of photographic paper. A metallic taste was on her tongue.

Careful with that negative, her mother would say. *You're too quick with it.*

There were no scratched negatives or careless tones of grey in Vivian's work.

Greta adjusted the enlarger's lens to focus a cycad, the fine cross-hatching patterns in the trunk, the elaborate seed necklace. She admired these plants that survive months without rain, and burn yet live. Resilience. She wished she had more of it. There were people who thought she was strong, adventurous. But inside she was something else.

The quietness of the room, the darkness inside and outside, took her into another world. She lost track of time with the gathering prints. It was the witching hour and she was inspired.

She kept the bush stone-curlew until last. The quick appearance of that cautious bird gave her goosebumps. She pegged up the photograph. The dark room, the equipment, film and chemicals, the hours of labour were all worth it for this one image. Suddenly she felt a connection with the unkempt feathered messenger who called out its sorrow to her in the night. In this dim orange light, in this strange, dripping atmosphere, there was something in that haunting eye that could be a mirror.

12

'We've been here a month, did you know?' Toby called over his shoulder. He had a towel around his neck and goggles pushed up on his forehead. If you asked him who he was, he'd say Chuck Yeager.

'Time flies when you're having fun,' Greta said.

'I think it's slow,' said Raffy. 'The hotter the day is, the slower the time is.'

They were all feeling the heat of the build-up, and going to the creek often, especially now it was the October school holidays. This morning Greta had suggested they go through the gap in the fence and try to cross the rainforest bridge over the pool of water there.

The excitement of the idea was so strong the children didn't want to play too long in the creek. The two younger boys were drying themselves when Toby returned from a brief wade upstream. He'd spotted a fence ladder on Trapper's side.

They all went to look, careful to stay close to their bank.

'It's like a stile in a storybook,' Raffy said.

'Why is it there if he doesn't want us trespassing?' asked Toby.

'So he can climb over,' Griffin suggested.

'He fossicks on this property,' said Greta. 'And if you see him, I don't want you talking to him.'

'Why not?'

She led them away without answering, hoping their excited voices hadn't travelled up to Trapper's ears. She went through the gap in the fence first. 'Go straight across and wait for me on the other side.'

Joel had assured her there would be no crocodiles but she didn't want to linger on the bridge to who knew where.

It swayed under their feet. Greta kept her eyes on the shadow water. They passed the shaggy trunks of paperbarks, the corkscrew necks of spiralus pandanus. The forest darkened around them.

A few metres along, Raffy stopped. 'What is it?' he whispered, staring at a large shadow hanging among dark, leathery leaves just ahead of him. He hugged his towel to his mouth. His skin was beaded with creek water.

'It's a car, don't you see?' Toby was incredulous that his brother hadn't realised.

The rusted carcass hung upside down, clutched by a tangle of branches, woody vines and green tendrils. Headlight casings protruded with a gaping stare.

'It's old,' said Toby. 'Older than those wrecks up at the homestead.' He put a hand over his mouth. The homestead was out of bounds.

Greta let it pass. 'You're right. It could be from Second World War days.'

'Take a picture,' whispered Raffy.

Toby wasn't waiting for photos and carried on across the uncertain footbridge. Greta framed the car in the viewfinder. There wasn't enough light, it would be a shadow. As she took the shot Griffin's foot broke through the bridge. Half of him disappeared into the water. She hurried to pull him up. A white graze on his back inked with blood.

'Go on, Raffy.' She lifted him over the gap.

He hurried on to Toby, who'd reached an archway of light.

'Are you right to keep going?' she asked Griffin in a low voice.

He'd cut his shin. Watery blood trailed to his foot. But he assured her he wasn't hurt and limped on through the forest and out into sudden daylight.

'What is this place?' he wondered out loud, taking in the small flood plain ahead of him, the pandanus laden with orange fruit, the rock face that rose to the outcrop.

There was only sky and sun above the cliff. No shack or homestead. No world on the other side. Vines hung down from crevices in the rock. A brave, slender tree reached out for sunlight, straggly roots clinging to stone.

It was the hut though, that excited Griffin most once he saw it. Greta had almost expected it not to be here, to find that the rocky labyrinth above had sucked it into a crevice, or the magical wings of the geese had vanished it away.

The soft ringing of chimes wafted towards them. As they drew near, Greta saw several sets dangling from the verandah roof's beam. Most had just one or two threads knotted with a shell or wishbone, a few shards of brown bottle glass or tiny mirrors, a twist of rusted metal or a bolt.

Toby slipped inside before she could tell him to wait.

'There's nothing in here,' he protested when she called him out.

She glared at his brazenness. He sulked to one side of her, and then followed Griffin to the mango tree. A flock of magpie geese saw the boys coming and waddled away, pink faces raised, bills tapping at air.

Raffy stayed near Greta to peek through cracks in the hut walls. He wouldn't go in without her. She hesitated. There was no door, only the dark entrance. She leaned in a little way.

'Hello?'

No reply. Just a slender breath of wind that brought the smell of magpie geese and made the chimes sing, *Come in, come in!*

It took a few seconds for her eyes to adjust from the glare outside. Shapes came to her slowly. A curtain wavering at her left. A round table with two chairs. A concrete trough, identical to the laundry one at the shack. A window above it with three closed louvres draped in cobwebs. An aluminium teapot alone on a shelf under the trough. She picked it up and looked inside for damp tea-leaves. None.

'Do you think someone lives here?' asked Raffy.

'Maybe,' said Greta. 'Maybe not.'

Raffy looked at her. 'That's a funny answer.'

It seemed lived in and abandoned at the same time. She couldn't decide if the girl had been here or not.

He moved to rifle through clothes on a rack—a pair of overalls, a couple of dresses, a workman's shirt. He waved the shirtsleeve at her. A microbat flew out and terrified him, swooping low, brushing his hair.

He fled behind the curtain. 'Look! Someone sleeps here!' cried Raffy.

The bat was forgotten. He held the curtain aside for Greta to see a single bed pushed snug into a narrow alcove. It had a faded pink chenille bedspread. Propped against the mould-speckled pillow was a threadbare calico rabbit with gangly arms and legs and drooping ears. One eye was missing. The bedhead had a shelf. A musical trinket box sat there, similar to one Greta had as a child.

Above the bed, nine nails were hammered like pegs into the alcove wall. A wire loop hung on each, except for the middle one, which was empty. It could have been a game, like hookey, except that the loops were decorated with charms, like minuscule replicas of the trinkets on the chimes outside. They were bracelets, the same kind as she'd seen the girl wearing.

Raffy sniffed the air. 'This place smells of something.'

Greta agreed. There was a damp smell to the room. Watermarks stained the lower sections of the walls. And the bed had an odour that reminded Greta of the girl. Raffy moved away from it.

'Go and play with the others,' Greta said. 'You don't have to stay in here.'

He left, pleased with that idea. Her hands went to the trinket box. She sat on the bed, mattress sagging under her, to wind the key at the back of the box and flip open the lid. A ballerina doll popped up and turned to 'Greensleeves'. Greta laughed softly.

The doll wore a mint green tutu. She'd lost her leotard, but someone had drawn a bikini top on her in green texta. Behind her was a mirror, stuck into the lid. There was no jewellery in the box; instead, an audio cassette, four photos and three Kodachrome slides held by a sticky rubber band that broke when she touched it. She hesitated and glanced up at the bracelets, the cobwebbed window and the rack of mostly adult clothes.

No one has been here in a long time, she reassured herself. There was no harm in a quick look.

In the first photo a teenage boy was knee-deep in a creek. He held a fish on a hook in each hand. Something made her think it must be Danny, brother number five, the one Joel was closest to in age and friendship. He was in the next photo too, with Joel and another boy. She laughed to see her husband so young and fresh-faced. He had the same intense gaze she knew. The third photo showed Joel on a horse.

Her worry eased. Obviously these weren't the girl's photos.

The last print was black and white. A woman held a baby in a stiff white dress, clutching a painted Easter egg. The woman's hair was as dark as the child's was white. Maria and Magdalen, Greta thought. Beside them an unsmiling Joel stared up at the camera. Greta's fingers gently touched his face. She wanted to pick up that little boy and hold him.

The music box slowed its tune, the ballerina jolted to a stop.

Greta went to the doorway for better light to see the slides. There was the homestead before it burned, with lush greenery around the house; and a wicker chair on the verandah, with a peacock woven into the back; and Maria sitting in it, smiling at the camera.

A shout came from outside. Greta held her breath. What if she'd been wrong and the girl did live here? What if the box and its contents were part of an obsession with Joel?

Her children's voices settled down among honks of geese. She went back to the jewellery box and took out the cassette.

A white chrysalis was spun over the plastic cover. She broke it open to see inside. *The Six Swans* was handwritten on the front of the insert. A piece of paper was folded behind the tape. She opened it to see a pencil sketch of the boy with a swan wing. Underneath his foot was the letter *J*.

She knew what this must be. Joel's sister didn't read, he'd told her, so his mother read books onto tape. Joel did too, or he made up stories and drew pictures. Greta imagined him in a branch of the mango tree, with Magdalen nestled into him, listening. Perhaps this hut had been a cubby where they'd all played by the creek.

A chair scraped the floor near the table, startling her. Raffy shuffled over. His brothers were ganging up on him, he said.

'Look what I've found.'

He took the cassette from her. 'It's like Dad's old music tapes.'

Joel played them often along the highway.

'I think it's your grandmother telling a fairytale. *The Six Swans*.'

'I know that story!'

Did he? Greta wasn't sure she liked it for bedtime. She'd clipped the pages together in his fairytale book. But a clip will come undone. Toby would relish the horror notes of this tale and embellish them for his wide-eyed little brother.

'Who drew this?' He held out the picture of the swan-wing boy.

She pointed to the initials. 'Your dad.'

She opened the box and took out the photos. He laughed to see his father so young.

'My guess is that's Uncle Danny,' Greta showed him the boy with the fish.

'Who keeps these here?' Raffy asked.

'I don't know.' She packed everything back in the box and turned the music key for him to delight over the ballerina while she took photos of the kitchen area and the clothes rack, and then came back to focus on the bracelets.

Raffy was lying on the bed whispering to the rabbit. They were peering through a knothole in the wall to spy on the outside world—brothers, friends, enemies.

She decided not to disturb him and turned to the opposite wall, which had sections covered in newspaper to keep out rain or stop outsiders looking in through gaps between the wall panels. Lindy Chamberlain caught her eye, with those sunglasses. Greta remembered the news stories from her childhood. A newborn taken.

A mother judged. A nation caught in a frenzy, spinning convictions. Most of the other newspaper cuttings were local, unknown to her, from the late 1970s, into the 80s, 90s. Last century, Toby would remind her.

Behind her, Raffy called out, 'Can I take a picture? Through this little window.'

She helped him line up the lens with the knothole, but then he wrestled the camera from her.

'Let me do it, let me.' Click. Click. Click. Click. 'There! Whatever I've taken will surprise you.'

She smiled. 'Come on. Let's see what's outside.'

He replaced the rabbit carefully and crossed its lanky legs. She led him around the back of the hut. A cast-iron oven lay belly up on the grass. Raffy called her over to a mound of dirt clogged with shards of glass and rusted metal, brown longneck bottles, burned beer cans, a star picket draped with barbed wire.

She let him photograph it, then took the camera back to walk among the cycads. She passed her hand over the fronds. They were exotic feathers, soft and velvety to touch. *Cycas calcicola*, Griffin had told her. Rare, and here with the dinosaurs.

'Look,' Raffy called her over. 'It's a cauldron.'

He'd found an iron bowl with a hole in the bottom of it, sitting on a stand. Not far from it was a hand crank blower and an anvil in the grass. Raffy picked up a pair of blacksmith tongs.

'Wherever you go it's stranger and stranger,' he said very quietly, and passed her the tongs so he could run off to the mango tree.

Yes, thought Greta. Stranger and stranger. And she wondered whose homemade forge this had been.

She set up the camera and tripod, feeling like a photographer at the scene of an unnatural event, where the people had vanished but left parts of themselves. The fire bowl, the hut, the chimes. Bracelets on a wall. What were they trying to tell her?

She remembered her mother picking up an abalone shell out of wet sand. It had a hole in it, which she put straight up to her eye and then gave to Greta to do the same.

It's all about focus, how you frame the shot.

Vivian. Vivian, whispering down here in the secret valley.

What happened to that shell? Greta asked herself now. She'd kept it in her coat pocket and used it often. At the beach, at school, walking along the main street.

She checked her father's watch. It was time to go. She called the children and went to photograph the chimes along the verandah. It was harder than she thought. The strings insisted on moving, twirling in an uncanny air, a numinous breath that hovered under the eaves.

Raffy was the first to appear. 'Who made these do you think?' he asked, gently tapping them.

'I'm not sure.'

It's the girl! It's the girl! sang the chimes.

Who else could it be, this careful scavenger, seeking little pieces of metal and foraging for small bones to whittle and shape? Greta could see the girl sifting through that pile of dirt out the back, wandering from car wreck to car wreck and combing the grass by the old forge bowl.

Again she wondered if perhaps the girl *was* here from time to time, after all. I hope she doesn't mind we've visited, she said to herself. And taken photographs. She snuggled the camera into its bag.

Raffy had the whole row of chimes singing. He moved up and down the verandah, tapping his instruments.

'Boo!' Griffin leaped from the hut.

Raffy froze, shocked. Greta stepped back into dangling strings. A little wishbone caught in her hair.

'See?' He grinned and held up her backpack. 'I catch the things you miss.'

She freed herself and planted a kiss on his forehead.

Toby arrived then to upset Raffy's game. He smacked the row of chimes with a stick. They swung out and up, ready to fly off.

'Leave them!' she told him and grabbed Raffy's raised fist. 'We're going now.'

She settled the rattling objects and glanced up the slope behind the mango tree to the outcrop. If she were alone she'd try to find her way to the other side. For now, with the children, she led the way back to the bridge. Before crossing they all turned to look back.

'It's like a magic place,' mused Raffy. 'But I don't think we should visit without you.'

'Yes. You mustn't come here alone. I think this is the only time for you.'

'Why?' Griffin was disappointed.

'The bridge is broken. And it's too far from the shack if you hurt yourself. I'd never know.'

'A troll could half eat you and take out your eyes and you'd just have to lie here dying,' confirmed Raffy.

'There's no trolls here,' Toby told him. 'We're not in your fairy-tale book.'

Trapper might pass for one, thought Greta. She warned them to tread wisely and remember the gap Griffin had made. Toby went first with Griffin following. Raffy was more hesitant.

'It's very dark in here,' he said in a low voice.

He didn't like the way the bridge shuddered with their foot-steps, or the shadowy water underneath. He tightened his grip on

Greta's hand as they approached the hanging car. He edged past it with one hand over his face, peeking through the gaps between his fingers.

'I keep seeing it as what it's not,' he breathed through his hand mask. 'I keep thinking that car's a creature.'

13

They arrived home from the hut adventure to find a faded blue ute parked outside the shack.

'I hope that's not Trapper,' said Raffy.

But the man who eased from the car was a stranger.

'Joel around?' His eyes were a gentle blue-grey. He was thin, edgy.

'He'll be back soon,' Greta said, and introduced herself.

'Gabe.' He shook her hand.

So this was him. Brother number seven, Joel called him. Separated from family, Greta didn't know why. Maria took him in as one of her own when he needed it. He might leave for a few months, a year, and then return. He and Joel had worked together for years on this and other properties, meatworking, fencing, mustering, haymaking. They were a team. More than that, Tori said. They were like blood.

'Got you a couple of geese.'

He leaned over the side of the ute and pulled out two dead birds. They were large, big-winged. Greta thought of the swan story. Toby came over to hold one by the neck and feel its weight, and ask about the goose-hunting season. He was interrupted by Joel's quad bike.

The two men greeted each other.

'Been looking for that cow of Trapper's,' said Joel.

'She tried to eat our vegies last night,' Raffy added, 'but we chased her off.'

Gabe smiled about the cow and handed Toby the other bird. 'One for now, one for the freezer,' he said.

'You'll stay and eat with us?' Joel asked.

Toby and Griffin lit the campfire near the cabin, where they'd made a firepit with a circle of rocks and a log for seats. They went to find more wood, while Greta boiled water in a metal bucket to pluck the birds. She worked under a tree, a little way from the fire. Raffy watched her dubiously.

'What is it?' she asked him.

'I was wondering,' he whispered, as she rhythmically pulled feathers, 'if these come from the hut.'

'I doubt it.'

'How do you know?'

'Because I don't think they look like your magic geese,' she said. 'I think these are normal.'

He wasn't sure they were, on account of their half-webbed feet. 'I have never seen bird feet like it,' he told her.

Back at the fire, they raked a bed of coals for corncobs and sweet potatoes, and then joined Gabe and Joel at the cabin site. They were looking over the new floor, and talking about starting wall frames. Gabe was keen for the work. Raffy proudly mentioned the ironwood stumps that were termite-proof. And that both parents had worked on the foundations—kids too if you counted carrying away dug-up rocks. It had been an effort, Greta agreed, cementing in posts, making sure they were all level. She'd felt like an overly taut stringline by the end.

When the time came to cook the meat, no one could find the campfire grate. Joel and Gabe dragged over the old bed frame from the shed and set it over the fire. The springs were soon red-hot coils.

'You could cook a lot of food on that,' said Raffy.

Gabe cut the meat into a butterfly and threw it flat on the bed. He grinned. 'Best way to cook goose.'

Fat dripped into the flames. The meat sizzled.

The smell of it through the smoke reminded Greta of the girl and the hut.

When the food was ready, Griffin clanged a saucepan. Toby rolled the vegetables out of the coals. Joel cut up the goose meat. There was little talk at first apart from murmurs about the good food. But then Raffy piped up, 'We found a hut today, down in the valley. You can't see it from here.'

'The meatworker's hut?' Joel glanced at Greta. 'I thought that would've fallen down by now.'

'No.' Raffy's cheeks were bulging with sweet potato. 'It's fully standing.'

Joel peeled the burned sheaths from a corncob, and let them fall into the coals. There was a sudden flare of the papery skins, a quick return to nothing.

Griffin leaped up and ran over to the shack, returning with the musical jewellery box. 'We found this.'

He offered it to Joel who seemed bewildered at first, as if he didn't want to take it.

'You should have left that where it was,' Greta told Griffin. She understood now what he'd been up to with her backpack in the hut.

'Why? No one's there.'

He wound the key at the back and pressed the box to Joel's chest. Joel took it this time, though Griffin had to open the lid. The ballerina popped up and started her dance. Specks of glitter on her tutu glinted in the firelight. The texta bikini was a poor match.

'She needs a shirt on really,' said Raffy.

Greta laughed, and Gabe echoed her softly.

Raffy was solemn, unsure of what he'd said.

'Whose is it?' asked Toby.

'Magdalen's,' replied Joel.

Raffy put a hand on his father's shoulder.

'I didn't know,' Griffin said quietly, closing the lid.

Greta breathed a secret relief it didn't belong to the girl.

Joel put the box between his boots and picked up a goose bone to nibble off the last of the meat. 'She wouldn't mind.'

'If she did, she can't do anything about it now.' Toby threw his chewed cob into the fire. The flames hissed.

'Toby.' Greta frowned.

Everyone was quiet again. Then Joel and Gabe dragged aside the bed frame and built up the fire. When Joel sat down again, Griffin reached for the box and opened the lid just enough to take out the audio cassette without starting 'Greensleeves'.

'Look, Dad,' Raffy said. 'It's a tape, like your ancient music stuff.'

'Mister Looky-Here with his ancient stuff,' said Joel, shuffling along the log to make room for him. He seemed to have recovered from the unexpected box.

Raffy snatched the cassette from Griffin to pull out the insert. 'And there is your picture!'

Joel took it from him, amused.

'Can we listen to it in the four-wheel drive?' Raffy stood up, ready.

Joel shook his head. 'Tomorrow, matey. We've got a visitor.' He nodded towards Gabe.

'What is this tape?' Toby took the insert from Raffy.

'It's my mother telling a story for Magdalen,' Joel said. 'We recorded heaps of them. The others went up in smoke with the old place. I don't know how this didn't go the same way.'

'*The Six Swans* is in my storybook,' enthused Raffy. 'Six brothers are turned into swans and their sister has to save them, but she's not allowed to talk for six years and has to make them six nettle coats. It's all about six.'

'It's all about wicked stepmothers, actually,' said Toby. 'The kids' wicked stepmother turned the boys into swans. And their sister ends up marrying a prince, and his mother is a wicked stepmother too—'

'That'd be a mother-in-law, not a stepmother,' said Greta. 'Neither are much loved in fairytales.'

'Sexist,' noted Griffin.

'Yes, well.' Toby paused to check his logic. 'The mother-in-law steals the babies and lies to the prince, her son, that his wife killed them. His wife can't tell him it isn't true because she's not allowed to speak. So the prince puts his own wife in jail.'

'Bastard!' shouted Griffin.

Gabe grinned.

Raffy gave the tape to Griffin to look after while he acted out the rest of the story.

'When the sister is about to be killed—'

'Executed,' corrected Toby.

'—she calls out to her swan brothers and they fly in! Quickly she throws the nettle coats over them and they change back into men. But the last boy's coat wasn't finished, the left arm was missing. So he ends up with a swan wing forever. He was the youngest.'

Griffin took the picture from Joel and waved it to the audience. 'This is him.'

Raffy's fingers lightly touched his father's scarred arm. 'Did she save you, your sister?'

'Dad saved *her*.' Toby spoke with passion. 'Dragged her from a burning car, didn't you, Dad?' He looked to Gabe, who must know the story.

Gabe nodded with a quick glance at Joel, who said nothing.

'But she still died.' Raffy was confused.

Griffin held out a photo for Joel to identify.

'My mother, Maria. And Magdalen. Before she was sick.'

'What made her sick?'

'Magdalen? Ear infections. Screamed for days, poor kid. First one was the worst. Her ears were never the same after that.' He licked his fingers clean and dropped the bone into the fire. 'Neither were mine.'

Raffy fizzed a nervous laugh.

'Just kidding.' Joel smiled weakly. 'It was nothing for us compared to her. She always had infections after that, wonky hearing.'

'Wonky how?'

'Sort of muffled, like hearing underwater. Not all the time, but enough to frustrate the hell out of her. Other times her ears turned super sensitive, and every sound was magnified. Then she'd hear things we never could.'

'Who's this?' asked Griffin, holding up the boy with his catch of fish.

'That's Uncle Danny,' said Raffy, with a quick look across to Greta.

'No,' said Joel, 'that's not your uncle.' He handed Gabe the photo.

'That's Lennie,' said Gabe. 'Lived down the hut with Devil. His father.'

'Devil?' Toby moved nearer to Gabe, keen for more.

'Meatworker,' said Gabe. 'But Lennie, he was more a metal-worker. Horseshoes, hooks, knives, frypans—anything you wanted, Lennie could make it. He had a forge bowl, you know? Made one from a brake drum off an old truck. He could make anything that Lennie. Young fella, but clever.' Gabe paused. 'I reckon Devil was jealous.'

Griffin took the photo to see Lennie close up. 'How'd he get in Magdalen's jewellery box?'

'She was sweet on him.' Joel stood up to hook a stick under the full billy's handle and lift it onto the coals. 'Him too, for her.'

'Before she died?' asked Raffy.

'Of course!' Toby swiped the top of his little brother's hair.

'How old was she?' asked Griffin. 'You know—when she died?'

'Fifteen,' said Joel. 'Just for one day.'

Toby picked up a stick to prod a branch deeper into the flames. 'She died on her birthday?'

When he sat down Joel took the stick and made an adjustment from a different angle. 'That's right.'

The children were silenced. Only the fire spoke with its soft hissing and the sudden pop of a stick exploding into flame.

———

'I like that drawing of the boy with the wing,' said Raffy from under his mosquito net on the verandah. Greta had promised them earlier that they could sleep the night there. 'It's not like his other drawings,' he added. 'Not like the ones for us.'

'True,' remarked Greta.

She stood on a chair to hang up Griffin's net. He pulled it around the swag and crawled inside.

'Dad never says much about his sister or that fire in the car,' Raffy went on. 'About how he saved her.'

'No, he doesn't.' Greta stepped down.

Joel never spoke about the accident with the children. She tried to shield him from their questions, and told them to ask her about it, not him. Tonight she'd wondered if she'd said too much to them.

'But why not?' Raffy persisted.

'Because heroes don't boast, that's why,' Toby mumbled into his pillow.

Greta struck a match to light the camping lantern on the table.

'Do you think she knows we're here?' Griffin asked her. 'Magdalen?'

'Of course she doesn't!' Toby's pillow flew into the side of his net. 'Once you're dead, you're dead! That's it!'

————

Joel shoved a log into the flames. Sparks shot up into the night. Greta set down three mugs with teabags and poured the water from the billy. Gabe nodded and smiled when she passed him the cup.

'Gabe and I'll have that roof on the cabin before we go out to Connor's,' Joel said.

'The kids say they're not moving from the bus.'

'More room for us then.'

'How far away is this station again?'

'A few hundred kilometres.' He glanced at Gabe for confirmation.

'Yeah, about that.' Gabe gulped his tea.

Greta was overcome with tiredness. She drifted in and out of hearing the men chat and laugh softly together, then drop into their silent bond. The fire held her gaze, the orange shimmer under a log. The coals were like coral, the heat like wavering water.

When Gabe stood up to leave, she stirred.

'I'm all good, mate,' Greta heard Gabe say to Joel, who was ready to walk with him. 'You stay with the missus. Fire's still goin'.'

As the ute pulled away, Joel stretched out on the ground to rest his head in Greta's lap.

'I hope it wasn't too sad for you, talking about your sister and Lennie.'

'Nah,' he said. 'I'm okay.'

She paused, 'What happened to Lennie?'

'He left in the end. Before Magdalen died.'

They were quiet then, listening to the fire, and sounds of the night. A masked owl winged over them.

'I wish this grass had been burned off,' Greta said.

'We have to wait for the rain now. Ronnie'll keep an eye on it; he's with the firies.' His forefinger lightly brushed her chin. 'Don't worry yourself.' He was charmed by the sky. 'We could sleep here. Watch those shooting stars.'

'We'll be eaten alive.'

'Not under a mozzie net. I can hang one from that tree behind us.' He stretched his arm back to point at it.

The fire had died down to hot coals when Greta woke to a sound drifting up from the creek. She'd heard it in her sleep, but here it was again for real. Joel wasn't beside her. She looked through the mosquito net to the fire, and beyond into the dark. The sound returned, the low moaning of an animal—a cow, perhaps.

She listened for Joel's footsteps. There was only the rustle of cane toads and the dull thuds of a wallaby on the move. She'd convinced herself she'd imagined the sound when she heard it again. This time she wondered if it was Joel. She left the swag and pulled on her boots. The torchlight was weak. She wished she'd thought to change the batteries.

She made her descent in line with the banyan tree to find the track she knew. Everything was cast in an unfamiliar light under this three-quarter moon. The heads of cycads, the faces of rocks took on a different character. She felt as if there might be spirits among them, watching the newcomer pass.

Above her the Milky Way was a spill of stardust. She thought of early sailors, longing for night's trusted planets and constellations. Navigation is everything.

She headed down towards the black boulders. They too seemed altered by the night. Their presence was intensified. Her hand brushed against a pandanus frond; it cut a sting along her finger.

She heard the soft moan again, and found Joel leaning against one of the stones, passing some torment of his mind into it. The moonlit fan palm behind him was so close he seemed part of it. An odd-angled frond stuck out at his shoulder, like a giant wing with splayed feathers.

Never wake a sleepwalker, her mother used to say.

She couldn't decipher his whisperings. The frond wing moved slightly with him. When he started walking away she let him go. He shuffled around to the other side of the boulder. After a moment she followed, to make sure she didn't lose him.

He wasn't there. All she saw were the luminous trunks of the paperbarks and the dark line of the creek.

Behind her came a deep sigh. A moonlit cow was watching her. Its hooves were shiny black. A tag was pinned to the animal's ear. Trapper's errant heifer, she guessed. Four other cows looked on from further off. Greta backed away slowly. The cow snorted and trundled over to its friends. They left in a line, heading for the mango trees.

'Joel,' Greta called softly.

He was nowhere. The night, the ground, the rocks had taken him in while she wasn't looking. Perhaps it was her who'd been sleepwalking, seeking the ethereal noise that could have been the creek or could have been the soft, low, secretive grief of a man.

The sharp crack of a stick sounded a little way up the hill. A dark shape moved between the silhouettes of trees and cycads. It was him.

The beat of a hammer on metal sings out and echoes back. The fire bowl is brimful of fierce coals, a rush of flame. With his tongs, Lennie holds a glowing piece of metal across an anvil. He hits it with the hammer several times then returns it to the heat. His chest is wet with perspiration. His face is a ruddy glow. Behind him are objects he has made or mended or twisted into a new form. Horseshoes, hooks, a bell. Iron spirals and curled shapes, pipes and shafts. The workbench is strewn with his tools and an array of metal parts.

Standing not far from him, Magdalen watches.

She is leaning into a red bead tree, her arm around the trunk. Curling pods are scattered on the ground. The seeds have spilled, are bright red like pellets of blood.

She is captivated by the dreadful fire in the bowl, the loud banging of the hammer. Fire and metal. There's a fierce mystery in it.

14

With school holidays and Tori's children coming for sleepovers, it was another week before Greta developed the photos. They reminded her of crime scene pictures, pegged up side by side. She felt sure the girl was there, hiding. She searched for any sign of her in the hovering shadows behind the curtain, the cobwebbed light at the window. The eight bracelets on the wall intrigued her.

It's all about how you frame the image, her mother would say. *How you see.*

'And what do you see?' she whispered to herself.

The one-eyed rabbit stared back at her, knowing.

As she was packing up, a woman's voice spoke outside. The words were distorted, amplified, riddled with static. Her words had a musical lilt.

Greta opened the door of the darkroom. The sudden sunlight was so strong she saw nothing at first, just a flare that hurt her eyes. The sound was coming from the four-wheel drive, parked between the shack and the new cabin. The children were crammed in the front. Both doors were wide open. Toby was behind the wheel,

Griffin in the passenger seat and Raffy perched in the middle, squashed to one side against the gearstick. Their eyes were all fixed on the cassette deck.

Greta reached in across Griffin's legs to turn down the volume.

'It's her,' Griffin said. 'It's Dad's mother. She's reading *The Six Swans*.'

'I don't think she's reading it,' Toby added. 'I think she's telling it her own way.'

'Yes, I know, but you can listen to her quietly. Your father mightn't want to hear her voice.'

'Why not?' asked Raffy.

'Because it's like waking the dead,' Griffin told him.

'You certainly have it loud enough for that.' Greta turned the volume down another notch.

'Oh, man!' Toby's hands grasped the steering wheel.

'I can't hear!' Griffin's fingers brushed hers aside to rewind the tape. 'You've lost the place!'

Joel's face appeared at the driver's window. 'You've got it working then?'

'Yes.' Raffy frowned. 'But now you've interrupted and we have to start again.'

Greta looked across the three of them to Joel. 'Are you sure you want to hear it? They can listen another time.'

'Doesn't bother me.'

He was cheery enough. He might have stayed to listen, but the sound of Gabe's electric saw drew him away. They were working on the wall frames, kneeling on the cabin's floor to put together studs and noggins.

Maria's voice resumed, turned up louder so they could hear it over the intermittent sawing.

Greta went inside to make bread. By the time the yeast was frothing she was mesmerised by Maria's soporific voice. She could see Maria in the armchair and Magdalen's head resting against her mother's knee. And Joel drawing each feather in his swan boy's wing at the family table, and the doors open to the hot night.

The dough was hard to knead, her fingers felt weak. She rested in the hammock while the bread rose in its tin, and the fire she'd lit in the oven settled to coals. Hearing Maria tell the story changed it for her. She wondered if Joel's mother saw a connection between her own six sons and daughter and the ones in the story. It saddened her to think of both mothers losing their children through their own untimely deaths. Maria wouldn't have known it when she recorded herself telling the tale. Greta felt a new poignancy in the plight of the dead queen trapped in a ghostly realm witnessing her children's abuse and metamorphosis.

What had Magdalen thought of this tale's cruelties? Greta wondered. Or was it the end she loved, when the swans return to be brothers and the sixth one lives in her castle, always there to put his wing over her?

The story finished. There was a stretch of crackling static.

'Turn it off!' she heard Raffy say.

But Maria's voice returned in a haunting song. The notes passed down into the valley and out to the escarpment. A lament, a supplication. The children were quiet. The power tools stopped. Greta felt the song move through her. It had a strange effect, like a gentle current bearing her into dream. She saw Joel walking the fence lines seeking comfort for a grief he couldn't speak. And his mother too, traipsing the land, holding her anguish and her children. While the bush stone-curlew stepped ahead, or behind.

'It's finished!' yelled Griffin.

The spell was broken. The children's voices babbled over the sudden absence of Maria and moved across to the banyan tree.

The car was abandoned, the doors still open. Greta went to retrieve the tape. It was warm from playing. She put it on the shelf by her father's tin. There was something in it, the dead man's ashes and the dead woman's voice, up there on the shelf.

———

'I'm sad for you,' Raffy said to her that night. 'You don't have *your* mother on tape.'

Greta wasn't sad at all. She was quite certain she wouldn't like to hear a recording of Vivian. She adjusted the mosquito net around Raffy's bed and cleared toys from the bus floor.

'Mum?'

'Yes, Raffy?'

'You know that hut down near the creek? With the rabbit and the music box?' He propped himself up on his elbows. 'I think it's exactly like the hut in *The Six Swans*. The sister finds a wood-cutter's hut in the forest. Her swan brothers fly there every sunset and secretly change from swans back into boys. Just for quarter of an hour. Then they change back to swans.'

He was quiet, and she knew he was imagining himself shape-shifting from a boy to a swan and back again.

Griffin stamped up the bus steps and threw himself on his bed. Toby followed him in, whistling.

Raffy's voice drifted after her as she walked across to the darkroom.

'How long is a quarter of an hour?'

'Fifteen minutes,' came Toby's reply. 'Fifteen times sixty seconds.'

Greta could feel her father's watch ticking in her back pocket. Quarter of an hour. Enough time for swans to turn into men and back again. Enough time for a woman to walk into the ocean

130

and disappear. It was that short and long a time. From when her father last glimpsed Vivian and the moment she was gone forever. When he walked into the wind and the rain calling, calling her name, and found her soggy headscarf wound around a tree root sticking up out of the sand.

Greta took out her contact sheets from the photos she'd taken. She was thinking about a new photo series for Janna's art and craft show. She looked over the thumbnails with a magnifying glass— car wrecks, animal bones, the homestead. Dead cars and dead creatures. Dead house. They were reliable at least. They didn't move or do anything unexpected. The cycads are alive, she thought in her defence. And the bush stone-curlew.

She started developing the negatives she'd chosen, experimenting with different exposures and tones, not caring about mistakes. Unlike her student days she made sure she rinsed them properly.

It'll eat its own medium, Vivian had explained to a curious Greta, watching water run through a rack of prints. It was a mystery to Greta back then, why the magic solution that reveals a picture would later turn and attack it.

A knock startled her. She braced herself for Toby claiming insomnia.

'Who is it?'

'Brynn. Here on my weekly stickybeak. You're the only person I can visit this late.'

Greta opened the door.

'What's with the bus?' Brynn stepped inside.

'Joel's idea of the kids' bedroom. Toby says they're driving off in it if we work them too hard.'

'I thought it was my school bus come back to find me.'

Brynn examined the pegged-up prints.

'Griffin tells me they're bizarre,' said Greta. 'In a good way.'

'He's not wrong.' Brynn laughed. 'Show me this garden.'

They meandered around the rock-lined beds and tyres converted to planters, with Brynn shining her torch on the thriving plants.

'You *must* fence this vegie patch, Greta. It's a miracle the pigs aren't in.'

She stopped to see the cabin's few skeleton walls.

'When's this cabin going to be finished, the day you leave?'

'It's moving faster with Gabe here,' said Greta.

She diverted her friend to the dip of land below the shack. The cycads were waiting for them.

'I love the nights here,' she said. 'The darkness.'

'And these cycads, I see from your photos.' Brynn's hand touched a frond.

'I can imagine them moving around at night,' said Greta. 'Swapping places, watching us sleep.'

'You really are odd, Greta, on top of being a southerner.' Brynn cupped her hand to light a cigarette.

A curlew wailed from the rocky outcrop. There was a silence between the women. When the bird called again, Greta shivered. 'It goes right through me that cry.'

'Harbinger of death, some people say. Or endings and beginnings.' Brynn wandered closer to the edge. 'Undid those first white settler women. Poor things. Sail to the antipodes, set up house in the bush like a white sore thumb, and then hear that in the night. It'd scare the living daylights out of you, wouldn't it, if you were on your own, a fresh know-nothing from the other side of the world.' She peered downhill as if she might spot the bird. 'Reminds me of you Greta—only you're a know-nothing from this side of the world.' She smiled over her shoulder.

The bird wailed once more.

'Again! It knows you're listening.'

Greta thought of Hazel's poisoned water, people who'd lived in this place before it was made farmland, before they were uprooted, shifted. And those who'd come after. A family unravelling on a hill. Her own family, herself. 'There must be stories for that cry.'

'For sure. Different stories and meanings for different people and places, you know? About how the world works, or a sign. I heard one about a curlew who stole the moon's heart. Don't quote me, ignorant whitey that I am.' She paused as if the bird might sound again. 'We can't know the deeper meanings. But they're there.'

'We don't know the stories under us,' said Greta. 'Right with us, all around. Bring in our own instead.' She was thinking of *The Six Swans*, Pavel's whimsical castle, fairytales in Raffy's book. 'Those old paperbarks, the black cockatoo, the boulders down by the creek. They're the fabric underneath, holding us, know it or not.'

'Listen to you, drama queen!' Brynn stubbed out her cigarette and turned to the shack. 'I need a drink. I hope you've got one for me.'

Greta walked beside her, shining the torch along the ground.

'There's something in that curlew, though, you're right,' Brynn added. 'Doesn't matter who you are.'

A cane toad hopped in front of them. Brynn tried to kick it but missed. 'Bastards. They're all the way over in WA now, can you believe it? No more frill-necked lizards at my place. Wiped out. Gone.'

She checked the melons by the water tank. 'Here's a couple of fruit starting!'

Greta lit the candle on the green table and cleared Toby's juggling balls and cricket bat from the chairs. Brynn left a little jar of billygoat plum seeds on the table for the children to plant.

Joel came out with three beers.

'Why thank you. I'd take you home if I thought you'd finish anything,' Brynn said to him, lighting another cigarette. 'What's the story with that cabin? Your woman needs space.'

A breeze floated through the verandah. The chimes tinkled. Joel took a swig of his beer rather than talk about the cabin. Brynn flapped away her exhaled smoke. She was amused by him.

'I've heard about you. The kids told me everything.'

He tried to look light-hearted. 'Yeah, they say my reputation precedes me.'

'Brynn's a relative newcomer,' Greta smiled. 'She's only been here eight years.'

She saw Joel realise Brynn was a joker, and relax.

'I'll be back to work then. Measure up a few things for that cabin.'

Brynn let him go and settled into a cane chair. She blew a smoke ring that Raffy would admire.

'When's that man of yours off to Connor's, did you say? I know you told me.'

'In a fortnight.'

'Are you up for it?'

'Have to be, I guess. Though I am a southerner, as you point out. I'd be a liar if I didn't say the thought of it makes me edgy—here on my own with the kids. The grass gives me nightmares. Fire. And Trapper storming in after his wandering cow.'

'Trapper's cows are on the loose?'

'Only one that I've seen. Down at the creek, near the mango farm, with a few other wild roamers.'

'Jumped fence for a new herd, eh? Can't blame her.'

Greta laughed. 'Cow politics, Tori tells me. Didn't like her own boss or thought she'd be one herself.'

'Just like us,' said Brynn. 'Grass is always greener.'

Yes, thought Greta, just like us. She had a vision of her and Joel with the boys in the back, driving through barren land, heading for where the road converged into a green mirage.

15

Greta swung an old tyre into the back of the red ute. She was taking another load from the homestead to use for planters. She'd just called Janna, and heard about her father's place at Fishermans Creek—how the soil had shifted and the house collapsed. And Janna's ex wanted his shipping container back in the new year. Greta had promised to organise the removal of her mother's photos, her father's furniture and boxes.

'You must enter the art and craft show too,' Janna reminded her.

'I'm hardly a local anymore.'

'Place where you're born owns you forever.'

Greta was thinking on that when she heard Tori's troopy drive in after picking up the children from school. The car stopped at the shack first, and then revved up to the homestead. Greta could see Toby and Axel were with her. The younger ones' voices drifted from the shack.

'Thought I'd deliver him direct,' said Tori, opening the back of the troopy. 'Come on, tough guy, out you get.'

Toby sidled out and looked away from the two mothers. He had a bruise on his cheekbone.

'What is this, Toby?' Greta asked.

'You wouldn't get it!' He shrugged her off.

She felt a pang watching him slip away towards the shack. Axel loped down the hill after his friend.

'They're at that age,' Tori observed.

Greta wasn't ready for that age. She was caught up in the one before it.

'There was a flare up,' Tori said, sticks that went too far. 'It'll blow over. Rhianna'll call you.'

'Toby,' Greta sighed. 'Only the second week of term.' She shook her head about him locking horns with Joel, his brothers, now schoolmates.

'I brought home young Raymond too. I didn't think you'd mind. He wanted a play with Raffy. I cleared it with his Nanna. Gabe'll give him a lift home; he's minding the place next door while he's in town.'

'Ah good, they've been asking for a while now. I'll go down and find them all something to eat.'

Tori brushed her hands lightly and squinted at the disintegrating home, the cars doing the same.

'Can you believe this tip of a car joint? I mean the whole darn place. Must be hundreds of dumped cars, I reckon.' She swept a fly from her face. 'Gawd. Lars and his cars. Seb and his hot wheels, back in the day. An' then the wrecker's yard!' She clicked her tongue. 'Not that all this junk is theirs. If you wanted to steal, dump and burn, this is where you did it.'

'I can't see how we'll move them all before we go.'

'Is that a joke? You'll be dead before that happens.'

'Mick wants them cleared.'

'Mick.' Tori blew out his name. 'Mick's a Sydney man now. Trust me, the cars are here to stay.'

She walked around the front of the homestead to have a look at the old place. Greta went with her.

'Hard to believe he did this, isn't it?' Tori glanced at her friend.

Greta didn't know what she meant.

'Fedor! Settin' fire to the house. After Maria died, and Magdalen.'

'Fedor lit the fire?' Greta was shocked.

'Joel never told you?'

'I assumed it was a bushfire.'

'That was no bushfire. That was Fedor.'

Greta stared at the ruin, trying to absorb the words.

'Yeah, ol' Fedor. Didn't like somethin', had to kill it.'

'He didn't like the house?'

'Didn't like the memories. On the anniversary of Maria's death, Fedor just loses it. Makes a pile of her clothes, books, sheets, jewellery, headscarves—anything he can find—and starts a bonfire right there in the living room. In the dead of night. All Magdalen's stuff too. Up in flames.'

'God.'

'He was tormented, you know? Possessive. Especially with Maria, like someone might take 'er off 'im. Hate 'n' love, the two together. God, did the shit hit the fan with Pavel for bein' too kind to Maria. Talkin' too much together, playin' that accordion. Fedor kicked 'im out. That's why Joel and Pavel built the shack.' She sighed. 'I never could work 'im out, old Fedor. You know, livin' in this house, workin' so hard, till Donegan's goin' broke an' gives Fedor a deal to buy the block and the house, even the meatworks, though that was finished. But soon as 'e owns the place, he burns it out!'

Greta was silenced.

'I have to take my kids and go,' said Tori. 'Our house is full of hungry workers.'

Greta drove the ute back down to the shack with an odd feeling. Why hadn't Joel told her Fedor lit the fire?

He and Gabe were finishing the cabin roof. The heat and sunlight up there must be intense, she worried. Gabe arrived early every day and had a coffee and a quick chat with the boys before joining Joel. They worked with an old rhythm, a synchronicity. And a pride in their craftsmanship, erecting wall frames plumb and straight, cutting timber for roof battens. It was the little house with no history, no blood and salt on the kitchen bench, no bullet through the floor.

She parked the ute. Toby was sitting on the step, checking his toolbox of lures and fishing gear.

Griffin rushed out to her all excited. 'Come inside.' He ushered her to the main room. 'Look up!'

Sunlight flared down through a skylight in the roof.

'It's a stargazer window!' Griffin gently pushed her to stand directly under it.

Joel's face appeared in the square of light. He kissed his fingertips and pressed them against the perspex.

I do love you from this angle, she thought.

Raffy tugged her hand. A shy boy stood next to him.

'This is my friend Raymond,' he said. 'He's here till Gabe finishes work.'

She recognised the boy she'd seen riding on the back of the mobility scooter on the first day of school.

'Hi, Raymond.'

'Hi,' he whispered.

'We were going to draw pictures on the steps under the verandah,' Raffy continued. 'But my chalks are stolen.'

'They're not stolen!' laughed Griffin. 'You leave them out everywhere!'

'Can we buy more?' Raffy's eyes shone with hope.

'I think you need to put them back where they belong, Raffy.'

He sighed. 'Anyway, we're off down the creek for a fish. You could come with us to be croc spotter.'

'There's no crocs in that creek,' Toby called from outside.

Raffy pressed his face against the new flywire. 'Miss Rhianna says you never know what's lurking.'

———

Toby and Griffin kept ahead of the younger boys and especially Greta. At the black boulders they turned right towards the secret valley.

'We're going upstream,' Greta insisted, pointing the other way.

Toby gave her the look of death. Griffin hovered near him, uncertain. She stood firm. Toby huffed exasperation and pushed past her to march upstream. He called the others after him. They would go up near the mango farm, he yelled, away from adults. He glanced behind him to see who were his allies. Raffy and Raymond stayed by Greta. As they were about to enter the water, Raffy spotted a set of slender bones on a flat rock. They were picked clean, and arranged in a pattern.

'Who did that?'

'I'm not sure,' she replied. 'A bat maybe, or a possum.'

He paused, considering it.

Greta waded into a shallow rock pool and sat with her back to a frothing tumble of water. The heat, Toby's defiance, Fedor's fire were snatched into the babble of the creek.

Next to her a St Andrew's Cross spider web stretched between the paperbarks. The trees were very close, quiet guards, shedding skin and standing in still water at the creek's edges. A rainbow bee-eater darted from a tree branch to the water and back again.

We live in paradise, she thought. Immediately she heard women laughing from Trapper's side of the bank. She half expected to glimpse them watching her from behind the pandanus leaning over the water, but she saw no one, just brown ferns clinging to rocks, waiting for rain to turn them green.

'What is it?' asked Raffy, bemused.

'I thought I heard people laughing.'

'It's the creek gone inside your head.'

He and Raymond sat on a rock midstream to cast their hand-lines and their hope. She waited to hear the laughter again. People from before, she felt, but here now. She wished she could know them, talk to them. Ask them about this place.

Griffin and Toby's voices drifted down the water to her instead. She watched Raymond and Raffy, heads close together, all concentration on threading hook and sinker onto the line. They could be Gabe and Joel, she thought.

She imagined them here, with Danny and Lennie too, and Magdalen watching from a warm rock, a red dragonfly hovering at her toes. Joel was telling his boys last night how he used to come down to the creek and the dark boulders at night, to smoke tobacco sneaked from Fedor. It was one of his favourite haunts. Sometimes he came alone, sometimes with the others. Or just Magdalen. Greta could see her moving between the old rocks, resting her ear against one to hear its inner hum.

The longer I'm here, the more your family seeps into me, she'd told him.

The hour ran on swiftly with its minutes, the sound of the water, her thoughts. Suddenly she remembered she hadn't asked Gabe when he would be leaving. She called out to the boys nearby and further off. Toby and Griffin yelled back they'd be there soon.

'We'll go ahead,' said Greta to the younger boys.

She meandered uphill after them. Raymond turned to look back at her. She smiled at him, and he grinned back so broadly she felt carried.

'Gabe's left already!' Raffy called from the top.

'Not to worry,' Greta assured Raymond. 'We'll take you home. I have to go to the post office. We can buy ice creams.'

Aunty Hazel wasn't at her usual seat on the shop verandah. Greta hoped she wasn't sick. She gave Toby money for the ice creams and went into the post office. Dee had a magazine open on the counter. A photo of a hairless cat had caught her attention.

'Can you believe it exists? Who wants an animal like that? It's unnatural. People have gone unnatural.'

Dee rewrapped Greta's parcel of jewellery to fit in a smaller envelope with a cheaper rate. Greta thanked her profusely, paid, and ushered out Raffy, who'd come to find her with his dripping ice cream.

On the verandah they met kids from school, at a table with a woman who had a box of hot chips open for everyone to share.

'There's Sandy, Aunty Hazel's daughter,' said Raffy.

Sandy called them over and offered them chips. 'I was just sayin' next year when I'm teaching part-time, we'll go out on bush days with Aunty Hazel, so she can teach us a little bit about her country, plants she knows, what they're called in language. We might make a little book for people.' She smiled at Greta. 'Get you whitefellas learned up, eh?'

'See,' said Griffin, on their way past Uncle Pavel's castle to the tall slide in the park. 'We should be calling things by their right names. Trees. Birds. Dragonflies. So we're talking their language, you know.' He was quiet for a minute, then added, 'Language comes from the land and the animals, Aunty Hazel told us that.'

He ran from Greta then, to mark a football careering across from the oval. The next generation, thought Greta, they show us the way. She sat at the picnic table to watch them playing.

You could stay here, the voice in her head said. You could make this your children's home. Learn with them.

She thought of Uncle Pavel building his castle in the thicket just behind her. Was it his ode to Maria, to a fairytale that never came to be? Make a wish. Or was it inspired by the stories she told Magdalen, the castle where the swan boy lived ever after with his sister and family?

When they pulled up at Agnes's place, her mobility scooter was parked in the front yard.

'Gabe keeps Nanna Agnes's scooter running like a dream,' Raffy explained. 'She's going to take us to Darwin on it one day, isn't she, Ray?'

'Nah, you're crazy!' laughed Raymond.

Greta wondered if Gabe was related to Agnes and Raymond. Everyone around here seemed to have a connection, a vast network of relatives.

Not you, came that voice again. Only child with your own children your only family.

A mother dog trotted around the side of the house, with a host of puppies scampering after her. Raffy opened the car door and hopped out so his friend could slide across the seat. They both went to the house. The front door was open. A girl appeared there. She waved to Greta.

'Thanks for having me,' Raymond called.

Raffy came back to the car.

'That's Lanie,' he said, clambering back in. 'She's the fastest runner.'

'Fastest swimmer too,' added Toby. 'She'll thrash everyone at the swimming carnival.'

———

After the children had gone to bed, Greta went to the darkroom to find Henry's slide viewer. She was curious to see the slides from Magdalen's jewellery box, after what Tori had told her. She slotted in the homestead first. The saturated colours made the house look surreal.

Pavel only took one roll of Kodachrome, Joel had told her a few days after she'd found the jewellery box at the hut. Fedor crushed the camera in a fury over a photo of Maria.

It didn't make sense to Greta, the obsessive, angry love of Fedor, his pyre of belongings.

'He wasn't always like this. It was that prison, what they did to those people,' Maria had told her children.

What prison, where? The details were sketchy. It was never talked about. All Joel seemed to know was that Pavel secured Fedor's freedom and the three brothers escaped across borders, ending up hidden in the same freight train as Maria, who'd survived her own journey across mountains and sea. It was just her and her suitcase and the songs in her heart. Questions made her nervous. Fedor didn't suffer them either.

'Why do you need to know? Why? Here is enough for you. Here where I have made you the new life.'

The past was not discussed.

'We only spoke English,' Joel said. 'Fedor's rules.'

Too many memories with his own language, Maria's too. It was why she left the house to sing, Joel said.

'We didn't think about it. We didn't want to be singled out.'

No hard-to-say names, no strong-smelling lunchboxes.

'There was nothing enviable about our foreignness then,' he continued.

It had always been clear he disliked the conversation. Greta didn't push it.

The homestead glowed in the slide viewer. Fronds and leaves rose like green wings protecting it. Among them a crimson ginger flower peeked out, a sexy pink, the fiery red of a heliconia. The lime tree by the front steps was laden with fruit. The frangipani's dome of white flowers nestled by the kitchen window. To the side of the kitchen was the Hills hoist, and behind it a poinciana tree flared red. At the other end of the house a vegetable garden sprawled out to a mini orchard of banana and pawpaw trees. Uncle Pavel!

The casement windows along the verandah were open. The living room doors were wide open too. Greta tried to see inside but it was all shadow.

She looked at the second slide—the wicker chair on the verandah with its peacock woven into the high, arched back.

You could enlarge those, she heard Vivian say. *Make something of them.*

'Yes, yes,' whispered Greta.

The idea grew on her. If she could send these few slides and photos away to be enlarged and printed, she could set them among her photos of the ruin. Life as a montage of the past and present. Janna would love it.

She slipped in the last slide. There was Maria in the chair, with her wistful smile.

She heard footsteps and Joel's whistle outside. His fingers tapped the door.

'Come in,' she said.

The door opened slowly.

'I haven't wrecked a prize-winning pic?'

'Lucky for you, no.'

He sat next to her.

'I was looking at these slides of the old place,' she said.

He was silent at first, seeing his mother.

'Mrs Donegan passed that chair on to us. My mother loved it. She loved peacocks. I don't know why. Fedor hated them. All those evil eyes in the tail looking at him.'

He swapped to the homestead slide in the viewer, and then picked up the jewellery box, winding the key at the back. His fingers gently opened the lid. The music started.

'My mother actually had a peacock for a while,' he said, watching the ballerina turn. 'Pavel bought a few chicks. Only one survived, the blue prince we called him.'

He told her how it used to strut along the verandah and perch on car bonnets, until Vadik cracked his stockwhip and the bird flew to the poinciana tree. Maria kept the feathers in the linen cupboard and sometimes put them in a vase.

The music stopped. The ballerina froze. Joel shut the lid of the box.

'There's a surprise for you over at the cabin.'

Greta followed him to the balcony off their bedroom. A tarp was draped over a bulky object.

'Tell me that's not a dead body you're hiding.'

He pulled the cover away. There was the old enamel bath she'd seen at the homestead, filled with water and floating frangipanis.

Joel lit a camping lantern on the chair next to it. 'Thought you might like it for cooling off. Or growing waterlilies.'

She shed her clothes and climbed in. The water rose with her and slopped over the edge. Joel lowered himself in too. The lantern cast a warm glow over his scars, the bleached welt from his shoulder to his midriff, the six thinner scars creeping towards his back.

He flicked water at her. 'Did you know Jupiter and Saturn are closer now than they'll ever be again in our lifetime? Closest for four hundred years, in fact. Since Galileo.'

She flicked water back. 'Is that right?'

'Toby's facts. I could go on a quiz show.'

She'd overheard Toby's chatter as he helped Joel measure wire and ram in stakes for a new python-proof chook pen. The planets were a recurring theme. A secret astronaut still hovered in him.

'It's the strangest thing,' she said, 'how we're turning but can't feel it. Rising and setting sun, moon, planets—it's all an illusion. We can be upside down and never know, just keep thinking we're the right way up.'

He drew her in close, and cupped his hand to trickle water across the rash on her neck. She rested her face against the scar on his shoulder. Behind him the indigo night stretched up with its speckled path of stars.

She thought of Maria feeding the peacock breadcrumbs from her hand and of the feathers with glowing eyes hiding in the cupboard. And of Fedor with his rage and his grief. She closed her eyes. In her mind was a picture in Kodachrome colour of a metallic-blue bird singing from a tree that grew orange-red flames for flowers.

Fedor is sitting on the verandah after the grind of the day. A black shawl is over the back of the cane chair. He is washed, pristine. The blood and the carcasses have left him, the smell of them, though sores along his arm still itch. They are a constant irritation, these raised pustules. A long-sleeved shirt usually hides them. For now he is in a singlet, to let the late afternoon breeze reach his skin. His white-blond hair is combed back from his forehead, and scented. His eyes are ice blue.

Maria goes to him. She walks with the slight sway of a dancer, and her eyes are full of sadness, and full of love. She holds out a tall glass of cool water with a wedge of lime. She grew the fruit herself. Its taste is bitter and alluring.

He takes the glass. And she sees in him the old torment. It returns from time to time with the last kill of the day. It is the way the animal looks at him that undoes him. Those eyes become the eyes of a man he knew once.

The last glance before a body crumples in snow.

Years have passed since that moment, when the look of another man cursed him. The hours since then can't be counted. And yet the eyes of that man are always with him.

16

It was dusk by the time Greta left Tori's place. There had been great excitement when she dropped off her three boys for the weekend. Tori was taking them up to Darwin for Axel's junior sedan race. The rough old car was ready on its trailer. Greta realised too late that Griffin had left his binoculars on the dashboard. Hopefully he wouldn't miss them. She would have liked to see the car race too, but she was keen to blitz the garden, finish beading a few necklaces and make frames for her photos. She'd decided to send a range of jewellery and photographs to the Fishermans Creek arts and crafts show. She phoned her friend now on a stretch of road that ran like a spine along a hill and was known for good reception.

'You have seen the light,' Janna's voice smiled from the phone cradle.

Greta warned her the photos mightn't fit with the seaside vistas and vessels. A bush stone-curlew, cycads, car wrecks and the homestead's abandoned rooms could seem out of place.

'They sound fantastic!' Janna enthused.

Greta's car came over the rise. Janna's voice vanished. Ahead an unnatural orange cloud hovered above the tree line. It was close, Greta realised as she came to the T-intersection with the road home. It felt like an odd rerun of the night they'd arrived at the property and found a fire along the way. She had a sickening feeling it was at the lake or the hut.

A raised yellow ute powered by and clunked over the empty floodway. It swerved right onto the track leading through bushland to the lake. Greta followed it. The unmistakable noise of a blaze disturbed the quiet. The flames soon came into view. She pulled up next to the ute. An arc of fire surrounded the water on three sides. The slope up to the homestead was not yet alight, but Greta could see it would be soon. There was an odd wind pushing in that direction, fanning the flames. The pandanus were giant candlesticks wrapped in spiral ribbons of orange light. Each head of fronds caught fire with a sharp crack and flare of light. The fire gathered strength, chasing its way around the banks. The lake was a silent darkness in the middle. Orange reflections shimmered across the water around the edges but the centre was a void.

The driver of the yellow ute leaned on the open driver's door to film it with his phone. As she eased out of the car he grinned at her and hitched up his low-slung trousers.

'Fuckn' brutal, eh!'

On the opposite bank, shadow animals moved uphill. But one stepped in a different direction, onto the spill of rocks leading into the water. It was a person.

Greta reached for Griffin's binoculars. The heat was a mirage, the flames wavered. She tried to focus. Joel sharpened into view. He was looking across the poison water to the ring of flames. He was a shadow behind the fire. Like the dingo she'd seen run through the blaze that first night on the highway. She called out to him but the noise of the fire ate her voice. He turned and walked to the firebreak. His ute was there, ready with the slip-on water tank.

No sooner had Joel driven up the incline than a fire unit rumbled in behind her, flashing red and blue lights. It was Ronnie. He pulled up close by. Voices and static crackled over the radio. The yellow ute started up, reversed and drove away.

'Who was that?' Greta asked.

'Logan's son,' he said. 'They live a couple of kilometres away.'

She paused, unsure whether to ask Ronnie about the hut. She wished the girl would appear so she could take her up to the shack.

'What if this goes into the valley?'

He gazed over that way. 'I don't think it'll head there,' he said. 'But it'll light up that gamba in a minute,' he nodded at the hill. 'The wind might send it back this way too. Best follow me up the firebreak, eh?'

His truck meandered through clumps of gamba until they came out on the firebreak. She kept close behind. The smoke was thickening. His lights were a comfort.

At the top of the hill he parked by the ghost gums. Joel was there, and so was Tori's partner Jed, in a fire unit.

Joel came over to her. 'I wondered where you were.' He kissed the top of her head.

While the men discussed how they would monitor the fire, a breeze came through and carried sparks onto the slope above the lake. A fierce new crackling filled the air. Sparks flew up from the understorey, reaching for the leaves of trees. One crown burst alight. It sounded oddly like pelting rain. Underneath, the flames passed up the hill like batons. The sand palms' fanned fingers turned to fire. The cycads burned like torches. Clumps of gamba flared. Among them boulders and termite mounds shimmered.

Embers floated across in orange twists and drifted into the gamba below the shack.

Joel walked along the edge of the hill and down into the amphi-theatre of cycads, Greta behind him. They watched the first smoke curls down near the outcrop. Fire sprang to life. In seconds a ravenous wall of flames was advancing. It was a roaring wind, a voice. Trees were enveloped. Saplings were tossed left and right in a crazy dance before the flame. Leaves disintegrated, sparks rocketed into the night. The force of it pushed upwards in a wave. It had a mind of its own, a consciousness. There was a grudge, an argument to settle.

Joel's face glimmered orange light. He stared down into the inferno. Did he see Magdalen? Was he in the burning car on the highway? Or was he at the homestead, beating flames with a blanket, standing back to hear the iron roof buckle, windows shatter, walls peel into flame? The scar on his arm flickered reflections.

He shook off his quiet, and said, 'We'd better hose down the cabin and shack, and then I'll head up behind the old place. It'll rip through there.'

Ronnie's red and blue lights flashed near the homestead.

Greta told him to go and started soaking the roofs and ground around the buildings. She'd just filled the bath outside the cabin when Brynn's ute rattled in.

'Come to see if you need a hand.' Brynn grimaced at the fire below her. 'It's a curse, this gamba. Makes fires too hot. Stunts the trees. Kills everything. In a few years we'll be a wasteland. They're meant to be cool fires, you know, good ones, cleaning up the land. Where's Joel?'

Greta pointed up to the old house. While she was looking, the turkey bush sprang into flame. She wished the curlews away.

They would have escaped early on, she told herself, with the first hint of smoke.

In the woodland beyond the lake, spotfires were starting.

'Are your photos safe?' Brynn asked. 'I can take them for you, out of the smoke. You too, if you want to stay the night.'

'I'll wait for Joel.'

She went and found a spade each, to keep an eye on the ground. Leaves, ash and embers were floating down around them.

'Just as well Gabe burned off before you arrived,' Brynn said.

Yes, thought Greta. Gabe's safe passage.

The paddock behind the collapsed house leaped into flame. A surge of vicious crackling grew there. An orange glow pulsed above the homestead. Smoke mushroomed into the night.

Simultaneously the fire across the hill lost breath. The monster that might have raced up to devour the shack had diminished. The grasses were mostly vanquished.

Greta packed a couple of boxes of her prints into Brynn's ute and waved her off into the night's smoke haze.

A strange silence pervaded the land. Earth and sky were the one darkness, except for snakes of orange flame creeping over the ground, fiery eyes in blackened trunks, and a flickering light inside the homestead. Her ears strained for the familiar cry of the bush stone-curlews. She heard none. There was just the last sighing of the fire, or the crackle of grass that had escaped before, now catching alight.

Joel returned after midnight. He blew dark snot from his nose and sat on a stool at the kitchen bench. She nudged a glass of water to him. His eyes were bloodshot. The scar on his arm was smeared with grime.

'Who lit it?' she asked.

He shrugged. 'Piggers maybe.' The glass shook a little in his hand.

'I think it was Trapper,' she said.

He sighed. 'Is there water in that bath?'

'It's waiting for you.'

He eased himself from the stool and headed for the door. She followed him into the smoke-filled night. Blackened leaves were scattered across the cabin's verandah. She lit the camping lantern on the chair by the bath.

Joel stripped and slid into the greyish water. Fine wisps of ash floated around him. She watched him submerge, hands over his face. He was very still, holding his breath. Then he surged upright, blew water, smoothed his hair slick over his skull.

'Are you all right?' she asked.

She could hear the sound of the fire in him.

He wiped the watery dirt from his shoulders. 'I'm fine.' His arm rested wet on the edge of the bath.

Her fingers lightly touched the scars. 'I'll get you a towel.'

She leaned in to kiss his smoky mouth once, twice, and the crease above the bridge of his nose that was pulled tight against her questions.

When she reached the shack she saw a flash of light up near the homestead. She found Griffin's binoculars and searched the darkness. Flames slunk along the ground in front of the ruin. She followed them down to Magdalen's birth car. Inside it the giant tuft of gamba was alight. The car was aglow, a beacon in the night.

———

Smoke still drifted through the valley the next morning. The land was transformed. Stripped, denuded. Black and grey ash stretched down to the outcrop and across to the lake. Most of the gamba had been razed to the ground. The trees were blackened, their leaves crisped brown. The colours of the escarpment were dull. A yellow cloud masked the sun.

There was a great stillness all around. The land was in shock.

Greta looked out on it with a thumping headache and nostrils stinging from the acrid smell of burned land and smoke. Joel might sleep for another couple of hours yet. Her father's watch said 8 a.m. She gathered her camera gear and headed for the homestead to ring Tori. The incline seemed more exposed, the ruin more abandoned.

'Blaze at yours last night,' said Tori.

'It's as well the kids weren't here.'

'You'll be sneaking around with that camera, right? Watch out for the ground. It'll be burning hot.'

'Yes, Mother.'

'And stay away from the trees. They drop with no warning.'

A burst of static interrupted. Tori disappeared.

Greta stood up into a wave of giddiness and nausea. She wondered if it was more than the smoke; if she was sick. She walked down to Magdalen's birth car. The red bead tree had survived, though its trunk was licked black. The car was freshly burned out. Its tuft of gamba had disappeared. The body had sunk lower into the ground and was encircled by a line of ash. It reminded Greta of sand sculptures she'd made with Gavin. Cars, whales, monsters. She could see him driving over the sea to the horizon in a winged sand car draped with seaweed and studded with shells.

She photographed the birth car and then walked along where the turkey bush had been. It was obliterated except for the blackened skeletons of a few contorted branches. Magdalen and Maria's stones were naked white. The ground was scoured clean. There was no sign of the curlews.

Below her the slope to the lake was a charred silence. The termite mounds were sooty towers. The cycads had bleached fronds in a whirl, like a memory of flame.

A needling pain bit through her ankles and her knees. Her legs felt weak. She checked her father's watch and returned to the firebreak. How changed the place seemed, like another world. Everywhere, once hidden debris was now exposed. The upturned tray of a truck, concrete blocks stuck through with metal pipes, tin cans, beer bottles, corrugated iron, fencing wire, steel drums. Rusted, burned, burned again.

When she reached the far side of the lake she set up the tripod.

A bluish haze hung among the trees and across the water. Blackened pandanus trunks stuck out of the ground at odd angles like abandoned oars. The only movement came from the kites, spinning their intent high above the water. They passed through drifts of murky cloud. And yet the lake was clearer than ever. Greta stood at the edge of the bank to see the submerged prisoners. The silent and gutted car. The bones in their dreadful whiteness.

She didn't walk far around the water. The ashen ground was too warm and powdery. When her boots sank in a mound of hot, shredded gamba ash, she stumbled out with a hideous sense of her mother sinking in front of her.

'Get a grip,' she told herself.

She moved to firmer ground and distracted herself with framing camera shots. Tongues of fire wavering from the end of a branch like a flag. Blackened root knots in a crater left by a vanished tree. The line of its ashes had spilled along the ground to make a white tree cut-out on a black earth.

You could lose yourself here, she thought, and the little voice in her head claiming, *I know where I am, I know where I am,* became a far-off sound.

A little way deeper in among the trees Greta saw one bleeding bright red sap. Now she'd seen one she noticed others. As if the bark had slit open just before her eyes settled on it. A bloodwood weeping. There was no colour in the landscape as rich or alarming as this sap. She wandered from one to the other until she came to a semicircle of flames burning low to the ground.

A jarring laughter disturbed the quiet. She looked around but saw no one. The sound came again, this time directly above her. She stepped back to see up the tree in front of her. It had burned to where the branches started and they were bleached silver.

Why aren't they black like the trunk? she wondered. They have been skinned.

The ground tilted under her. She looked up again, squinting against the sun. In a fork where two bony-armed branches met she saw the girl.

'What are you doing?' Greta cried.

'Making coats for my brothers! To turn them from swans into men! I must finish. There isn't much time.'

Sunlight flared around the girl. She was hard to see. Greta shifted to bring her into focus. She seemed younger and was wearing a grubby pair of shorts and a faded pink singlet. Pandanus fronds rested across her legs. She was weaving and sewing them together. Five finished pandanus coats hung on rusty clothes hangers around her.

'My fingers hurt!' The girl held up her hands to show bloodied, swollen fingers.

Cut by those serrated leaves, Greta thought. Pricked by the needle.

'If only the green ants could help me. They are so clever. The way they stick their leaf nests together.'

Greta spotted several green tree ant nests hanging from bare twigs. The more she counted the more she saw.

'I must keep on against all odds,' the girl was saying. 'It is my task.'

Greta smiled and nodded to her. The world spun.

'And your task, do you know it?' The question floated down in a distorted voice.

'I'm not sure I understand you,' Greta replied.

The girl stopped working and was quiet, as if she couldn't believe a grown woman didn't know her task.

'Go back to where you came from,' she said solemnly. 'Fly south.'

Heavy pinpricks stabbed Greta's arms and legs, abdomen and back. Feathers took root in her skin; she was weighed down by giant wings on either side, sprouting from her arms.

The odd laugh sounded again, this time from a distance, across the lake behind her. When she looked up into the tree once more it was empty. The girl, the coats were gone. All that remained were the ant nests in the branches and burned pandanus fruits scattered on the ground.

'Strange,' mused Greta, because she thought the orange fruits had finished their season.

You are not from here, a voice in her said.

The skin along her arms prickled. The wings had vanished with all their feathers.

Find Ronnie's track, go home, she told herself.

And though she meant to avoid the lake there was a pull in the water, a slow spinning that reeled her towards it. The bank rocked under her. A bolt of pain shot through her head. Her hand floundered for the nearest tree trunk. She grasped its charcoal bark, leaned over and vomited. Her mouth was dry, her lips sticking.

The firebreak was a blur. Still, she must go there. She hauled herself up and began the slow climb. The sun was a cruel eye. She lost count of her footsteps. A far-off voice called her name.

When she reached the top of the track her legs buckled. A voice, a shout, swam through the air. A watery silhouette ran towards her.

'Greta, it's me—Joel.'

Her body and her head felt quite separate, though her brain told her he must be holding both. She could feel his breath.

'I've got you,' he said.

The earth was falling away from her now. The sky was spinning around her husband's face.

17

Greta watched as her blood was drawn up into the specimen tube.

'You'll have to watch this fever,' the doctor warned Joel.

Joel rang Brynn and Tori while Greta waited out the nurse's observations and the doctor's insistence that her temperature drop before going home. The sound of Joel's voice, the fierce light shining down made her ill. In the end he was quiet, but she could feel him watching her, hands ready to stop her rolling from the narrow bed. The blue curtain wavered slightly whenever a nurse passed. She imagined herself on a boat at sea, with the horizon ahead and a breeze behind this curtain that was a sail.

'Do you ever think it was a miracle the way we met?' she asked him. 'I mean, in that moment. If I'd left the rocks. If you'd been swallowed by the sea. None of this would have happened.'

He shifted uneasily on the stool, unsure if this was fever talk.

'I mean the kids. Us. Why we're together.'

'I never thought about it.' He pressed her fist against his cheek. His skin was cool.

'It makes me think of fate,' she said.

He held a paper cup of water for her to sip.

'We don't talk much, do we? I never minded before. No questions asked.'

'No questions asked.' He patted her arm. 'You need to rest.'

'It's odd we're both orphans, don't you think? Both lost our mothers young. I'm afraid for the boys sometimes—that it'll happen to them. Like a curse. Fate again.'

The curlew's eye stared into her own, under her closed lids.

'There's no such thing as fate,' he said. 'Fate's dead.'

'I'll take your word for it.'

Brynn was waiting for them when they arrived back home. She had the fan set up by the bed in the cabin, and one of the wicker chairs too. She'd brought a swag.

'I'm moving in to help nurse and kid wrangle,' she said to Joel in a low voice. 'I'd have thought they'd take her to hospital, myself. When do you and Gabe leave?'

'Gabe'll go tomorrow, as planned. I'll wait and see.'

'Do you have to go?'

'We need the money. Mick's not paying us much and we don't know when he and his mate will buy us out.'

Greta's migraine clamped tighter. The voices in the room became distorted whispers, like garbled cassette tapes. The hours were a blur of fevered waking and sleeping. Night came. The world shrank inside her crimson mosquito net. She vaguely registered movement behind it. Light, shadows. A camping lantern on the dresser. The shape of Brynn or Joel in the wicker chair. Above her the stars turned in the ceiling window. Joel kept sweeping aside the net to take her temperature and wipe her with a cool face washer. Sometimes she woke to find him lying next to her, his hand over hers. Her skin was wet with perspiration. The sheets were always damp.

And then, as if a switch snapped, it was day and the children returned. They stared at her through the mosquito net. They had soft ruby ghost faces. She reached her hand out to touch them, to feel their skin.

'You're sicker than sick,' said Raffy.

'It won't be forever.' Brynn guided him outside.

She'd taken on a gentler presence. The angular, bony body was a whispering movement through the room.

Perhaps we have all died and become spirits, Greta thought. It might be possible.

And yet she could hear her father's watch ticking on the pile of books by her bed.

'What is the time?' she kept asking, and one of the people outside the net would tell her.

'Ten o'clock at night.' 'Seven o'clock in the morning.' 'One o'clock in the afternoon. The children are having lunch.'

We're still here, Greta assured herself, in the land of the living.

Griffin brought her the spider conch shell from the shack and pressed it into her hand. 'Here, listen to your beach.' He held the shell up to her ear.

The sea was far off, the winds of the place. She thought she heard a child's words in that airy sound. The singsong notes of Gavin's voice.

She clung to the shell through the night. The migraine returned and consumed her. The sound of sand sifting down, down, down filled her ears. She could hear nothing else, just the sand pouring in steady streams, covering the bed, rising up the sides of the mosquito net, spilling into her mouth. It was weighing her down and she was breathing it in, grain by grain. She was being buried alive in one of Gavin's sand cars, and he was there, right beside her, flicking more and more sand at her and laughing and not hearing her cry, 'Stop! Stop!'

The mosquito net swept back. Brynn's face loomed near. She shook a thermometer in her hand and put it under Greta's tongue.

'Try not to thrash around.' Her eyes were stern. 'And don't bite the thermometer.' She gave her tablets to swallow with water.

Greta knew nothing else until she woke up in another sweat, and a face was pressed against the mosquito net, just like the girl had done at the flywire that night on the verandah.

'Who is it?' she asked. 'Who are you?'

It wasn't the girl. This was a younger child. Her eyes strained to make sense of the distorted visage. A little boy. Climbed out of the spider conch shell. He'd come to her for real this time, Gavin.

'What are you doing here?' she asked. 'You're dead.'

He laughed at that and said, 'I'm not dead!' And the net floated apart to reveal Griffin with a lemonade icy pole. 'Brynn says these are the cure for killer fevers.'

He tore open the wrapper and held it to her mouth. Her lips stuck to the icicles.

'Thank you, thank you,' she said, one hand holding on to his precious little arm.

And he was pleased and beamed a smile to her and promised her he wasn't anywhere near dead.

———

'I know what all this is about,' she whispered to Joel. She could see him moving behind the net. 'I know what it is, this sickness.'

He parted the net and put his hand on her forehead.

'It's that girl. I saw her.'

A frown played across his brow.

'The girl, Joel. The one I told you about. I saw her at the lake, up a tree. She was making pandanus coats. Six. For her brothers.'

'She's off her head,' came Brynn's voice from the shadows.

'She's at the hut.' Greta grabbed Joel's arm.

'Shh,' he said softly. 'No one's at the hut. I checked.'

'But I saw her.'

'You're delirious, Gret.'

He planted a light kiss on her forehead and let the mosquito net drop again. He told the shadows he was going to check on the children.

Brynn took form in the cane chair. 'If you don't calm down I'll give you something to knock you out,' she said.

Greta feigned sleep. At first she felt sicker with her eyes closed. The bed was turning. It became the lake, a whirlpool sucking her into its vortex.

She waited for the world to steady before checking her father's watch. The glowing hands told her 3 a.m. Hours had passed. The sheet was damp under her. The bed had stopped its random spin. Above her the misshapen moon peered through the ceiling window. She was weak, but she felt compelled to walk. She slipped out from under the net and stood up. Brynn's chair was empty. Joel was asleep in a swag.

She stepped out into the night as she might step onto a new planet. The gleaming rocks, the moonlit fans of the sand palms welcomed her. She crouched behind one of the boulders to wee. Very near she heard the cry of a stone-curlew. Alive, she thought, alive! And close!

She stood, using the boulder to steady herself, willing the curlew to come to her now, silver in the night, stepping across the prickly ground.

She heard a cough and saw a figure emerging from the dark. It was the girl, hands cupped in front of her chest. She hid something. Before reaching Greta she stopped.

Slowly she unfurled her fingers. A curlew chick lay dead on her palm. Its feathers were sooty and damp. The dusky blue legs were stiff, the little claws curled in a last contortion.

'It is the younger of the two,' said the girl.

Greta's eyes blurred. She reached out. 'Give the chick to me.'

But the girl's hands closed over the feathered corpse. She turned and walked away. Greta followed, calling softly for her to stop.

An adult curlew shrieked from the valley. The girl turned again, her face all moonlight. And her mouth was a bright red smudge, sewn shut with black stitches.

Greta gasped and stumbled. The girl kept moving downhill. A dark cloud sliced through the moon. Trees, cycads, rocks became night souls. And the girl was one of them. Greta would never find her.

She was struck again with vertigo. Her muscles ached. She took a few breaths and shuffled back to the cabin. Her foot knocked Joel's swag on her way to the bed.

'What is it?' he mumbled.

'The girl, she's out there.'

'I'll go,' he said. 'I'll find her.'

'No,' insisted Greta, 'you can't.'

'Why not?'

'Darkness ate her.'

By morning the illness had lifted. She felt drained, but the vertigo was gone and her visions of the girl had faded. They were delusions. Fever bred, she told herself.

Magdalen huddles in the old tin bath. Water drips from the tap with a soft beat. She's listening to her father's belt buckle tap-tap on the door. The flame wavers in the kerosene lantern on the floor.

I know what you're up to, Magdalen!

The belt whips the door. She jumps.

Slut!

The lock rattles. Magdalen lowers herself under the water where the sound of him is dulled. She holds her breath until she hears her brother's voice. She sits up quickly. Water sloshes to the floor. There is a scuffle behind the door, a shout from Fedor. Silence. Magdalen submerges herself again.

On the other side of the door and down the hallway, Maria's voice calls.

Joel. Joel.

He walks down the hallway to his mother. Her body is a sunken shape on the bed. Her hair is damp on the stained pillow. The sheets smell of her sickness.

Look after Magdalen, Joel. Don't let her wander.

She's with me all the time.

The lake, it frightens me.

She doesn't go near it.

His mother struggles for breath; he gently lifts the pillow to raise her chest.

Don't ever leave her.

You know I wouldn't do that, Mama.

I know. But promise me.

I promise.

She lifts her arms from the sheet to reach for him, but trembling mid-air, clasps her hands instead. He takes them in his and lowers his head to her chest. Her eyes are closed, she is somewhere else.

The quiet of the house has its own breathing. And the night is long. It's longer than ever.

18

'Are you sure you're all right for me to go?' Joel asked. He was leaving for Connor's in the morning.

'Yes, yes,' Greta assured him.

It was almost a week since the illness struck. She'd recovered from the worst of it in a few days, though she still felt off balance. Mundane details she'd known before would come to her like news, and then she'd remember, ah yes, that's how it is. The cabin had surprised her, with alterations like bathroom walls and a lino floor, a sink even, and a bay of louvres in the second bedroom. All happening while she was there, delirious.

Joel zipped up his clothes bag. 'I don't think you should go to this Halloween party on the weekend.'

The invite was from one of the school families, at a station. It was a slumber party too, for their daughter Poppy's birthday. The boys were sleeping over.

'I said I'd paint faces,' Greta said. 'The kids want me to go. I'll drive Brynn and Tori back here for the night. They'll look after me.'

Griffin wandered in and lay down next to Joel's bag. 'You could stay and come with us, Dad, go as Count Dracula. I'll be your vampire kid.'

Greta waved off Joel before dawn.

The boys were quieter than usual over breakfast. The absence of their father made them solemn. This is just like any other day, she told herself, and made the boys' sandwiches. Toby held the door open for his mother as they left the house—he knew a few tricks.

The way out felt longer. She kept seeing narrow tracks she'd never noticed before, winding into bushland. Where did they lead?

We are nothing, she thought, nothing. We could be snuffed out and not missed.

'Mum?' Griffin said from the back seat.

'Yes?'

'If anything happens, you're it.'

'Yes.'

Ahead, dust was propelling a ute towards them. Greta slowed. The other vehicle screeched to a halt beside her. It was Trapper. He got out and slammed the door behind him. The ute had a canvas canopy. She wondered what he hid under it.

'Where's yer old man?' he demanded.

'He'll be back later.' She stepped out to face him.

She could feel the children's gaze on her. Raffy would worry she'd told a lie; Toby would call it tweaked truth.

'He can buy that heifer or I'll shoot it.'

'There's no shooting here, sorry.'

'I'm not givin' it to ya!' He pointed at her face.

If he didn't move the finger she'd bite it. He dropped his hand just in time.

'Guess I'll have to bring 'er in with a salt lick up at those old yards.' He cast his eyes to the back seat. 'Kiddies, eh? Off to school?' His laugh had a sneering note. 'Well, when yer done learnin' numbers, come an' see my critters.' He waited to see if that stirred them. 'I've got freak animals. Goat with three horns. Mind-readin' cockatoo. An' a giant albino lizard!'

'What about a thylacine?' asked Griffin. 'Tasmanian tiger.'

'Not yet. But I'm gettin' one! Raaaaagh!' He roared at the window, fingers in an ugly curl.

Raffy leaned away.

'It'll cost ya, but!' Trapper grinned.

'How much?' asked Toby.

'Five bucks a head.' He sucked in his breath. 'Mate's rates.'

'We need to go or we'll be late.' Greta forced a smile. 'Good luck with the heifer.'

She drove on, watching Trapper in the rear-vision mirror. She wished she'd mentioned the fire. She'd have liked to see his reaction. He took his time to follow them out. She waited for him to pass through the gate and closed it behind him, snapping the new padlock through the chain.

———

Throughout the day, Griffin's words knocked inside Greta's head. If anything should happen, if anything goes wrong. She felt the land whispering it back to her, with its russet atmosphere of singed leaves and fronds, and the rusted vehicles matching them.

In the afternoon, while the children were still at school, the silence closed in around her. There was an underground will to this place. She felt it keenly now she was alone. And at the heart of it was the lake, beating a secret pulse, drawing lines to the shack, the hut, the homestead.

'Can we go to Trapper's critter world?' Griffin asked the day after the neighbour's invitation.

'No, we cannot.'

'What would you do if I went by myself? Took Trapper's stile over the fence?'

'I'd worry he might lock you in one of his cages, make me pay to come and look at you.'

Raffy gave her a serious look and took the jar of shells to his louvre museum, as he called it, either side of the front door. Along the glass slats he'd arranged feathers, red seeds and conical gum nuts. Cicada shells, a dead butterfly with blue wings. A piece of bark stuck with globules of blood-coloured sap. He sat a few seashells beside two bleached snail shells from the bush. Sand leaked onto the glass alongside grains of red dirt.

'Do you think Trapper ever climbs over his stile and goes to the hut?' he asked.

Greta had a vision of Trapper creeping over the bridge to the secret valley and the hut where the girl hid, innocent, unawares. She decided she should speak with the local policewoman, Eileen, the mother of one of Griffin's school friends.

'Oh no, where's it gone?' Raffy rattled the shells in the jar and poked his finger inside to shift them. 'Vivian's necklace has disappeared.'

He came over to give her the jar. The black and red beads were missing.

'Do you think she'll mind?' he whispered.

'I think she'll understand,' Greta whispered back.

'Griffin says you're not allowed to collect shells from beaches these days.' He put the jar on the bench. 'But I'm wondering where this came from?' He brought her the spider conch shell.

'A friend gave it to me.'

'Your best friend?'

She paused. 'Like a brother, actually.'

He turned the shell in his hand. 'Are you still friends?'

'He died. A long time ago now.'

'Oh.'

Toby called him out to the green table to watch his four aces card trick. She listened to the slap of cards being dealt.

'See how you can hear the ocean?' Gavin had said, holding it up to her ear. 'Keep this and you'll hear it forever.'

His face there, smiling at her! Hair stiff with sea salt, freckles across his nose, the sunburned streak on his cheekbones.

She clutched the shell now and remembered one, two drops of red spotting the white, a penknife cut on Gavin's finger, and one on hers too. Blood sister, blood brother.

She pressed her finger onto the few grains of sand inside the opening and put them on her tongue. Grit crunched on her back teeth.

'That kid! That kid's the devil!'

The words whipped across her forehead. She could see it all again. Gavin's mother flinging open the door of her father's cottage so hard it sent a crack line up the wall. Rain blowing inside. The house rocking with the fury of the dead boy's mother. Greta's twelve-year-old self kneeling on the floor, pressed against the cold metal leg of the bed, by a pile of books that might topple. In her hand a damp matchbox hid a curl of Gavin's hair.

His mother knew nothing of the matchbox. She only knew Greta and her dead son. Her eyes were wild and her hand reached for the child on the floor.

Greta's father stepped between them, his hands seeking a truce.

'Livvie, don't.'

Her eyes bulged in disbelief.

'I'll drive you home.'

She shook her head. 'Never, never!'

'Take this then.'

He held out his raincoat. She shook her head again. Raindrops flicked from her head, no, no, no. To his offer, to the death of her son. He watched her walk out into the lashing rain and stood there long after she'd gone, staring into the storm.

When he turned back inside he said, 'I'm going to take you away from all this, Gret.'

He kept his word. They went inland. No memories for either of them. No sea, just the legend of an inland one. No talk from the waves, with their pounding of the inevitable truth. No constant staring at the rip and the quicksand that took her mother.

Instead of fish, her father searched for rocks. Gems, opals, crystals. He taught Greta how to sand the residue away, polish the stone. She had held on to them, these talismans. Stones are solid. They are before the sand.

19

Just before sunset, Tori drove Greta, Brynn and the children to the Halloween party in her troopy. They took a turn-off twenty kilometres south along the highway, onto a dirt road. Cattle stopped to stare as they passed, and termite mounds glowed in the late sunlight. A cardboard witch greeted them at the gate, her long, skinny fingers like the birch in her broom. From the driveway, Tori followed signs to a clearing with a bonfire and a teepee. A line of skull and pumpkin lanterns were strung up above a small stage, with a mirror ball turning in the centre.

'Hippies,' muttered Brynn.

'You're not very dressed up,' Tori admonished her, 'though you're skinny as a skeleton.'

'I'm not into this American hoo-ha.'

'Halloween's from Europe,' said Toby. 'All Souls' Night. Leave food for your dead relatives. Kill your beasts before winter. Blood on snow!'

Greta remembered her aunt's goats pushing inside the farmhouse when the butcher came to kill the sheep. They never liked the smell of him.

'We should've left food out for them,' said Griffin.

'Who?' Raffy asked.

'The spirits, on Halloween night. Maria and Magdalen. Vivian, Frank. There's a few in the family. They might drop by the shack.'

Raffy paled.

'Don't worry,' Toby put his arm around his little brother. 'We're sleeping here.'

Greta lugged her basket over to the food tables. The children carried the face paints and card table. A crowd had already gathered. Tori quickly disappeared. Speakers on the stage thumped out music as Greta looked for faces she knew. With each beat she felt more uncomfortable, a stranger. She wasn't part of this town, of any town. *It's how it is if you're always moving,* Janna would remind her. *Perpetual fish out of water.*

'I feel like an alien—do I look like one?' Greta asked quietly.

'Put your mask on,' replied Brynn. 'That's what it's for.'

Greta secured her homemade cat face. She'd painted it gold, with black whiskers and eye markings. The op shop lace wedding dress she'd dyed black scratched her skin. Her black lace-up boots were too snug. The leather had turned stiff.

She set down the kangaroo lasagne and urged her children to eat, but Griffin and Toby were off to the bonfire with friends to light sticks. Raffy hurried after them, an odd sprite in leggings and a skivvy, and a stocking balaclava with holes for eyes and mouth. He was a blood-sucking burglar, he said. He was back before long to give her the stocking.

'Too sweaty.'

She tucked it behind her pentacle belt buckle and pushed the cat mask up onto her head, overheated too. Her face was an elongated reflection in the stainless-steel urn beside her.

'Here,' said Brynn, handing Greta a thick orange cocktail. 'Mango daiquiri. Surely you can have one.'

A drummer and guitarist started playing on stage. Rhianna swept in and took the microphone. She wore a red taffeta dress with black dots. Her voice soared across the crowd, all jazz.

'Isn't she great?' smiled Raffy. 'Ray says she's going to win those big music awards next time. That's her brother on the drums.'

It was dark now. The mirror ball's lights circled the ground, while the pumpkin and skull lights grinned on people below. Griffin yelled out as he whirled by, balancing on a rolling pipe, arms flailing. Greta set up her face-painting table. Children lined up to become witches, vampires, zombies.

'No one has their real selves on tonight,' Raffy noted.

Toby had a white square fountaining red arcs on each cheek— the new washing machine spewing blood, he said.

Raffy asked for his stocking head back and urged Greta to become a cat again.

He led her to a food table and offered her a red jelly eyeball. Greta had just shifted her mask to pop one in her mouth when Erin sidled up. She wore a tan glittery dress, tight-fitting and very short. Her fake leopard-skin shoes were high-heeled and chunky. Raffy hurried off with his brothers to a piñata showering lollies.

'Joel's out at Connor Station with Gabe, I hear.' Erin lit a cigarette.

Greta nodded and sipped her daiquiri. The mask slid down her face. Everything contracted. Erin kept talking.

'Used to stay out there for months those two. Get away from family. And us girls.' She drew on the cigarette. 'How's it out on the block? Can't be easy for a southerner. All by yerself.'

'So far so good,' said Greta, and instantly heard Vivian. *Don't speak too soon.*

'Sink or swim, my mother used to say. "An' if you sink, Erin, I'm not raisin' those five kids." She reckoned she'd done 'er time.'

Greta looked over to the jack-o'-lantern table where children were scooping out pumpkin flesh and carving faces. Griffin's hands were draped with orange innards. He might be Jack the Ripper or he might be a surgeon.

'You've only got three, right?' Erin asked her.

'That's right.'

'That you know of, never could tell with those boys.' She dropped the cigarette butt and crushed it under her shoe.

Greta's face tingled.

'Not that I'm sayin' anything. You 'n' Joel look real solid. Just lettin' you know—there could be kittens in the cupboard.'

Erin slunk away. A child in a fluoro skeleton costume minced past. Griffin followed, holding palm twiggery as antlers. It was a parade of gory painted faces and garish costumes. The masks, the faces, real and unreal were blurring. It made her feel giddy.

She went to find water. Remnants of that fever still lurked in her.

Kittens in the cupboard. She could hear them mewing.

A sudden vision of her father sliced in.

He was knee-deep in the creek, clutching a pillowcase. His fist was a knot at its neck. The pillowcase squirmed on the inside, a bundle of pitiful wails. His face struggled against the cries, the wriggling under water. 'It has to be done,' he grimaced.

She saw him fight with himself. He lost his footing and fell on his knees. And though he stood up quickly, the weight of his wet clothing and of what he held made him unsteady.

'Your mother won't have them. You know that.' He bent over his task.

'You don't have to drown them,' she'd pleaded, sobbing from the bank.

'I do.'

And the way he said it begged her to forgive him.

'God, that moon's big!' Brynn's voice cut across the pitiful kittens. 'Harvest moon, is that it?'

'Blue moon. Second moon in a month.'

'I'll believe you.'

You and Joel look real solid. Greta remembered the girl's lantern-lit face hovering behind flywire. There is no solid, she thought. We're all masks in the strange-lit night. Questions spiralled into her with the mirror ball's turning lights. About the Joel she knew and the one who'd been here before.

Raffy came up to take her and Brynn to the sleepover teepee where a crew of giggling children welcomed them inside. Felt monster lights were strung around the canvas. The party's host and mother of the birthday girl introduced herself. Red tagua nut earrings dangled by her jaw.

'Do you think it's all right to leave them here?' Greta asked Brynn, after she'd helped the boys set up their swags.

'Absolutely. I'd leave my own if I had any.'

Greta waved Toby over to remind him to look after his brothers, and she would pick them up in the morning. He gave her a high-five. Then she and Brynn went to find Tori, who was at the stage, jiving to the music.

'I'm not leavin'!' Tori declared. 'I'm dancin' all night long!'

'We'll have to lasso her,' said Brynn.

Greta waited until she turned onto the highway to ask her question. 'How old are Erin's children?'

'Teenagers,' Tori called.

'Were they there tonight?'

'Sure! Out in the dark, trying not to be seen.'

Kittens, kittens, sang the voice in Greta's head.

There was the click of a cigarette lighter and the first whiff of Tori's joint.

Greta kept her eye on the white line up the middle of the highway, the winking red reflectors on the side. Behind the rise ahead, a road train's headlights beamed into the night. The sky went dark again briefly, before the truck appeared, bearing down towards them, lights piercing bright, flaring an aura around the cabin. Three trailers thundered past. The troopy shuddered.

The sign to Old Mine Road was a welcome sight. The tyres slipped on gravel when she turned.

'Dangerous!' Tori called.

Greta laughed and remembered the trepidation she'd felt when she first drove along this road. It was familiar now, and didn't seem to take so long to travel. As they came to the T-intersection before the stretch that took them home, a brightly lit scene met them.

'Film crew?' asked Tori. 'I heard they're making a film.' She put her head out the window to see.

'Accident,' Brynn said.

'Holy fuck.' Tori moved forward to see between Brynn and Greta.

Just before the floodway a cattle truck had jackknifed and tipped. Flashing lights twirled. From the side of the road shocked cattle stared at the slowed cars. Inside the trailers shadows moved. A battered car was on the other side of the road.

Two men in fluoro orange waved Greta on. Snippets of their

talk floated to her. A tourist on the wrong side of the road. A truck driver in shock. The vehicles ahead picked up speed. As Greta crossed the floodway she glanced between the paperbarks. She saw a shadow person holding up a lantern. The pale face was unmistakable with its halo of white-blonde hair.

Greta slowed to glance in the rear-vision mirror, but the headlights of the car behind were too bright and she saw nothing.

———

Once home again, Greta lit the camping lanterns on the shack verandah. She had a mind to take one to the hut in the morning and ask the girl for her father's in return. Tori found beers in the fridge and brought out three.

'It was a mess, that cattle truck,' said Brynn.

'Terrible,' said Tori. 'Poor truck driver, poor tourist. Can't bring 'em back if they're gone.'

No, thought Greta. We can't bring them back. She couldn't stop thinking about it. The stranger taken from the car. And the dazed, wounded cattle, which seemed strangely connected to Toby's slaughtered Halloween animals.

'But I'll give you a dare!' Tori perked up. 'Let's go down to Trapper's and break free his critters!' Her face was shiny with the idea, as if it could right the way the night had tipped.

'He's invited the kids there,' said Greta.

'It's a nightmare, I've heard,' Brynn warned.

'Someone should do something,' agreed Tori.

'What's anyone to do? The guy greets everyone with a rifle.'

'You can't stop these people,' said Tori. 'It's why they're here.' She stood, ready to go. 'That's why tonight's the night for a dare!' She stepped off the verandah. Her laugh skipped out across the valley. 'Bring me the boltcutters! You've gotta run to the cages, free the animals and make it back! Person who snaps the most locks wins.'

'Who's dragging out the humans downed by Trapper?' Brynn asked.

'Trapper? He'll be horizontal from his homebrew. Out to it after sundown.'

'How do you know?' asked Greta.

'I've lived here all my life.'

The night swam in this foolish, watery idea. Tori did a ragged waltz to the shed. She reappeared triumphant, waving boltcutters, and then disappeared.

'We'd better go after her,' said Brynn.

They caught up with her on the track down to the boulders and the creek.

'You show a sense of direction when you're drunk, I'll give you that,' said Greta.

'Turn that thing off!' Tori waved away Greta's torch. She was wide-eyed, a rabbit in the headlights. 'All we need is the big light in the sky.' Her arms swung up to love the moon.

At the creek she stripped off her jeans and flung them over her shoulder to wade across. Greta hitched up her dress and followed. The lace hem dragged in the water. Stones bit into her feet, the current pushed against her legs. She remembered the creeks of her childhood, spotlighting yabbies with Gavin, him with the net and a torch, her with her father's lantern. Tori was already at Trapper's fence ladder.

'Who's first?' asked Brynn.

'I am,' said Greta. If she waited she might lose her nerve. Come to her senses.

Brynn nodded, then pointed to Greta's torch. 'Keep that off unless you want his dogs after you.'

Greta switched off the torch and grabbed the boltcutters. The lace stuck to her legs as she climbed over the fence. She gave Brynn a thumbs-up and followed a line of rocks up to the cages. Above her the Milky Way was a chalky curve, the smudged arc of a wing bone.

The cages were bathed in moonlight, and Trapper's demountable, too, at the top of the slope. The cages were about thirty metres from him. As Greta came to the first one the stench made her gag. She couldn't see what was inside though she could hear shuffling. She switched on the torch, shielding the light with her hand. A mangy wallaby stared back at her, its tail was an infected sore. The next cage was tall and narrow. Inside a cockatoo huddled over a shallow bowl of greenish water. One scaly leg was manacled to a metal post.

A fuel drum banged loudly at Trapper's. One of his dogs started growling. Close by a twig snapped, and another. Greta ducked behind the cockatoo cage. There was a whistle like a bird then a twang of wire, the rattle of a chain.

The girl came into view, cast in full moonlight at the next enclosure. She took something from her pocket and pushed it through the wire. Greta thought she heard a quiet singing.

The cockatoo began squawking. Trapper's dogs barked and pulled on their chains. Heavy footsteps shuddered inside the demountable and the door swung open with a bang.

The girl fled, a flash of white through the trees. The dogs were in a frenzy. Trapper roared at them. They quietened. Greta heard him pissing into the grass.

As soon as his door slammed shut she made her escape. She was almost at the fence when she tripped and fell. The dogs were wild again, chains clanging as they pulled against them.

Trapper's door swung open. 'Who the fuck are you?'

She scrambled to her feet and ran.

'I know you're out there!'

Any second Trapper might turn the dogs loose. Greta leaped over the stile. The hem tore on the barbed wire. The boom of a rifle punched through the air. She reached the water and waded downstream to Brynn and Tori, who were waiting where the fence crossed the creek. Tori snorted laughter.

'Shut up,' said Brynn.

'What's funny?' Greta whispered. 'I nearly got shot!' She sat down on a rock and tugged at the torn skirt of the dress, which had wrapped around her legs. She yanked harder, tearing it off, so only the bodice remained and a frill of the lace below it.

Tori laughed, 'That's a look! You've got new swimmers.'

'So much for you two taking up the dare.' Greta caught her breath. 'It's like you said, Brynn. The animals. Though I didn't see a white lizard or a three-horned goat.'

'Where's the boltcutters?' asked Tori.

'I must have dropped them when I tripped.'

'He'll be findin' them tomorrow,' said Tori.

You idiot, Greta said to herself and ducked under the metal flap at the fence. She hoped to feel safer, here on the other side. The water quickly became deeper and she could feel a current. She was level with the dark pool under the footbridge and the rainforest around it. Tori and Brynn joined her.

She shivered. 'Are you sure there's no crocodiles?'

'Never seen one here.' Tori let herself be carried downstream.

Greta followed her with Brynn close behind. She held the torch in her mouth. At the next gathering of rocks she hauled herself up and shone the torch beam across the water, looking for red eyes.

'That girl was there. Feeding the animals.'

'Who's this girl you keep seein'?' Tori asked, finding a rock to sit on. 'How old?'

'Early teens,' said Greta. She left the torch on the rock and slid into the water. 'Hard to tell. I think she visits the old meatworkers' hut.'

'That'll be a McKinny. They squat round here. Your place, my place, anywhere they don't get caught. McKinny'll be out stealin' cattle.'

Greta wondered if the girl was hiding among the trees, watching the women float down the creek. In the distance Trapper's dogs started up their barking.

'Listenin' to those hounds, maybe the McKinnys're campin' on Trapper's,' said Tori.

Greta left her rock and floated down to a series of boulders where the water gushed loudly, forced through unseen channels. All three women stood and balanced their way to where the creek flowed smoothly again.

They'd reached the hut. It was an eerie lean-to in the moonlight. The iron roof shone bright. The mango tree was a dark shape. The pandanus stood around like wise old ones with their grey-silver beards.

'There it is,' said Tori. 'Devil's camp.'

'Really?' Brynn cut a sharp laugh. 'What a name.'

'Before your time.' Tori looked over to Greta. 'Does Joel ever mention him?'

'Just in passing.'

'Came and went, old Devil. Used to shack up here with Sal. God knows what she saw in 'im. Evil bastard. Twisted.' She smacked a mosquito on her neck. 'Sal was the only one could keep him on a leash. And only some of the time.'

She floated to a fallen tree and grabbed one of the roots sticking out of the water to hold herself there. Brynn and Greta joined her. They were all three in a row up to their necks to escape mosquitoes. The creek tugged at them.

'Devil and Joel's uncle Vadik were mates,' Tori was saying. 'Vadik used to be down here too, till him 'n' Devil'd fight an' Vadik'd go back up to the homestead, take his chances with Fedor.'

'Joel mentioned Devil had a son,' Greta said.

She tried to imagine him here in the hut with Devil, Sal, Vadik— the boy with the beautiful smile, surviving.

'Lennie.' Tori sighed. 'Lennie wasn't cut out for this place.'

Lightning glimmered behind clouds, far off. A curlew's wail rent the quiet. Tori released her hold and drifted to a boulder peeping out midstream. Her arm hooked onto it. She was half in, half out of the water, staring down the rolling line of the current.

'Things turned bad for Lennie.'

There's a sharp crack from the burning log, a flurry of sparks up into the night. Joel adjusts one of the jaffle irons in the coals. Four faces shimmer in the firelight, and behind them the dark boulders are allies.

Magdalen sits close to Lennie, twisting a bracelet on her wrist. It is hand-forged, black steel with a gentle twist in the metal, and charms dangle from it, little metal curls, shards of bone. A matching heart pendant hangs around her neck on leather cord. Danny is leaning against a tree, pressing tobacco into a paper. He twists the end and lights it. The sound of the creek, the dance of the flames mesmerise them into quietness. Until a shuffling in the dark startles them, and a face appears out of the shadows.

Devil's razor laugh clips the air. He steps closer and takes shape in the wavering firelight. His belt is in his hand and his trousers are loose on his hips, buttonless. Danny's torch shines on him but he ignores it.

What're you doin' 'ere, boy? he barks at Lennie. I told you to stay away from that girl.

He points at Magdalen. The belt dangles from his hand like a snake.

Fedor don't want it! He clears phlegm from his throat and spits on the rock between him and his son.

Not me either. She's fuckin' loopy.

The belt sways beside him.

Sal moves in out of the night. No one has heard her.

Leave 'im, Devil. Come on, we're goin'.

Fuck off! Devil raises his arm but she's too quick for him tonight.

He turns back to Lennie. Y'know what you are, boy? A weak fuck. A lazy fuck. Ya wanna stay with me, ya fuckin' work. An' not with yer fuckin' fire an' tongs. It's time you was pullin' yer weight in the meat house.

He whips his belt on the rock. The boy jumps. Magdalen is frozen, staring at the fire as if in a trance. Her breath is laboured, frightened. Devil is slightly unsteady. His breath is whisky-drenched. His words start off quiet this time.

Y'know what I'm thinkin'? I'm thinkin' you're a fuckin' fake! Ya don't even look like me! Ya sick fuck. What do ya take me for, huh? Stupid?

He laughs softly and his eyes wander to fix on Magdalen.

How is 'e for ya, girl? Does 'e do it good for ya, huh?

Fuck off, Devil. Danny comes over to the fire, shining the torch in Devil's eyes.

The older man laughs. Ya wanna see how it's done, do ya, Magdalen? You come with me, girl. Get yerself a turn with a real man!

There's a smack of glass on a rock. Joel is on his feet with a longneck bottle sliced off halfway.

Sal's voice comes from the other side of the fence.

I'm crossin' this bridge, Devil. Better hurry up if you wanna cross it with me!

Devil stalks towards the fence. Come 'ere, ya fuckin' bitch! He stoops awkwardly to go through the gap and catches his shirt on a barb. Wait! Wait up!

The shirt tears when he pulls himself free. A little piece is stuck on the fence.

KAREN MANTON

Magdalen's gaze is on the fire. A tremor runs through her. Lennie grasps her hand and holds it tight. Tight like he'll melt both their hands together.

20

The starter gun cracked. The boys dived in. A surge of voices cheered. Greta edged alongside the pool, urging Griffin on. His fingertips touched the wall first. A sea of blue flags waved madly. He emerged from the water shivering. She handed him a towel.

'Well done,' the woman next to Greta said to him.

It was Eileen, the policewoman. She was thin and neat in her dark blue uniform, with a strawberry blonde plait.

Griffin smiled at her and went to collect his ribbon. The next race started.

'Swimming was never my thing,' Greta said to Eileen. 'Griffin takes after his father.'

Eileen smiled. 'As long as you can stop yourself from drowning.'

Greta took her chance to ask about the girl. 'She seems to be alone, I'm not sure where she's living.'

'I haven't heard of her,' said Eileen. 'Let us know if you see her again.'

She excused herself to answer her mobile phone. Greta moved away. Tori waved from a bain-marie where she was serving chicken wings. Greta recognised some faces from the Halloween party, but not many. That was already a couple of weeks ago, she realised, hard to believe.

'Greta!' Miss Rhianna held out a tray of orange quarters. 'Do me a favour and pass these around?'

They chatted briefly, about an upcoming gig Rhianna had in Darwin and a story Griffin had written, until a girl with a cut foot drew Rhianna away. Greta moved through the crowd as hands darted at the tray with calls of, 'Thanks!' Raffy and Raymond appeared and took the last three quarters.

They ate one each and, with Greta following, headed over to Nanna Agnes on the mobility scooter. She was parked in the shade of a rain tree growing on the other side of the fence, the toddler Greta had seen with her on the first day of school was asleep on her lap. A group of girls huddled around her. Raymond gave her the last piece of orange and gestured to Greta with his peel.

'This is Raffy's mum.'

Agnes smiled. 'Ray's keen for your place again.'

'You're welcome any time, Ray.'

The boy smiled shyly and stuffed his lunchbox into the bag hanging off the back of the scooter. Lanie arrived with a fifth winner's ribbon to pin to Agnes's shirt. Water from her hair dripped on the toddler. The child woke and flung her hands up to Agnes's neck. The starter gun cracked again. The girls rushed off to watch the race. Raffy and Raymond wandered away.

'Lanie's taking home a few ribbons,' Greta said.

'Yeah, she's sporty that one. Ray says she's headin' for the Olympics!' She had a deep laugh.

The cheering became too loud for them to hear each other. As the race finished, Agnes said, 'Well, I gotta take this one back home for a feed.'

It was time to go herself, Greta thought. She looked for her boys among the children milling outside the change rooms. They eluded her. Red hair, black hair, brown hair, blond hair. She couldn't see them. Instead, she noticed a white-blonde ponytail drift through, now seen, now obscured. Greta went after her, but when she entered the girls' change rooms the group had dispersed. There was a smell of chlorine. A wooden bench along the wall was strewn with towels, wet bathers, thongs. The cubicles were empty. She went outside again.

Where are you, where are you?

Griffin tugged her arm. 'Who are you whispering to?' He had a way of appearing.

'Myself.' She smiled at him and found some icy-pole money in her purse for him to share with his brothers and friends. 'I'll see you after school. You're catching the bus this afternoon, remember?'

He nodded. 'Our bikes are at the front gate.'

She wanted to hug him. He knew and edged away.

'I'll see you later then.'

He gave her a sideways glance, a quick nod. She looked once more for the girl and went to the car. Over the road, one of the old church's bowed doors was jammed open. She might be hiding there, Greta thought, and hurried across.

There was a hush inside, an unusual stillness. The loudspeaker and surge of cheers from the pool sounded far away. Like the school, the church had louvres down both sides. Several were missing or broken. A panel had fallen from the ceiling and split across the font. Greta walked down the aisle between wooden pews. Broken glass crunched under her boots. The altar still had its once-white cloth and a candle in a jar at each end.

She looked through the louvres for any movement in the bushland. A blue-winged kookaburra flew through the quiet up to a branch. Had she really seen the girl?

Once home Greta decided to go to the hut and put her question to rest. If the girl is there, she told herself, I've been mistaken. If not, she's possibly wandering around town. And what did that mean? Did she have a home, relatives, friends in Lightstone?

The children wouldn't be home for a couple of hours. She had just enough time. She emptied Raffy's basket of feathers, seeds and cicada shells and lined it with a red tea towel. Then she filled it with two of her home-baked bread rolls, snake beans from her garden and a pawpaw from Brynn.

She set off with her camera and the basket, taking a shortcut by stepping down from the cycads just below the shack, to the cleared hill that went straight down to the outcrop. It amazed her how quickly the land rejuvenated. Greenery was sprouting through ash and stubs of burned gamba. New fronds waved from the blackened trunks of sand palms and cycads.

In no time she arrived at the rock formations overlooking the valley. The air around them shimmered. She found the passage-way she'd walked along before and entered unafraid. But once she turned the corner into that narrow corridor she again felt its walls were too close, as if the stone might unexpectedly shift, reconfigure, lock her in. She scuttled through to the archway that opened onto the valley.

Immediately she breathed easier. Birds called and the creek sounded friendly. The fire hadn't reached here, everything was as it had been. She wound her way down between rocks and the silvery blue-green cycads.

The hut was still there beyond the mango tree. For some reason she was always ready for it to have disappeared. Upstream she heard a slap, slap. It came from where the water gushed fast between boulders; where she, Tori and Brynn had been on Halloween night. She followed the sound and saw the girl knee-deep in the water, her dress hitched up to her undies. She wore a belt and had a net bag slung low across her back. Two fish were already in the bag, glinting in the sunlight. She was bent over, hands invisible under the rollicking flow. The water was noisy, rushing between rocks.

You should call out to her, Greta thought, so you don't give her a fright.

But the sunlight and spray from the foamy water made an aura around the girl, and Greta knew she must capture it now or miss the image forever.

She put down her basket and took up the camera, wishing she could see the girl's hands under water. They would be open like traps. Click, click. The girl drew out another fish and whipped it on a rock before slipping it into the net bag. Then she waded ashore. Her hair hung in long, wet strands. She didn't see Greta until she stepped onto the sand. Immediately she flung the fish to the ground and grabbed the knife from her belt, aiming it at Greta. Sunlight flared from the blade.

'What are you doing here?'

Greta took a step back. 'I came to see if you're all right.'

The fish were laid out on the sand, popping air. The girl crouched low and slit the first fish through the gills. Blood leaked onto the sand.

'You're clever the way you catch them,' Greta said.

'I don't like hooks.'

She killed the others with her knife and picked up one to scale. She worked the blade down the body, scratching away at it. Scales flew in all directions. One stuck on Greta's shin. When she was done, she slit the fish along the underbelly and delicately scooped out the guts with her fingers.

A kite landed in a tree close by and whistled.

She stood up, smiling at the bird. 'Every day she visits.' Her eyes flashed blue at Greta. 'I leave her treats.'

The girl tossed the liver upwards. The bird flew to catch it mid-air.

'See that?' she laughed and cut off a fish head for the bird as well. Then she gutted the other fish, and washed them all in the creek before returning them to her bag. She glanced at Greta, as if to say, 'Come on,' and headed down a narrow track leading to the hut.

Greta stepped in behind her. They were almost there when the girl moved to a cluster of rocks and a dead bush, all twigs and no leaves. A bowerbird's arch was under it. The entrance was decorated with snail shells, delicate bones, mica and a string of diagonal mirrors. Three of Raffy's blue chalks lay there too. 'Evidence!' Toby would shout. Mean mother I am, Greta thought, not believing a boy about disappearing chalks. She took a photo for her confession.

The girl snatched up the string of mirrors.

'We steal from each other,' she said, and made her way back to the hut's track.

Sunlight darted from the mirrors as she walked. She kept close to the creek, as if her feet and her ears were listening to its sound.

The hut seemed smaller this time. The girl went straight to the kitchen trough with the fish. Greta glanced around for her father's lantern. The curtain was pulled back. She could see everything. The bed and the rabbit and the bracelets above them. The newspapers on the opposite wall.

'Here, sit down.' The girl pointed to a chair with her knife.

Greta did as she was told and put her basket on the other chair. 'I brought you some food.'

The girl smiled at it. 'You are very kind.'

Greta rested her camera on the table, near a small brass bowl filled with coloured beads, screws, hooks and snippets of wire. A pair of pliers rested across it. She tried not to stare at the beads, but her peripheral vision recognised four as her own.

'I've been wondering what your name is. Mine's Greta.'

The girl turned away to sharpen her knife on a stone by the trough.

'Elena,' she said at last, with a quick glance at Greta. 'Call me Elena.'

Maria Elena—Greta remembered the name carved on the memorial rock for Joel's mother. No doubt the girl had seen it and was stealing the name for cover. A blowfly buzzed through the doorway to find the fish, the cobwebbed window. The girl had her back to Greta. The knife made a song on the stone.

'I saw you earlier today at the swimming carnival. I was talking to Eileen, the police lady, while I was there and I wondered if . . . if you need anything.'

The girl quickened her rhythm with the knife. It looked home-made to Greta, the handle was bound with leather.

'Elena?'

'Don't tell them I'm here!' The girl spun around so fast Greta jumped. Her knife was pointed at Greta's chest.

'Only you can know. Only you can see me. No one else!'

The girl's hand was shaking. Her eyes were a vibrant blue. 'If you tell them, I'll go. I'll leave and you'll never find me.' Her voice was urgent. She flicked the hair from her face and said more quietly, 'You have to keep my secret.'

'I understand.' Greta lifted her hands in surrender.

'Promise!' The knife lunged forward.

'I promise. I won't say a thing.'

The girl's hand relaxed. The fly buzzed in the sink.

'You took things,' she said. 'You took them from the shelf above my bed. They're gone.'

Greta felt she was inside a reversed tale of the three bears, with the girl an angry Goldilocks and herself a befuddled intruder bear under interrogation.

'That was Griffin. I can bring them back if you like.'

'Perhaps that little boy should bring them himself.' She leaned against the trough, arms crossed.

Greta blinked. There was an edge to the girl's voice. She remembered that night on the verandah, the girl's fixed gaze on Joel and Griffin. What had it been? Jealousy? Retribution? A grudge?

'Joel said the tape and jewellery box belonged to his sister.'

The girl's gaze intensified.

'You shouldn't take what isn't yours,' she said. 'There's consequences.' She spoke each word carefully. 'Punishments.'

Her crossed arms flexed nervously. Greta was uncertain if this was an adolescent pose or a real threat. She was tempted to point out the girl had taken Griffin's amethyst, beads from Greta's work boxes, trinkets from the bowerbird. And her father's lantern.

'Where is your family?' she tried.

'Gone. I left.'

Greta shifted in her chair. She wished she could record the conversation. 'That night on the verandah, when you were looking in, I thought maybe you wanted something. From Joel.'

The girl ignored that suggestion and said, 'Your son. He was there also.' There was a bitterness in her tone. She unfolded her arms and steadied her right hand on the edge of the trough. 'He likes to hide.'

So she had been watching them. Especially Griffin.

Why? Greta wondered. Because a curiosity about Joel had

switched to his son? Or because Griffin was a wanderer, like this girl? Her fingers picked at the trinkets in the bowl and found a metal button, tiny glass balls, a silver feather earring. She tried to pretend she wasn't searching for pilfered beads. She hooked out a wire bracelet, similar to the ones on the hut wall but smaller, for a toddler. It had a single charm attached, a miniature stick figure made from little bones bound with red cotton.

'The bracelets—do you make them? And the chimes outside?'

'I didn't make those.' The girl looked up to the wall and then moved the basket to sit opposite Greta. Her hands wrapped around the bowl. 'I add to the chimes. My charms.'

An almost imperceptible breeze wafted around the hut. The chimes murmured and the news clippings breathed out from the wall. As if someone had called her, the girl went outside.

Greta found her leaning against the hut wall, eyes closed. Her whole body was listening to the soft ringing of the chimes. The fury of before was gone. The exquisite sounds of the chimes had altered her.

Greta lifted the camera. Click.

The girl's eyes snapped open. 'You ask a lot of questions.'

The breeze gathered, teasing loose flaps of corrugated iron on the roof. Dead leaves whirled into spirals and skittered across the ground.

'Hear that?' asked the girl, her head tilted slightly. 'It's the wind, from the lake.'

She was still holding the knife, gently pressing the blade to her fingertips. Greta waited for her to speak about the poison water. It took her by surprise when the girl said, 'You should go now. Your children will be home. From school.'

Greta took out her watch to see the time. It was much later than she'd expected. She went inside for her hat and unpacked the food from the basket onto the table.

'Wait,' said Elena.

She came and dragged a chair to the trough, and stood on it to reach inside a cupboard above the window. 'I want to give you this.'

The chair wobbled under her. She handed Greta a postal cylinder. Greta prised off the red plastic lid. Inside was a roll of paper, A3 size. She spread it out on the table to see a detailed sketch of the boy with a swan wing. The intense, questioning face took hold of her. And the wing with its painstakingly intricate feathers. He wore a singlet and shorts with the letter *J* on the pocket. He was standing on a cliff edge, toes curled over the rock as if he might leap forward and fly.

'Joel did this?'

'You know his drawings.'

Greta didn't answer, her eyes still on the boy, the wing.

'Thank you, Elena. The children will be excited to see it.'

Especially Raffy, Greta thought, who had sticky-taped the smaller sketch on the window above his bed. She returned the drawing to the cylinder.

'And Joel. Joel will be pleased.' The girl's smile was strained.

'How do you know him?' Greta asked softly.

The blue eyes darkened. 'I don't.' The words slipped from her mouth like two pebbles, one to hold in each hand.

Greta picked up the cylinder. 'I'll be going then.'

'Visit me again if you like.'

Greta smiled. 'I might do that.'

She had started to walk away when the girl called from the doorway. 'Greta!'

Her voice was so clear. She was standing at the edge of the verandah. Her blue eyes shone. Behind her the chimes gently moved.

'I trust you,' she said.

21

Greta set her camera down on the green table and looked at each boy with his handful of cards. She waited. Not a word.

'Which one of you has fiddled with my camera?'

Toby was first in. 'Not me!'

'Not me,' echoed Raffy. He wouldn't look at her.

Griffin was insulted, betrayed by his brothers' swift thinking. 'What are you looking at me for?'

Even the boy with the swan wing watched him, set inside his new frame and hanging from a nail in the verandah post by the table.

'Someone wound back the film without telling me, and now I've taken photos over the top of other ones.'

She placed three prints on the table. They leaned in to look. Wherever Greta had expected to see Elena, the girl was obscured by her sons. Toby's legs, Griffin's torchlit horror face and Raffy's cheeks pulled wider than a wide-mouthed frog were superimposed over ghostly impressions of boulders in the creek, fish on the sand, the hut and its chimes, the bowerbird's arch. The girl had disappeared.

'Double exposure. All my careful photographs overlaid with yours.'

Griffin slid the playing cards to himself and shuffled them around the table.

'Maybe that fairy did it,' Raffy suggested. 'The one that leaves the chimes and the bones.'

'There're no fairies here, Raffy,' Greta sighed.

'We're not in your storybook,' added Toby.

Greta could swear she saw the swan boy's feathers ruffle in the corner of her eye.

The familiar toot, toot of Tori's troopy saved her children. Griffin and Toby bolted, Raffy smiled sadly at his mother before sliding away.

'What's with you?' Tori was impressed with her friend's scowl.

'Nothing. I should get over it.' Greta pushed the photos towards her.

Tori looked through them. 'Creepy! You could sell 'em.'

Axel marched past wielding a pair of mango pickers. The handles were long, with a mean beak at the end.

'We're going to raid the old mango farm next door,' Tori said. 'Save the fruit from pigs and cows. Bring a bucket.'

They had to drive out to the road to access a track on the other side of the orchard. It went down to the creek, where Tori parked. The children slipped through the fence to the trees. Tori held the barbed wires apart for Greta.

'Aren't we trespassing?' Greta pulled her bucket after her.

'Of course, but no one's here, so no one's to know.'

It was a dark cathedral under the mass of evergreen leaves,

with the trunks as close-standing pillars. Greta climbed barefoot up a tree. Tori passed her pickers and a bucket, and climbed a neighbouring tree. Greta had expected the orchard to be cooler, a relief from the sweltering heat. Instead she felt closed in.

Tori exclaimed there were too many green mangoes in her tree. Greta found the same and climbed higher. She was tired, after interrupted sleep—Griffin had woken her a few times saying he could hear a dog yelping. She'd heard nothing.

'Must be Ronnie's bus, givin' him strange dreams,' Tori said.

'That reminds me, Ronnie said Joel came back here with Danny about fifteen years ago.' Greta tried to sound indifferent. 'I was wondering where they stayed.'

She pulled a ripe mango from its stem. The milky sap stung her fingers.

'They'd've been in the shack with the wild pigs and horses,' said Tori. 'They weren't here for long. Went travellin' around, you know, chasin' work. Does it matter?'

'Not really. Just something Erin said at Halloween.'

Questions she wanted to ask needled Greta, but Axel and Skye came screaming to the base of Tori's tree in a fight.

'Outta here, you lot!' their mother commanded. 'Or it's all over an' we're goin'!'

The children made themselves scarce. Tori chattered on, while Greta moved to another tree. They'd climbed a few by the time the buckets were full. Tori picked up a golden one with a rosy blush and smiled at its perfection, then called to the children.

Only Raffy, Barney and Skye drifted in from the shadows. The other boys were missing.

'They went through the fallen fence to our place,' said Raffy. 'They wanted to play at the creek.'

'I'll find them,' said Greta. 'You help Tori with the buckets.'

She spotted Toby and Axel near the boundary fence. They'd discovered a burnt-out car twisted around a dead tree.

Toby hurried to speak. 'Trapper said this is the car Magdalen died in.'

'Trapper?'

'He said Dad and his brothers took her for a joy ride and crashed into the tree. And then it burst into flames.'

'When did he tell you this?'

'Just now. He was here with his gold detector.'

Greta scanned the spaces between the trees. The bushland gawked back at her. Trapper had vanished.

'I don't want you talking with him.'

'Why not?'

'I don't like what he puts in your head.'

'But it's true. This is the car. He said.'

'Yes, but he's wrong, Toby. Magdalen died in a car accident on the highway.'

'I told him that. He just looked at me and said real slow, "Is that right?"'

Three long car beeps sounded from Tori.

'Go on,' she told the boys. 'Everyone's waiting for you. Where's Griffin?'

'He walked home ages ago,' said Toby.

They pulled up at the shack with a blare of the horn for Griffin, but there was no sign of him. The other children divided the mangoes into two piles, one for each family. They lined up the green ones along the verandah to ripen. Greta sliced a few ripe ones for everyone and made tea for herself and Tori. She kept expecting

Griffin to appear, boasting that he'd beaten them home, but half an hour passed and he still hadn't turned up.

'When did you say he set off home?' she asked Toby.

'Ages ago. He was bored at the mango farm.' He added, 'Maybe he's run off.'

'What for?' asked Axel.

'Because of the camera. Wrecking mum's shots.' He looked sideways at Greta.

She stared back at him.

'Well, it wasn't me!' he protested.

'And it wasn't me,' chipped in Raffy.

'So you've said.'

She sent them off to look in the usual places. The darkroom, the tree house, the bus, the cabin, the shed, the four-wheel drive. She crawled under the verandah. Bare feet thumped overhead. She could smell the mangoes. Their shadows interrupted cracks of light. She moved further in under the house.

'Griffin,' she whispered, as if she wouldn't give him away to the others.

Remnants of life above dug into her knees—beer bottle tops, walnut shells cracked open by Raffy's brick. Griffin's knapsack was slumped against a foundation post. Inside she found a pocket guide to snakes, an ant-eaten muesli bar and her head torch. She heard the scuttle of a lizard but nothing more. She retreated back into daylight. Above the homestead a dark band of cloud loomed. A streak of white curled along the front.

'Storm on its way,' said Tori.

Greta pulled her father's watch from her pocket and tried to remember when she'd last seen him. 'He's been gone an hour— more maybe . . .' Her words petered out.

'I'll go back to the mango farm and the creek. Maybe we missed him.'

'Let's check the homestead first,' said Greta. 'And ring Brynn.'

Toby strode alongside his mother. 'He'll come back. He always does.'

She didn't look at him. She felt sick. As well as the lake, the hut and the creek, there was the bushland up behind the homestead and out to the road. There was Trapper's forbidden property and the wasted paddocks his cattle roamed. The possibilities kept expanding.

The old house creaked its usual welcome. Tori checked inside while Greta and Toby wove between car wrecks calling for him. Above them the cloud drift intensified. Greta walked away with her rising panic. Near Magdalen's birth car she found a boulder to stand on for a better view down to the lake. Maria's fear bloomed through her like an exotic flower. There was a strange vine, a pulsing cord between the two mothers. She had a terrible misgiving that the lake might have taken her child.

Raffy ran over to her carrying Griffin's bird book.

'What is it?' She took it from him. It was open at the hooded parrot page.

'I found it in the bus. He said he saw one'—he pointed at the picture of the bird—'down near the lake.'

'How near?'

'In a log on the edge.'

The ground tipped under Greta, the clouds and the sky spun.

'Go to the shack, Raffy.' She gave him the book. 'Wait for me there. You mustn't leave until I come home.'

She watched him head across and then started down the firebreak. The sound of the quad bike chased her. Toby pulled up next to her.

'Have you seen his binoculars?' she asked.

He shook his head and climbed off the bike.

'Stay with Raffy. Don't let him wander anywhere.'

Toby nodded. He seemed older in this moment. A rumble of thunder came from over the homestead. She glanced to the ruin and hated it all of a sudden, the curse of it, the souls lost to it. Lightning crackled across the sky.

Greta drove down the track, fingers vibrating on the throttle. The smell of fuel smarted in her nostrils.

'You'll see him,' she told herself. 'You'll see him if he's there.'

The lake was a silent glass.

'Griffin,' she called, edging her way around the banks, where new grass was sprouting fire debris.

There was no sign of him in the water. The half-submerged tree lay in its skeleton pose. The ghost car was a drowned song. Still, she believed he might be here, unseen, made invisible by the malicious dam.

'*Where is he?*' she screamed at the water.

She threw in a stone to provoke an answer. The reflections of clouds moved across the speechless mirror.

There was no boy. The place was a vacuum, a vanishing.

Fear gripped her and with it the terrible accusation. *You did this! You did it!*

She was surrounded by angry voices, the pointing finger. Vivian rattling a strip of ruined negatives. Gavin's mother spitting her grief and her fury. Joel's dreadful silence, the children's bewildered gaze on her. *You lost him.* If she hadn't been up the mango tree with distracting thoughts; if she'd been counting children as a mother should . . .

She heard a heavy tread behind her and spun around.

A wallaby bounded out of the bush and scuttled down the

bank into the water. Seconds later a dingo raced to the edge. The wallaby was swimming to the tumble of boulders on the other side. Greta watched, astounded. She'd never seen a wallaby swim before. The dingo sniffed the air and watched the wallaby scramble out and hop away. It waited for a moment afterwards, one paw off the ground, then was gone into the mosaic of rocks, cycads and termite mounds.

The lake resumed its quiet. Disturbances in the bush settled. The air was humid, damp to breathe. Perspiration trickled down Greta's face, her chest, her arms.

Above her a sea eagle drifted in and out of merging clouds.

'Watch for him,' she whispered.

A slight breath of air passed low over the ground, bringing with it faint noises. A far-off tapping, soft ringing. The more she listened the clearer it became, as if it would strengthen for someone who heard. Greta's eyes searched for where it was coming from. She saw nothing at first but the flash of a lizard's fiery red tail. It darted up a rock to a stick she recognised—it was the divining stick. From each twig a string dangled down to a star of delicate bones. The lizard watched her, sides breathing in and out, red tail flicking. The stick was pointing to a blackened branch with a single new leaf on one of its twigs. A line of miniature mirrors hung from a branch under it. They were square, like the ones from a mirror ball. She spotted one on the ground ahead, and another, and another, until she came to a cycad with luminous new fronds curling upright. It had a rusty bicycle chain around its neck. A black cockatoo feather was jammed through the chain. She pulled the handsome feather free.

It is not a sign, she told herself of the blood-red mark. It is not an omen.

But clearly she was being led along a trail. She was sure of two things. That Griffin had been here. And that the girl had planted these curious messages—not as markers to keep herself from being lost, but to lure another child. She shivered and remembered the girl's fascination with the birthmark on Griffin's neck, his father's mark.

Be good, my child, come go with me! I know nice games, will play them with thee!

Vivian used to read 'The Erl-King' out loud. What kind of mother reads her child that poem at night? And what games might the stranger girl play with Griffin?

The bushland called her deeper into an enchanted forest. Psychedelic green buds studded the dark arms of the ironwood trees. Cycads boasted new heads of feathery green. The charred trunks of sand palms were crowned with vibrant fronds. She could almost see the vivid threads of grass sprouting, as if the pressure of her boots had triggered this magic. It is the work of perched aquifers, tubers and rhizomes underground, she told herself. The secret sustenance. Brynn had told her about them. Subterranean networks keeping plants alive for months without rain.

A line of burned cycad nuts, like dark marbles, led her to an odd sculpture balanced on a rock—a pyramid of rusted metal rods and skinny bones, with a delicate bird skull suspended in the centre. A red bead plugged each eye socket. She followed the skull's line of sight. It took her to a doorless fridge lying in the red dirt. Two lines of barbed wire had been strung across the front and caught a flying fox. It was long dead, wings stretched wide, legs out stiff. A pink bead glinted at its ankle, bound with yellow cotton.

Greta's heartbeat quickened. Steady your breath, she told herself. Her mind kept spinning wild horrors, like the malevolence of the lake had crawled from the water and entered the girl to move on land. She stopped, disoriented. The bush closed in around her. Find a reference point, the voice in her urged. An anomaly, a unique feature. There must be one. But in each rock and tree she found a repeat of another. Her shirtsleeves clung damp to her arms. She breathed a humid fear. I cannot find him, I cannot find him.

Thunder rumbled again. The dark clouds from the homestead had spread. The rejuvenated forest petered out. She no longer heard the gentle sounds that had drawn her along. Great tussocks of gamba rose around her, whipped with black marks but not burned. Her heart sank, until a red shirt among the stalks caught her eye. Griffin! She dived after him, calling out. The untucked shirt flitted ahead, just out of reach.

'Griffin!' she shouted. 'Griffin!'

She was close, her fingers almost touched him. The boy's head spun around to face her and instantly disappeared.

'No!' she cried out.

He'd vanished. The grass spilled her into a clearing. A cow's bones lay scattered at her feet, stark white against the cracked, orange earth. Sun-weathered hide clung to an arch of ribs. It was the skeleton from the lake, escaped in the night only to fall apart at daybreak.

She drank the last of her water and checked her phone. There was no reception.

Beyond the bones was a disintegrating car. Rubbish lay strewn around it, a detached bicycle wheel, a swollen esky, a shoe. And Griffin's blue cap. She stooped to pick it up.

Perhaps that little boy should bring them himself.

Her chest tightened. She circled the vehicle. No one was there, but a muddied tarp draped over a small mound was pushed up against the front wheel. She stared at it, sickened.

There's consequences. Punishments.

A crack of thunder split the silence. Large spots of rain hit the tarp.

Get yourself together, she told herself. You can't know it's him until you look.

She snatched away the tarp. Underneath was a grey dog. Long teats drooped from its swollen belly. A bullet hole neatly marked the forehead. The dog's eyelids hadn't quite closed. A fly buzzed in to clutch at the eyelid, explore the snout.

Greta stepped away. Behind a nearby rock was a newborn pup. Dead, like its mother. She found two more and, just beyond them, Griffin's thong. She snatched it up.

The rain came down fast, slanting sideways to sting her face. In moments she was sodden.

'Griffin!' she called again, knowing there would be no answer.

The rain intensified, became a veil. The land was altered, she couldn't see far ahead of her. The trees and gamba, rocks and termite mounds were vague presences. Only one shape moved, walking towards her. Too tall for Griffin.

With every second Elena became more real. Rain pelted her body. Her dress was soaked, clinging to her skin like the hair over her skull. Drops of water beaded her eyelashes.

She must see me in the same way, thought Greta. We are each other's mirror.

'What have you done with him?'

'Come with me,' the girl said above the clamour of the rain.

She led the way across ground pockmarked from pigs and buffalo to a track flanked with new grasses. A *Keep Out!* sign was nailed to a woolly butt tree. Elena walked along the glistening track; the red dirt was carved with rivulets. She held out her hands, palms up, to feel the rain. Her dress was transparent. Beyond her the world was shrouded in rain.

They stopped at a large shed Greta knew must be the slaughter-house. There were no windows. The door at the end of the building had been pulled off.

A spasm of light jerked across black clouds. Thunder bellowed. The girl ushered Greta inside.

Rain drummed on the corrugated-iron roof. Greta stepped up onto the killing floor and called for her son. No answer. She moved further in, past the rusted knocking box and platform. The walls were scrawled with graffiti. A perished hose lay on the ground. Beside her were two skinning cradles, bolted to the floor, and an offal chute down to a trailer outside. She stepped around the carcass hoist and its dangling winch cables. The hooks on the hoist and the meat rail still had their stainless steel gleam.

She looked behind her, expecting to see Elena, but the girl was gone. Across the killing floor, one section of wall was missing. It made a giant, accidental window onto a small cattle yard with a ramp up to the knocking box, and an open shed with a bench where Joel would have salted and folded hides. In the distance a tree line edged the creek. She could just make out a figure heading towards it, fading between vertical lines of rain and grass.

'Elena!' she called out.

The girl didn't turn. A flock of black cockatoos flew slowly past, screeching their love of rain.

The building tightened against the pull of the wind. Greta walked alongside a drain with a grate, to the coldroom at the end. The sliding door was jammed open. The meat hooks hung still and empty. As she went to step inside, a ferocious bark leaped out at her. She yelled and ducked sideways. A dog surged at her again, but was yanked to a halt. Its high-pitched yelp shot through the space. She saw a trail of barbed wire running from the inner thigh of the dog's left leg, out through a hole in the wall. Thunder rumbled overhead. The walls and roof vibrated. The dog cowered momentarily, then started its hoarse barking again. So this was the dog Griffin had heard.

'Mum!' He stood behind her, as if he'd never left. He held a metal bucket with a scoop of water in it.

'Careful!' she warned, as he set it down for the dog.

'He's hurt,' said Griffin.

She waited for him to be clear of the dog, then grasped his shoulders and pulled him close. 'I thought something had happened to you!' Her voice echoed around the building. She couldn't repress a sob.

He was mortified by her tears and tried to pull away. 'Nothing's happened. I'm safe.'

She covered her face for a moment.

'The bush isn't a monster,' he added. 'It can't eat you.'

'What you don't understand is there are places that can.' She fought the tremor in her voice.

The dog tried to move forward and yelped.

'How can we get that barb out of his leg?' Griffin asked, crouching to see it. 'And whose dog is it?'

There was no tag on the collar, just a short length of broken chain. Greta suspected it might be Trapper's dog, possibly the mate of the dead female she'd just seen. She wouldn't put it past Trapper to lead a pregnant dog onto a neighbouring property and shoot it.

'How long have you been here, poor thing?' She knelt by Griffin and instinctively reached out her hand.

The dog lunged.

'God!' She clutched the puncture marks above her wrist.

'We can't leave him.' Griffin raised his voice over the dog's high-pitched yelps. 'He'll starve.'

212

Greta stepped outside the coldroom. The rain had stopped, everywhere was the sound of dripping. She was overcome with the pain in her arm, the knowledge Griffin was safe, and shame that she'd suspected Elena of child-snatching when in fact she'd led her to him.

'Did you follow anyone here, Griffin? Trail markers or a path? How did you find your way?'

He looked at her and didn't say yes or no.

A car horn tooted outside.

'Go and see who it is, Griffin. Quick.'

Her wound throbbed. The dog watched Griffin go, eyes never leaving the space where he'd disappeared.

He returned with Brynn.

'Just the kind of hoo-ha you'd expect from southerners,' she remarked, marching up with a pair of wirecutters she kept in her ute.

Griffin persuaded the dog to let him hold it still. Brynn was quick with the cutters. She left a last curl of wire. It was too close to the embedded barb.

'That'll be a vet job,' she said. 'I'm not game to hook that out.'

'What about Mum's arm?' asked Griffin.

'We'll just cut that off.'

22

The day after finding Griffin another fall of rain swept through. Greta went outside to feel it tapping on her skin. It had shifted something in her, the storm that brought her son back home with the surprise dog. She felt the mud across her feet claiming her, the land taking her in.

She and Toby went up to the graves to plant a young kurrajong and a grevillea tree for Magdalen and Maria. Toby started digging a hole, because Greta's arm was sore from the dog bite, but he soon stopped. Though she assured him no skeleton hand would poke out, he was curious, afraid.

'Not much will be left by now, Toby. It's the tropics.'

'Bones last forever,' he said, with such conviction she believed him.

She motioned for Toby to help her position the kurrajong.

He filled in the rest of the hole with the dirt mix Greta had made. She pressed it down with her boot. He was braver about the second tree and took up the spade again. He worked hard, determined to equal her efforts.

'You'll let us keep the dog,' he said, 'now we've called him Rex.'

'I don't know that your father wants a dog. We're foster carers for a few weeks until he's re-homed, that's all.'

'A few weeks!' Toby huffed, more vigorous with the spade.

'Someone might claim him yet,' she said, though the council had told her no one had reported a dog missing.

'What's Dad got against a dog?'

He was digging like a man now, foot on the edge of the spade, pressing in. Greta wiped her face with her shirt. The rash on her neck prickled. She pulled her hair into a bun and stuck a pencil from her pocket through it.

'His sister's dog took a poison bait. Died under the house while they were out looking for him.'

She saw Magdalen on the floor of her room, distraught, and the dog lying beneath. 'Your father said he'd never have another dog.'

'Rex'll change his mind.'

Rex was recovering at the shack, doted on by Griffin.

Toby handed the spade back to her. He didn't trust the bones. Greta powered on. She was no longer thinking of Rex, but her visit to the State Library in Darwin the day before while the vet extracted the barb. She'd searched microfiche pages for death notices or an article about Magdalen's fiery car accident. No obituary, no report of the highway tragedy. She was beginning to think Trapper might have been telling the truth. Perhaps the car near the mango farm was the one.

The groan of a cow crossed the hill, and then a shout, steel clanging, the grunt of an engine. Greta stopped to listen.

'That'll be Trapper come to claim his cow. Up at the old yards, sounds like.'

Think of him and there he is, she noted.

'Tori says good luck to him with those yards,' said Toby, helping her lift Maria's kurrajong into position. 'She says a stockman died there once, and no cows ever went in again. Donegan had to build new yards.'

Greta poured water from a drum onto the trees. 'We'll have to water these until the proper wet comes in.'

She gave the clouds a hopeful look. They billowed in white towers above her. The cow's noise became more urgent.

'I'm going to see what's going on.' She headed up behind the homestead.

The clanging sound returned and then a series of shouts and the low groan of an engine. A tilt tray truck slowly approached, with two quad bikes either side. Trapper was driving. As the truck chugged past, Greta saw a hog-tied cow roped onto the tray.

'I offered to sell it to ya!' Trapper yelled.

The quad bikes sped down the track out to the road.

'If Tori saw that she'd be wild,' said Greta.

Tori who was always saying, 'We look after our animals. Don't frighten the cows.'

'He heard you,' Toby said from behind her as the truck slowed to a stop. He was standing on a tall, stately termite mound.

'Get down!' she told him, ready for the mound to crumble. 'You'll damage it!'

Toby stood where he was, eyes on Trapper striding back to them.

'You can mind yer own business, girly! An' keep off my land! Next time youse go snoopin' round me prize animals I'll blow yer bloody brains out.'

Greta narrowed her eyes at him. Toby was a silent giant behind her.

'Got it? Stick yer nose in yer own shit. I seen ya down at the hut! Lookin' for another fella, eh? Like young Magdalen. Sniffin' roun' Devil while 'er ole man's away workin'!' He laughed at her.

'She mighta been missin' somethin' upstairs, but there weren't nothin' missin' downstairs!'

'You can go now, Trapper.' Greta kept herself calm.

He didn't move, squinting up at Toby instead. 'Whatcha lookin' at, boy?' He sniffed, shot a last fierce glare at Greta then marched back to his heifer. The truck crawled away.

'Toby.'

'Yes?'

'I said get down from that mound.' She turned to him.

As he jumped she saw a hunting knife strapped to his right leg. Stab injuries flashed through her mind. A knife through a boy's skull, heart, thigh. A mother looking on too late. He thudded to the ground, scrambled up unscathed and dusted his hands, smiling under the broad-brimmed hat.

'What's that on your leg?' She asked him.

'A knife.'

'Bring it here.'

He didn't move at first, but she stared him down. The blade was long and glinted in the sunlight.

'It's my pigging knife,' he said proudly.

'Where did you get it?'

'Down near the hut.'

She gave him a displeased look.

'You'll have to take it back,' she said. 'It's not yours.'

'It doesn't belong to anyone!'

'Lucky Trapper didn't see it—what if it's his?' Or the girl's, she thought.

It looked home-crafted to her, like Elena's fishing knife.

'Dad said I could keep it!'

'Dad's not here!'

'I asked, on the phone.'

'We'll see about that.'

———

When they'd finished planting and returned home, Greta hid the knife on the shelf above the laundry trough. Toby was distracted already, dressing up in Axel's motorbike gear to ride the dirt bike that was on loan.

'Don't go far,' She told him.

Under the shower, she ran the water hard on her back to shake the picture of Trapper's cow in that truck.

When she came out, Rex was at the back door of the shack, whining.

'Who's there?' Greta asked.

He followed her inside. She crossed to the front door, which was wide open. Maria's voice drifted from the four-wheel drive. It was parked by the pizza oven. The front passenger door was ajar. No one was inside, but the dog rushed out to it, barking.

She had the sense someone had just been here, even more so when she noticed two melons and the pigging knife on the table.

Griffin suddenly appeared to reach inside the car and stop the tape.

'Where have you been?' she asked.

'Here and there.' He sounded vague. His binoculars were around his neck. A bird guide was in his back pocket. He brought the cassette tape to her, brown ribbon trailing.

'I don't think you should play this so much,' she said, taking the pencil she was using as a hair pin to wind the tape back on its spool. 'It might break for good.'

'I wasn't playing it!'

'Who was then?'

He shrugged.

Raffy's chatter floated over from the banyan tree.

'He's with his imaginary friends,' Griffin said.

In the distance was the buzz of the dirt bike.

'Well, I don't know who's picked these melons,' she sighed.

He left her to the mystery and wandered into the shack. She sliced one melon in half. Inside the pulp squirmed with caterpillars. Now she saw a hole bored at the end of each fruit and a dusting of black mould across their skins.

She hurried to inspect the vine by the water tank. Stems had shrivelled, the leaves were leached of colour. When she touched it her hand was instantly covered in orange beetles with black spots. In the vegetable garden she found the same damage, ragged holes in leaves, white mould spots. She tore at the ruined plants, uprooted them and shook each one.

'All this work for nothing, nothing! *Nothing!*' she yelled.

Raffy and Griffin called to her from the banyan tree's platform. She waved, conscious they were watching her lose it, and crossed to the cabin. From there she looked back to the shack, the surrounds. Everywhere was very still. She felt sure the girl was near, watching her. Like she was creeping around waiting to bump into Joel and say, *Here I am!* Or coax Griffin on another walk.

'I know it was you,' she said in a low voice about the melons and the tape. 'I know you're there.'

Greta went inside and sat down at the rickety desk in her bedroom. It had a mirror propped up on it. There was a time when she'd refused to look in one. She braved the truth now. Black hair, tanned skin with a tinge of sunburn, hazel eyes with a rim of green that Joel said bewitched him.

Who are you in the end? Vivian used to ask. The question wasn't addressed to anyone in particular, though a bitter note rang through it.

Vivan's old sewing scissors were by the mirror. The da-da-da-da-da of the sewing machine came back to Greta, her mother's gritted teeth, the snap of cotton. And her aunt's pursed lips, 'If all the money wasn't going to those cameras you could *buy* the child clothes.'

Greta picked up the scissors now. Snip. They sliced a strand of hair stinging her eyes, then dived to the hair at her neck. She found a slender, matted twist. Snip. And another. Snip, snip. She liked the sound of it.

Half an hour later Raffy bounded in to tell her Brynn had arrived. The casual way he said it made Greta suspect the children had stolen her phone and found reception up the tree. 'Come quick—Mum's troppo!'

He stared in shock at the floor. 'There's black feathers,' he said and crouched to touch them.

Brynn said nothing of the haircut at first. She looked at the uprooted plants and destroyed melon vine. 'Yes, well,' she sighed, 'it's the melons that break you.'

She settled into her favourite chair on the verandah and lit a cigarette. 'What's with the sexy hairdo? Was it planned or did one of your kids find shears in the night?'

'Too much of it in this heat. Can't stand it scratching my neck.'

'Ah, thought it might be the upcoming lunar eclipse, stirring us to our stranger selves.'

A smile played across Greta's mouth. 'When is that? The children might like to see it.'

'A week and one day. Two in the morning. Nice way to start December. Blood moon.' Brynn exhaled her smoke and regarded the haircut again. 'I like it. I think it suits you better.'

'I've done it before.' Greta's hand ran across the new feel of it. 'Cut it all off, number one on the clippers, when I was twelve. Gave everyone a fright. My teacher persuaded Dad I needed a shrink.'

Brynn laughed. 'Adults desperate for diagnoses.'

'Motherless was mine.'

'We're all orphans in the end.' Brynn was quiet with her thoughts. 'What happened to her? She was a photographer, right?'

'She left us for another world, you could say. When I was eleven.'

'Accident?'

'They tried to tell me that. Quicksand. A rip. But I don't believe she was sleepwalking into the river mouth.'

'That's tough.' Brynn drew on the cigarette. 'Life's tough. Some learn it sooner than others.' She looked over to Greta. 'When's that husband of yours back?'

'First week of December. There's a water tank to do, bathroom tiles, painting.'

'No cladding on the outside?' asked Brynn.

'No, flywire like the shack, though there's a few fancy louvres, so the tourists know they're in the tropics.'

Rex nudged Greta's leg with his nose. She tickled behind his ears.

'I'm no clairvoyant,' Brynn said, 'but I'd say something's eating you, girl, and it's not pumpkin beetle.'

Greta laughed nervously. Her fingers played with a loose twig of cane from the chair.

'I've been thinking this for a while now. But it sounds stupid to say it out loud, you know?'

'Say it.'

'I keep wondering if that girl I've seen belongs to Joel.'

Brynn looked at her. 'It's quite a question, if you've never asked it.'

The dog found a ball under the chair and dropped it in Greta's lap. She threw it for him.

'Since when have you had these thoughts?'

'Since the night she visited. The way she looked at Joel as if she wanted to reach out and touch him. And the way she looked at Griffin. That was the more unsettling thing. Like she was jealous of him. I think she *is* jealous. That Joel has these kids, looks after them, does anything for us.'

'You have been brooding.'

The dog came back with the ball.

'Why don't you ask Joel about this girl? Or Tori?'

Greta went to find a dog bone in the fridge. She didn't know how to ask, was the answer, or what to do with his reply. As soon as she reappeared Rexie took the bone and slunk away.

'And you know something else? I always thought Joel said his sister died of burns from an accident on the highway. But the other day Trapper told the kids she died in a car fire down near the creek. Went on a joy ride with her brothers, crashed into a tree.'

'Would you believe Trapper?'

'The car's there, wrapped around a trunk.'

Brynn shook her head. 'It's all before my time. Ask Tori. She'll know. What she doesn't know she'll make up. You'll get a good story, if not the truth.'

'Fabulous.' Greta knew what Tori would say. *Don't go there. What you don't know doesn't kill you, but what you do sure can.*

A breeze swept down from the hill. The chimes tinkled softly.

'Truth is, I don't want to ask Tori or anyone else. I feel like a fool. Like I don't know my own husband.'

'Do you think I knew Henry? Not likely. None of us ever knows anyone.' Brynn stubbed out the cigarette with a forceful twist.

23

On the night of the eclipse Greta emerged from the dark room close to 1.30 a.m., leaving a new set of prints dripping along the line. The moon had begun its transformation. A reddish smudge blurred the silver light. She wished she had the right camera equipment to capture it.

The hum of a vehicle distracted her. She listened to the engine accelerate then slow, stop and start. It was near the lake. She walked over to the firebreak to try to see it. Rexie trotted after her, whining. She hushed him so she could hear the engine more clearly. Every now and then she saw the flash of headlights. The driver was looking for something. She could hear music, like one of Joel's tapes, and that familiar rattle jolting over the sound of the engine. When she heard the fan belt squeal she was sure it must be him, home early. But he didn't come up the firebreak and after a while she began to wonder if something was wrong.

She went to check the children were asleep. Rexie followed her inside the bus and curled up on Griffin's bed. She stuck a note on the door saying she'd be back soon and closed them in together.

She found her boots and a torch and started down the firebreak. The lake was a dark shadow. The headlights were gone but she could still hear the car further on, near the meatworks. Everywhere else was strangely quiet except for the noise of her boots. She whistled softly to comfort herself.

At the lake she stopped to listen for the vehicle. She couldn't hear it. She shone the light into the water. The forty-four-gallon drums, the bones and the drowned car were dark shapes. A curlew wailed. Greta shivered. The bird and the lake knew something. She could feel it in the aftermath of the bird's cry and in the quiet breathing of the lake, the wavering reflection of the altered moon.

The vehicle was idling.

She took a track off to the right from Ronnie's firebreak, certain it led to the meatworks. The tree with the *Keep Out!* sign loomed. A new sound penetrated the quiet. Like the distressed moan Joel had made that night he was down at the boulders. She hurried on. The torch blinked out.

The curlew cried again, urging her forward. She could hear the car engine and the tape playing The Church's 'Destination'. She headed towards it and found the red ute parked between boulders near the meatworks, but no sign of Joel. The headlights beamed into the dark. She turned off the tape deck.

'Joel,' she called.

There was no answer. The car, the bushland was empty of him. Blood was spattered along the bumper bar. Her fingers came away from it sticky.

'Joel!' she called again.

Only the curlew answered.

She switched off the headlights. Her mind raked through scenarios. He'd been injured. A hitchhiker had attacked him and was lurking nearby. She jostled the torch. It gave a feeble glow.

Trying not to be heard, she walked around the meatworks, past the cattle ramp and open shed to the gap in the wall. In the torchlight she saw steps up onto the killing floor. She couldn't see anyone inside, but there was a shuffling behind the knocking box. It could be an animal or it could be him.

'Joel?' she whispered.

She heard another sound, a metallic ding near the coldroom. She hid in the shadows. The blood on the car unnerved her, and the state Joel might be in. She wondered if he'd hit an animal, a person even.

A soft clink came again from the killing floor's shadows. Greta looked there and saw the girl's face emerge, lit by Frank's lantern.

'Elena!'

The girl was oblivious to Greta. Instead, she approached the back wall and set the lantern on the ground. A soft light beamed across the floor to a shape inching along the wall. It was Joel.

He didn't notice Greta but the girl must have been clearly visible to him, illuminated by the lantern. She wore an olive green velvet dress with sleeves to the elbow and four bracelets up each arm. Blood glistened on her skin. She edged closer to Joel, whispering, and then stopped, though her left hand was held out to him. 'Joel,' she called softly. 'Joel.'

Her strange cooing travelled around the walls. *Joel, Joel, Joel*, his name multiplied.

She picked up the lantern and moved forward. Her face was a mask in the soft yellow light.

'Take me with you,' she pleaded. 'I'm begging you, Joel.'

Her hand reached for him, nervous. He wouldn't touch her.

She set down the lantern roughly this time. It wobbled from left to right and almost tipped. Her left hand tugged at the bracelets on her other arm. They were stuck, embedded.

'Don't leave me, Joel,' she sobbed. 'Don't.'

Her hand worked frenziedly to shift a bracelet. She tore one over her wrist and held it out to him. 'Take it! Give it to him. *Give it!*'

She shook with the words. Her eyes stared at Joel through the O of the bracelet. Behind her the gap was a window onto the trees, the grasses, the shadows of the boiler room, the hide shed, the cattle yard. The moon was a scab in the sky. There was a new hush. On the killing floor the lantern was the only light.

Greta heard the soft shake of feathers. The girl turned to see who or what was there.

A piercing cry entered the room. No one moved. The cry sounded again, reverberating around the walls. The building was a dark silence. It was breathing them in.

Outside a second stone-curlew wailed.

The bird in the slaughterhouse took flight, long legs trailing behind its tail. Elena ducked as a wing skimmed her hair. The lantern tipped. Glass cracked, the flame was snuffed out.

The girl was gone, taken in the slipstream of the curlew. Greta peered out to the darkened landscape. She saw no one. All she heard was the swishing of grasses.

Joel stumbled to the gap in the wall and jumped to the ground. Greta ran after him and caught his arm.

'What are you doing here?' he gasped and staggered backwards. 'I told you not to come down here.' He was off, walking back to the car.

'Joel, you're hurt.'

His pace quickened. He might try to leave without her. The headlights flicked on. He was inspecting the damaged bumper bar.

'What's happened, Joel? There's a cut on your head.'

He touched his temple and lowered his fingers to the headlights.

'I hit a wallaby.' He spoke slowly, piecing events together. 'I tried to find it. I thought . . .' He turned to the meatworks. 'I thought it went in there. I was trying to find it, to kill it, finish it off.'

Greta scanned the bush for an injured animal. The landscape was turning visible again, the moon was easing out from behind its blood cloud. There was no telling where the wallaby might have dragged itself for an agonising death. She listened for it, and for Elena.

'The car didn't hit *her*, did it?'

'Who?'

'The girl, Joel. Elena. We saw her just now. Her arms are bleeding from those bracelets.'

'There was no one else, Greta—just you!' He sounded confused. 'You scared the hell out of me.'

'She was holding a lantern, talking to you.'

He shook his head, dazed. 'I saw you. I saw you with a lantern.'

There was no point arguing. 'Where's Gabe?' she asked.

'At Connor's. He's doing another week.'

She looked again at the bloodied bumper bar, the dent.

'If I'd hit anyone I knew, Greta.'

'Yes, yes.' Her thoughts were scrambled.

He dabbed the side of his head with his sleeve. She might have believed that he hadn't seen Elena if the girl hadn't been so close, holding out her bracelet. *Give it to him.* Who was him? *Take me with you.*

'What do you want?' Joel suddenly barked at her.

She jumped, startled. His eyes were wild. Joel was changed; she didn't know him. His hand smacked the bumper bar. The beam from the headlights wobbled.

'There's times I really wonder about you, Joel,' she said slowly.

'What times?'

'I could name a few.'

He was fully lit by the headlights and yet he was a stranger. She saw the shape of him, and that alone. He'd been drinking, she could smell it on him. But it was the head injury making trouble, she told herself.

'Get in,' she said. 'I'll drive us back.'

He was silent next to her. She tried to stay calm while her mind replayed the scene in the meatworks, the girl's desperate face, the smeared blood on her arms, Joel's disoriented look.

'God, Greta!' he yelled out. 'The lake!'

She skidded to a halt. They were right near the edge of the bank. Just a red patch of earth was between them and the drop to the water. She had no idea how they'd arrived there.

'Look at that,' breathed Joel.

Out of the shadows stepped a silver wraith, a feathered mystery. Thin and fragile. An apparition, a ghost in the headlights. Propped high on grey-silver legs, velveteen and long and gangly. And a golden eye, watching. It was poised in perfect stillness, with the lake a dark void behind and the night a vast, black mirror.

24

She might have convinced herself the meatworks was a dream, or a return of her fever visions, if the red ute wasn't parked there the next morning with its dented bumper bar. And if Joel wasn't crouched in front of it to inspect the damage.

'How is it?' she asked, frowning at the bruise and cut on his head.

'Not too bad. My ears are ringing.'

'The children are awake, so I can't talk about this now.' Her hand tapped the bumper bar.

'Sorry to come back like that. Unannounced.'

'You should go to the clinic after that knock to your head,' she said, knowing he wouldn't.

His hand touched the nape of her neck where her hair had been.

Raffy squealed from the verandah. Rex bounded after him. All three boys rushed to their father. He let them pummel him.

'This is Rex!' Griffin crouched by the dog, holding him back from jumping.

All three boys fixed their eyes on Joel.

'I'll explain later,' Greta said.

The children ushered their father into the shack for the chaos of breakfasts, lunchboxes, a lost shoe and a split school bag.

'Come with us to the gate,' they said, setting off on their bikes and shouting for him to catch up on the quad bike.

Greta smiled to herself, knowing they'd be working on him to keep Rex, who was doing the faithful thing and running alongside them all.

She went to check on the garden until Joel came back. She could tell he was going to pretend the night before didn't happen. He'd say, *It was you I saw with the lantern.*

She had a mind to go and photograph it shattered on the killing floor.

Take me with you. The girl's face was etched into Greta's mind.

The quad bike returned. Joel stood at the vegie patch fence, hearing about mould and insects. 'The water tank's arriving today,' he said when she was finished. 'They rang yesterday.'

'No rest for the wicked.' She squashed a grasshopper between her fingers.

Neither of them spoke for a moment, each looking at the other, as if there might be an answer in their eyes.

'I thought you were out there for a couple of weeks longer,' Greta said at last.

'Changed my mind.' He smiled at her. 'Missing you too much.' His hand was on the rickety gate between them. 'And I want the cabin finished.'

───────

The truck with the water tank drove in as Brynn and Greta were leaving to go up to Darwin. Greta felt a hint of guilt but was glad for a few hours away. A ride to town with Brynn would be a welcome distraction.

Her eyes followed two brown pipes running parallel to the road that went all the way to Darwin.

'One for beer, one for water,' Joel had said the first time they'd passed them.

Toby had believed him.

'You're a quiet one today,' said Brynn, accelerating to pass a road train.

'And you're a leadfoot, my friend.'

The highway had an apocalyptic look, with steam rising off the tarmac after a downpour they'd just missed. Up ahead a kite was feasting on a dead lizard. Brynn beeped. It flew off just in time. She switched on the radio and delved into her tobacco pouch. Greta took it from her, rolled the cigarette, lit it and put it in her friend's mouth.

'Ta,' said Brynn, blowing smoke out the window. 'Find me some music on this radio, will you? I can't stand these endless talkers.'

Greta went through the channels until she found a blues song.

'Do you want to hear my news?' Brynn asked.

Greta turned to her.

'Someone stole my giant pumpkin.'

'Are you for real?'

'Carted it away in the night.'

'You didn't hear anything?'

She paused. 'I was back late.'

'Over at Ronnie's, eh?'

'What's with your mind, girl? I was on my way back from Katherine.'

Greta wondered what Brynn was up to in Katherine, and who'd steal an overgrown pumpkin.

Brynn shrugged. 'It was starting to rot,' she said. 'Would've lost it in the end.'

She turned up the music and said no more. Greta dozed off into a surreal world of giant pumpkins and carcass hoists. A car horn startled her awake. The hot glare of concrete, tarmac and tall offices with windows like mirrors leaned in on her. Brynn pointed to a metal arch over the main street.

'Latest solution to hot cities. Grow a vine shade and cool us down. Uproot trees for car parks and other architectural wonders. The oldest milkwood in town went yesterday. Can you believe it?'

She dropped Greta at the supermarket with a request for haloumi cheese. Greta braced for queues, jingling Christmas music, fluorescent light. Hazel was a pleasant surprise, over by the fruit and vegetables. She smiled to see Greta, and asked her to fill a bag with oranges that she couldn't quite reach.

'Young Griffin says you're going south for summer. Swapping crocs for white pointers, eh?' She chuckled.

Greta laughed. 'We're not sure where we'll go yet.'

She put the oranges in Hazel's trolley and asked her if she needed anything else.

'No, all good dear.'

'We'll see you before we go I hope,' said Greta. She wanted to say something more, to say she would miss Hazel, and that she wished they could stay longer, get to know her.

The old woman smiled and said, 'You'll be back, for sure. No one leaves forever.'

———

As they neared home Greta asked, 'Do you mind a quick detour?'

Brynn glanced at her. 'Is this an adventure?'

Greta told her to slow down and pointed at the track to the lake.

'You're not going to murder me, are you?' asked Brynn.

'I was thinking of it.'

Brynn moved carefully along, watching out for the points of young termite mounds.

'What's this for exactly?' she asked as they pulled up at the meatworks.

'Photos.'

'I didn't realise you'd sneaked the camera along with us.'

Greta took the camera bag and tripod from the boot and brushed through grass to the missing section of wall. Up on the killing floor the lantern was gone. Only scattered glass remained, scattered across the floor. It could have been from years ago. She searched for other clues from the night before. All she found was a curlew feather.

The light was shifting. She'd have to be quick. Practice shots, she told herself, choosing the knocking box, the hoists, hooks and skinning cradles. In the chiller she found an old vat for cleaning meat hooks. A pile of them was still inside. At the end of the building she discovered the butcher room, with a stainless steel table, a meat band saw, and Vadik's old mincer. The blast freezer's door was stuck half open.

There, she was done. She'd come back when the light was better. On her way out she picked up the curlew feather, and heard Vivian say, *Nothing's ever as it seems.*

There was a hush through the building. Rain pattered softly on the roof. She stuck the feather behind her ear.

'Are you finished yet?' Brynn called from the hide table. 'Your frozen peas'll be melting.'

The car skidded softly up the muddy firebreak.

'Did you find what you were looking for?' Brynn asked.

'Not really.'

'Me neither. I've never found what I'm looking for.'

―――――

Later that afternoon, Greta and Joel started tiling the cabin's bathroom. It was a cramped, hot task. The fan gave little relief. The tiles were cheap and slightly different sizes. They didn't match the spirit level's line. Joel cursed while Greta kept on with her section, pasting glue on tiles and trying to see through a blur of perspiration.

After a couple of hours the fan screeched to a halt. The room filled with the smell of burning plastic. Joel said he was finished— for the day and with bathroom tiles in general. Greta sat next to him on the bath rim. The children's voices drifted over from the banyan tree.

'I have to know, Joel.' The words were suddenly out.

'Know what?' He put the lid on the glue.

She could have killed the question then. She could have swallowed it back down.

'Is she yours?'

He looked at her nonplussed. 'What are you talking about?'

'The girl, Joel. Down at the hut.'

'God, Greta,' he whispered.

'I know you think you didn't see her, but she was there last night, so close she could've touched you.'

He looked at the floor. His jaw muscle twitched.

'I've had enough of this.' She sighed and stood up.

'What?'

'The way you avoid, avoid, avoid. Every time.'

Rexie followed her to the shower behind the shack. She was still clutching the glue trowel. She stabbed it in the ground by the door.

She turned the water on hard. Mud spattered across her feet.

Joel's boots came crunching over gravel. The shower door swung open.

'What kind of an accusation is that?' His body blocked the doorway.

'It's a question,' she said through falling water.

He smiled incredulously. 'She's not mine, Greta. You are. You and Raffy. Toby. Griffin. There's no one else.'

'How would you know, Joel? You shot through after the house fire. Came back and shot through again.'

He was stunned. 'What are you talking about?'

'You always told me you left and that was it, but you came back, fifteen years ago!'

'It was a month, two maybe. Fifteen, twenty-three years—what's the difference? It's ages ago.'

'Her name's Elena!'

He reached under the water and turned off the tap.

She snatched her towel from the hook. 'Your mother's middle name, Joel.'

'So?'

'So it makes me wonder if there's a connection. If she's part of us, our family.'

She held the towel against herself. He stormed out. She listened to him march off and skid to a stop. The footsteps were quicker on the way back. He was in the doorway again.

'I'm going down there to tell this girl to clear out!'

'No, Joel, you can't do that.'

'Why not? She's squatting illegally on my land.'

'It's not yours—not entirely.'

'Oh, come on!'

'You're just passing through, Joel. What if she has nowhere else? What if her home isn't safe?'

'Home's never safe, Greta.'

She let him go. Above her the clouds were shifting. Thunder rumbled in from different directions. At her feet the reddened water swirled in patterns. Grains of dirt that had splattered apart were converging, spiralling in.

———

Joel was the last to the table for dinner. He settled into the chair with an odd smile for her. A challenge or a triumph. The children looked from one parent to the other. There'd been a rift, they knew, and their father had disappeared until sundown. The air was taut.

'These are delicious omelettes you've made, Toby,' Greta said.

'With our own chickens' eggs,' noted Griffin.

'Not mine,' mumbled Raffy, whose newest hen had gone the way of the old, under the rufous owl's claw.

They ate in silence then, until Joel said, 'Danny'll be here for Christmas.'

An electric fizz passed between the boys. Raffy knocked over his water. They broke into chatter about the uncle they'd never met, where he'd sleep, the fishing trips to arrange.

Joel took a toothpick from the belly of a grinning ceramic koala in the middle of the table. One paw was up in a permanent wave. Raffy had bought it from a second-hand stall at the markets. Greta found it ugly but he wanted it on the table.

'They're going extinct,' he'd argued. 'They won't be here when I grow up.'

Slaughtered under clear-felled trees, burned by ferocious bush-fires, mowed down for development. When she was a child she couldn't have imagined they might disappear.

She told the boys to carry the plates inside and wash them.

'He's taken his time to show up, your brother.'

Joel picked at his teeth. 'Danny's on a different clock.'

'One that doesn't go tick tock!' Raffy sang through the screen door.

'Still knows when to fly in from outer space for turkey and plum pudding,' Greta said, smiling.

Toby called Raffy to the sink. Joel tossed the toothpick to the heliconias.

'No one's there,' he said. 'At the hut.'

'Is that right?'

He looked out to the escarpment, the softer light across the country. His fingers tapped the beer bottle.

'Have it your way then,' she said, knowing the girl would have been hiding up in the mango tree.

He went inside and helped the boys finish the dishes. Before long it became a soapsuds fight.

She set up at the outside workbench to make frames for her photos and repair the swan boy's one, which had taken a knock and come unstuck. Her ears stayed with the action inside the shack. They'd calmed down and were all cosied up on the couch. Joel was reading a chapter of *Journey to the Centre of the Earth*. The lilt in his voice made her hands dreamy, so the hammer nearly slipped when she aimed for a nail.

We're travelling to the centre of the earth, you and I, she thought, but from different hemispheres. *No one ever really knows anyone.*

She'd never pried into Joel's past, or he into hers. It had worked for them. But something was shifting in this place, on this land;

under the gaze of the old house, and in the presence of the quiet, breathing lake. The respectful silences they'd kept were tipping. Now it was concealment.

Insects flew at the lantern. The swan boy watched her from his frame. How long did it take Joel to sketch the wing? Each feather was drawn so delicately—the shaft, the tiny strokes of a vane.

She'd glued and clamped two photo frames by the time Joel finished reading. The boys started asking him questions about the old meatworks. He took them through the steps from kill to skinning, cutting quarters, boning. How he cleaned up hides, took off hooves and tails. Salted and folded them. Some hides were covered in ticks. They came off like fish scales on the back of his knife.

Toby wanted to know about skinning and boning knives.

Vadik sharpened them, Joel said. There were no fancy air compressor ones. A saw was used to quarter the animal.

He ushered them to the laundry trough to clean their teeth. They kept on with their questions, about 'the chiller' and 'the blast'—how cold they were; and who worked where.

'Old Devil was on the killing floor with Fedor. Vadik was in the butcher room making mince and salami. Radek, Danny, Gabe and I worked where we were told. The other boys too sometimes. But whoever was in the butcher room stole the best cuts for our mother. Say goodnight to yours now.'

'Goodnight,' they called in unison, as they passed her.

'Your dad Fedor was the boss at the meatworks, right?' Griffin stepped up into the bus first.

'That's right. Donegan owned it, Fedor ran it,' Joel explained. 'It was small, unregistered, but people knew Fedor's meat was good. They had bigger plans but Donegan lost his money.'

'And Devil ran it when Fedor was sick with his gammy leg?' Toby confirmed.

'Tori says Devil was a weirdo,' Griffin added. He'd learned to be all ears around Tori. 'And everything stopped when the law changed and all the unregistered meatworks closed overnight.'

'You know your history,' Joel said.

'Not mine, yours.'

'Why did we close down?' Raffy's voice chimed in, confused.

'Someone died of salami.' Toby had his facts. 'Not Vadik's, though.'

Joel told them goodnight and came to find Greta at the workbench. The questions had wearied him. He rested his chin on her shoulder to look at the swan boy sketch.

'Is that you, do you think?' she asked.

'Nah.'

'I think it is.'

'Have it your way then.' He rested his hand on her shoulder, and then left for the cabin.

She stayed on to make two more frames. How different tonight is from last night, she mused. She wanted to make sense of it, the eclipse night, but the scene in the meatworks kept misting over in her mind.

Joel was asleep when she finally went to bed. The moon's face was in the sky window. The mark on his chest gleamed white, and the six scars reaching for his back were the skinny fingers of a moon wraith. The streaks on his arm glimmered. They could be feathers in the swan boy's wing.

25

Greta spread out her photos on the old door she'd set up as a make-shift table in the cabin's spare room.

Outside, Gabe's angle grinder screeched through metal. He and Joel were building a platform for the cabin's water tank.

Greta had a fan blowing behind her. The photos were held down by small pebbles. The tendril roots of the banyan tree, the boulders near the creek with their ghostly knowing. The cycads in their stages, from the first elegant curl of a new frond to a burned trunk with whitened fronds to a pod holding seeds like treasures.

She liked these images with all their black-and-white tones. They had a truth that colour missed.

She'd decided on a few different series—cycads, the homestead and hut, car wrecks. A portrait of the bush stone-curlew. And a triptych of chimes.

Raffy had taken a photo through the knothole in the hut's wall and caught the nearest set. She found her photo of the same ones. The odd thing was, in her photo there was an extra string.

She looked at it more closely and saw a run of diamond-shaped beads. Vivian's necklace.

We steal from each other.

She'd thought Elena was talking about the bowerbird.

Joel whistled to her through the louvres.

He appeared in the doorway and leaned wearily against the architrave. 'Ronnie's coming tomorrow with the crane to lift the tank.'

'Is Gabe still here?'

'He's gone to pick up someone from the clinic.' He came to the table and walked around it, admiring the photos. 'You could be a professional.'

'That was my mother. I'm amateur all over.'

'They're looking pretty flash to me.'

'Any of these cars familiar?' she joked.

He smiled and pointed out a few. Seb's first Holden driven to death. Vadik's ute, left to rot where it stopped up behind the homestead. The station wagon Danny stole and then burned in a panic. He perused the others. Magdalen's birth car, and the many vehicles Greta had discovered after the fire.

'You must've walked the entire place,' he said.

He wasn't far wrong. The abandoned cars obsessed her. The angle of a vehicle, the way a door was jammed open or a bonnet had buckled and lifted. She wondered about the vanished humans who'd driven them and been passengers. The cars took on a character of their own. Forlorn, forsaken. With a scurry of cloud overhead or a watchtower termite mound behind. Forgotten vehicles made present.

She was glad she hadn't photographed the car near the mango farm. She had come to believe Trapper's story must be right. Tori had seemed hesitant to talk about it.

Joel moved on to the homestead photos. The empty, burned-out rooms. The peacock chair. Magdalen's jewellery box, the ballerina.

He whistled softly at the enlargements of the bush stone-curlew. It had such an ethereal, other-worldly look, it could be the night-bird they'd seen at the lake.

'Clever.' He smiled at her. 'I hope you're not giving it away.'

The photos from the meatworks silenced him. His fingers nudged the knocking box and skinning cradle.

'What happened there, Joel, down at the meatworks? Not the other night—back in the past.'

He frowned a little and kept his eyes on the photos. 'What do you think happened? It was a slaughterhouse.'

'Not that. Something else. You can feel it whispering around the walls.'

He moved away from the carcass hooks to a corkscrew pandanus.

'Did Lennie work there?'

Lennie's boyish, smiling face stared up at them both. It was one of the enlargements she'd had done up in Darwin.

'Tori said he wasn't cut out for here,' she persisted.

Thunder sounded overhead. Joel's forehead was beaded with perspiration.

'The meatworks was no good for Lennie.'

He peered out the louvres. The sky was dark grey. You've done it now, thought Greta. He'll tell you nothing.

The pedestal fan whirred behind her. She could smell rain. As it came sweeping in he sighed and spoke without turning to look at her.

'Devil sent Lennie into the meatworks to keep him from Magdalen. She hated the place, wouldn't go near it. Fedor was sick at the time, so Devil was running the show. But my father had told

Devil if he caught Lennie and Magdalen together that'd be the end of it—no hut, no work.'

Thunder cracked nearby. The room dimmed. The rain settled into a steady rhythm. Joel became a shadow at the louvres.

'Vadik reckoned he saw Lennie and Magdalen up at those rocks above the hut. Did or didn't, doesn't matter. Devil got wind of it and put Lennie on the killing floor. We all thought that was a bad idea. I tried to get Devil to let him do the hides outside. But no, Devil wanted sport.'

'How do you mean?'

Joel turned back to the table to find the photo of Lennie with his catch at the creek.

'Lennie wouldn't do his first kill,' he said after a pause. 'Or skin and gut. Vadik forced his hand. There was a fight.'

'Lennie fought back?'

She couldn't believe it of the gentle-faced boy in the photo, proudly holding up his fish.

'I did,' said Joel.

He's a dog, a dog!

Lennie's voice is hoarse. He's hurrying behind Joel through the grass, clutching his purple ear with bloody fingers.

True, thinks Joel. Devil is a dog.

He sees the mad scrum again, Devil's teeth latched on to his son's ear like a pit bull. Vadik dancing around them both with a meat knife. Slashing the air. Closer and closer to Lennie's face.

The meatworks is behind the boys now, out of sight, but another Vadik scream chases them.

Joel can still feel the bone in his uncle's arm. Twist, twist, snap.

He's dreading the return to the hill, the homestead, his mother. Vadik will get there first, wailing and dangling the broken arm. Maria will turn her head to look at her son. The way she does. Out of that tired pillow. Already he's sick with shame.

He tells Lennie to walk faster. There isn't much time. They'll only just make it to the highway for the bus.

You've gotta get out of here, Lennie, he says. You have to pull yourself together. Get on that bus to Katherine or Tennant. Wherever.

Lennie's stumbling behind him, gasping or sobbing or both. This never would've happened if Sal was here.

No, it wouldn't have, thinks Joel, and he's hoping Lennie won't faint.

Joel's thinking about what he'll grab when they get to the hut—a few tins of food, a change of clothes. He'll have to raid Devil's cash. There's a slash in the mattress Devil sleeps on, Magdalen told him once. Put your hand in, you'll find it. She can see in the dark, that girl.

26

No one was at the hut. The mango tree was a dark umbrella. Rotten fruit littered the ground underneath. Magpie geese were feasting there. They raised their pink faces and honked at Greta, and then dipped back to their food. The air smelled of them and overripe fruit.

Greta slipped inside the doorway with a gentle 'Hello?'

The place was empty. The bowl on the table had no trinkets, and the fishbones on the sink had been picked clean. One of her homemade bread rolls was on the floor, half eaten, over by the clothes rack. Two dresses and a shirt were missing.

She has run away, Greta thought.

But when she looked around the curtain she couldn't be sure. A small case was on the bed. It was old-fashioned, pale blue with crimson piping and a maroon handle. The rabbit was propped up against his pillow, staring at it. Greta clicked open the latches.

Inside was a black shawl embroidered with blood-red tulips. She pulled it aside and found a sketchbook lying on a shoebox full of photos. A square biscuit tin held cassette tapes. Jammed behind it was a small icon, and a little glass salt shaker that smelled faintly perfumed.

Greta opened the sketchbook to find every page filled with drawings. Wings, bird faces, eyes and beaks, children's arms and legs. Hybrid bird children. The head of a bird, claws for feet. Wings instead of arms, feathered legs. The swan boy in different poses. Some of them were rough sketches, others were skilful drawings. No colour, all grey lead. She placed it on the bed for now.

The tapes were labelled with story titles. The photos were in bundles tied with black ribbon. She undid one. There was Joel, showing off a fish. Maria with an armful of pawpaws. Joel, Gabe and Danny on the back of a ute, proud of their hunted pig.

Between the shoebox and tin was a woven mat, wrapped around a crystal candlestick. It was for one candle, with a crystal column and prisms hanging from the candleholder's dish. The foot was a swirl, like water.

Thunder rumbled in the distance. The room darkened, as if someone had moved to block a window. The clouds were hiding the sun, she knew. She'd seen them gathering earlier.

You must go, she told herself.

The wind picked up outside. She listened to it pass through the valley, rustle the pandanus fronds, stir the mango tree. A breath sighed through the doorway. On the walls the newspaper clippings murmured. Airy fingers picked at the roof.

Greta returned the candlestick to the case with the photos and tapes. But she hesitated over the sketchbook. Her husband's precious drawings. The shawl was soft in her fingers. A tremor ran through her. She'd found parts of a dead woman, of Joel's family, of him. And the secret intent of whoever had smuggled these treasures away. Where had the case been all this time? Behind the clothes rack? Under the bed?

The chimes at the doorway rang brightly with a gust of wind. It was a pretty sound, whirling, whirling, until they were suddenly jostled.

Greta spun around. 'Elena,' she breathed.

The girl was at the curtain looking in. Greta half expected her to seize the case and slam it shut.

'I've been looking for you,' Greta started.

The girl wasn't listening. Her eyes were a strange shining. She was like the Lady of the Lake, emerged from a watery underworld. Around the hut, the sounds of the magpie geese wings whirred. The girl looked up to the departing song of them, as if the roof wasn't there and she could see them heading through the sky in their V formation. Greta waited for the slow honk, honk of their call.

Instead there was a fierce thunderclap, an electric white-blue spark. The girl shrieked. Greta was thrown against the wall of newspaper clippings. Outside came the blistering tear of thunder, a searing light.

Greta stood and searched the shadowed room. Elena had fled. On the floor was a bracelet. Only seven were left on the wall. This one was heavier, black with gentle twists. Its charms were exquisite carvings in bone and wood, miniature emblems crafted in metal. A feather, the face of an owl, a bird's claw.

The hut shuddered; the roof lifted in the wind. Lightning flickered outside and inside. Light, dark, light, dark. The rain fell hard now, so that when Greta called after the girl, her voice was whisked out the door and lost. The creek was becoming a rush of water.

Greta withdrew into the hut again. Joel's sketchbook had slid to the floor and let loose a photo, face down. *Magdalen, 14 years* was penned in the corner. Greta flipped it over.

The girl was pale, pale. White blonde. With eyes that were a vivid blue.

Greta checked the name on the back again, and then flipped the photo once more to stare into the face she knew. She couldn't believe it. Elena, Magdalen. One and the same.

It's all about the way you see things.

———

Greta rushed to the door. The valley was shrouded in a silver curtain. The creek gushed white rapids, the rocks were disappearing, changing shape.

The chimes swirled around her, spinning rainwater from their dance.

Tricked! Tricked! they sang.

Rain fell in steady lines from the roof, pelting down truths that had always been there.

'My God—you're not real,' Greta breathed over and over into the wind, the rain, the laughing chimes.

She slipped the photo of Magdalen inside her shirt to keep it dry.

The air shook with thunder. Earth, sky, rushing water trembled light and darkness.

I trust you.

Inside the hut, water eased across the floor. A feather floated over Greta's foot. She looked again at the photo, into those piercing blue eyes. The smile was alive.

Another gust of wind pulled at the hut. The walls bled rust and water. The hanging bracelets gently tap-tapped. Greta stood on the mattress and unhooked them. She bound all eight bracelets with the black ribbon from the photos and tucked the bundle into the suitcase with the tapes. Then she slipped Magdalen's photo inside the sketchbook's back cover, placed it on top of the shoebox and draped the shawl over everything. She jammed the lid shut and clicked the latches into place.

The rabbit stared at her. *You fool*, the little pink mouth said.

Greta picked up the case and, on impulse, the one-eyed rabbit. At the doorway she hesitated. Rain flew in on the wind.

The land had altered beyond what she knew. The creek was white, tameless, pulling at the dirt, flattening grasses, the green hair of mermaids. The mango tree was surrounded by a moat. The track to the footbridge had vanished. The sun had been carried away. The afternoon had fled, twilight was descending.

The chimes rang loudly as she went out into the wind and the rain. *Farewell, farewell.*

The boulders in the creek were sinking. She feared that the bridge would be gone, swept under not just by water but shifting ground.

The track to the rainforest was disappearing. She hurried on against the wind and rain, dead fronds catching her ankles, mud sucking at her boots. The valley wanted to keep her. She gripped the handle of the case tight. The rabbit had slipped from her and gone.

The bridge was still there, partly submerged. The vines and trees made a dark tunnel ahead. Before trying to cross it, she turned. A bolt of lightning dived into the valley and Greta fled into the rainforest. Rushing water pushed against her legs. She passed the hanging car. Vines grasped her wet hair. Her clothes were a second skin. She edged along to where the bridge had sunk. Beside her a rock peeped through. She stepped onto it and from there to a fallen tree that took her to the bank.

She ducked through the fence, barbs picking at her shirt. Ahead of her the gentle paperbarks stood unfazed by their rising creek, and the giant boulders loomed with quiet surety.

She came to the base of the hill. It was a weeping face of rivulets. Lightning spiked above, cycads and rocks flashed silver.

It isn't far, she told herself. It isn't far.

27

'Where were you?' two silhouettes called from behind a sheet that was pegged up on a makeshift line and backlit with a desk lamp.

A dragon and a boy shadow puppet dropped. Griffin stood up. He made a strange figure, with his legs shadows behind the sheet and his upper half normal. He stared at Greta, her face streaming water, the suitcase by her side. She'd been dropped from a storm cloud.

She felt stunned into a new corporeality. The solid floor under her feet was a comfort. Raffy shone the desk lamp on her.

'You're wetter than wet!' He came out to see her more closely.

Griffin touched her arm. She wanted to grab hold of him and never let go. Raffy held out his palm where a paper cut bled. She kissed it. The metallic taste of his blood was a relief.

'There was wild thunder,' he said. 'The house shook and you weren't here.'

His eyes remembered their fright. She cupped the back of his neck with her hand.

'Where's your father?'

'Up at the graves,' answered Griffin. 'They're sinking.'

She slipped back out the door and looked up to see flashes of torchlight in the dark. It seemed no accident for it to happen this night. A mother rising to reclaim her child. A sister facing her brother. *Take me with you.*

Toby emerged through the rainy darkness.

'The ground's caved in up there.' He panted from his run down the hill.

Greta wondered what Joel was seeing, if Toby's fears were right and bones were still there.

They went inside. Toby peered over the scrim to annoy his brothers. A shadow puppet appeared with his sword raised.

'Where did you find these puppets?' Greta asked. 'The boy and the dragon?'

'Miss Rhianna gave them to us, one for every kid in the class. From her trip to Bali.'

'I cut out my own great feathered hunter,' said Griffin. 'I thought him up.'

Toby's shadow puppet had broken in the bottom of his school bag. He thought he might take Griffin's dragon now. Greta wiped down the suitcase and listened to the squabble unfold.

The children are mine, she told herself, they are my own flesh and blood.

She'd had a thought while climbing out of the valley that perhaps the shack would never appear; perhaps it wasn't even real. Maybe Joel and the children and herself were imagined.

She put the suitcase on the lowest shelf in the pantry and went out to the shower. She hugged herself against the storm she'd passed through and the girl who had vanished.

'She is gone, she is gone,' she whispered.

Greta felt a sudden absence; as if she'd lost someone. Her fists gently knocked at her skull. Is it related to the sickness? she wondered. Or is it me? And there was always the niggling question about who'd called her mother to the quicksand. Was it the depression everyone suspected? Or a vision like this girl? Did it run in families?

She listened to the boys' voices rising in the shack, a thud. She turned off the tap, tight, as if she might turn off the ghost of Magdalen too.

Why had her husband's sister, who she'd never met, appeared to her and not him? It didn't seem right. Or fair. You're an easy target, the voice in her said. Gullible.

'We're hungry,' Raffy called from the back door.

She wrapped a towel around herself and went to the cabin for clothes.

It was a new moon again, the night felt very dark. The wind had returned and whisked away the rain to gather its own strength. The mahogany branches swayed. Lightning strobed through the clouds above them. She wondered if a cyclone was forming off the coast. Raffy was on the shack verandah shining a torch in her direction. The chimes spun outwards into the wind.

'It's a creepy night,' he said as she joined him, and went back to the scrim. 'Get ready for the puppet show.'

Toby had been ousted for being bossy. He was at the bench slicing kangaroo meat. 'Stir fry tonight,' he said.

A chef was merging with the astronaut lately. She cut vegetables beside him. Every scent, every colour was more potent this night. The fluoro green tinge between a zucchini's white flesh and evergreen skin; the bright orange of a sweet potato spotting white milk.

Real, real! they sang out to her.

When she went to the table with cutlery she found her father's lantern. She must have walked right past it before. The glass cover was intact, not a scratch on it.

'Did you kids find this?' she asked, but none of them answered.

She lit the wick. Her face was a long distortion in the glass.

When she came back inside she was greeted by a giant bird shadow. Long-legged, hook-beaked. Vicious claws. It had knots for knees like a curlew, and a wild crest like a cockatoo.

'Watch, watch!' Griffin called.

The bird and the boy with the sword were on a journey. She tried to follow the story but kept seeing other images. Magdalen's shining face raised to sounds of flying geese. A thousand reflections in Maria's candlestick. And the silhouettes of her father and aunt on the calico screen around her bed in the living room at Fishermans Creek. Greta had slept there after her mother died, for warmth and company, and because when her aunt came to help she slept in Greta's bed. Her aunt's shape had loomed larger than her father's, and her voice spoke over his. *Be careful what you dredge up. Let sleeping dogs lie.*

Outside the wind dropped. An ominous silence grew until a deep moan sounded beyond Greta's garden. She went outside. The mahogany tree leaned forward. Suddenly a searing crack split the air. The tree's arms flailed towards her. A mighty thud shuddered through the ground. Branches splayed up against the bus. Woody fingers slid into the verandah.

Toby rushed out to his mother. She was frozen in shock. Joel's quad bike zoomed down the hill. He pulled up where the tree met the shack. His face was a frightened mask.

'God, I thought I might have lost you.'

Griffin jumped down from the verandah to inspect the pizza oven nested among branches, miraculously untouched. Then he climbed onto the back of the tree and walked along it to where roots stuck out in a wheel of stiff tendrils. Toby's torchlight flickered around them.

Greta ran her hand along the trunk. There is nothing ghostly about a split mahogany, she thought. How odd it should fall this night. After the girl became Magdalen, whose grave was sinking.

28

The next morning the sun rose with burning clarity. The clouds had been sucked away. The tree was a felled giant between the shack and the new cabin. Greta felt realigned to see it, calmed in some way. The tree was solid. An undeniable truth.

Raffy came with her to see the garden damage. Two banana trees were flattened. He solemnly tiptoed over the broad leaves. The storm had taken its toll too. Stakes were blown over, shade cloth was ripped free and tossed aside. Stems were snapped, leaves shredded.

Ronnie arrived early with his digger and the chainsaw.

Raffy greeted him. 'Where's your possum?'

'He's too big for this pocket now. I left him at Brynn's for today.'

Raffy had doubts over the safety of that, on account of the pig that bit.

'Nah, don't you worry. That possum's too smart for her. Like you, eh? Too smart for your brothers.'

Raffy's grin widened. Ronnie noticed a front tooth was missing. The boy fished in his pocket and held up his trophy. Ronnie bent down to see it properly. His grey eyes were magnified behind his glasses.

'What's that worth from the tooth fairy?'

'She's not having it. I'm keeping it in my museum.'

He pointed to his collection on the louvres. He'd recently added a bandicoot's skull and a nest.

'I'll give you a tour if you like. Doesn't cost a thing.'

'After the graves', he smiled, and then mentioned to Greta, 'That storm come in like a tornado along the ridge there. Lifted Dee's demountable right off the blocks. Set it down facing a new direction.'

Raffy squinted up at big Ronnie, unsure whether to believe that or not. They had a *Six Swans* hut, and now a *Wizard of Oz* wind. And a salmon-coloured castle. His storybooks were leaving deposits all around.

———

'Do you believe in ghosts?' Raffy asked his mother, watching Toby and Griffin run up the hill behind Ronnie's digger to the sunken graves.

He wasn't so keen to join the men and his brothers, offering instead to help Greta with grasshoppers. He was armed with a jar for the job.

'I don't believe or not believe,' she told him. 'Things just are.'

'I'd like to see one,' said Raffy. 'I would like a conversation. With dead relatives.'

He held up the jar for her to see the first grasshopper.

Yes, dead relatives, thought Greta. They had her in a jar just like that.

She set to work with besser blocks and a few old screen doors to make shelters over her more fragile plants, and repaired shade cloth where she could. She spoke to them as she worked, her cherry tomatoes, kan kong and Brazilian spinach. Raffy hummed alongside her, checking his tomatillos, their little green lantern husks.

She thought about his question. And the haunted look of her father after Vivian was gone. His return from a night fishing trip, when the seawater glowed phosphorescence.

'I saw her,' he'd breathed, walking in the door with that stunned expression, the shining eyes of a convert. 'Out on the water.'

'Nonsense, Frank,' his sister replied. She pushed a cup of tea to him like a cure. 'It's grief. Does things to your mind.'

'But I saw her.' And his face turned to the dark window, the sound of the waves beyond the finger of land that separated him from where she had gone. 'I saw her feet.'

Greta had seen Vivian's feet too, luminous under the water. The dream she had that night was so vivid she came to believe she'd been in the boat with her father. She saw herself floating under the stars, and the quick lights in the water were greenish silver, like underwater fireflies. While ahead the mysterious shimmers moved through the dark water: yellow, green, silver light. And then her mother's feet, right there by the hull, just below the lilting wave.

There were no more sightings after that for Greta. Vivian was framed and hung on the wall. After a few months she would turn the photo around when her father was out fishing. A blank square or her mother's penetrating gaze. She could choose which one.

The graveworkers returned mid-morning. Everything was back to normal, Griffin claimed. He had a rhino beetle crawling up his arm, making a noise between a hiss and a buzz. Greta put on the coffee, and pounded galangal, ginger and miniature chillies in the mortar and pestle for a green pawpaw salad. Her mind was on Maria's suitcase in the pantry. How to find the right time with Joel; how to explain what she'd found.

He was outside with Ronnie at the green table. The trill of cicadas drowned out the words she tried to hear. And between these moments, the beat of the pestle, the smell of crushed ginger, the gritty taste of coffee at the bottom of the cup, the girl's words and face kept coming back to her.

You will never see me again.

It gave Greta a feeling she couldn't pinpoint. Disbelief, perhaps. The future will prove you wrong, Toby was fond of saying. She opened the fridge to find the half a mango cake she'd kept, but only one piece was left. Griffin took it out for Ronnie.

'Well, now,' he said, 'can't eat that all by myself, can I? Any extra spoons?'

When every crumb had disappeared, he stood up to his full giant height and announced he would deal with the mahogany. He was going to cut flitches for table tops. 'I'll give you a dried and prepped one in exchange,' he told Greta. He had a couple ready at the timber yard.

The chainsaw's high-pitched noise seared through the air. Sawdust fountained from the tree and fluttered to the ground, with its fresh wood perfume. It was hard to believe such a mighty tree could be so reconfigured.

Ronnie said he'd bring Greta some ready-cut pieces of timber for table legs and stump chairs. He was so keen on the idea it started to take shape for her—long and narrow with slightly wavy edges. When he was done she gave him a bag of long purple eggplants and a loaf of home-baked bread.

Raffy reappeared with his t-shirt stretched into a bowl for red hibiscus flowers.

'You can make tea with these,' he told Ronnie. 'Pour boiling water on them and the water turns dark purple. Squeeze in lemon juice and the water turns pink!'

'Magic, huh?' Ronnie said.

'I'll make it for Christmas,' said Raffy. 'Only nine days away! I'll show you how then.' He lifted Ronnie's hand and placed one of the flowers in his palm. 'There you are.'

Ronnie's smile quivered. He glanced at Greta and back to his hand, to the fragile red love of the flower.

In the late afternoon, Joel and Gabe drove up to Darwin to see a rodeo. Gabe's long-lost cousin had come across from Western Australia to ride. Joel thought they might go to a band after, even stay the night. But by 11 p.m. she heard the red ute pull up outside the cabin with an old cassette playing JJ Cale's 'After Midnight'.

He'd parked so close the headlights shone through the flywire to their bed where she'd knotted up the mosquito net and had photos from the suitcase spread out with a fan drying them. She met him on the steps. He smelled of sweat and cigarette smoke.

'Turn the music down, you'll wake the kids!' She kissed him so he knew he was loved, and sent him to the shower.

Back in the cabin she gathered up the old photos with a sense of mild panic and put them loose in their shoebox. The cassettes were in their tin with the bracelets. Should she pack everything away in the case again, put it under the bed? Or leave the contents revealed?

Leave everything out, she decided. She had opened it and she must show him. The flame in her father's lantern gave her courage.

When Joel came back he immediately noticed the case.

'I found it at the hut,' she said.

He sat on the bed and slid it onto his lap. 'In the hut, you say?'

Greta nodded. His hand smoothed the top.

'It was my mother's.' He opened the lid and saw it was empty.

His eyes went to the shawl on the chair, the candlestick on the desk, with all its reflections from her father's lamp; and the small icon against the mirror.

'The hut was flooding so I brought it home,' Greta told him. 'I was worried about the photos and tapes.'

He put aside the case to look in the shoebox.

'I had the photos spread out on the bed to dry,' she explained.

He flicked through them, remembering, and then took up the cassettes to read the handwritten titles.

'These'll keep the kids entertained.'

He grew quiet when he found the bracelets.

'Lennie made these for Magdalen.' He undid the ribbon to look at each one closely, as if looking for a catch or join.

'He used to leave her gifts. Chimes mostly, like the ones you found, and little tokens. He'd hide them in a crevice or hang them from twigs, or leave one among the rocks down at the outcrop. They'd meet there in secret. If one of them was early, they'd hide, lead the other through the passageways and around boulders with clues. It was a game. Magdalen spent hours at those rocks. It was her haven, her favourite place.'

'The bracelets were above the bed in the hut,' Greta told him. 'One's missing, I think, the middle hook was empty. There should be nine.'

Joel shook his head, bemused. 'Can't think who would've taken them there. Or the case.'

He gave Greta the bracelet she'd found on the hut floor. 'That's the best one, the first. The ones Lennie sent after he left aren't made so well. I guess he didn't have his tools or the time.'

She'd already noted the difference between this beautifully made one and the others. They were roughly crafted and decorated with simpler tokens—a grimy feather, a sharp sliver of bone. A screw fastened with fishing line.

'Who delivered them?' she asked.

'They came in the usual mail run. We had a mailbox on the highway in those days. One sack for Devil and one for us. Now and then a bracelet arrived for Magdalen, sent care of Devil—so Fedor didn't find it, I guess. He'd tell Vadik, who would get word to Magdalen.'

'Why would Devil help Lennie and Magdalen?'

'I think Lennie threatened him in some way—real or in Devil's mind, I don't know. He had some kind of hold over Devil; knew things he'd done. I used to worry Devil'd take him out one day. Shut him up for good.'

'Did you ever see Lennie again?'

He shook his head. 'No, we didn't.' He was quiet for a moment, holding the bracelets in his hand like he was feeling the combined weight of them.

'I had to cut them off her once.'

'Cut them off?'

'When she was bitten by paper wasps, down by the creek. Her arms swelled up so bad I had to do it. She never wore them up at the homestead, only when she was on her own or with us. Kept them hidden over at the banyan tree.'

He showed her a bracelet that had been fixed with wire and leather thong.

'She mended them, every one.' He sighed. 'And never forgave me for it, said it was proof I didn't want her to have Lennie. She couldn't understand why he had to leave, thought it was because of me.'

He put them down and stood up to hold the candlestick. 'Mama'd be glad you found this. She'd want you to have it.'

Every facet and prism reflected his red shirt.

His fingers touched the fringes of the shawl. 'My father gave her this.' His face was tender, for the love that had been there once.

Greta waited a moment, and gently passed him the sketchbook. 'There's this too.'

'God!' He smiled at her and shook his head. 'I thought this would've gone up in flames.'

He sat down on the bed again to turn the pages, remembering the bird children he'd invented, the children who could fly away.

'I can't believe you drew these pictures. They're incredible.' Greta moved next to him.

He drew them for Magdalen in the beginning, he told her. To amuse her or illustrate the stories on tape. It became his obsession. An escape, perhaps. He'd filled sketchbook after sketchbook.

He flicked through the pages. Faces of horror and delight, feathered beasts and beauties.

'Go slower,' Greta said, because she wanted to see the images more closely, the private language between him and the girl who didn't read. How alive the stories were here in these drawings, more vibrant than words on a page. One thread multiplied into myriad fantastical images and tales.

'When Magdalen died I just stopped,' he said.

He turned the last page before Greta could warn him about the photo inside the back cover.

Greta wanted to say, 'It's her, the girl—your sister.'

But the sad way his fingers touched his sister's smile undid the words. She didn't dare tell him yet—I've seen her, talked with her, Magdalen who called herself Elena to me. It might cut too deep.

He held the photo up like a mirror and stared into it. Then he lay back on the bed, with the photo face down on his chest and his eyes closed. He looked as if he were sleeping.

Greta packed the shoebox, tapes and sketchbook into the suitcase and shifted it from the bed. She undid the knot in the mosquito net to let it fall in place and leaned in to kiss his forehead. His hand shot out and gripped her arm, pulled her to him.

29

A few days after the tree fell, Greta began work on the mahogany slab Ronnie gave her. Joel helped her now and then. He seemed quiet after the suitcase. She wondered if she'd been wrong to bring it up from the hut. He was happy for the crystal candlestick to be used, and for Greta to frame Magdalen's photo and sit it by her father's ashes. And for the children to pore over the sketchbook. Yet he was weighed down with his thoughts. You have trespassed, the voice in her whispered. Not that he said it. Not that he would.

These thoughts were preoccupying her the afternoon the children finished school for the year, when Griffin appeared signalling for her to stop. He went before she could ask him the reason.

Out the front of the shack she saw an off-road motorbike. The rider took off a metallic blue helmet. Threads of blond hair stood up in a static funk. Danny, the brother, returned. He might have ridden out of one of those old family photos, morphed from image to flesh.

He tousled Raffy's hair and held his hand out to Greta. His handshake was firm.

She smiled at this blond version of her husband, slightly taller and thinner, not as muscular. He gave Griffin his helmet to hold while he took in the shack's new verandah, the cabin and the mahogany tree's remains.

'Railway van hasn't left.' He smiled.

'You won't know it on the inside,' said Raffy.

He led his uncle onto the verandah. Griffin donned the helmet and went to find Joel. Danny gazed out to the escarpment and snatched a glimpse of the old homestead.

'Can't believe it's all still here.'

'It might not be,' said Raffy. 'You could've made it up.'

Danny smiled quizzically at this boy philosopher and made him happy by sitting in the cane chair the boy offered.

Raffy fished two oval stones from his pockets to show his uncle. 'You'd think these were eggs.'

Danny scooped them up and pressed them against his own eyes. 'What a very strange creature you are,' he said in a high-pitched squeaky voice.

Raffy shrieked laughter and collided with Greta as she passed Danny a beer.

He drank with a deep thirst.

'I want to show you something,' said Raffy.

Danny followed him inside to see the louvre museum. Then Raffy pointed to the photo up on the shelf. 'That's your sister.'

'Yeah, that's her.'

Next stop was the swan boy which they admired together. Raffy put his hand on his hip like his uncle.

'Your dad could draw all right.' Danny sipped his beer. 'Not like me. I only draw stick figures.' He struck a stick figure pose and Raffy laughed.

Joel called from the verandah.

Danny went to shake his brother's hand. 'I've moved in already.'

'Where have you come from?'

'Three ways.'

Joel nodded and said, 'I'll take you around the place, see what still needs doing.'

They set off in the red ute up to the burnt-out house, with the boys and Rex in the tray. A car full of brothers.

Greta wondered if Joel would take Danny to the graves. The girl and Maria kept coming to her. The girl's lips sewn in blood and black stitches. Maria's scalp beaded with dried blood.

They are gone, she told herself. They have been sent back to the deep. Their bones are covered.

She returned to sanding the table. Scouring the wood to a clean layer was a comfort. Somehow it cleared her thoughts of the dead women. Instead she was curious about this suddenly arrived, congenial clown Danny. Joel had whisked him away too quickly, as if he was on guard, wary of his unpredictable brother.

'You never know what Danny'll say or do,' he'd told her in the past.

They came back before sunset, eager to light the campfire and cook sausages.

'Glad to be here, Danny?' Greta asked, as the boys slid marshmallows on sticks to hold at the coals.

'Yeah, I am. Best time of year to be here, huh?'

He looked across the greened-up land, the colours of the escarpment, the strip of gold cloud against the deepening sky.

Toby took a flaming stick to his uncle, who blew out the fire and popped the melted marshmallow in his mouth, sucking in air to cool it before swallowing.

'Think I might stay on when you guys go. Think I might just live here all my life.' He grinned at the boys.

'Mick's business partner Dawson is arriving any day,' said Joel. 'Wants to see how much we've done.'

'Hope he's rich!' said Danny. 'We're all getting a cut when they buy it, right?'

'Yes, but you'll be getting less,' said Raffy, ''cos you turned up so late.'

Toby's eyes bulged fury at his brother, but Danny laughed and licked marshmallow from his fingers.

'What about the others then, eh? No show from them either.'

Raffy didn't have an answer. He held out his stick with another marshmallow for Danny.

'You can sleep on the verandah with us tonight,' Griffin told his uncle.

Danny nodded. 'Good idea, I need to turn in—I'm wrecked from the long ride.'

While Danny had his shower, Greta found Raffy and Griffin at the end of the verandah with their faces up to the lattice. They were looking at the night ruin on the hill. She put her eye to one of the gaps as well.

'I've been thinking,' said Raffy. 'You know how Fedor burned down the homestead?'

'Who told you that?'

'Danny and Dad. Today,' said Raffy.

'Axel told me,' said Griffin. 'He reckoned it was because Fedor hated everyone.'

'I don't think he hated anyone,' said Raffy. 'I think it was because his heart was on fire.'

They were both quiet and then Griffin added, 'I think he was setting it free.'

Greta wasn't sure if he meant Fedor's heart, the house or everyone in it.

———

Joel stretched out on the bed, exhausted from the day, from an unspoken tension between him and his brother, perhaps. Greta couldn't put her finger on it. There was something between them.

From the desk she looked at his reflection behind hers in the mirror.

'Joel, you know the case?'

'Uh-huh.'

'Are you going to show it to your brother?'

'I don't know. I haven't thought about it.'

'There's something else I have to tell you.'

As soon as she said it she wished she hadn't. He moved his arm from across his eyes to see her. She went to sit close to him on the bed. He sat up against the wall.

'The girl at the hut—the one I told you about . . .' She looked quickly at him and then focused on her hands. 'It was her, Magdalen. I know you won't believe me.'

There was a long silence between them. The night insects beat in time with the pulse in her head. He thinks I'm unhinged, she told herself. His voice startled away her thoughts.

'Did she say something to you? Like a message?'

She took a breath, taken aback. 'No. Not directly. She was more . . . cryptic.' She paused. 'Are you sure you didn't see her in the meatworks that night? She was there, saying, "Take me with you." She was wearing the bracelets.'

He sighed. 'I didn't hear or see anything. Like I said, all I saw was you.' He closed his eyes. 'I'm sorry.'

'For what?'

'For bringing you here. Us. I thought it'd be all right. I thought we'd come and work for a few months then leave.'

'I'm not sorry. The kids have loved it.' She touched his hand. 'You should sleep, you're tired.'

By the time she'd settled the mosquito net back around the bed he was drifting off. She turned down the lantern. In the ceiling window there were no stars.

On her way out she heard him say very quietly, 'Help.'

Over the next few days, Joel and Danny worked to move cars at the back of the ruin with Ronnie's tow truck. Mick wanted them gone. On one of these mornings Greta was sitting next to Raffy on the front steps with her coffee when a vehicle purred in and veered up the hill to the homestead.

'Is that Uncle Mick's friend?' Raffy asked.

'The one.'

'Flash car, don't you think?' Griffin noted.

Toby came around the side of the shack dragging what looked like a collapsed human dummy. It was a diving suit.

'That's like a selkie skin.' Raffy touched it cautiously.

Greta laughed. 'She's a long way from home if it is.'

'There's SCUBA tanks in the shed,' said Toby.

'Your father used to dive when I first met him,' she said, unsure whether that explained anything. She hadn't realised he'd brought diving gear with him, or hired it. What for? Diving in Darwin harbour? It was possibly a Danny idea.

'Step inside.' Toby held open the suit for his brother.

Raffy climbed into it and almost overbalanced. Toby righted him and zipped it up to the neck. Raffy disappeared.

'Let him out, or he'll cook in there,' said Greta.

Toby spread out the diving suit on the verandah floor like a floating man.

Greta suggested they go to the hill to fly the kite, she could see the trees swaying there. Raffy said he'd rather play marbles by himself under the house, but the others were keen—Toby with his diabolo and Griffin with the kite.

By the time they reached the homestead, the visitor was leaving. He gave them a broad, artificial smile from behind the car's closed window. Danny was at the back securing a car wreck to the tow truck.

'Where's Joel?'

'Around,' said Danny. 'He was here a few moments ago talking with the dude.'

'Dawson, was it?'

'Sole buyer! Says Mick's run into financial trouble.' He walked with Greta around the side of the house. 'He's keen, wants it now. Wants us all out one week after Christmas.'

Greta smiled, amused. 'Sure.'

'I'm not joking. And he wants a fence around the lake for health and safety. As if he's built all his tourist cabins and the backpackers are arriving tomorrow.' He entered the old kitchen, saying, 'Joel's not happy Mick didn't tell us it's a Dawson-only show.'

She followed him into the gutted living room.

'Sold, sold, sold,' he said. 'All this will go.' He went back into the hallway.

'At least it might help you a little, some money coming in.' She shadowed him.

'Not much. Mick sold it for a song.' He poked his head into Magdalen's room. 'My sister's haunt.'

She peered into the room too. The mattress had been chewed since she saw it last.

Danny moved to the boys' room. 'This is where all the action was—girls sneaking in windows, guys escaping for the night.' His hand closed around a bunk rung and shook it. 'Some of us trying to sleep.' He grinned. 'Do you have brothers and sisters?'

'None.'

'They can be overrated.'

He had a quick look at the collapsed bathroom and disappeared out the back of the house. She found him peering through the empty window of a car wreck.

'Joel's thinking of bringing up his old bomb at the bottom of the lake,' he said. 'We've done it before. Dragged a car out of the river. Gabe brought it back to life.'

Greta laughed. 'It's parked there in the back paddock, right?'

Danny squinted at the shadow vehicles. 'Yeah, one of those'll be it.'

Greta stopped laughing. 'You're not serious about this, are you? The lake is poison!'

'It'll be okay if he wears protective gear and washes afterwards.'

Toby called out from a car roof where he was spinning the diabolo. It whizzed crookedly to Danny, who caught it and demanded the sticks. Toby tossed them over and came to watch his uncle's style.

Greta's phone dinged a message. 'Your brother Mick,' she said to Danny.

'You'd better ask Joel to speak with him.' He was spinning the diabolo higher and higher, never missing a catch. 'Mick's not my type.' He smiled at her, but wasn't taking the phone.

'I'll leave you two then,' Greta said. 'Put Toby to work, wear him out if you can.'

She walked down the slope to the newly sprouting turkey bush, and found Griffin. The kite was caught on a tree branch. He was lining the fresh grave mounds with colourful stones and had made a third and fourth circle by Maria's one.

'These are for the grandfathers.'

She smiled. 'That's very kind of you.' Joel had never said where his estranged father was buried. But for Frank she said, 'It's not really his place here.'

'Better take him where it is then. He'll be asking what's taking you so long.' He squinted up at her for an answer.

'Do you know where your father went?' she asked.

He pointed down to the lake.

The hill was transformed now the rain had arrived, luminous with young spear grass, and fluorescent cycad fronds atop black trunks. She felt revived walking among them.

Joel heard her footsteps and turned around.

'Danny's told me about the sale.' She passed him the phone with Mick's message.

He kicked a stone into the lake. 'I thought we might have stayed another month or so, if there was money enough. But Dawson wants the space freed up. He might take on Gabe short-term.' He looked to the homestead. 'They're going to bulldoze the old place.'

'I'm sorry.'

He shrugged. 'Nothing lasts forever.'

'I hear you're planning to raise your drowned car.'

'I'm thinking about it.'

'Must've been your first, for all the effort.'

'Yeah, I bought it off Mick. Seb and I had it running like a dream, till we trashed it.'

He sauntered towards the firebreak and then stopped to wait for her. 'We need a Christmas tree, I'm told. There's plenty of turkey bush out near the crossing. I'll take the kids there with Danny, do some fishing as well.'

The boys set off mid-afternoon with their fishing gear in the four-wheel drive and one of Joel's cassettes blaring. Greta sank into the hammock for a moment's peace.

The gentle rocking made her drowsy. The humidity was intense. Her thoughts travelled out of her brain and floated around her. She drifted into a half dream, where everything was black and white, like a grainy film.

She was dressed in Joel's wetsuit and an old metal diving helmet. Her legs moved in slow motion, puffs of sand rose as she walked across the floor of the lake. The drowned car loomed ahead. When at last she reached it she bent to look through the vacant windows, unsure of what she might find. There was nothing but the rusted steering wheel and seats. The boot was open, like an invitation. A suitcase was inside. It was just like Maria's except the latches were shiny and new. How enticing they were. Greta so much wanted to see inside. But no matter how hard she tried, she just couldn't pick open those little latches.

30

Greta finished her table the day before Christmas. Everyone helped her carry it onto the verandah. When they'd set it down she ran her hand along the top with pride. There would be a feast. An event.

Inside the shack, the kitchen was a frenzy of utensils, food and Dee's recipes torn from magazines.

'This turkey'll be an experiment in Pavel's oven,' Greta confided in Raffy as she wrestled the herb-buttered breast into a butcher's net.

He was earnestly stoning cherries for a sauce, using Dee's cherry stoner. His fingers were smeared in crimson juice. Globules of cherry flesh sat among ousted pips. He'd hoped Gabe might shoot another goose for Christmas, but Gabe was off fishing with Toby.

Greta waited until late at night to make the chocolate ice cream plum pudding, hoping the ice cream wouldn't turn to liquid so fast, but it did. Danny found her stirring dried fruit and glacé cherries into melted chocolate. She gave him the spoon to lick. He was all chatter about his family's Christmases.

'We had two,' he said, one at Donegan's, and then Maria's feast. There was always an argument between Fedor and Vadik. One time they upturned the table, trampling food, plates, glasses. Maria and Joel buried the meal in the garden. Through it all Pavel would play his accordion on the homestead verandah or the shack steps, or down at the theatre of cycads.

He paused to splash extra brandy into the chocolate ice-cream mix and steal the last red glacé cherries. Greta slid the bowl into the freezer with a good luck wish for it to work.

Danny offered to help her wrap presents, since Joel was over at the shed finishing a billycart. She dragged a secret crate of gifts from the pantry to the tree. The boys had done well with the turkey bush. Several branches were embedded in a bucket of sand, decorated by Griffin and Raffy.

Greta switched off the main light in the room. The coloured fairy lights on the tree looked magical.

Danny sat on the couch. 'I was a professional wrapper once.'

She handed him a roll of paper, sticky tape and scissors.

'They sacked me,' he added, running the scissors through candy-striped paper.

She laughed and opened the packets of embroidered stockings she'd found in the box from Fishermans Creek.

'Those are pretty flash,' Danny said of the red, green and white embroidered stockings.

'My mother never liked them,' said Greta, 'which is why they're still in their packets.'

'Our mother knitted us Christmas stockings,' Danny said, 'for socks and boiled lollies.'

Greta could imagine Maria in her armchair in the living room, needles clicking, cursing the wool in this sticky weather. And her mind on Christmases a world away, with muddy snow and rugged-up people huddling around a metal drum sprouting branches and fire.

'I had a pillowslip,' Greta told him. 'No knitted stockings in our house.'

You're a dead giveaway, she used to think of her father, who'd fill the pillowslip at the end of her bed while she pretended to sleep.

Danny pulled a length of sticky tape and tore it with his teeth. 'Is your mother still around?'

She shook her head. 'No. Both parents gone. I'm an only child, so it's just the kids now for me.'

'Better do Christmas perfect then, eh?'

He ran the scissor blade down the gift ribbon to make bouncing curls. Perhaps he really had been a professional wrapper. When he put the present under the tree, twigs caught his hair. A bauble fell and broke.

'Sorry.' He tried to steady the wobbling tree.

'Don't worry. They're cheap, silly decorations.'

Greta swept away the pink and gold shards. Danny picked up one of Toby's devil sticks and hooked a decoration from the tree. He held it out to her like a gift. Greta stared at it, unbelieving. It was one of Magdalen's bracelets. She looked at the tree more closely. Seven others were hanging from twigs among wooden stars, snowflakes and felt angels.

'How did they get there?' she asked herself out loud, mortified.

Danny looked confused, slowly recognising them himself. He went back to the tree and hooked up each one on the devil stick, then shucked them off one on top of the other to make a tower on the floor. The heaviest bracelet fell from the tree by itself. Danny picked it up.

'I found them down at the hut,' Greta explained. 'Joel said Lennie gave that one to Magdalen and sent the others to her after he left.'

Danny sank back into the couch and sighed. 'Yeah.' He closed his eyes briefly.

'But I can't understand how they ended up at the hut.' She watched him turning the bracelet in his hand. 'You know Trapper?'

'Real charmer.'

'He said Magdalen was always down at the hut, even after Lennie went away.'

Danny gazed intently at her, almost the way Magdalen had.

'He seemed to be implying she was having it on with Vadik or Devil, which I couldn't—I don't believe. But it was odd.'

He leaned back, the bracelet in his hand. Then he stretched forward and flicked the stack on the floor.

'Lennie didn't send those ones. Lennie only ever made this.' He passed her the one he was holding.

'And the others?'

'Devil. For the Devil's game.'

'Joel didn't tell me that.' A liquid chill was moving through her legs.

'Joel doesn't know.' He paused. 'Magdalen was lying dead, in the same bed our mother died on. Fedor had put her there with candles, for a vigil. He insisted. Said it's how our mother would have done it. When I came in Sal was standing over her—must've come in the window, 'cos Fedor wouldn't have let her in the house. That's when she told me what Devil an' Vadik had been up to. But she put the promise on me, y'know? Magdalen had told Sal, but she made Sal swear she wouldn't tell Joel. It'd kill Joel if he ever found out, that's what Magdalen must've been thinking. She never loved any of us like she loved him. I don't mean it jealous-like. It's just a fact.'

His words came quickly then, overlapping. Pictures lining up, converging.

'The last thing Lennie told Joel was, "Tell Magdalen I'm coming back for her." She held on to that hope like nothing else. So you can see how the plan was hatched.'

The Devil's bargain. A bracelet for a favour.

Devil spins a story: Lennie sends his Magdalen a gift when he can, using Devil as a go-between so Fedor doesn't find out. No letter or note since Magdalen doesn't read. And no need of it anyway. A gift is worth a thousand words. But nothing comes for free from Devil. Not even a passed-on gift. There's special favours required, or no Lennie. And no telling anyone what Devil likes for favours. Not a word, or you're dead, and your brother Joel too. Devil knows how to kill a man and hide the body.

So Magdalen visits the hut in secret when Vadik gives her the sign. The game is on. Devil is the ringmaster and Vadik peeks through a knothole in the wall. Vadik and Devil make the bracelets at night. They're not beautifully made like Lennie's but they do the job. Devil tries the forge bowl once or twice, but doesn't have his son's talent.

Greta sees Magdalen close her eyes against Devil's spider-leg fingers, whispering, 'Lennie, Lennie,' to save herself.

Roused from his thoughts, Danny slowly stood up. 'Do you mind if I grab us both a beer?'

'Sure.'

He went to the fridge and came back with one each. 'Joel says this is your favourite.'

She thanked him. 'Did Magdalen ever notice the bracelets were different?'

'In the end Sal told her. That's how the accident happened. Magdalen was running from Devil, and came across Joel's car with the keys in it.'

He went quiet. The Christmas lights shivered on the turkey bush.

Greta could see the girl fleeing the hut, crossing the rain-forest bridge, ducking through the gap in the fence to find Joel's car parked there like a miracle. She saw Magdalen at the wheel, erratic, panicked, driving to the mango farm. There had been no joy ride, only a desperate escape by a child who ended up wrapped around a tree trunk, engulfed in flame.

Danny closed his eyes.

Greta thought, He thinks Joel's told me the car crash was on the property, at the tree. He thinks I've known all along.

And she couldn't remember now if Joel had told her it was the highway or she assumed it.

Danny opened his eyes and sat forward, clutching the cold beer. His fingers were wet with condensation. 'Later I had this weird thing where I wondered if Sal had been there in the room with Magdalen's body or not. It got me thinking—maybe she wasn't really there. The mind plays tricks, you know.'

Greta knew. Magdalen was looking down on them from beside her father's tin.

'But then who else told me what happened? Devil and Vadik, the bracelets and all that. She must've been there.'

He gulped his beer, downing the forbidden truth.

'I never saw Sal again after that. Or Devil.'

'And Vadik?'

'He hung out down the hut, horizontal drunk twenty-four seven. I went there once, had him up against the wall, when Fedor comes in and says, "Let him go." I'll never know why I did.'

'I met Vadik once,' she said softly. 'Not long after Joel and I first got together. He was in a hostel in Adelaide. Sick with a racking cough and skinny as death. He'd tracked Joel down, wanted him to visit.'

She remembered the old man clutching Joel's arm, the cracked lips spitting unintelligible whispers, until the cough took over and he lay back defeated.

'I hope he burns in hell,' said Danny. 'Him and Devil both.'

There was a creak on the verandah floor. Greta looked up, anxious. Was a child out there listening? She stood up and opened the door. No one was on the verandah or to the side of the shack. She went back to Danny and the Christmas tree.

'I thought I heard someone.'

'Me too.'

'No one's there.' Her fingers adjusted an angel on a precarious lean.

He took a sip of beer.

'I won't say anything,' she told him.

The Christmas lights winked.

Somewhere inside her a voice cried out, *How does this happen?*

Magdalen. What are you doin' here, girl?

The child's shadow is in the doorway. She's carrying a suitcase and wearing a moth-eaten velvet dress of her mother's, olive green with three-quarter sleeves. Sally wasn't expecting her.

Magdalen doesn't enter. She's shocked to see Sal is back.

I've come to get my present from Lennie.

She's taking in the purple flower across the woman's right eye and cheek.

Sal in turn is struck by the change in Magdalen. She's been away a few months, Sal, since Devil busted her collarbone. Long enough for the girl to be different, to be no longer a child. But still. The hint of blue eyeshadow, the pink lipstick, painted fingernails—none of it matches the kid Sal remembers.

Four bracelets sit tight up each of the girl's arms. She's nervous, her fingers hover up and down the bangles.

He's sending them to me, she says, and pulls one bracelet lower to show Sal. He's sending them till he comes back for me.

Sal is quiet in the dark of the hut. She hears a tremor in Magdalen's voice. She wonders if Fedor knows the girl's down here, or the brothers. She's wondering if the girl's willingly dim.

Lennie's not comin' back, love. Lennie's gone.

Sally takes hold of Magdalen's arm. The girl's pink mouth grimaces.

Don't be angry with me, Sal. It wasn't my idea.

She tries to pull away, but Sally's grip is too tight.

He said you were gone. He said it was all right by you, an' if I just do a little bit like he says, Lennie'll come home.

Sally wasn't letting go.

Magdalen sobs, caught.

It wasn't my idea. Promise. Devil said I had to or he'd tell Fedor 'bout Lennie taking me with him.

She whispers the last words, twisting away in case Sally strikes her.

Instead the older woman takes her out to Lennie's forge bowl. She stirs the coals with the poker and fishes out a rough circle of metal.

That's not Lennie makin' you bracelets, girl. That's the Devil's work.

Magdalen stares at Sally.

Never tell Joel, she whispers.

Suddenly she turns and runs.

Magdalen! Sally calls. Magdalen!

But the girl has gone—past the mango tree, up between the cycads that lead to the outcrop above. She's left the suitcase behind.

When Devil stumbles out from the rainforest bridge and along to the hut he finds Sally at the forge bowl. She's holding the poker like a weapon.

You keep away from that girl, you sick fuck, she says.

He swipes at her once, close as he dares, then takes off up to the outcrop.

Magdalen doesn't see Devil sneak into the haven of rocks where she hides. Her ear is pressed against a rock wall to listen. She does this because the stone will help her hear underneath the watery sounds that plague her ears. She'll find the right notes, clear as bells tinkling through the rock—footsteps, whispers, a soft whistling.

There's still a flicker of hope in her that it is Lennie playing their old game of seeking each other out in narrow gaps and hidden alcoves, the dark spaces.

A shadow appears at the end of the corridor. The afternoon sunlight is behind him, sifting through the trees. He's a silhouette moving through the dust motes. She knows this gait.

He whistles an odd little song. Magdalen, Magdalen.

The air smells of his sweat, his alcohol breath.

Magdalen, I have a present for you—it's from Lennie!

He kneels in front of her, holding a bracelet.

She doesn't take it.

His hands swim to her. Grab her wrist and force the bracelet on.

The fish knife is so swift he doesn't even see it.

Fuck! Aiya!

His shrieks spike around the rock walls.

She's stuck me! She's stuck me like a pig!

The warm rocks have dulled their colours. Devil's hands are striped red.

Magdalen is quick to disappear. She knows how. He will never find her in this labyrinth of secret chambers and passages that only she can navigate. Her breath is loud in her ears, and the hum deep inside the stone walls leads her on.

Behind her she hears Devil calling, his footsteps pursuing her. She must be fast, and not take a wrong turn.

She emerges where the rock formations end, where the land leads down to the lake.

Joel, Joel, she breathes, willing him to be there.

Her feet are swift across the ground. She believes in the earth, the stones that have eyes and whisper the way.

And there it is suddenly, his car, stopped at the edge of the lake, with the driver door open and the keys still in the ignition.

31

'Here we are then, the orphans of Christmas,' announced Brynn, unwrapping a ham on the bone.

Ronnie's face calmed when she appeared. He was spruced up in a cornflower blue shirt and jeans that hadn't been worn often. He'd brought a CD player for carols. Toby put it on an upturned crate near the table. Joel found everyone a drink and Greta raised a toast to friends and to Christmas. For a moment they were hushed by the escarpment's sunset colours, the brilliant white trunks of the ghost gums and the warm glow of the termite mounds.

'Best time of day,' Ronnie said.

'Best time for Christmas dinner, I say,' added Brynn. 'Too hot earlier.'

'We've been down the creek,' Griffin told her. 'Gabe caught the biggest fish.'

'With some help from you fellas,' Gabe said.

He'd arrived early that morning, making a trio of older brothers to mirror the younger. He gave each boy a lure for a present. They'd gone downstream to a magic spot he knew. The three boys were all smiles on legs when they returned, with Raffy holding a fish that was almost as tall as him.

Griffin and Raffy claimed seats next to Gabe and Danny.

The mahogany table was looking festive. Maria's candlestick was among an odd assortment of crockery, cutlery and glasses from the op shop. Raffy had found a pair of pâté knives, one with Santa on the handle, the other with a reindeer.

The turkey was sliced and the cherry sauce admired. The barramundi was a glistening pride on the baking tray.

'Will you eat the eye?' Raffy asked his uncle.

'Yes,' said Danny, and he dug it out with the tip of a sharp vegetable knife and sucked it while Raffy looked on, revolted.

Toby called on everyone to pull their bonbons. The volley of crackers confused the dog and frightened the chickens tiptoeing along the verandah.

'Who let them out?' Joel shooed away a hen with his bare foot.

'It's too wet in their hutch,' Griffin told him, planting a bright orange paper crown on his father's head.

Joel seemed relaxed enough. Greta kept glancing at him, wondering if he'd heard the horror tale Danny had shared the night before. It gave her an unreal feeling, as if there were two of her—one Greta going through the motions of Christmas Day, from opening presents, to chasing overexcited children to preparing food; and the other under water, trying to catch up with the dark shape of her husband swimming into the deep ahead of her. *What did you hear last night, what did you hear?* she asked him through the watery silence.

'Come on now, eat up,' Greta urged.

Before long, remnants of meat and limp salad were scattered across plates. Toby slipped morsels to Rex under the table.

'You'll make that animal sick,' warned Greta.

'If you feed it my ham I'll chase you with a stick,' said Brynn.

'Dad's father chased him round the garden with an axe once,' piped up Griffin. 'And when he couldn't catch him, he chopped down Uncle Pavel's banana trees. Every one.'

'Those were the days, eh, bro?' Gabe raised his beer to Joel.

Danny raised his beer too. Joel smiled and swigged away the memory.

'If you can get through Christmas without any blood on the floor, that's a good thing,' declared Brynn.

Ronnie chuckled and nodded.

There'd been no blood on the floor for Greta's Christmases, no axe-wielding relatives. It was the undercurrents, the silences, the voices behind a closed door she remembered. Either at her aunt's place, where there was a sea of unknown faces and discarded wrapping paper, or at home alone with her parents, where the turkey was undercooked and the oven out of gas. Her mother would drink the last of the brandy, gather up the plates and take them outside. Then the sound of each one breaking. A sharp crack over the tap above the gully trap. One, two, three.

And her father would say, 'Come on, Gret. Let's see how it is out on the water.'

'Time for ice-cream cake, Mum?' Toby asked.

The adults claimed they couldn't eat any more. But when Griffin brought out the pudding there was a change of mood. It hadn't quite set with so much brandy in it, but was a hit all the same.

A soft rain began, thickening to a downpour. They were cocooned in together, melting into the humid atmosphere with leftovers on plates, perspiring faces, snippets of talk and dripping candles. Raffy yawned and slid onto his mother's knee. His paper crown sagged over one eye. A blue stain marked his cheek.

Toby came out from the Christmas tree with presents for Gabe,

Brynn and Ronnie. Greta stirred, suddenly shy. Raffy offered to unwrap Brynn's present for her. Each one was a framed photo of a car wreck with a dramatic cloudscape above it.

Gabe nodded to Greta and thanked her. Ronnie did the same. Brynn was distracted, pulling another bonbon with Griffin.

'You know something,' Griffin said to her. 'A while ago I saw Trapper's cow eating your pumpkin, back behind his fence.'

'Ha! I might have guessed!' She raised her glass. 'Here's to a happy heifer.'

———————

It was past midnight when Ronnie guided Brynn to his ute to drive her home and the children stumbled across to the cabin, lugging their Christmas booty. Danny and Gabe followed Greta inside, bringing dishes.

'Thanks for the feed,' said Gabe as she parcelled up leftovers for him.

Joel went out to wave him off. He came back with the last dishes and promised to wash them tomorrow.

He kissed her lightly on the nose.

'We're up early don't forget,' he reminded Danny on his way down the steps.

'You should both sleep in,' Greta said. 'It's Boxing Day.'

She returned to the table, poured herself a drink and pushed one over to Danny. Maria's candlestick was between them. The CD player sang on. *O Christmas tree, O Christmas tree.*

'I've been thinking about what you told me last night,' Greta began.

'I shouldn't have said anything,' he cut in quickly. 'I don't know why I did.'

'Where did Devil go after Magdalen's accident?'

The candle flame wavered. Wax pooled around the foot of Maria's candlestick.

'He . . . disappeared!' His hands glided through the air like a magician.

'Not that anyone would miss him,' Greta said.

'Nah, no one's missin' Devil,' he agreed. 'Except Vadik. He might've missed him.'

Greta remembered Joel clutching Vadik's wrist to make him let go of her shirt.

Danny leaned down to ask Rex how he'd liked Christmas. Their noses almost touched.

'Yeah, Devil never came back after Magdalen died,' he went on. 'I heard a rumour he was out the back of Pine Creek.'

'Gold country.'

'I saw him once, not far from there.'

'You saw him?'

'Yeah. Strangest thing. I was down that way with Gabe. We were drivin' past these old gold digs, stopped for a break. Heard that laugh, you know, the Devil laugh.

'He was just a shadow at first, by this fallen-down house. Then he moved and I saw it was him. No doubt. He comes down all smartass-like, says he can smell us. It was hot and still, and we're looking at him when a breeze picks up, rattling dead leaves over the stones. Devil didn't like it, started cursin' us both, said we were hexing him. And then he dared to sleaze on about Magdalen. That was it, I snapped. I wanted to kill him, you know? He takes one look at my face, and runs. I went after him. The ground there—it's all cut up, loose stones. You can't put your foot down solid. We were slipping all over the place. I was thinkin' one of us'll fall, break an arm, twist a leg. But I wanted to get him. Not for me, for

Magdalen.' He took a breath. 'I was real close and he was panting hard like he might collapse, when he looked back at me. His face was white, terrified, you know? I'd never seen him look like that. "You'd better hurry up, Devil," I said, and reached out my hand, and *fffwit*—he's gone!'

'Gone?' Greta saw the ground suck him under and zip up the gap.

'Mine shaft. Even if you had X-ray vision you couldn't have seen it, there was that many branches and leaves covering it. Would've gone in myself if Gabe hadn't grabbed me. So the two of us are staring down this shaft. You couldn't see a thing. It was dark as night. I said to Gabe, "Fuck! I killed him!"

'He had to hold me up I was that freaked. And he said, "Nah, that Devil killed himself. Stepped in the wrong place. That wasn't you, Danny."'

A beetle flew into one of the candle flames and dropped to the hot wax, fizzing.

'I asked him again, "Gabe, was it me that did it?" Because I'd been so close, my hand ready to grab him, ready to smack him one.' He punched his fist into his hand. 'I see it sometimes.' He sighed. 'Like I said, sometimes the mind plays tricks.'

A light breeze wafted through. The candle flames leaned then bounced upright again. 'The Holly and the Ivy' drifted out to the dark.

Rain fell again around the shack. The green tree frogs started up their chorus.

Danny stood to leave. The dog was ready to walk with him, tail wagging. 'I'll see you then.' His fingers might touch her hand. 'Thanks for Christmas.'

He walked across to the cabin where the children had put their swags with his in the spare room. She stayed on alone, listening to the rain. She couldn't go to Joel. Not yet, with all she now knew. What she couldn't fathom was why—why had Danny let her in on it? So she could tell Joel without Danny breaking his promise to Sal? She wasn't sure she had the right to do that. She was carrying secrets that weren't hers. *I trust you.*

Rain mist blew across the table. The candles went out. At last she went to the cabin. Joel was asleep under the mosquito net.

She lit a candle on the desk, and quietly opened the top drawer. A gecko clicked from the ceiling. Her hand felt for where she'd hidden Magdalen's first bracelet. She slid it over her wrist, and then slipped under the mosquito net, careful not to disturb Joel. She wasn't sleepy at all. She could stare through the skylight at the stars all night. Her fingers slowly turned the bracelet around her wrist.

There was something still alive about the girl, something near, despite her grave being refilled, tamped down, fenced in by new stones.

'Are you still here?' Greta whispered into the dark.

She'd expected the silence that followed. And yet she had a distinct sense that Magdalen wasn't finished with leaving.

32

'Where is everyone?' Greta asked Raffy.

She'd slept in. The sun was well up and she could hear the steady hum of a tractor down the hill.

'They're taking that car out of the lake,' said Raffy. 'They're going to drag it up.'

This must have been the talk between the men yesterday after the meal. She'd seen Joel, Ronnie, Gabe and Danny in a huddle, intent on a project.

Raffy walked down the firebreak with her, noting the camera was always with her these days. Danny, Joel and the other two boys were at the edge of the bank looking down to the car. Ronnie's tractor was parked where Joel had pulled up when he first showed them the lake. A long chain led from the tractor to the bank. Joel was in diving gear with tanks on his back, holding a yellow-and-blue rope attached to the end of the chain.

'Is it safe?' Raffy asked Greta, as Danny lowered Joel to the water with a climbing rope.

The sun was high and the poison water clearer than ever. They watched Joel swim to the car. Danny fed the chain from the bank.

Toby helped, bristling with purpose. Greta and Raffy could see Joel moving around the car in slow motion, checking the silt inside. He attached the chain to the tow bar. When he surfaced with a thumbs-up, Danny gave Ronnie a shout. The tractor revved and the chain pulled tight. Griffin shouted. Joel ducked under again to check the chain was secure and swam to the bank. Danny helped him up on the climbing rope. Rex circled them both with wild excitement.

The poison water is all over him, Greta thought.

Joel took off his mask and the tanks and peeled the wetsuit down to his waist. Then he showed Toby how to check the chain was ready and signalled to Ronnie. The tractor groaned and pulled. Nothing shifted. Again the tractor revved. Still there was no movement in the water.

Danny went to talk with Ronnie then returned to the edge of the bank. 'We'll try again.'

The tractor's engine strained louder. There was a rumbling in the lake. Silt billowed across the steel drums, the bones, the debris on the lake floor. The surface of the water bubbled and spluttered. The back of the car appeared. There was a tug of wills then, between the water and the humans. The tractor moaned. Mud skidded under the huge tyres, while sucking, gurgling noises came from the lake, until finally the water parted and let the car go.

'There she is.' Danny whistled as it eased over the edge, water gushing from it.

Ronnie hauled it well clear of the bank. Two deep wheel lines gouged the red dirt. When he stepped down from the tractor everyone converged on the car. Rivulets of mud water laced the rusted shell. Silt and blood, thought Greta. The ground might have been birthing or burying it. Again she remembered those sand cars she and Gavin would sculpt to sit in and wait for the tide.

'Whose car was that?' Griffin wanted to know.

'Your dad's.' Danny circled the car.

'Our dad?' the boy asked.

'Sure. I thought you knew that already.' Danny looked through the driver's window to Greta.

She shrugged and smiled at him. She'd assumed Joel had told the children about it.

'Stand back,' she warned Toby, who was too close to the car that dribbled poison water.

'The seats are like skeletons,' he said.

He meant the front ones. They'd lost all their padding. Only the rusted metal frames remained. One was leaning forward, the other had fallen sideways on its mate.

'Nice work, thanks,' Joel said to Ronnie, moving around to the open boot. He peered inside.

'What are you looking for?' Greta asked.

'Nothing. Just seeing what's here.'

'You're stressing me out with that poison water.' She frowned at the drops dotting his skin.

'One-off like this doesn't count.' He gave her one of those smiles that knew it mightn't convince but would try anyway. 'It's sustained exposure.'

'You need to wash it off.'

'Don't worry, I will.'

Ronnie shook hands with Joel and Danny, and nodded at Greta before leaving. She moved away a little from the two brothers at the car.

They were solemn, remembering their youth.

As the tractor started up and chugged off to the firebreak, Toby and Griffin ran after it, urging their uncle to keep up.

Danny sprinted to catch them, but soon dropped out of the race. 'Old age!' he called back to his brother.

Joel didn't seem to hear. He was taking off the diving suit.

'It was a burn and dump then, was it?' Greta asked him. 'Insurance scam?'

He laughed at the idea of insurance, and picked up the chain lying like a fat snake next to him. She helped him drag it across to the four-wheel drive and hoist it into the back.

'What was the upgrade?'

He found a laugh. 'Another vamped-up ute from Seb.'

He seemed fatigued by the dive, the drama of the car, the weight of the chain.

'Will you finish the fence?' She looked down to where it stopped further along the bank.

'Guess so.'

Only now did Greta register that Raffy hadn't left with his brothers. He was leaning against a rock draped with Joel's wetsuit, arranging empty cicada shells across his singlet.

She felt a dart of guilt that she'd not been counting heads. No wonder things slip from you, a voice in her said.

'I like your cicada brooches,' she told him.

'Will you give me a lift up the hill?' he asked hopefully.

'If you help your dad pack up,' she said. 'I'm going to take a few photos.'

There were five left on the roll of film. Her fingers had a tremor. Raffy's chatter floated behind her. He lifted the air tanks with Joel and carried the wetsuit to him, draped across both arms like a gift.

33

Do you know where we're going? Greta asked Joel.

'Always,' he replied as he drove along.

Danny was leading the way on his dirt bike along mud tracks that disappeared into grass and came out again. As he pulled up at a weatherboard house with a *Land Rights* sign leaning against it, Sandy came around to meet him.

'Aunty Hazel said you lot might come by for a swim.'

When he suggested she come with them, she laughed and leaned her arms on the children's window.

'Keep an eye on those grown-ups—no leavin' me cigarette butts, no beer bottles.'

'Not us!' Raffy laughed.

'And no jumping from the waterfall!'

She gave the car a friendly thud with her fist as they ambled away.

They passed a billabong covered with green lily pads, and purple flowers rising through the water, open to the sun. Griffin spotted a white-bellied sea eagle clutching a limp magpie goose. It hopped to a low branch to watch them pass, then bent to its prey.

Danny was waiting for them further along by a creek. They walked single file beside the rollicking water, through a narrow rock gorge where the stones were deep purple with jagged white lines. The boys stopped to pick up glinting mica, or marvel at a curled leaf spun into a cocoon and hanging from one thread. The sound of falling water drew them on into rainforest, where damp tree roots sprawled across the ground and above was a mosaic of green. Danny and Joel led the way, remembering. They passed old figs with swarming cable roots and were brushed by glossy dark leaves. Greta felt as if she was passing through a womb. Before she expected it, the shadows opened out onto a rock pool. Spray drifted to them from the surge of white water tumbling over the cliff.

They were all silenced, as if to speak might break some element of its beauty.

Then Danny dived into the water and Toby went after him, with Griffin quick to follow.

'Are you sure we're allowed here?' Raffy asked Joel from the edge. 'I don't want to be illegal.'

'Your father's been illegal all his life,' Danny spurted water from his mouth, 'but not as illegal as me.'

Joel took Raffy in on his shoulders, saying, 'Aunty Hazel wouldn't say yes if she meant no.'

Greta went in after them. Griffin called to her to follow him up rocks to a ledge behind the falls. Joel assured her he and Hazel's children used to climb up there. Her muscles strained as she made her way from one rock to the next. Griffin grabbed her hand to help her up the last step onto the ledge. They stood side by side in a veil of spray, the rush of water mesmerising them both.

'If you stare at it long enough,' said Griffin, 'then look at the rockface, you'll see the stones moving.'

She tried it, this water illusion, seeing rocks dance to the same rhythm as the falls. Joel appeared beside them with a grin. He stood with his toes curled over the rock ledge. He seemed different here, stripped of that heaviness she'd noticed in him over the weeks. Cleansed of the poison water, she thought, come home to some point in himself. They didn't speak, there was only the pounding of the waterfall, the soft spray. She breathed it in beside him and felt she could face anything. There was no time, they could be the only people in the world; protected by these rocks and their fierce curtain of water.

'What are you thinking?' Joel asked her.

'I want to leap into it.'

His arms slid around her and his chin hooked over her shoulder. 'Not without me, but not here.'

He kissed her shoulder. Drops of water hung from his eyelashes, beaded his skin.

'Danny says a tourist drowned here once,' Griffin's voice interrupted. 'They shouldn't've been here without asking.' He paused to check both parents were listening. 'But that's not why they died. It was because they forgot they couldn't swim.' He stepped aside to see the rock pool below. 'How can you forget you can't swim?'

He left his parents to wonder on that while he explored a ferny alcove behind them.

Afterwards, when they came out of Hazel's track to the road, Joel stopped the car so they could farewell Danny. His paniers bulged either side of the bike, bespattered with good-luck mud, he said. He'd wanted to make the waterfall the last place he was with them before leaving. An old favourite spot, Joel had explained. And a soft spot for Sandy, Greta suspected. The children held onto him, begging him to stay.

'See you when I'm lookin' at you then, bro,' said Joel.

'Yeah, I'm lookin' at you,' said Danny, stretching on his gloves.

'Hug each other!' Griffin commanded, and they did for a brief moment, before racing to grab the other's arm for a light-hearted punch.

Greta went to him last. 'Goodbye you,' she said.

'Thanks for everything.' He eased the helmet over his head, but kept the visor up to add, 'You can tell Joel if you want.'

She nodded, and then said, 'I'm not the judge of you.'

Danny pulled down the visor and started up the bike. She gave him the peace sign. The children ran after him as he sped away and were met by a curtain of rain that had passed over their uncle and settled in above the four-wheel drive.

The rain became a deluge through the afternoon. The children complained that nothing was the same now Danny was gone. About four o'clock Greta drove them out to Tori's for a last sleepover. As they crossed the floodway sunlit arcs of water fountained up beside the car.

'This'll be it for goodbye to you lot,' Tori had said on the phone. They were going to Bali in a few days for the rest of the holidays. 'Send me a postcard from this Fishermans Creek place, so I know it's real.'

When they arrived at the bridge on Tori's road Greta under-stood her friend wasn't joking about flying to the airport in a mustering helicopter. It was a new river, swollen into a swift body of brown current and white foam, carrying branches, leaves, flotsam. The wet had truly arrived. The bridge was submerged and water lapped up either side of the road. The give-way sign showed only the word *Give*. Tori, Axel, Barnie and Skye waved from the other side. Jed put-putted across in a tinnie. As Toby, Raffy and Griffin climbed in, Axel yelled out a warning about crocodiles. Raffy kept his eyes on Greta all the way across the river.

On the way home she passed errant creeks cutting through bushland, rollicking over grass and between trees. The land was remapping itself. She wanted all the creeks and the rivers to rise, to cut off the property like an island and keep her there in a secret time and space where no outsider could enter.

She drove in along the track with this thought, that they could remain here, cocooned, witnessing a transformation of land and water in which every human element, construct and invention might be cleansed, carried away, submerged.

She found Joel sitting at her table with a mug of tea. He'd spread out Magdalen's chimes in front of him like he might dismember them or was looking for a sign in them. There was a restlessness in him.

'We'll paint those walls in the cabin tomorrow?' he asked.

'Sure.'

When the rain eased he set off to work on the new lake fence.

Greta set up her beads and wires. She felt compelled to make bracelets, as if by making new ones she was expelling the counterfeit ones made by Devil and Vadik.

Of the three brothers, Vadik had been the clown once, she'd heard Joel telling the children.

'What happened?' Griffin had asked.

'He made friends with Devil,' Joel replied. 'Devil ate him up.'

Greta cut a long piece of wire and started threading on beads. She kept arranging and rearranging colours and combinations. The design eluded her, like obstinate clues that wouldn't line up. In the end she left them, escaping to the darkroom to develop her prints of the dredged-up car. All five were good enough, she thought.

She had four pegged on the line when the strangest thing happened. As she adjusted the focus on the enlarger for the last negative, she saw—for a fleeting second—Gavin and Magdalen sitting in the car. They were in colour, though the car was black-and-white. Gavin was driving with a look of sheer exhilaration, as if speeding down the highway. Magdalen laughed beside him, her mother's shawl twisted as a scarf around her neck. The embroidered red tulip rested at her throat.

Focus, blur, focus. They were there and then not.

There was a bang in the distance, like a shot. The orange safe light flickered on and off. Greta finished exposing the negative and hurried the paper over to the developer. The safe light fizzed off. She slipped outside.

Already it was dusk. The four-wheel drive hadn't returned. She went to the fuse box and shone a torch inside. None of the fuses had tripped.

'Must be a problem out at the transformer,' she told Rex. 'Where's Joel?'

He thumped his tail eagerly.

She lit her father's lantern on the verandah. The full moon was easing up over the escarpment. Microbats darted around, flying in close and out to the darkness again. She cupped her hands and called Joel's name. No answer, and no sign of him over at the cabin, or of torchlight at the homestead.

She decided to cook a curry.

'If he's not back soon,' she told Rex as she lit a fire in the oven, 'we might have to go looking.'

Rex kept his eye on her through the flywire door while she chopped vegetables and meat and scraped them into the cast-iron pot. When it was sitting snug in the middle of the coals in the oven she made her decision. She whistled to the dog and, tying him up on a long rope, promised to return soon and told him to guard the house. If she could trust him not to run off after wallabies she would have taken him.

A search for torches led to nothing. Joel probably had the best one and the boys kept losing the others. The phone torch would have to do. She took the lantern as well.

The track was slippery, the red dirt embossed with water-marks. On either side of her the slender blue-green stalks of spear grass were knee-high. A python with a jet-black head and a creamy brindle body emerged onto the track. She let it pass. *The light and the dark, the light and the dark*, she heard Vivian say. Beside her the barbs on the new fence glinted in the moon-light. She followed its taut strength down around the poison water to the raised car.

It was an eerie shell in the moonlight. The four-wheel drive was further along the bank where the unfinished fence ended. Joel was sitting on the other side of the wreck, looking over the water. His shirt glowed unnaturally white. The scarred arm was alive, a rush of silver feathers.

The damp earth was soft underfoot. Spider's eyes glinted up at her like stars. He jumped a little when she sat next to him on a low, flat stone. The lantern sucked air in the quiet. Insects flickered against the glass. Quietness settled around them, drew them in. She felt the presence of the lake, the same breathing that Maria and Magdalen had known.

'I never really told you the story of this.' His hand lightly brushed the marks on his arm.

'The car fire,' she replied.

He kept his hand on the scars.

'I always thought it happened on the highway,' she added.

She saw in her mind the car twisted around the tree near the mango farm.

'It was here,' he said. 'By the lake.'

'Here?'

She was shocked. Here! She'd been wrong and wrong again. From thinking it was the highway to believing what Trapper had told Toby.

His boot kicked the dirt, cleared a space.

'We were clowning around—pissed. Just over there.'

His hand indicated the spot. He licked his lips; she could hear the dryness of his mouth, smell it.

'Me and Gabe, Danny. A couple of others. I'd run the car dry the day before. We came back with fuel. I started filling it, but Danny couldn't hold the funnel straight. I tipped the jerry can too far and dropped it. Petrol everywhere. We were laughing, carrying on; legless, you know. I flaked out on the back seat to get myself together. The others were mucking around outside. Someone must've dropped a cigarette. Bang. The car was alight. Real fast, the whole thing on fire. And there was a thumping behind the back seat, right by my head, coming from the boot. Gabe had me by the leg to pull me out. I said, "Wait, wait," because I couldn't work out that other noise. It was always hard to shut that boot. You'd slam it and two seconds later it'd pop open. When we'd arrived it was up. A couple of us jumped on it real hard, to close it. None of us thought someone'd be in there.'

Greta stared at the moonlight shimmer on the lake, the stiff arms of the drowned tree.

'It was Magdalen,' he said.

The words leaped from his throat. Even he looked surprised to hear them.

'God,' breathed Greta.

The story rewound on high speed in her mind and played again on this new track.

Magdalen was running from the outcrop, but instead of turning right to the mango farm, she turned left towards the lake. Devil was after her, but she had a head start, and there was Joel's car! What a relief to see it, with the keys ready to go! And then the car wouldn't start. She tried it again and again. Devil would appear any second. There was no time to run. The boot was the only place to hide.

Tell him, Greta, she told herself, tell him what Danny said. Tell him why she was running.

But Joel had more to say.

'Magdalen was in the boot. She must've wrapped herself in the old tarp—that's why we didn't see her. I'll never know why she did that. Maybe we were too rowdy drunk for her. And she was wild at me, over Lennie. For helping him leave, and for cutting off those bracelets.'

He ran his tongue over his lips.

'I heard her too late.'

Greta saw it all playing out before her.

The flames were licking the ceiling, the doors, the front seats. The car was an inferno. Gabe was pulling his leg, but Joel was hanging on to the back seat, to the voice he could hear behind it. He had a knife. He was cutting into the seat to reach that muffled voice. God knew how long she'd been calling out. The vinyl started melting into Joel. The air was a thick fog, his skin prickled with vicious heat. His own self might peel from his body. And pounding against his skull was that desperate thudding. The other boys dragged him out, with Joel screeching what he'd heard. His foot set off the handbrake as they hauled him out. He scrabbled upright and went for the boot.

'Joel, Joel, she's gonna explode!' Danny screamed.

Headlights zinged onto them. Gabe yanked Joel aside. Radek's ute roared forward and rammed the burning car. As it left the bank, the boot popped open. Inside was a fiery wraith. Joel leaped after her. For a brief moment he caught hold of her arm. They were all one creature, Magdalen in the car and Joel reaching out. An airborne phoenix over the deep. And then the car plunged, and Joel dived into the poison water.

'It was all too late,' he said to the moonlit lake.

'It was an accident, Joel. A terrible, terrible accident.' Greta's words were slow in her mouth. They belonged to someone else.

'Maybe. But however you look at it we set her alight. Her own brothers.'

'You couldn't have known she'd be in there,' whispered Greta.

'Truth is I didn't get her out of that burning car fast enough. I killed her.' Every breath was a sob now. 'Look after Magdalen. That's all our mother ever asked of me.' He shook his head. 'Six brothers. Not one of us could do it.'

A curlew wailed, and another set up its echoing cry. They called in tandem, faster and faster until one gave the final shriek. Joel took in a breath and wrestled to find a steadier voice.

'There were people who used to say Magdalen wasn't all there— because of how she was, with her wonky hearing and quirky ways, you know? People couldn't work her out. She didn't match their idea of normal.' He'd found his usual voice again, his words were very clear in the quiet. 'But in the end it was us who weren't there. We weren't there at all.'

Suddenly Greta could see all the way through—the water and Joel and the secrets of this place. The car, the fire and the burning girl. Magdalen. Maria. Fedor. None of them was missing. They were all there under the surface. They had been there all this time, staring back at her.

The moon guides Joel in through the passageway. He is thin and vulnerable, passing between walls of moonlit stone. The rock breathes into him. At the end is a tumble of boulders and stones. They have fallen from higher up, from the outside world, the sky even. He looks up at the steep spill of them to the dark night, the spray of stars that shiver.

He walks up the haphazard steps to a smooth platform. The moon's light casts a silver clarity over the landscape. He can see in every direction. From the dark shade of the mango orchard, through the valley, to the lake. And up the hill to the homestead.

Behind him the shack has a soft glow inside. His wife has tethered it down with ropes of vine and stem. But above all his own children earth that little house to its ground. They wake up fearless, and live.

A bush stone-curlew cries. He hears its wail in a different way, standing on this ground of stone in the dark. He hears a different note in the lament, an appeal, a salutation, an announcement. He is struck by it.

The last cry courses through him. The rain is a mist, drifting in. Fine spray gathers on his skin. The rain thickens and the rocks gleam water.

Below him where he cannot see a dark filament passes. It is Magdalen, his sister. She has paused beneath where he's standing. Her palms are held flat against the stone, her ear is pressed to the rock. She is listening to that breathing, the quiet noise of him under the rain. It is the softest keening.

34

Greta walked up the firebreak alone with this new truth. She'd been stripped of a cloudy film. The image of the burning brother carrying his burning sister had seeped into her. She understood everything in a different light. The car, the lake and every anecdote Joel had told about his family. The photos and audio cassettes, Maria's candlestick, the blood-red tulips on her shawl. And above all, Joel.

The camping light on the table and Rex's bark greeted her. It was like stepping out of a time warp. Rex came to her from under the verandah. She untied him.

Everything was as she had left it. The beading boxes and the half-done necklace. The pot of stew snug among coals in the oven. She ate some of it, hungrily, and put the rest in the fridge for Joel.

After a shower she set up her father's lantern on the shack's verandah as a beacon for Joel, and went to the cabin to wait for him. She found taper candles and lit one in Maria's candlestick, and stood others in jars. Then she settled herself on the day bed on the balcony to wait for him. Rex curled up underneath.

She wondered if Joel was at the hut. He might sleep in the very bed where Magdalen was abused. It sickened her. She would have to tell him Danny's hideous secret, she would have to find a way.

Beyond her the rain fell with a steady gentleness. She imagined again that shadow child Joel, slipping out a casement window to tiptoe along the verandah; stepping onto moonlit stones leading down past the red bead tree and in among the woolly butts and boulders. His mother was a silhouette in the spear grass. The stalks were almost as tall as her. Did she know he was there, a smaller silhouette behind her? She never turned. He cupped his ears and listened to her sing.

'Where is he now?' Greta asked Rex.

She closed her eyes to listen for her husband's footsteps. She kept seeing the car on fire over the lake, and the homestead ablaze, with flames reaching from every window, and Maria's voice crying out, *Greta! Greta!*

A hand shook her leg.

Joel leaned over her. She moved back so he had room to sit.

'Now you know.' He touched her arm lightly.

'Now I know,' She found his hand to lock her fingers through his.

He sighed and stretched out beside her. She waited for his breath to slow, the soft whistle in his nose to start its song. The deeper he slept the more alert she became. She turned to watch him. His face twitched with a frown. She wished she had Maria's healing talents, to twist an illness of the heart or mind into an imaginary rope and pull it out through the top of his skull.

All Greta had were words. *It's a terrible, terrible accident.* This hideous guilt.

She slipped away from him to see if the electricity was back on. She'd have liked a fan. No luck yet. She walked out to the garden to feel the night air. The rain had stopped. A dark finger of cloud curled through the heart of the moon. The vegetable garden, the cycads, sand palms and trees were touched with ethereal light. She shone her torch on leaves and stems, looking for any fruit to pick. All she found was a ripe golden eggplant on the ground, pierced with needle-point tooth marks. When she bent to pick it up her torch flashed ahead onto a child's foot. She stood up and aimed the light at the nearest pawpaw tree. A boy the size of Griffin hid among the leaves. His face was a white mask. She recognised him immediately, though he was so out of place.

'What are you doing here, Gavin?' She hardly knew her own bewildered voice.

He turned and fled to the darkroom. She heard the door bump against him, and his footsteps inside. There was an uncanny stillness then. He'd left the door ajar. She stepped gingerly up into the room and flashed the torchlight around the walls, under the table and in the dark space at the end. When she heard a squeak from him it gave her such a fright she dropped the torch.

'What do you want?'

He was cowering in the darkest corner. She went to shake him, but a scuffling at her feet interrupted. She scooped up the torch and shone it down on a bush rat escaping through a hole in the lino floor.

There was no Gavin. Of course there wasn't. *You fool.* She remembered the lanky rabbit on Magdalen's bed in the hut.

On her way out the torch flickered over the developer trays. A print lay sunk in the first one. The image had morphed into dark shapes.

Did I do that? she wondered. Leave a print to distort itself? Yes, yes, it must have been you. The children are away, she told herself. She had rushed out of the darkroom when the power went off, then left to find Joel. She'd forgotten this last image.

A version of the car from the lake. She shone the torch on the prints already pegged up. How innocently she'd chosen those negatives just a few hours before, without an inkling of the story that lurked there.

She crossed to the shack with the chant of frogs ringing in the air. They sang with a quick beat that matched her heart rate. The lantern was still flickering on the table. She took it inside and went to the kitchen sink to splash her face and fill a glass with water. Hadn't Magdalen said it to her, from up in the tree with the silver branches where the coats hung on their rusted hangers?

Go back to where you came from. Fly south.

She took down Magdalen's photo.

'You have cut a weakness in me.'

The blue eyes shimmered behind the frame's glass.

Was this how it was to be from now on? Visions, images, presences slicing in. Or had they always been there, unrecognised? Something in her wondered if it was Gavin, not Magdalen, who was the puppeteer of these bizarre visitations.

From his place on the wall, the swan boy watched Greta bind up the photo in bubble wrap and sticky tape. She did the same to him. The parcels sat side by side on the kitchen bench, ready for a box.

The electricity still wasn't restored by morning. Greta was up early to make coffee. She thought Joel might have mentioned the night before, but as he had been after his sleepwalking and the strange night at the meatworks, he didn't discuss any of it.

'I've been thinking,' she said, as they prepared the paint and rollers. 'Maybe we should go to Fishermans Creek so I don't have to send the picture frames. It's too expensive. And I need to take my father back to where he belongs. It's time.'

He smiled at her. 'I thought you might say that.'

They started with the end wall in the children's room, and then did the bathroom walls. The paint fumes soon made Greta giddy. She went outside and sat on the cabin steps. Joel's story was spinning in her head; and with it she felt that vortex she'd seen in the lake when she was sick. It was the tug Maria had felt, and Magdalen.

There's nothing there, she knew Joel had said to them. And now the car was lifted out, he might say the same to her. He might say, 'All of this is nothing to do with you.' But here on the steps, with the sticky walls of the cabin behind her, and ahead the old ruin falling into itself, she knew that it did. Maria and Magdalen had made sure of it. She'd felt the ominous pull of the lake from the moment she first saw it.

But she hadn't expected glimpses of her own life to bleed into that poison water, or into the burned, gutted, buried vehicle now raised and exposed and ready to drive at her with Gavin behind the wheel.

———

By late afternoon the river near Tori's place had dropped enough for Joel to pick up the children. They came home to find open boxes stacked neatly against the room's inner wall. One marked *Op Shop* was by the front door.

'Why can't we just stay here?' Toby protested. 'Axel thinks it's weird we've got no real home.'

'We're it,' said Greta. 'We're home. Wherever we are.'

Toby was unconvinced. 'Axel's grandma came here when she was a kid, and Tori was born here, like Axel and Barney and Skye. They've never left Lightstone. Axel says they never will.'

'That's boring.' Griffin was looking through the flywire with his binoculars. 'And it's not true either. Tori used to drive road trains.'

'We don't even know where we're going.'

'We will soon.' Joel called them out to the mahogany table where he'd spread a map.

The divining stick had been rediscovered under the verandah. It would be Greta's pointer. Griffin found a tea towel for her blindfold. One, two, three, they turned her around. Five, six, seven. She pointed her divining stick. Both twigs had to count, she said.

'Bullseye!' called out Joel. 'Esperance via Fishermans Creek.'

'She peeked under the blindfold!' claimed Toby. 'I saw!'

Joel circled each place several times with a pencil. 'Done, no changes.'

'You're cheats,' said Toby. 'You talked about it before.'

'How do you know?'

'I can tell.'

'Don't you want to see our Mum's beach?' Raffy pushed him. 'We're taking Grandpa Frank back!'

'What's with Esperance?' said Toby sulkily. 'What kind of a place is that?'

'It's near where your mother and I met. Where you began, in fact, Toby.'

'Yeah, right.'

'There's no pleasing some people, is there, Raffy?' Joel swooped the boy up over his shoulder. 'Personally, either place suits me. Surf's great at both, they say. Beats once-a-year cyclone surf here.'

Toby picked up the divining stick and snapped it.

'Where's Magdalen?' Griffin asked. 'What have you done with her photo?'

Greta showed him the frames in bubble wrap on a shelf in the pantry.

'I don't want her packed away,' said Raffy. 'I want her out with us. Like we have Grandpa.'

'She can go in the glove box with the maps,' suggested Toby.

Like an icon, thought Greta.

———

The last few days passed in a whir, spinning faster and faster. Boxes were taped and packed into the trailer. Others waited for the op shop—the now-headless T-rex poked his neck out of one of those. Wood, bricks and all the items Joel had collected over the months were stacked in the open shed. The shack and cabin were cleaned, ready for Gabe, who would be caretaker of the property and oversee the cattle agistment for Dawson. He dropped in a couple of nights before they were due to go, to find Griffin raining olives onto a pizza base and Toby stoking coals in the oven.

'Thought I'd come and see what you mob are up to,' he said.

He stayed for pizza, and sat up late into the night with Joel at the campfire. Greta left them to themselves. From the cabin she could hear their voices, and then long silences, with the fire holding their memories and the bond between them.

'He's the best person for this place,' said Joel the next day. 'Knows it like the back of his hand.' He paused. 'First thing he'll do is smoke it for healing.'

Greta could see Gabe there by the lake, and the kites watching him from the clouds.

On their last day, Ronnie came over for a cup of tea, to say goodbye.

'If you settle somewhere let us know, I'll have this table trucked down to you.' His hand smoothed the wood.

Brynn arrived in the late afternoon to see how the packing was going, to mop the floor that Greta had just done, and to drink a beer with her on the verandah. Then Brynn said, 'Well, I'll be off then,' and she went down the steps as briskly as ever. No kisses, no hugs invited. Just a last deep stare before she slipped into her car.

Afterwards Greta walked down to the small stage of cycads. The sky was aglow with pink and gold clouds. Thunder still talked in the distance. She wished she could see the bush stone-curlew one last time. It would be hiding somewhere, keen to step out in the dark.

Joel came and stood with her to watch the escarpment's deepening colours. It held them both silent. Like the dark boulders near the creek. A place will go into you.

'Are you ready, do you think?' Joel asked softly.

'Who's ever ready?' She smiled. 'Not me.'

It always caught her out, this feeling before moving on, this knowing that what she saw now would soon become an imprint in her mind. The long highway with its red earth and spinifex tufts would shift this landscape memory, with its magnificent clouds, and the cleansing storm that returns lost children and reveals truths. The burning sands, the crashing waves would become real.

'Walk with me down to the lake?' he asked.

Magdalen's death car was still there, with the new fence behind it.

'I don't think I showed you this yet,' he said. 'I found it in the boot.'

It was the ninth bracelet. She held it flat on her palm, not sure her fingers wanted to touch it. Devil's last treacherous gift.

'I heard what Danny told you on Christmas Eve. It was me you heard on the verandah. I was shocked. And not.' His boot scuffed at the dirt. 'I couldn't bear to talk about it.' He looked at the bracelet in her hand. 'I had to get it out. The last one.'

'I put those other wrong bracelets in an envelope if you want to throw them out. The one Lennie made is wrapped up with everything else in Maria's case,' she told him.

'If I could light up Lennie's old fire bowl, I'd melt those wrong bracelets to nothing,' he said.

Greta slipped away to the new fence and pressed down one of the wires to duck through and stand at the edge of the bank. The water was very still. Above, wisps of cloud wafted downwards in golden shafts. Others curled and drifted across the darker presences behind. The sky and the water had identical dancers, moving in mirror opposites.

She took the bracelet and spun it out across the lake. It skimmed close to the water and sank.

'Not long till you're standing at your water's edge,' she heard him say.

'No, not long.'

They left after breakfast as the sun climbed above the escarpment. Greta locked up and put the keys under a rock behind the front steps for Gabe. She'd left him the coffee pot on the bench.

The car horn tooted. Raffy called for her to hurry up. She took a last look at the escarpment and went to them. The children had stacked highway entertainment underfoot. Frank's tin was hidden in the toolbox strapped behind the back seat. Rex jumped up beside him.

'How long till Fishermans Creek?' asked Griffin.

'Five days, a week maybe,' said Joel. 'If the car doesn't break down.'

The track out was muddy; wet dirt spattered the windows as they splashed through puddles. The land was luminous green. A black-necked stork paused its red-legged step through flooded ground. Sunlight glinted on its emerald neck.

'Are you excited to be taking us to the beach where you lived?' Raffy asked Greta.

'Of course,' she lied.

It felt so much more like dread. Like she was on a conveyor belt with no way off. And the car was a time capsule, crammed with its humans, dog and gear, and their past, present, future. Depending on how you look at it, Griffin would say. He spoke up now, 'It's been a good home to us this place, hasn't it?'

Raffy leaned forward and tapped Greta's arm. 'Where's Magdalen?'

Greta opened the glove box and passed the photo to him. He pressed the frame against the window.

'Goodbye, goodbye,' he called softly.

The green grasses passed by the window and stones flicked up at the car. Greta thought of Magdalen running after her brother, calling for him. He would stop and wait for her, scratching his legs where grass seeds had spiked his skin.

Rex pushed his head past Toby's shoulder to rest his snout on the open window.

At the gate Raffy handed Greta the photo. She shut the girl away in the glove box and stepped out to open the gate. A pheasant coucal was on the ground with its tail feathers displayed.

'Goodbye!' Raffy called to it.

'You're nothing to a pheasant coucal!' Toby protested.

As Joel drove through, the bird leaped up to a tree branch and squawked farewell.

Greta dragged the gate across wet stones, wound the chain into place and snapped the padlock shut. She waited a moment, hand on the top rung, secretly willing Magdalen to show herself one last time. The image of the girl in the long, green grasses had taken a hold. The ever-present sister, following, following. As a human child and then a spirit one.

She looked back up the dirt track that had carried her family in the first night.

Clear as Magdalen's voice she heard the words. *I only ever wanted to look after him.*

The angel shadow.

35

A week later they pulled into Fishermans Creek. Joel drove down the main street and parked at the end where there was a sea wall and steps down to the beach. Next to them was an old bluestone church enclosed in a white picket fence. It faced the sea and a windbreak of pine trees. A labyrinth had been raked in the sandy soil under the pines. The paths were scattered with pine needles. The boys tumbled out of the car, Rex on their heels.

'Did you ever go there?' Joel asked Greta, gesturing to the church.

'Out of hours. My friend Cassie's father was the priest.'

He turned his back on it and sauntered to the pine trees. Raffy was on the beach building a sandcastle. Toby was at the shoreline, jeans rolled up. He yelled out that the water was freezing. Greta pushed open the gate into the churchyard. A sign on the church said *Community Hall*. The green copper bell was still on its post. Gavin and Greta had been given detention once for sneaking out of the school next door to ring it. *I am supposed to punish you*, Vivian had said and left a chocolate on the bench.

The door was as heavy as Greta remembered it. Only a few pews were left, pushed against the white walls. All the other trappings of a church had been removed except for the altar. Too difficult to extract, she guessed.

Hard to believe she was standing where Gavin's coffin had been, with him inside, like and not like himself. His eyelids sunken. His forehead a cold stone. She'd dared to touch the hairs at his wrist, snip a curl from behind his neck with her dead mother's nail scissors.

'Quick,' Cassie Blake said then, because Gavin's mother had arrived for a last viewing before the funeral.

Greta was not allowed to attend. Cassie whisked her out through a side door into the laneway before Mr Blake came to comfort Gavin's mother. Greta ran off, clutching the white spider conch shell in her pocket like it was her friend's bony hand. She'd forgotten to leave it with him.

Griffin's far-off voice called her outside. He'd reached the centre of the labyrinth. Joel was walking an outer path. Greta started it herself.

The thing about a labyrinth, Janna would say, *is there's a clear way out. Forward. It's not a maze.*

Joel drew up close to her on the path next to hers, caught her hand, let it go again. He gathered speed and leaped over into the path Griffin was on and raced him to the end.

When Greta finished she stood between the pine trees. They whispered high up in their branches and she realised she'd missed them. On the beach Toby was infuriating Raffy by tunnelling through his sandcastle. It imploded.

'You're a wrecker!' shouted Raffy.

Toby danced around him laughing until Joel started towards him.

Janna's place was a nine-acre block about twelve kilometres out of town. She came out to greet them. A magpie carolled welcome from the balcony railing.

Janna squeezed Greta tight. 'I haven't seen you for so long.'

They spent a moment remembering each other, smiling at their older faces, flecks of grey hair. After bringing in bags and setting up the children to sleep in the living room, and herself and Joel in the spare room, Greta unwrapped the photo frames.

'Perfect, perfect,' Janna smiled, handing her a cup of chai. 'Sarah will pick them up tomorrow. She's organising the show, she'll love them. She's keen to meet you.' She quietened, taking in the homestead images. 'You know you can stay here, come to the opening.'

'We'll move on before then,' Greta said. 'But thanks.'

'I don't think there's anyone left here who'd remember you,' Janna said.

'Art shows aren't my scene, even friendly amateur ones.'

Greta set her father's tin on the windowsill.

'You're taking him to the quiet inlet?'

Greta nodded. 'Tomorrow. I've booked a boat.'

'You waste no time.'

'I'll settle him first and then concentrate on those boxes. Gives me the chance to visit him if I want.' She sipped her tea. 'Show me this shipping container.'

They walked through the house paddock, past candlebark gum trees and red gums with burls and long, peeling strips of bark. A brown kookaburra laughed the old way Greta knew.

The door to the container opened with a screech. A musty, damp breath exhaled from the dim space inside. Greta shone her torch across boxes stacked to the ceiling and furniture draped in old sheets. She lifted a cover from an armchair. It had tilted to the side. The leg was chewed short. Deposits of wood dust spotted the floor. Behind it her father's fishing nets were disintegrating.

It gave her a surreal feeling to see her mother's photo boxes. She remembered how they'd lined the shelves in their house. Now they were damaged from damp and insects. Greta's heart sank. The prints were stuck together and eaten away. When she touched them silverfish streamed from the sides. The next box fell apart in her hands. Shreds of paper slipped out in a waterfall of powdery dust.

Janna covered her mouth in horror. 'Oh God, Greta, I'm so sorry.'

'It's not your fault. I shouldn't have left them here like this. I don't know why I did.'

'You had to leave, that's why,' said Janna.

'Yes, I had to leave.'

She felt a surge of guilt to discover corroding cameras and mould-spotted lenses. On the back shelf was a last box of black-and-white photos. She managed to prise a few prints free. Among them was a self-portrait of Vivian looking out a window. Light was cast over her face, but her body was part of the room's shadows. Which window was it, Greta tried to remember. She found one photo of her father's fishing boat. None of him. At the bottom of the pile was a photo of a small beach cave set into sandstone rock. Vines dangled over the entrance. An unreadable sign stood to the left. The photo had a haunted, timeless look. It could have been taken years ago or yesterday. There was no date on the back.

She took the photos of the cave, her mother and her father's boat and said, 'Not much point keeping on looking for now. Most of this is for the tip.'

The river was a few kilometres from Janna's place. They pulled up not long after sunrise. Greta wanted to avoid people. They were the only ones in the car park. The children followed her to the remains of the riverside cottage her father had loved and her mother hated. Greta felt herself standing between them, feet parted evenly in the sand. The house looked as if it had tried to walk to the sea.

The front room had nosedived and broken free from its other half. Sand mounds had gathered inside. Orange tape surrounded the site. A council notice flapped in the wind: *Condemned.*

The cottage was the last in a row of five fishing shacks and sheds on a rib of land that edged the river. They were all abandoned. Vandalised by humans and the weather. The river had changed its course, widened, eaten away at the earth.

In front of the collapsed house a finger of land jutted out to sea. The water was a confused swirl there, where the river and the sea met to converse, to pull with and against each other.

'Did you ever bring me here?' asked Raffy.

She looked down at him and remembered her own salty innocence.

'Yes. You were two the last time.'

Raffy had sat on the floor and clutched the old man's toes. Her father had looked at her with the sea still shifting in his eyes. Griffin had asked to see through the binoculars. Frank drew his grandson in close and held them up for the boy at first because they were heavy. In the end he said, 'Keep them.'

'We'll be back, Dad,' she'd promised.

But they hadn't made it in time.

Rex barked, jolting her back to now. She breathed in the place, the beach to her right where the land swept around in an arc of sand and the sea churned hidden currents into waves. The calmer town beach was around the point. It had seemed far off to her once, another world in the distance.

Behind her, Toby dragged a belt of sand-coated kelp and called his brothers for tug-of-war. Rex leaped around him.

Raffy ignored them. His gaze was on a flying pelican. He ran underneath it, arms held out like wings. Griffin didn't respond either. He was at the river.

'Careful, Griffin!' she called out.

Careful of the deep, swift river with its deadly pull beneath the surface.

I can feel it snatching pieces of me away, Vivian used to whisper.

Greta let the wind push her in Griffin's direction. He was inspecting her father's old jetty. It had sunk a little way underwater and was ensnared by reeds.

'Don't try to walk on it,' she cautioned him.

He crouched to find a flat stone and skipped it out over the water. A moorhen came running and jumped into the adjacent reeds where her chicks peeped.

Joel whistled to Greta on his way across the sand. He was carrying the tin.

They all walked upstream to a pontoon. It was much sturdier than the one she'd known. Made to last, her father would say. How strange to be on a floating platform, holding him this way. It was like waiting for a boat to the underworld with a temporary pass.

'Can I take a photo?' Griffin asked.

She nodded and he took the camera.

He crept up behind a cormorant on a pylon drying its wings. She heard the shutter click. The bird didn't move. Clever boy, she thought. Frank would have liked to see it. He would have liked to see all three children here where the river and the sea met.

The burbling engine of a vessel came through the quiet. The sound of it and the whiff of fuel clothed her in an old self, the child that used to stand here.

The boat was called *Kingfisher* and the owner, Sol, was cheery enough. Crab pots, fishing lines, buckets and nets were stacked on one side of the deck. The engine room had a slim berth in it. He didn't say much but was happy for the boys and Joel to stand with him. Greta sat with her back to the engine room and her father's tin beside her.

They went upstream to a bend in the river and entered a narrow estuary lined with rushes. A pelican flew ahead of them.

Sol manoeuvred the vessel alongside a small jetty. He helped each of them step out over the gap between the boat and the pier. The jetty shuddered under the children's feet as they hurried ahead, calling out thanks. The boat honked a farewell.

Greta led the way along a track through bushland.

'Are you sure there's not quicksand here?' Raffy asked.

'Positive,' said Greta.

He hooked his finger through a belt loop in her jeans because both her hands were carrying the tin. It seemed heavier than usual. She wondered if it was because she was about to release him.

The beach was a quiet inlet. She'd often camped here with her father. They'd fish and melt marshmallows in the campfire and lie back to watch shooting stars. The dunes she'd known had eroded to low platforms. The beach was strewn with fallen trees weathered to a silver grey by rain and wind, sand and water.

'Do you think Grandpa will mind that it's not his beach near the river?' Raffy wanted to know.

'You can't own a beach,' growled Toby.

'It's all the same water in the end.' Greta led them across hot sand to the shoreline where they could walk without burning their feet.

'You could've done this over the side of the boat,' Toby pointed out.

'I'd rather stand with him.'

She found her spot in the end, where a dead tree's branches met lapping waves.

Joel followed her into the water. Griffin kept by her side. Raffy walked behind, placing his feet in the dents she left on the sandy floor. Toby waited at the shore, his toes just touching the foam edges of a broken wave.

'I don't want them sticking to me,' he said about the ashes.

Rex stayed with him, darting left and right and then stopping to watch Greta.

The sun burned her shoulders. A faint smell of bushfire smoke wafted in. She waded into the water, relieved at the coolness, the clarity of the sea.

'Stand upwind of me,' she told the others.

If she'd thought ahead she might have brought some words. Instead she looked to the horizon, that thin blue line between sea and sky that had always fascinated her. The line that doesn't exist.

A Pacific gull glided low to the water to skim up a fish and fly on.

It was enough. Frank wouldn't have wanted more.

The stream of ash sifted quickly down. Sand meeting sand.

'Now they will find each other,' said Raffy. 'Vivian and Frank.'

He kept watch over the water for his grandmother's spirit. She would come through the water and find her man. Griffin patted the surface of the water softly. Joel put his hand on Greta's shoulder.

She rinsed out the tin. She was tempted to let it sink and become the home of sea creatures. Toby would tell her she was littering. She held it out for Joel to carry. Griffin waited behind. His left hand was raised. Her mother's broken necklace was threaded between his fingers. He smiled at her and let the beads slip into the water.

'Frank might like them,' he said quietly, without a flicker of guilt.

They waded back to shore side by side.

Toby gamely checked inside the emptied tin while his parents loitered at the shoreline. The breeze picked up, and with it a gentle swell. Waves curved, sighed, broke, pulled back and made themselves again.

'Well,' said Joel, 'we have buried them.'

Greta smiled but didn't answer. The hot sun made her cheeks tingle. She turned to look at the dunes, the melaleuca, the banksias. She half expected to see Magdalen there, watching. Vivian even, with her bright headscarf. Or her father in his green-and-black flannel shirt, moving along in that steady, stooped-shoulder walk.

They are never buried, she thought. They are only set free, or not.

36

After Greta's last run to the op shop and the tip she parked at the beach wall and took the main steps down to the sand. Joel was there with the children. Toby and Griffin were floating on lilos near the lone pylons of a long-gone jetty.

'Don't let them go out too far,' she reminded Joel. 'There's tricky currents.' She licked her lower lip. It was cracked and peeling in this dry, hot weather.

Raffy tapped her arm. 'Shut your eyes!' He pressed a secret into her hand. 'Open!'

It was an abalone shell, rough side facing her.

'You'd think it was nothing,' he said, and flipped it over to reveal the pearl and rainbow shimmers on the other side. 'You can have it,' he said. 'It's my gift to you.'

Like the girl with her amethyst and her insights. *You have lost someone. Someone very young.*

She called out her thanks, and then said to Joel, 'I think I'll go for a walk around the point.'

There was a reef there, where the waves turned rough like the beach near the river mouth.

Joel stood to brush sand from himself and see where she meant. 'That's quite a way.'

'I like a long walk. You can drive over when you're finished here. Take a look at the surf. There's a lighthouse the boys might like to see.'

'Uh-huh.' He looked out to the horizon where clouds were gathering. 'That cool change'll be here soon.'

Already they could feel the wind's new direction and a drop in temperature.

'Will your camera be all right if there's a downpour?' He pointed to the bag over her shoulder.

'I'm taking my chances.'

He lifted her cap and kissed her nose. 'We'll see you there.'

She walked close to the waterline, where the foam sneaked over her toes. The tide was coming in. A child shouted for her to beware a flying cricket ball. She ducked just in time. The smell of freshly ground coffee wafted from the beachfront cafe that had been a store when she was young. It had a balcony now and tables with brightly coloured umbrellas. She passed the pine trees in front of the labyrinth and church. The bluestone wall ended. The white-yellow dunes of her childhood loomed near.

The sandhills had more vegetation than she remembered. Coastal tea trees had taken root, and the green-blue grasses were a thick chorus, all blowing in one direction. She paused at the tallest slope, where she and Gavin used to toboggan on plastic bags. In the wind she heard his excited shrieks, that distinctive shout.

Behind the dunes the caravan park flag flapped, its ropes clanging against the pole. It whipped so fiercely she thought it might rip.

She hurried on to the point, eager to leave this beach and find the surf around the corner. It took her longer than she expected to climb across the rocks. She kept losing her footing and changing her mind about which way to go. Waves licked at the rock platform. Spray flew to her on the breeze. Puffs of foam wobbled in rock pools. Sun-hot stones bit her underfoot. She was puffed out by the time she jumped down to the sand on the other side. A timber post met her there like an entry guard, decorated with a seaweed scarf and a small tower of sea-smooth pebbles and shells. Raffy would like it.

Ahead of her the crescent beach was cast in a mist of spray and sunlight. Perfect waves curled and broke along the slope of the shoreline. Shells rattled backwards with the retreating water, only to be flung forward again with the thud of a new wave. Midway along the beach, wooden steps led up to a slat path that wound back through dune grasses to a car park she couldn't see.

The next point was a cliff with the lighthouse perched on top. It was automated now; no lighthouse keeper lived there. When she was young she had thought of the lighthouse as a friend, the searchlight that might find her mother out there in the ocean. She had trusted it. Until the nightmares came. Then she was creeping behind the rocks at the bottom of this cliff, trying to escape the fierce light with its endless sweeping rotations and glaring truth.

She listened for her children's voices in case they had arrived at the car park above. They would go to the lighthouse first, she predicted, before coming down to the beach. Each boy would want a turn with the tourist binoculars and have to hunt for coins. She could smell a hot chips or doughnut van. It made her hungry.

The wind sang a high-pitched tune and flicked her hair back from her face. Her eyes stung.

What are you waiting for? she heard Magdalen say, so close she might be hiding behind that tumble of rocks outside the cave entrance. It had been blocked off with a metal grate. The creeper was gone and there was no signpost as there had been in Vivian's photograph. The sign hadn't been there when Gavin found it either, a year after Vivian's death. What a discovery that was, and how excited he was to show her this little haven where an animal or shipwrecked soul might shelter when the tide was high and furious. For a child aged twelve and her nine-year old friend it was perfect, especially when sandstorms swept along the beach or the weather turned quickly into lightning and rain.

Closer, closer, the voice inside Greta said.

Inside her and outside her, flitting across the rocks in that singsong way that could be Gavin or Griffin or Magdalen.

When she first saw the cave all those years ago, it had looked like a mouth, and the sandstone rocks above made eyes and a nose. The clinging creeper was hair. Now it was an erased face, swept flat by the wind, the waves, an invisible giant hand. Stones and rocks were piled up in front of the grate.

Greta remembered her camera and fumbled with the lens cap. It dropped on the sand. She picked it up, blew away the grains and put the cap in her back pocket with her father's watch. Her fingers had that annoying tremor when she tried to focus. She could have sworn Magdalen was behind her. I will look in a second, she thought. Click.

———

They think the cubby is for just the two of them, Greta and Gavin. But the older boys move in on them like engineers. Muddy Cooper reckons it's his, because it was his dad's idea to dig out a tunnel for hiding contraband stuff. The vines hanging from the rocks were a useful curtain. Hardly anyone knew the cave was there back in the day. There were no steps up to a car park.

He says he and his mates are going to start up the tunnel again. He declares Greta and Gavin are out of the picture. They watch from a distance and spy from behind rocks. There are fights and secret conversations among the older gang. But in the end the project is their bond.

Over the summer the cave deepens. The boys bring in spades and mattocks. They drag railway sleepers from the old train line and carry them to their tunnel. They use them for supports inside.

One morning Greta asks to see the progress. She's chased off with rocks and flying seaweed and verbal abuse. She reports back to Gavin. The place they'd thought was theirs is even more forbidden.

Until the day of the football match. The bus draws away to cheers from a small crowd of parents and locals whose boys are fighting for a place in the finals up in the big city. They head for the pub to wait for news of victory.

Gavin and Greta aren't waving off the footy team. They're sliding down dunes on plastic bags.

'Let's go to the point,' says Gavin when they have wearied of their game.

He flies off with the wind, an eager sprite. Greta can't hear all the words of his song. The wind snatches them away. Sand streams ahead in floating ribbons. Clouds move swiftly in from the horizon. The waves leap higher and alter in colour from turquoise to navy blue. By the time the children reach the point the moods of the sea and sky have turned. The clouds are one great stretch of deep grey. Underneath, the waves heighten and curl white lips. Lightning forks into the sea.

'Let's hide in the cave around the point,' Greta says. 'Wait for the storm to blow over.' Rain stings her face. Gavin looks uncertain. His plastic bag flaps in the wind.

'We can leave the bags here,' she says, and weighs hers down with a rock, signalling for him to do the same.

They start the climb around the point. It's high tide. Waves spill across the reef's rock pools and tumble into crevices. Now and then a bigger wave races up to break against the first line of boulders. Water splashes over the children. Greta feels a shudder beneath her. The weight of the sea is pressing in. It is a relief to reach the other side and clamber down. Rain bites into her skin. She struggles up the sand to the cave. The wind buffets her sideways.

'What if the others find us?' Gavin is breathless at the entrance.

'They're gone for hours.'

'They'll kill us.'

'They don't know we're here.' She grins. 'Anyway, it's just till the rain stops.'

She smooths away her footprints. Gavin leaves his. He relaxes once they're inside. He's curious about this tunnel, the wooden supports, the packed sand and earth walls.

'Pretty fancy,' he says from further in.

Greta's hair brushes the ceiling. The smell of the walls changes. They are damp and earthy.

'Don't go too far,' she says, unsure of the darkness ahead. 'I think we should go back.'

She retreats closer to the entrance. The temperature has dropped, and she's cold. She faces the sea and sits on the ground, hugging her legs. Outside the waves leap along the shoreline, foam chasing foam. Rain darts inside on a slant. The wind whistles and keens. Lightning skits across the water.

Her mother disappeared into a storm like this. Greta used to think a similar one might return her. She's given up on those fantasies now.

'I wonder how far it goes?' Gavin calls to her.

'Come back now,' urges Greta.

'You're such a scaredy cat!'

He disappears.

'Gavin!'

She creeps in after him until it seems like night. Beyond her is utter darkness. Suddenly Gavin jumps back to her with a curdling scream. She shrieks and clutches her head. He laughs and dances about, bumping into her.

'We should go back out,' she says again. 'I can't see in here.'

'I've got a lighter.' His thumb flicks at one he's stolen from his mother. 'Come on.'

Greta looks back to the entrance, the rocks there and the waves beyond.

'It's not much further,' he says. 'I just want to see how far they've gone.' He flicks on the lighter. The flame wavers in front of his face. He's braver than she knows.

Thunder reverberates through the tunnel walls, the roof. Grains of sand sift onto Greta's hair. Gavin's thumb works at the lighter, bringing up a flame, losing it. His face is a flicker of light, dark, light, dark.

'Here,' she says. 'Give it to me.'

She pushes down the button. The heat burns her thumb. She lets go and tries again. She might hold the flame this time. A smack of thunder sounds outside. The tunnel shudders. The ceiling showers sand. Greta runs, but she is too late. The roof parts, and the walls come marching in.

———

'Greta . . . Greta!'

Her ears popped. Joel's voice was urgent.

Everything tilted. The sea was climbing to the sky.

Joel was at her back. He wrapped his arms across her chest. Her legs were all pins and needles. She regained her balance, though he kept her resting against him.

'I didn't think you'd be here yet,' she said.

'I thought I'd better follow you.'

'Where are the children?'

'Eating hot chips.'

She looked behind her to the cliff steps. There they were, stepping down to the sand, holding out their hot cups to the wind.

'There's a plaque up at the lookout,' he said.

The unexpected collapse of a tunnel. One child dead, one survived. He could see the twisted mess of her.

Dark clouds hovered low over the water. Lightning flared and crackled across the waves.

'I can never get away from it,' she said at last. 'No matter how far I go.'

The taste of sand was in her mouth. Everywhere was the water, spreading and rising.

'Then bring it with you,' he said.

Around her was the scarred arm, the feathered wing of him.

They huddled against the gale and the wave and the tide. The sharp grit and points of shells bit into her feet. Fine grains of sand blew loose across the rocks, stinging her bare skin. She could see the hungry wave coming for her. She could dive into that cloud of foam, let the tide swirl and pull her in, the rip snatch her body out.

Behind her were the voices of her children. They were running across the sand. She could hear their words, somersaults in the air.

A last curling wave broke upon the rock, shattering spray and water.

She took in a sharp breath of the salty wind and clutched the feathered arm, ready to wing away.

37

Greta set the film in the camera and wound it on. The river was a calm presence under the dawn light. She walked beside it to the waves and the sound that had gone into her from when she was in utero. Draw back, breathe in, curl over. Break, foam, stream forward.

She took her time with the camera. The early sun was in her favour. Toby framed a few shots and then lost interest. She went on alone. A montage was forming in her mind. Of her mother's prints, her own, her sons'—in black-and-white film. The untrained eye wouldn't be able to tell whose photo was whose. Or when they were taken. The day, the hour, the year.

She looked at the world through her lens. Black swans, feathers ruffled like wavelets on the river. A pelican on a marooned wooden post. Clouds scudding overhead. The unpieced house on the sand.

There's only the shadows and the light.

At the car Joel spread a map across the bonnet. Griffin leaned in to look at his mother's circle around their next destination.

'Will we ever go north again?'

'Eventually, I reckon.'

'We'll head back home there one day, is that it? Back the way we came?' Griffin asked.

'Nah, different way next time.'

Greta called to ask them all to smile. She was a few metres from the car, with the camera focused on them. Click.

Out on the river there was a disturbance among the swans. One took flight, and suddenly the sky was full of the sound of flapping wings, as they rose in a cloud of black bodies and song.

Take me with you, take me with you.

The car groaned through its gears up the main street. A familiar rattle began under Greta's boots. In the side mirror she watched Fishermans Creek recede—the sand and green-blue water, the beachfront cafe, the bluestone church, the fish-and-chip shop with its ice-cream light, the post office and pizzeria and *Welcome to Fishermans Creek* sign. They grew smaller and were gone.

All that was left were the black swans. They flew en masse, a vast cape of dark wings, calling, calling the way on.

AUTHOR'S NOTE

Cultural note: this text mentions the name of a person who has passed away.

The first night I spent in Darwin, the heart-rending cry of a curlew went right through me. I still remember the outline of trees and the stars above at that moment. Since then, every time I hear a curlew wail it stirs a poignancy, not only on a personal level, but for many losses—human and environmental, including this country's wounds from the past and now.

While writing this book I had several encounters with curlews, and with every draft they emerged in the story more strongly. The bird's gaze reminded me of the saying 'the eye is the window to the soul', and the Irish proverb 'the eye of a friend is the best mirror'. Increasingly, I felt the curlew's impact on Greta, with its cry calling up grief to be held and healed by acknowledging it and carrying it in a new way.

Associations of the curlew's cry with loss, grief and separation, and new beginnings or change are found around the world, including in my northern hemisphere heritage. I want to clarify that my interpretation is not through the lens or perspectives of Australian First Nations' Traditional Knowledge, stories and culture, in which curlews often have a significant role. The character Brynn does acknowledge these stories in a general way, but owns her ignorance of deeper cultural meanings. Her words 'a curlew who stole the moon's heart' refer to a Wambaya story *Indilyawurna and Wardangarri* [*The Curlew and the Moon*] as told by Molly Nurlanyma Grueman to Rachel Nordlinger, Tennant Creek, May 1992 (transcribed in *A Learner's Guide to Basic Wambaya*, Rachel Nordlinger, 1998); and later published as a book by Papulu Apparr-kari Language Corporation (2006). Thank you to Molly for her storytelling, Rachel for her insights, and Papulu Apparr-kari Management Committee for approving its mention.

The description of the bush stone-curlew and quote 'cryptic plumage' on p. 76 are drawn from: P. Menkhorst et al, 2017, *The Australian Bird Guide*, CSIRO Publishing.

As well as the curlew, this story was inspired by a friend telling me about a dam with clear, toxic water, the genesis of the transparent lake in this tale; and my interest in liminal spaces. They became the heart of this story and its 'not-knowing', in-between places, that 'could be a dream or could be real'. Just as visions and nightmares relocate and morph aspects of nature, towns and people— Lightstone, the old property and Fishermans Creek are collages of the imagination, not real points on a map. For the same reasons, the characters have no surnames or exact heritage disclosed. As in a dream, some have stereotypical, surreal or veiled aspects, and their exchanges might be fleeting yet leave a message or mark.

My thanks to Tibby Quall, Dangalaba Elder, Kulumbiringin tribe, Gulumoerrgin (Larrakia), for your wisdom and advice, and for listening and talking about this story with me, especially around curlews and cultural perspectives. Thank you for your calm, knowledge and blessing.

Thank you also to Uncle Speedy McGuinness, Kungarakan

Elder, for conversations about this book, and a shared appreciation for ancient stromatolites and cycads, and the life they inspire.

I acknowledge the Country on which this book was written, and Elders past, present and emerging who nurture these places; and the languages, culture and people before and continuing there—including Gulumoerrgin (Larrakia), Kungarakan, Rak Mak Mak Marranunggu, Warai, Ngarrindjeri, and Boon Wurrung/ Bunurong.

'Always was, always will be'

ACKNOWLEDGEMENTS

To all those people who have helped bring this book into being over seven years, thank you. I could not have done it without you.

Thank you to Allen & Unwin's team—Jane Palfreyman for your enthusiasm and expertise, Ali Lavau for illuminative editing and encouragement, and Tom Bailey-Smith for your tireless and cheery professionalism—you are legends. Christa Moffitt, thank you for the beautiful cover, and Mika Tabata for adapting Isak's map. Thank you also to Jenn Thurgate, Deb McInnes, the Marketing team, and all those who have contributed, and to Wavesound for the audio book. Melanie Ostell—agent extraordinaire—thank you for hours of work, savvy editorial and publishing advice, commitment and care. Thanks also to Sophie Hamley and the NT Writers' Centre Hachette Mentorship for guidance. I greatly appreciate everyone's devotion to literature and championing this work.

Many friends and family have encouraged, believed in and assisted me. I cannot thank you enough for giving me strength and sharing your knowledge—from story, narrative and drama; to cultural experience and knowledge, protocols and migrant journeys; to the practicalities of properties, meatworks and plants in the top end; and the wonders of film photography and developing prints.

Some of you have been there again and again to read yet another draft or be a sounding board, discuss concerns and give insights. Others have drawn diagrams, suggested research paths, answered queries. Thanks to those who offered a quiet place to write; and those who stood by me through struggles and urged me to keep going. To all of you, thank you for your time, expertise, thoughtfulness and generosity, in particular:

Sally Allard, Peter Bishop, Karl Brand, Mary Anne Butler, Michael Chew, Ju Yuen Chew, Francine Chinn, Nicole Conroy, Jim Cox, Kerry Crosbie, Margaret Fendley, Dr Payi Linda Ford, Grundo, Russell-Hana, Karan Hayward, Tina Higgins, Brian Hubber, Terri Janke, Adam Kalnins, Jenny Kemp, Cate Kennedy, Melissa Kerr, Prue King, Maree Klesch, Breda Knightley, Trina Kruse, Di Lucas, Carolyn McLennan, Uncle Speedy McGuinness (Kungarakan Elder), Cat McKay, Donna McKenzie, LeeAnne Mahaffey, Maree Molinaro, Julia Moriarty, Sue Mornane, Lynne Muir, Terry Morgan, Zora Naidu, Mick Newnham, Rachel Nordlinger, Papulu Aparr-kari Management Committee, Bruce Pertzel, David Pollock, Dani Powell, Tibby Quall (Dangalaba Elder), Tash Rabbidge, Markus Rathsman, Anna Reynolds, Therese Ritchie, Joseph Sherman, Leah Swann, Ania Tait, Narelle Verzeletti, George Watts, Sam Wells, Christine Wilton.

To my colleagues Helena Turner, Melissa Raymond, Gillian Terry, Lisa Capps, Colleen McBride, Amanda Bethel-Donaldson; and Ailsa Purdon, Melanie Wilkinson and Rebecca Green—thank you for your keen support. Thank you also Batchelor Institute Library, the CALL Collection, and Libraries and Archives NT.

My deep thanks to those who have been part of my broader

writing journey—Jill Morris, Barbara Pertzel, Catherine Waterhouse; my parents-in-law Wendy and Ian Pollock; and the many friends, relatives and colleagues who have been there over years with coffee, chocolate, food, massages, kindness and goodwill. Batchelor Book Club, thank you and I'll be there more often now.

I'm grateful to the arts organisations and workers who have enabled writing opportunities: NT Writers Centre, Arts NT and Varuna Writers House—without you we could not create and share our work.

Special thanks to my mother Jill and brothers Paul and David for your affirmation from the beginning, a passion for books and stories, and your reading, advice and support.

And all the heartfelt thanks in the world to my husband David, and sons Jethro and Isak for sustaining, comforting and encouraging me across these years with your patience, understanding and love. Isak, thank you for the map, and Jethro for your magic, and both of you for your amazing forbearance, energy, humour and wisdom. You are my soul's treasures.